DRUMS IN THE DAWN

JOHN T. MCINTYRE

GARDEN CITY, NEW YORK
DOUBLEDAY, DORAN & COMPANY, INC.
MCMXXXIII

PRINTED AT THE *Country Life Press*, GARDEN CITY, N. Y., U. S. A.

DRUMS IN THE DAWN

CHAPTER I

A CARRIAGE with high yellow wheels and drawn by a pair of sturdy horses stopped at the door of the Two Pilots at New Castle, and an old gentleman in a brown wig and a bottle-green coat got out. He had silver buckles to his shoes; there were white frills at his wrists, and his neckcloth was like snow; and as the landlord of the tavern awaited him on the door stone, the old gentleman spoke to the driver.

"See carefully to the horses," he said. "Cool them and give them a reasonable ration of grain and water. And have them in the carriage by two o'clock, for I must go forward to get the afternoon coach at Wilmington." Then he turned to the host of the inn. "Food and drink, landlord," he said, with a gesture of the silver-topped staff he carried. "I trust I am in time."

"You could not have come at a better hour, sir," said the landlord, smoothing down his apron. "There is a fine leg of mutton, done over a hardwood fire, and stuffed with oysters brought up from the bay only this morning; and there are fresh greens from the tavern's own garden, a few broiled pigeons, sir, and a fowl. Or, if you'd prefer a cold cut in the heat of the day, there's a rare ham, sir, or a good round of beef."

But the old gentleman in the brown wig motioned these things away.

"Draw up a table to an open window," he said as a black boy brushed the dust from his garments; "get me a bottle of port, some ship's biscuit, and a pipe of tobacco. That, I think, will serve my needs while I am here."

Orders were given that this be done. A table was placed at a side window overlooking the river; a high-shouldered bottle was put upon it, together with a deep glass; also a dish of hard biscuit, a canister of tobacco, and a long-stemmed pipe. The landlord opened the wine with expert fingers.

"It's an excellent sort, sir," he said. "It was in the schooner *Enterprise*, two years ago, when she came up the river with as fine a cargo of Spanish and Portagee wine as a man ever tasted. A rich vintage, already gone ten years old at that time." He poured a ruddy stream into the deep glass. "A rich wine, heavy and full of purpose; none of your bubbling trash that our young men drink; a man of years, I've always said, requires a liquor that has body and substance."

The old gentleman merely nodded his head to this, nibbled at the biscuit, and sipped the wine; he gazed through the window at the windbound ships in the river. He had a thin-lipped mouth and many wrinkles; he had bright, shrewd eyes under heavy brows. The landlord, who had moved away from the table, after observing him a space, moved back again.

"Your pardon, sir," he said. "It may be you are Mr. Hasty?"

"I am," said the old gentleman, immediately. "What of it?"

"About an hour ago," said the host of the Two Pilots, "a carriage drove up and you were inquired after."

"Ah!" said Mr. Hasty. The shrewd, bright eyes gained in attention. "By whom?"

"A lady, sir. A young lady."

The thin-lipped mouth tightened; there was a deep indenture between the eyes.

"Did she give any name?" asked Mr. Hasty.

"No. But," and the landlord waved a hand toward a wide-balustraded staircase, "she is still here. She had driven a long way, she said, and is resting."

Mr. Hasty motioned with his wineglass.

"If it will not disturb her," he said, "you might mention that I have arrived. Also, that I shall be going in a short time."

When the landlord left him, Mr. Hasty went quietly on with his ship's biscuit; he poured more wine into his glass, and watched some fishermen on the river bank mending their nets. The wine was sound and crossed his palate with a grateful touch; a pleasant breeze stirred; but still Mr. Hasty frowned, the shrewd, bright eyes carried hard lights, and questionings were in them: sharp, sudden questionings. And anger! Then there came a step upon the stair, a light step, but resolute and quick; there was the rich rustle of silk.

Mr. Hasty arose.

"Charlotte!" he said, sternly. "Why are you here?"

The girl was tall; her flowing draperies were more French than Colonial; her mass of bronze hair was worn in a great knot at the back of her head; she had widely separated brown eyes with long lashes, and a flash in them that told of spirit. She stood before the old gentleman, a smile upon her lips; a quiet smile he did not seem to relish.

"I asked for you at this inn, Mr. Hasty," she said, "thinking you might stop here in your journeying up and down the bay shore. Indeed, I have inquired for you, in the last two days, at all the river-side taverns between here and Philadelphia."

He placed a chair for her, the frown still indenting his forehead; she sat down, folded her hands composedly in her lap, and looked at him. Mr. Hasty, as learned in the way of human folk as he was in the principles of the law, saw a readiness beneath this composure which disturbed him; he frowned more than ever.

"Can I ask them to bring you something?" he said.

"No, thank you. I was so anxious to be on the road this morning that I left the Sloop Tavern at Wilmington, where I'd stopped overnight, without breakfast. But I've seen to that since I've been here." She studied him, amused, as he ate of his biscuit and drank his wine and nodded his brown wig at her.

"You do not approve of my going adventuring alone upon the highroads, I see."

"I do not," he said. "I am opposed to such things, whether in you or any other young woman. But, now that you have ventured here, may I ask what you mean by it?"

"To be sure." Her beautiful, candid eyes were fixed upon his face; the slim white hands were quietly folded in her lap. "Two nights ago I heard from some shipping people, while at Mrs. Gaylord's, that you had left the city and were engaging in some business along the lower river."

"They told you of this?" said Mr. Hasty, pausing with the wineglass halfway to his lips.

"No. The matter chanced to come into the conversation. When I learned, Mr. Hasty, that you'd been gone upwards of a week I became interested; and I made up my mind it would be best if I saw you at once."

The old solicitor received this with little favor.

"I suppose," he said, with some bitterness in his tone, "you did not see fit to mention the matter to your uncle?"

"No," she said. "That never occurred to me. But even if it had I doubt if I should have done so; for, Mr. Hasty, I have learned what to expect from John Claridge in any matter concerning myself. He'd have looked at me, coldly, and would have gestured in that absolute way he has; and he'd have required me to remain at home."

The brown wig nodded; Mr. Hasty took a deep swallow of wine, put down the glass, and touched his lips with a beautifully white pocket handkerchief.

"It has been plain to me this long time," he said, "that you resent your uncle's caution. But, Charlotte, I ask you, now, to seriously consider the value of his advice. His experiences have been wide, and a well founded 'No' from such a man has often been the saving of an ill-considered situation."

The girl was looking through the window at the motionless ships, with their tall masts and empty sails; the gulls moved in rounded flights about them.

"There are a number of things, as you know, Mr. Hasty,

which you and I do not agree upon. And one of these is that any view I may have of my own affairs is ill-considered. I repeat now what I've said to you more than once before: I know quite well what I'm about, sir, and will permit no one—not even John Claridge—to dissuade me."

Mr. Hasty refilled his glass and held it up so that the light might strike through the ruddy dark of the wine.

"I've always said of you, Charlotte, that you are an outspoken young woman. It is a trait come to you, very possibly, from the Barreauts, who, while they were excellent merchants and built magnificent ships, permitted their women a too important voice in their affairs." He nodded at her across the brim of the glass. "Since you were a child newly come from the nuns' school at Baltimore, you've never hesitated to say what was in your mind. But is it not possible, my dear, that your judgment in a matter like this might be wrong?"

"I have considered it from every side," she said, "and my conclusions have always been that I am doing a just and fair thing." There was a silence for a moment; then she went on. "As I've said, I've inquired for you at all the inns on the way down from the city; and at each of them they had you in mind. 'An old gentleman who desired news of a brig expected in from sea.'" The slim hands were now tightly locked together, the great brown eyes were lighted with sudden feeling. "May I ask, Mr. Hasty," she said, "if the brig you are so interested in is the *Racehorse*, and if Philip Archer is aboard of her?"

Mr. Hasty put down the glass so sharply that its bottom rang against the table.

"You did not hear the ship's name at the Gaylords' supper party," he said, his look cold, and his voice with a new cut to it. "Some whippersnapper in your uncle's counting room has been talking of things he does not understand."

"The clerks in the counting room of Claridge & Company are quite well trained," said the girl, quietly. "They tell very little to anyone. To me they tell nothing at all."

Mr. Hasty lifted one hand, warningly.

"Charlotte," he said, "I tell you now, as I have told you before: put this nonsense out of your head. It has no substance, and you are doing yourself and your uncle a deal of injustice."

She sat quietly looking at him. He was just as she'd seen him so often before; the way he had of leaning toward her, that lifting of the hand in the cautioning gesture, the drawn brows and expression of impatient displeasure. She recalled the first time she'd gone to him, five years before: she was but seventeen and had been in the city only a short time. Her mind was distressed; she'd not known what to do; she'd thought of him and gone to him in his dusty office in Water Street to confide in him and ask his advice, for she'd been told he'd been her dead father's friend. The place was untidy; an old clerk in a scratch wig sat on a stool at a long-legged desk, writing with a quill in a great book of accounts. There were bundles of papers upon shelves, and upon hooks, and in cupboards; a strong box, doubly locked, stood with its back against the wall.

She'd sat opposite Mr. Hasty, at a table, that afternoon, much as she was doing now, and he'd looked at her from under his heavy brows. Yes, she'd said what was in her mind even that day; though but seventeen and timid, she'd spoken exceedingly well. And he had listened closely. She'd come to him, she said, because he'd been her father's lawyer, and was now lawyer for her uncle, John Claridge, and also for Claridge & Company, and she desired information and help.

"I have spoken to my uncle a number of times," she'd said, "but he tells me I am a child and must leave all serious matters to my elders."

"He is quite right," Mr. Hasty had told her. "Seventeen years is no age at which to obtrude yourself into the affairs of business. Your guardians have those things competently in hand."

There had been tears in her eyes at this, for she'd expected an answer of a different sort; but she did not permit them to be seen.

"My uncle's reply does not satisfy me," she had told Mr. Hasty. "For there were seven millions of gold louis named for me in the will of Antoinette Teresa Barreaut-Desfourneaux, my grandmother. Seven millions of gold louis that were part of the loot taken from the Spanish ship *Vision of St. John* many years ago. And as these were adventured in the dealings of Claridge & Company, is it not in the law that I should be told from time to time what fate has overtaken so large a sum?" Those were her very words; she recalled them well, for she had arranged them in her mind before going to the solicitor's office. "Is it not right and proper," she'd said to Mr. Hasty, "that I be told what profits have been made by this sum of gold money, and what truth there is in the claims made against it?"

Mr. Hasty had considered these things carefully; and then he'd said:

"On the whole, my child, you have done quite right in coming to me, if these things vex you. For, be assured, there is no one who knows all the sides of your business as I know them. And my advice to you"—it was then he'd leaned toward her for the first time and lifted the warning hand—"is to put all such questionings out of your mind. What you should know will be, in due course, told you. Claridge & Company is a great commercial house, and under the hand of your uncle it has thrived as never before. The sum of money you have mentioned, left by your grandmother, is quite safe. You need have no misgivings upon that score. And," Mr. Hasty had said, his voice lifting almost angrily, "as to any claim being made against it, that is preposterous! Quite preposterous! You must," he'd said sternly, "fix that in your mind. This money belonged rightfully to old Antoinette Teresa Barreaut-Desfourneaux; it was proper and lawful for her to leave it to you."

When he'd said that he'd arisen from his chair, taken a pinch of snuff from an ebony box, and paced up and down the floor for some minutes, quite agitated. Then he'd paused at her side and looked down at her.

"To be sure," he said, "there is rascality in the world. There are persons without conscience, or any sense of fair dealing; but matters having to do with such persons are not for you to concern yourself with. They must be left to your uncle and to me. As for you," he said, looking steadily down at her, "be advised, and think no more of these things that have been troubling you; give yourself to pursuits customary to girls of good breeding: embroidery, the harpsichord, riding in moderation, and possibly gardening. The cultivation of roses," said Mr. Hasty, "occupies the time very pleasantly for a young woman. Above all, you must not give heed to any silly talk."

That had been Mr. Hasty's attitude toward her five years before, and now, she, Charlotte Desfourneaux, a woman grown, saw the same expression in his face.

"You will understand, Mr. Hasty," she said to him, breaking the silence that had fallen between them, "the *Racehorse* brig and your interest in her would mean nothing to me if it were not for the letter my uncle received a month or more ago, and which he permitted me to read: a letter from a young man who claims to be the last of that family of Archer who have for so many years conducted the great suit at law against the Barreauts and the Claridges in the matter of the ship *Vision of St. John.*"

Mr. Hasty frowned.

"John Claridge sometimes makes mistakes," he said. "It was a mistake to permit you to read that letter."

"It was carefully worded," said the girl. "And it held a deal of questioning. There had been new matters come to his help, the young man said. To those proofs, and to the testimony his people had kept in hand over the many years of trial, had come a confession by one Fouquet, who had once been secretary to his grandfather; also a journal written by Fouquet's wife, and many documents sworn to in the Spanish courts at New Orleans. It was his thought, so the young man wrote, to come to Philadelphia and reopen the case, to take up all matters concerning it where his father had put them down."

"Charlotte," said Mr. Hasty, "I ask you to give no heed to these things; be guided only by those who speak with the authority of experience. In the first place this claim of the Archers to the booty in that old Spanish ship is without foundation; the law has always refused to recognize it. These people have pressed their claim in France, in England, and at New Orleans; and no matter how hard they have striven, they have not advanced their rascally cause one jot anywhere. And I, who have known them well, warn you against them; they are a brawling, hectoring race, and have no respect for the law and its processes. Furthermore, in the matter of this letter, your uncle is convinced the person who wrote it is an impostor, for there is no evidence that Richard Archer, now dead, had a son; indeed, there is none that he ever married."

"I may be wrong," said Charlotte, "but, Mr. Hasty, I have not the same confidence in the finality of my uncle's judgments you seem to have. I found his mind so fixed when he spoke of this letter that he left my thoughts filled with misgivings. And even you, Mr. Hasty, feel no assurance that he's right; for if you did you'd not troubled yourself these ten days, watching for a trading ship to come in from sea with, possibly, this young man on board."

Mr. Hasty took up the long-stemmed pipe which lay at his hand and charged it with tobacco from the canister.

"I hold the entire matter of the Archer claim in contempt," he said. "Nevertheless, in the past fifty years I have been called upon to make a defense against it no less than four times. Three times I have made sea journeys for this purpose; once to New Orleans, once to France, and once to England." He kindled the filled pipe at a lighted candle a waiter had brought for the purpose. "I have been so borne down upon, so badgered and bedevilled and knocked about by these Archers, that I have come to hate them fully as much as your uncle does; nevertheless," with a nod of the brown wig, "I do *not* agree with him as to this new claimant being an impostor. I was persuaded at once by the tone of his letter that he was the person he said he was; and," puffing at the pipe, "since seeing what I have seen this morning, I am more persuaded than ever."

"The brig is in the river, then?" said the girl.

He nodded once more.

"Yes. And I have been aboard of her."

"You have seen the young man?"

"Yes," said Mr. Hasty. "But it was certain things pointed out by Mr. Platt, master of the vessel, that convinced me. A hull scarred by solid shot," said Mr. Hasty, gesturing with the long clay; "masts bitten into by grape and musket balls; sails in rags; wounded men! These things were so like the footprints of an Archer that I scarcely needed anything more. When this youth's letter arrived some time ago, I, in spite of your uncle's belief that he was an impostor, set myself to learn more about him. As he said he was commander of a ship in the West India trade, I wrote to each of Claridge & Company's masters in those waters, asking for information. The skipper of the *Racehorse*, brig, received the letter I'd dispatched to him at Havana; and by looking over the list of arrivals and departures learned that a schooner mastered by one Philip Archer had made sail for Charleston only the day before. Captain Platt had taken in the *Racehorse's* cargo, and, when he sailed, he did not head for the Capes of the Delaware, as he'd meant to do, but for Charleston harbor.

"He found the schooner and went aboard her. She was owned in that port; but Platt was told her captain had given up his command because of some pressing business in the North, and was then ashore awaiting a likely ship that he might take passage in. Platt is a little ferret of a man who sees further into a thing than most of his class, and he located the schooner captain without a deal of trouble, offered him passage in the *Race-horse*, and they came to terms at once. A ship sailing that very night carried a letter to me; it said the brig'd follow immediately, and with the man on board."

"It was this letter, then, that caused you to leave the city so suddenly."

"Yes. But I might have delayed a fortnight and still have been in time; for it seems the ship which carried the message was one of the last to leave Charleston harbor for some weeks. In that city," said Mr. Hasty, bitterly, "the people have been taken with the same sort of madness we have here in the North; they are up and raving against the King's government. So great was their protestation against the laws that Sir Peter Parker, hovering off the coast with a fleet of British ships, made up his mind to move in and attack the city."

Mr. Hasty rekindled the pipe, which had gone out, and proceeded:

"Platt told me there was a great to-do when the admiral's intentions became known; Charleston city fell into a turmoil. The militia was assembled, material for fortifications, powder, shot, and pieces of cannon were taken to one of the islands in the harbor. Some of the foremost people in the city had sworn that no King's man bearing arms should ever again set foot upon Carolina ground.

"Platt saw the situation become suddenly menacing and immediately he got his passenger on board, put his vessel in order, and prepared to slip out to sea under cover of night. But what happens?" said Mr. Hasty, putting down the long clay and shaking an accusing forefinger. "This young rake-hell whom he has taken on board will not hear of leaving; Platt tells me he tramped the deck waving his arms and protesting!"

"He was not afraid!" said the girl. "He did not dread to make away through the blockade!"

Mr. Hasty smiled, wryly.

"No," he said. "It seems the young man is a patriot. He had the effrontery to assemble the crew; he swaggered up and down before master, mates, and ship's company declaring that no man who had a heart in his body would depart in that slinking fashion when help was so needed by the threatened city. There were men behind the earthworks, he said, men in rifle pits, on barges, all facing the place where the enemy must appear. Ships were needed; and the *Racehorse* must do her part."

"And she did, I suppose?" said the girl, her eyes upon him. "That is why her hull is broken and her sails torn!"

"Platt is a trading captain," said Mr. Hasty, "and a trading captain always looks, as he should, to his owner's profit. He would not hearken to persuasion; the brig, he said, would leave that night when the tide was right. And then, behold," said Mr. Hasty, "the passenger seized the ship! He harangued the crew once more; and when the mate, Mr. Partridge, tried to lay hands on him, he struck him down. More than that, our gentleman secured a pistol from a chest in his cabin; he took the brig's master by the neck and dragged him about, his heels rattling on the deck, declaring the man who would not strike a blow for home and country at such a time was no man at all. He demanded the key to the magazine; he stripped the tarpaulins from the two small guns and had them mounted forward; then he ordered out a boat and had the vessel towed to a place where they could not help being in the most terrific danger in the event of an attack."

"And the fleet came in?" said Charlotte Desfourneaux. "Sir Peter's fleet?"

"You may be sure it did," said the old solicitor. "King's men are not of the stuff that grows frightened at threats. Sir Peter came in. There were two fifty-gun ships that must have looked like floating fortresses, and a dozen others of smaller size; and they were crowded with men. Can you think of this shell of a brig with her six-pounder brass guns, each of which a man might slip into the tail pocket of his coat, lying there at anchor, waiting while such a peril approached? Captain Platt, so he told me, implored this madman who had taken his vessel to move her to a more possible place. But he would not; he had a pair of loaded pistols across his knees as he sat on the cabin-top, and he cocked his eye at the captain.

"'No colonial ship has yet run from the enemy,' he said, 'and we'll not be the first. Our guns are small, but I've seen their like give good service.' Mr. Hasty's eyes snapped and his brows were dark as he looked at the girl. "That was the saying of an Archer," he told her. "A true cub of a reckless breed; and when I heard it, my mind was completely settled that he was no impostor."

"And the brig kept her anchorage during the fight?"

"She did. I saw grapeshot in her mainmast; more than one plank is smashed in her hull, and, as I've said, her dress of sails gives her the look of a ragamuffin of the seas. Sir Peter's ships were driven off," said Mr. Hasty bitterly; "the *Bristol* was abandoned; and this rascal who had so mishandled the officers of the *Racehorse* boarded the frigate with a boat's crew and trained her guns upon the departing ships of the King."

There was a touch of color in the girl's face; her lips were smiling.

"I've been told," she said, "all the Archers have been strong-bodied men."

"This one is like an ash," said the old solicitor, pouring out more wine. "Big-boned and tall: as gaunt in the middle as a boy, but with shoulders that would fill a door." He looked at her, his wig nodding, his eyes hard. "His arrival, I think, will put things upon their old footing; he will take the place of his father in this matter, who, at an earlier time, had taken the place of *his* father. It will be the Claridges and the Archers face to face once more," said Mr. Hasty. "It will be strength against cold reserve; quick, heavy hands against eyes of ice; reckless strength against nerves of steel."

The girl stirred in her chair.

"It will be amusing to see John Claridge opposed," she said. "At least, it will be different."

"Once you've noticed the difference," said Mr. Hasty, "you'll find little to enjoy in it. The Claridges are people who have always liked to dominate; none of them, and I have served three generations, have held their heads higher than your uncle; none of them have looked more bitterly or coldly upon any who have approached them in an unfavoring mood."

"Well, at least, the Archers seem not to have dreaded them," said the girl. "Their opposition has gone on for years; there have been blows, there have been challenges and, so I've heard, duels. And, now, here is the last of them returned to the matter as unafraid as those who went before."

The old solicitor put down his wine untouched.

"Unafraid!" he said, nodding his head; "yes, he is entirely that. And for all John Claridge's place in the city, for all his strength as a shipowner, for all his money, his bank, his power in the ports of the world, he must take care what manner he uses toward this youth. This last of the Archers," said Mr. Hasty, "has an eye in his head, and a tongue, too; and as you've gathered from what I've told you, he's not one to hesitate when once he's made up his mind."

There was a pause; and then Charlotte said:

"There seems to be little or no wind; when you boarded the brig, was she in the bay or the river?"

"In the river, but making no headway. And young Archer had grown impatient with her slowness. He was for leaving her and making the remainder of the journey by carriage. He had his chest upon deck, meaning to do so at the next town."

"A chest?" said the girl, her eyes full of sudden questioning.

"A chest, and some other articles of dunnage," said Mr. Hasty.

"It was, perhaps, a large chest, bound with iron, and with a great Spanish lock?" said the girl. "And the name of Archer was on one end, the letters made of the heads of copper nails?"

"Yes," said Mr. Hasty; he searched her face with narrowed eyes. "And what then?"

"It is the chest my grandmother, Antoinette Teresa Barreaut-Desfourneaux, told me of. She had seen it at New Orleans, at Bordeaux, at London. It was the chest belonging to James Archer, grandfather to this young man."

"Ah," said Mr. Hasty. "She was right; quite right." He refilled his pipe from the canister and drew the lighted candle toward him. "It belonged to his grandfather, indeed. And he kept in it all things relating to his claim. I'm pleased you've recalled the matter to my mind. It is most interesting."

CHAPTER II

AT MID-AFTERNOON the sun was hot upon the river's face; summer was deep upon the banks; tall trees rose and went ranking away, thick, rich, whispering. A small trading brig, her sails hanging limp from the yards, was drifting around the bend below New Castle; some river birds floated in the heat above her topmasts; the helmsman dozed at his post.

A boat had put out from the west shore some time before, and Mr. Partridge, the vessel's mate, a stout man with a drink-blotched face, stood watching it.

"Two boatsmen, carrying a passenger," he said to the brig's master. "And the passenger thinks to come aboard of us."

Captain Platt was a ratty little man with close-set eyes and a sidelong look.

"If Hasty had not gone up the river road some hours ago behind a stout pair of horses," he said, gazing at the boat, "I'd say this was he, returning."

Mr. Partridge's eyes searched the boat earnestly, and surprise came into his face.

"Upon my soul, sir," he said, "upon my soul and body, I think it is. It is Mr. Hasty, indeed. Don't I know that bottle-green coat; and am I not aware of the way he sits and clasps his hands about the knob of his stick and rests his chin upon them when he's thinking? 'Tis he as sure as I'm telling you."

A few moments told it was the old solicitor, sure enough; and he paid his boatmen and came aboard at once.

"Well, Mr. Hasty," said Mr. Platt, with his sidelong look, "this *is* a surprise, sir; I fancied you'd be at Wilmington by this time, waiting for the coach."

The stout man stood by, curious and attentive, and Mr. Hasty drew the master toward the stern.

"I had hoped," he said, "to reach the city before midnight and so be ready for anything that Mr. Claridge cared to suggest in this matter. But, sir," and he tapped the stick upon the deck, thoughtfully, "my attention has been directed, by the merest chance, toward a subject which should have been very near my mind; so I had the horses put to the carriage at once and drove back to meet you."

The ratty-looking shipman said nothing to this, but his narrow glances questioned Mr. Hasty from head to foot.

"I see," said the old attorney, his eyes upon a great chest that rested in the waist by the rail, a heavy, oaken thing with rope handles and a Spanish lock, "your passenger has not yet left you."

"He means to go ashore at New Castle," said the master of the brig.

Mr. Hasty's eyes remained upon the chest; they were hungry eyes and covetous.

"No doubt," said he, "you'll be well rid of him. A damned hectoring young blade, to take you by the neck as he did, and to go blazing away with a brace of small pieces at fifty-gun ships. You'll be well rid of him, indeed."

Captain Platt moistened his thin lips with his tongue; his sidelong look had surprise in it, and curiosity as well.

"When you left the ship further down the river, Mr. Hasty," he said, "you were all for persuading him to stay aboard with me until we reached Philadelphia."

But Mr. Hasty seemed not to hear him; his eyes passed from point to point of the chest: he noted how the iron bands were riveted to the heavy oaken timbers, how the wrought metal corners had stood the blows and wear of years, how tight the lid fitted down, how secure the lock seemed, how heavy and durable it was altogether. It was like a merchant's strong box, or a thing in which a nobleman might secure his plate and jewels. The wood itself was so seasoned and hard, it might turn the edge of a sword blade. And the name upon the end of it, in burnished copper-headed nails: it was a chest in use, perhaps, for a century.

Mr. Hasty sat upon the rail, the point of his heavy stick digging into the deck, his hands clasped upon the knob; the sound of singing came up the companionway, a deep, rich voice with a rollicking lilt to it.

"A Spanish lilt," thought Mr. Hasty, with a wry face. "His father would sing them when we had him in prison for a space in Marseilles; he filled the place, so the jailer told me, with his ballads and love songs."

Mr. Partridge called down the deck to the master of the brig.

"The wind has stirred somewhat, and we're moving a bit; in a half hour we'll be abreast of the town. Shall I put over a boat for Mr. Archer?"

Captain Platt was about to reply, but he felt the touch of the solicitor's hand upon his arm.

"Wait." And as Platt turned an expectant face toward him, Hasty added: "I am not averse to the young man leaving the ship. Let him go, in God's name; but the chest must remain."

"The chest!" said Captain Platt. "He brought it aboard at Charleston. It is his property, Mr. Hasty. And," drawing down a corner of his mouth, "from the way he has guarded it on the way North, it would take a deal of persuasion to make him leave it behind."

Mr. Hasty studied the captain with valuing eyes; then his look went to Partridge, then to the watch on deck; man by man.

"How many of a crew have you?" he asked.

"Six, not speaking of the mate. Then there is the cook, and a boy that attends in the cabin and galley."

"From what I see of the crew they are not a sturdy lot," said the old solicitor. "But, then, one can never tell. What if a piece of gold money were put into the palm of each of them,

Mr. Platt? Do you think it would make a difference in their bearing?" But the shipman said nothing; he continued looking at Mr. Hasty, as though waiting for more. "Would you, or anyone in your ship's company, put a pistol to this fellow's ribs and order him out of the vessel without the chest—if a price were paid for the work?"

The close-set eyes of Platt went here and there among the watch as the old lawyer's had done; he licked his lips and seemed reckoning the possibilities.

"What money would you name?" he said. "The thing would be a dangerous one to do. What price would you put on it?"

Fear was plainly in his look and voice, but greed urged him forward; Mr. Hasty appraised him with precise calculation.

"Two hundred double louis," he said. "And paid down the moment the service is performed."

The greed in the captain's look grew greater, but as it grew it drew danger near to him, and he began to blanch about the mouth; his hand, as he lifted it to point at the companionway, shook.

"He's a swaggerer," he said. "I've seen him step; and there's a devil in him when he has the mind to show it. No man will affront him and come away unhurt."

Mr. Hasty's manner was cold, and there was scorn in his eyes.

"It is your own ship," he said. "You have a parcel of men vowed to do your bidding; also, there is a stout mate at your call."

"Partridge is broken with drink," said the captain of the *Racehorse;* "it is not in him to thwart a spaniel."

"Mr. Claridge will support you in any chance that might arise," said the attorney. "Five hundred double louis, full weight, minted money, paid down to you."

Platt wiped his gray mouth with his hand and swallowed. Then he said, with a choke in his voice:

"I like your readiness with your money, Mr. Hasty. But this matter is too venturesome a one for a man to go about alone. I'd need someone who could be depended upon to stand by me. None of those who were in the ship at Charleston will do, because this bully so awed them there they have not yet recovered from it."

"But," said Mr. Hasty, watching the man's expression, "for all that, there is someone you are thinking of?"

Platt nodded; he wetted his lips.

"There is the cook," he said. "We had a shot into us in the fight at Charleston that smashed the water casks, and we put in at an island off the coast to get more. We had no cook, and one offered himself, and I took him. A great, strong, dark fellow, from somewhere in the West Indies, and the devil only knows of what race or breed; but from what I heard tell of him he's one who'd turn his hand to anything if he were paid for it. Suppose," and the shipman's voice sank, "you add fifty more louis to your price, Mr. Hasty, for the cook. If he'll give his help, the bargain is made."

"Very well," said the attorney, coldly. "I add fifty double louis to the offer."

The brig's master nodded and rubbed his hands together; there were greed and fright in his look, but he said, steadily enough:

"I'll fresh charge a pair of pistols. I must take every advantage. Then I'll speak to Pedro."

He went down into his cabin, leaving Mr. Hasty at the rail, looking out over the river. The wrinkled face of the old attorney gathered more lines to itself as he smiled; he seemed much comforted. To set a cook in the path of an Archer! His smile grew into a chuckle. A dunghill fowl to face a gamecock! A half-breed scullion, of dirty blood; a mountain of straining fat; a greasy lout to go grappling about the deck with the son of Dick Archer! He tapped the deck with his cane, and his shoulders shook.

"This patriot youth! This mouther of great words!—this threatener, this singer of songs! By God, I'd like to hear the breath shaking in his throat," said Mr. Hasty, going livid with sudden rage. "I'd like to hear him beg. That would pay me for some of the insults I've listened to from his father, and from his grandfather, too."

But Mr. Hasty was not one to permit rages to hold possession of him; so he threw the feeling off and returned to his first mood of amused expectation. An interloping, presumptuous blackguard! A stout mongrel holding him in play; perhaps battering at him with some uncouth implement from the galley; an iron pot would be an excellent weapon and a comic one; swung by the handle a man might do good execution with it. And roars of laughter! The chagrin of the high-worded sworder, demeaned and beaten and stretched wretchedly upon the deck!

The eyes of the old solicitor went to the chest lying in the waist, and at once the laughing went out of them. The thing looked as durable as the Archers themselves: forged iron, toughened oak—a lock it would take a smith to open!

"And the flaunting of the name upon the end of it," said Mr. Hasty; "that's very like them, indeed. Cool. Impudent. Always putting themselves forward."

He'd known them well. In England, first. Then in France. Then in Louisiana. A ready race, with the pluck of bulldogs, careless and gay until the moment came for action, and then all desperation, all fire and steel. And shrewd! Mr. Hasty's nostrils dilated; his fingers gripped hard about the knob of his cane. He admitted they were that; and they were far-seeing, with intuitions that served them as well as wisdom. They quickly sensed what to expect, what to do. Their methods were mocking and checkmating; they kept one in a fury of uneasiness.

"A thousand times," admitted Mr. Hasty, "I have wished the devil had them all. My pride has suffered more through these people than through all the others chance has matched me against."

The singing voice continued to come up from below, rich, full-throated; and the old solicitor's hard mouth grew even harder as he listened.

"His grandfather, too, would sing that way when he'd lifted his spirits with brandy. Tavern songs were to his liking: he'd sing them by the dozen when at his ease, a bottle of drink before him, his belt slackened, and his boots thrown into a corner."

Visions came to Mr. Hasty of the Cheshire Cheese Tavern, of gambling places, of a dozen of clubs and inns frequented by Long Jim Archer. What an appetite the man had for ale and port, for thick slices of beef, for chops, and fowls, and pigeon pies; and his talk of Pons, of Pistol, of Falstaff and Prince Hal; of Doll Tearsheet and other gutter faggots; of Mercutio and Queen Mab. It had been enough to deafen one's ears. And in the midst of the talk and laughing, and the eating and drinking, let a word be said he didn't like, and he was up like a leopard! Up with his blade in his hand; or maybe an ale pot, or a tavern chair!

Mr. Hasty frowned and shook his head. He'd been waiting for almost a fortnight at the inns along the bay shore and the river for a sight of the *Racehorse* and her passenger; and during that time he'd thought a deal about the task he'd undertaken. The thing that came oftenest to his mind was that in the passage of years the breed of Archers may have weakened. Such things were frequent enough. Sailing the seas had misadventures other than battle and storm; it brought a man into strange ports where inferior women came to his notice. One dash of poor blood and the breeding of generations might be shattered. He'd hoped for something like that, but from what he'd heard he'd had his hoping for his pains. This fellow now in the *Racehorse* was as brawling a buck as his grandfather had been.

"If we are to have a slackening of either body or wits," said Mr. Hasty moodily, "it seems we'll need to wait for another generation."

The singing below ceased; and there came a springing step up the companionway; a rangy youth, long-boned and wide-shouldered, came upon deck; he was bronzed by the sun, and his blue eyes showed the lighter by contrast; his long hair was tied sailor fashion at the nape of his neck. He looked toward New Castle, which was now but a little way ahead, then over the side. And he spoke to the mate.

"Mr. Partridge," he said, "a little while ago I asked you to lower a boat for me so I might go ashore with my dunnage when we came abreast of the town."

"In a moment, Mr. Archer," said the mate. "The captain will be on deck to speak to you."

"There will be a night coach leaving New Castle, most likely, just before sunset, as that is a favorite time for them. And I desire to go by it. If we get much above the town, your men will have a long pull back against the tide."

A man was sent below to make the captain acquainted with his passenger's wishes; a tackle was rigged to hoist the chest into a boat; the boat itself was being made ready for lowering while Mr. Hasty inspected the young man with snapping eyes.

"He has the Archer nose," he told himself; "curved and none too small; his chin is the true type, square and solid as stone. The hair is lighter than either his father's or his grandfather's, and the eyes are another sort of blue. The mouth," and Mr. Hasty frowned over this, "is wider than it should be. What woman was his mother, I wonder? In some things she has put her stamp strongly upon him."

The boat slapped against the quiet water; a sling was passed around the chest; and while this was doing, the old attorney saw Captain Platt come out of the companionway with a brace of pistols stuck in his belt. At his heels was one whom Mr. Hasty took to be the cook—a man of dirty yellow color, and with coarse, flattened features. His sleeveless shirt showed immense corded arms, his legs were thick and bowed; his body was like a cask. The captain advanced, a hand upon a pistol butt and a furtive look in his eyes. The gray of fear was still about his mouth.

"What," said he, "going ashore, now, Mr. Archer?"

"Yes," said the young man; "my judgment is there is no hope of a wind in the river that'd carry us up to the city in less than two days."

Captain Platt motioned the men back from the chest; his shaking fingers fumbled at his chin.

"Let be, and stand away." As the seamen stepped back, the cook seated himself upon the box, grinning and snapping his great fingers. "It may not be known to you, Mr. Archer," said the master of the brig, "that it is not in accord with the usage of the port to take anything out of a ship until it has been inspected by the proper authorities."

The young man looked at the pistols in the speaker's belt, and he also looked at the man upon the chest, and his blue eyes narrowed.

"I will deal with any authorities that may be interested," he said.

"I am master of this vessel," said Platt, "and I, with my owners, will be held responsible for all acts such as this." He gestured toward the shore. "You may go if you are so pleased; but your chest must remain with us until we reach the city."

The giant half-breed squatted upon the box, chuckled, and wagged his head.

"Him chest no go," he said. "It stay in ship. It is Pedro Escallado who says it." He shut his fists and squinted at the passenger. "Him chest no go."

The young man hooked his thumbs in his belt.

"I am leaving the vessel because my business is urgent," he said. "And to transact that business, it is necessary that I have the contents of this chest at hand. So, you see, sir," his handsome teeth showing in a smile, "I cannot leave it behind. I will sign any papers necessary to release you from responsibility; and give my word that as soon as I reach Philadelphia I shall make a report of myself and my acts to any person qualified to receive it."

But Captain Platt shook his head; his hand was still upon the pistol butt.

"If my memory serves me right," he said; "when you came aboard of me at Charleston, your journey's end was named as Philadelphia. I have no means of detaining you, Mr. Archer," he said, "and no desire to do so; but your property stays in the ship until it is released in due form." He motioned to the seamen to throw the sling from about the chest. "And take it below—to my cabin," he directed.

As the men advanced to carry out this order, young Archer stepped in front of them, his hand lifted.

"One moment!" he said. "It seems to me," and he turned to Captain Platt, "you have taken a sudden fancy to my property; and I also note you have thought it necessary to provide yourself with firearms when announcing that fancy. In my first day in this vessel, Captain Platt, I was forced to carry things with a somewhat high hand so that we all of us should not be disgraced in the eyes of a brave body of our countrymen. I have no desire to do the like again, and so I request you not to interfere with my leaving your ship peaceably."

Pedro Escallado laughed; his black eyes twinkled; he sprawled upon the chest like a huge boar.

"You go," he said, "but him chest stay." He struck himself upon the brawny chest. "It is the captain's word, and I do what he say."

Without even a change of countenance, young Archer put his foot against the man's stomach and threw him to the deck. Then to the sailors he said good-humoredly:

"Now, my lads, we'll have no further words in the matter:

come forward with your tackle and hoist the chest into the boat." Then he turned upon the brig's master and said: "Perhaps it would be as well for you to keep your hands from those pistols, Captain Platt; I have a feeling you are not well instructed in their use, and may do yourself harm."

Though he still smiled, there was a crinkling about the corners of his eyes and a jutting forward of his chin that told he'd reached the end of his patience. Captain Platt, livid, but with a rat-like ferocity, drew a pistol from his belt and cocked it. Young Archer snatched it from his hand, and as he did so a heavy blow fell upon the side of his head, stretching him upon the deck. He was upon his feet in a moment, however, his head reeling; the massive arms of the half-breed cook hooked about him, and the great weight of the man bore him down once more.

Mr. Hasty smiled as he watched. A mongrel from some obscure island in the Caribbean, thick with the dirty backwash of the sea, had taken an Archer in hand and was beating the breath out of him! One of that fighting breed was flat upon his back with a yellow, greasy bulk holding him down. A cook, out of the filthy, roach-ridden galley of a trading brig, was——! But wait: the half-breed, to carry out what he had in mind, found it necessary to change his hold; and as he did so the face of things changed with it. Taking advantage of the instant's slackening, young Archer cleverly drew up his knees, planted his feet in the man's middle, and lashed out with all his force, tearing him loose. They came to their feet the same instant. Archer had a trickle of blood down the side of his face; the yellow man panted heavily, his face contorted with pain and fury. He plunged headlong, but Archer stepped aside and struck him as he passed, bringing him down.

Captain Platt had the second pistol in his hand; he rested the barrel of it upon his bent arm, but before he could fire, Archer threw himself sideways; then, as the weapon exploded, the young man caught up the one that had fallen to the deck, and glowering through the blood and sweat that was in his eyes, he menaced the ship's company.

"Mr. Partridge," he said to the mate, "into the boat with my luggage. Let there be no delay, for, by God, I've had enough of you all, and a few moments more may bring you no good."

The mate did not delay; the chest and the canvas bags which lay beside it were lowered over the side, and a pair of seamen were at the oars. Young Archer, holding to a brace, balanced himself upon the brig's rail and, for what seemed the first time, looked at the old solicitor.

"It has come to me in the last few minutes," he said, "that your name may be Hasty. In some documents I've read, your name was mentioned; I was told I'd meet you, but I'd not expected it'd be so soon. And I tell you frankly, sir, I'm sorry you are not a younger man; for I'm persuaded what has just happened is of your contriving, and it would suit my humor to settle the matter with you on the spot." He stepped into the boat and seated himself in the bow, so he'd have the brig and the two oarsmen in view as it pulled away. The hammer of the pistol was at cock; he fingered the trigger guard as he added: "However, sir, we'll meet again, I have no doubt; and I trust to arrange it so it'll be a meeting out of which you and your employer, John Claridge, will get little comfort."

The boat drew away from the *Racehorse*, moving toward the shore. Mr. Hasty stood at the rail and moodily watched it. He saw the figure of the young man silhouetted against the red of the evening sky; it had the true set to the head, the wide shoulders, the long, powerful, alert body, the suggestion of poise, of quickness, of strength.

"An Archer, to be sure," said Mr. Hasty. "A true son of the breed; and, so it may chance, with more devil in him than there has been in any of the others who have gone before."

CHAPTER III

A CARTER took Philip Archer's baggage to the Two Pilots, and as the young man stood in the passage watching the unloading of his chest, the landlord said to him:

"I'm sorry, sir, but there is no coach until the morning; however, you will not be uncomfortable overnight at the Two Pilots; and the mail leaves at a fairly early hour."

"I should like to finish my travels before then," said Philip. "Is there not a carriage or spring wagon I might engage, with a span of durable horses and a driver?"

The landlord shook his head.

"We have very little need of such things at New Castle," he said. "Our people are content to use the coach."

"Do I not see a carriage there near the stable?" asked Philip, pointing. "It may be I could engage the use of that."

"It belongs to a French gentleman, arrived in the last half hour," said the host of the Two Pilots. "And he will be leaving after he has had his food, and his horses are rested. Indeed," and the landlord smoothed the apron over his comfortable stomach, "there is no lack of carriages in the inn yard, sir; a lady came in one to-day, which is still here; and an old gentleman arrived in another. But none are for hire."

"At what hour is the coach in the morning?"

"Toward eight o'clock. And there is another leaves Wilmington at two in the afternoon. They are swift and with relays of good horses; you will reach the city while the day has still some hours to go."

As there was nothing to do to better the matter, Philip saw his chest up the stairs to a comfortable room, which had a raftered ceiling and was full of the cooling evening air from the river.

"I shall send a boy with hot water," said the landlord, looking at the dried blood on the young man's face, "for I see you have had a mishap."

"Hot water, by all means," said Philip. "And when supper is ready, let me know."

He cleansed his wound when the water came; also, he shaved and brushed his long hair, re-tying it at the back of his neck as it had been before. Then, with a large brass key, he opened the chest and took from it fresh linen, and as he dressed, he looked at the chest and the things bulging from it. The ship's carpenter of the *Manifred*, a New Orleans vessel which his grandfather had mastered, had made it while they lay at Lisbon many years before; Portuguese smiths had wrought the ironmongery and fastened it on. The *Manifred* had been a vast belly of a ship, slow, but stowing enormous cargo; Philip had heard much of her from time to time, for his father had been born in her, in the Bay of Biscay, while she lay amid a French fleet, with the British prowling to and fro waiting for strength enough to attack.

A stout chest, well made and strong; it had gone battering around the world, the property of grandfather—father—and son; in the holds of some ships, in the cabins of others, in taverns and tents, fastened to the backs of mules on mountain roads; and once it had been sunk in a depth of water at Porto Bello to save its contents from a galley full of half-breed buccaneers.

"It might well be filled with our blood," said Philip Archer, as he tied his neckcloth; "it might, also, be made of our bones: for it has held our hopes and fears, our thoughts and the hours of our days and nights: our very souls have been in it for more years than I have lived."

In his rummaging for what he required he'd dragged out much of the chest's contents, and he smiled as he realized its nondescript nature. There were sea boots and canvas jackets; there were uniform coats; there were a pair of well kept brass-mounted pistols, a hanger with a polished silver guard, dress shoes and frilled shirts and silk stockings; there was a deep Spanish saddle. Also there was a leather purse which had a plump, well filled look.

He pulled on a pair of soft leather boots, brushed a blue, tailed coat and put it on; by the time he'd finished with his dressing a black boy told him supper was ready below; he locked the chest carefully and went down. There was a gathering of travelers about the tables, drovers, farmers, and rough-looking men whose business took them on long journeys over the roads. Also there were a few pilots, and mates and captains of vessels in the coasting trade, then lying in the river. He sat at a round table with a few others; there were a pair of cold fowls upon it, a dish of chops, greens with butter, hot biscuits, and a huge pigeon pie.

"There is no tavern between here and the Capes," said a small round-headed man, who was master of a sloop carrying bricks from Bristol, "that puts the same good food upon the table as you get at the Two Pilots. No matter what the wind or tide, I always tie up here and pay the place a visit."

The landlord, who was busy near by, smiled broadly; the wrinkles of his fat face showed much satisfaction.

"Here," he said, "is an excellent countryside; grain and fowls and beef are of no great price; the kitchen women do not cost much for hire; fuel is for the cutting; fish are so thick in the bay that a blind man might prosper a-netting them."

The round-headed man cut into one of the fowls, and as he did so he shook his head.

"It is a fine condition of things," he said, "but how long will it last? How long will it be before the British come up the river with their ships-of-war? How long before their armies come swarming over everything like locusts?"

The landlord wiped his hands upon his apron.

"Well, sir," he said, "we are not altogether defenseless. Has not Congress provided us armed ships? Did not our fleet descend upon Nassau, in New Providence, take it quite gallantly, and load their vessels with many valuable things for the army?"

"They have some nine-pounder guns among them," said the master of the sloop, "and a few carronades which the British discarded as useless years ago. But, God save us, what protection are we to have from such things as these? The King's frigates are handy vessels; the snapping of a few gun locks will not frighten them away."

"We have a-plenty of schooners and sloops," said the landlord. "And more vessels are to be built—strong ships meant for fighting purposes; Congress has named one hundred thousand dollars as the sum to be paid for them."

They talked of the panic the merchants of the city had been thrown into at the menacing front of the British cruisers. Ships had been captured coming into port; outgoing vessels had been forced to return up the river; trade was at a stand.

There was a tall young man now engaged in talk with the landlord, at no great distance from where Philip sat. His English was without fault, but his rich and somewhat foppish dress had a foreign look; his hair was elaborately curled, there were gilt ornaments in his hat, his gold shoe buckles gleamed in the candlelight.

"A Frenchman," said a young ship captain, seeing Philip's eyes upon the dandy. "None other than the Duc de Chaulnes, who is engaged in some matters with Claridge & Company."

The host of the Two Pilots seemed disturbed in his mind as he listened to De Chaulnes; he gestured and blew out his fat cheeks and shook his head. But the Frenchman's handsome, dissipated face was set; there was command in his attitude.

"She is in the small room to one side there," the landlord said. "But she left word she was not to be disturbed unless Mr. Hasty returned."

"You may say to her I am a friend of his; also that I will intrude upon her for a moment only." But the host, anxious though he obviously was to please so high-mannered a guest, shook his head stubbornly; and at that Philip Archer saw the Frenchman's eyes fill with anger. "I am not only a friend of Mr. Hasty's, but I am a friend to her. You have my name; take it to her, and permit her to decide."

"It was her wish," said the landlord, "specially mentioned, sir, that you not be admitted."

De Chaulnes stood for a moment, a sneer upon his full lips, then he reached for the handle of the door. The landlord tried to prevent his opening it, but was thrust sharply aside; then De Chaulnes flung it wide and stepped into the room. Philip saw a girl at a small table, a girl with a great mass of rich bronze hair, with wide, beautiful eyes; he saw her start up as the man entered the room and stand facing him; and then the door closed, shutting them in. The landlord breathed heavily and rubbed his hands upon his apron.

"The lady does not desire his presence," he said, speaking to those in the room who were staring wonderingly. "She requested me to tell him so in plain words if the occasion demanded."

"Then," said Philip Archer, getting upon his feet, "why do you stand there? Take some action, sir! Have the door open at once."

"If I do," protested the comfortable host, "there will be violence. I can see by the look of the gentleman he's not one to be interfered with."

"Open the door," said Philip, pointing to it, "or I'll do it for you; and if I do I promise you to take this person by the neck without any words between us."

The landlord, bothered and vexed, called a brace of sturdy grooms in from the yard.

"Saul," he said, "do you get a cudgel, a stout, good one; and you, David, be ready to support me. Such goings on will not be tolerated in my house." Agitated, red of face, he threw open the door of the room. "Sir," he said, "this intrusion is not to be borne. You must leave at once."

De Chaulnes, with a white bitter face, turned; all in the public room were now upon their feet, food and drink forgotten; they saw the Frenchman strike the fat landlord upon each side of his head as one might strike a troublesome dog; seizing him by the shoulder, he whirled him out of the doorway; while Saul and David stood gaping, the man fell with a crash among the chairs and tables and lay still. Ignoring the dozen or more pairs of eyes that were upon him, De Chaulnes faced the girl at the far side of the table; she was pale, but her head was proudly lifted, her brown eyes filled with resentment.

"Charlotte," he said to her, "this is no errand for you, a girl, to venture upon alone. I carry your uncle's instructions: he demands that you return to the city. My carriage is at the door; have them bring your belongings, and we will start at once."

What the girl said in reply to this was not heard in the public room; but it must have been a refusal; at any rate, the man pushed the table aside and grasped her by the arm.

"I have been told," he said, "you are hard to control; that you will have your way, no matter what is said or done to persuade you. But, I'm afraid, Charlotte, they used only words, and sometimes words are not enough."

The girl cried out as he drew her through the door into the crowded room. And then Philip Archer arose, quietly, the wine bottle in his hand; he struck smartly, expertly; and he drew the girl back, out of the way, as De Chaulnes fell.

CHAPTER IV

PHILIP ARCHER stood in the doorway of the inner room so that Charlotte Desfourneaux might not see the limp form of De Chaulnes as the two grooms carried him out.

"I ask your pardon," he said. "I have startled you, I know. But my experience, a rough one, to be sure, but useful, has shown me when the moment comes as pat as that one came, the needed thing is to strike quickly and hard."

"It was very dreadful," said the girl, her fine eyes filled with trouble. "And I suppose you did no more than was needed."

"I assure you—no more." Philip studied her admiringly. Her voice, he found, was as musical as her face was lovely; she was tall, and of a marvelous figure; her hair was of the choicest red-gold; she had hands that were as white as they were slender, and yet as strong as—well, God help him!—they rather bewildered him; he could compare them with nothing he'd ever seen. "Your strapping fellows like that one," he said, "are not to be permitted any advantage. If a man is to deal with them at all, the advantage must be the other way about." He smiled at her, good-humoredly. "These are rules for the master of a ship," he said, "and have been found quite useful in the far seas with crews of men who are not always of one's own blood."

"You are a sailor, then?" she said. She was regarding him attentively, a sudden surmise in her eyes; a deep, quick look she had when her notice was unexpectedly taken.

"My days have been full of ships," he said. "Ships and sails," nodding his head; "wind and weather."

"American ships?" Her look was fast upon him.

"No, not always; not even," and he smiled, "most of the time. Spanish, Greek, Portuguese, French. Also, I once commanded a bark owned by a Moorish merchant, out of a port in Africa. Again, I was in a Dutch whale ship as far north as vessels might go."

Here the landlord appeared, bulkily, in the doorway.

"The gentleman is having his hurts attended to," he said. "Mr. Hasty has returned," to the girl, "and is with him. He is indignant that a person of parts should have been treated so. He says I, as landlord, shall be held responsible."

"Give no heed to him," said Philip. "He is not likely to consider your part in the matter, now or ever." And then, when the man had gone, he closed the door and said to the girl: "I have some small acquaintance with this Mr. Hasty. He seems an active person for his age, for only a little space ago I left him on board a vessel in the river, intending, as I thought, to make his way in her up to the city." The brown eyes were full upon his face; and as he looked into them they invited him to talk; they held an interest that flattered him. "I left the ship because she was making but poor headway," he said. "The old gentleman came aboard of us as we rounded the bend in the river just below; and, oddly enough, it was the second visit he'd made during the day."

"Mr. Hasty is a man who does not consider trouble if he has a matter he desires to carry on," said the girl.

Philip sat upon the edge of the table and smiled down upon her.

"That," he said, "was my own estimate of him." He considered a moment and then added: "On his first coming into the brig he gave me no attention at all; but matters seemed changed on his second appearance; for then he strove to inconvenience me as much as possible. I have a chest," he said, "a lumbering kind of thing which came to me from my father; and while Mr. Hasty was for bidding me Godspeed out of the *Racehorse*, he desired the chest left behind."

The look in the brown eyes inviting him to talk increased. Philip clasped his hands about one knee; he looked at her and admired her vastly; she had a way that bespoke confidence. He felt warmed; his blood flowed with a smooth beat; it was as though he'd known her always. So he explained matters to her.

It was possible, he said, the old attorney had more reasons than one for getting possession of the chest. If the information at hand were true, and he had every reason to suppose it was, that shrewd gentleman would give a year of his life for an hour, undisturbed, with the contents of it.

"What a ripping there'd be," said the young man, genially. "What a rending of wood and a bending of iron. God save us, I have a picture of him in my mind, breathless with eagerness and labor." .

He'd first heard of Mr. Hasty perhaps fifteen years before. Philip was then a lad, sailing with his father in the ship *General Wolfe;* they were in the South Atlantic and carrying a rich cargo for a house in Marseilles. His father was ill; he was down with the sickness that finally killed him, lying in his bed in the cabin. He was yellow and wasted; his hands had shrunken to bones, and there was no strength in them at all. At night the cabin was full of shadows; there was a holy candle which the sick man had seen blessed in the cathedral in Rio, and he burnt it, sometimes, beside him; also, there was a brass crucifix upon the wall, and in the dimness the boy saw the writhing Christ die a thousand deaths as he sat and watched. On the night Mr. Hasty was first mentioned, a gale was disquieting the sea; and the ship rolled deeply. Philip thought his father asleep; he'd lain so quietly, the candlelight touching him. But he was awake and thinking; and after a space he spoke.

It might be, he said, he'd not have long to go. He felt the thing, whatever it was, had his vitals in its grip; and if this was so there were some matters he should tell for the sake of the boy's future peace. A fear was in the lad's breast; he watched the hollow face, the fever-brightened eyes. And death seemed a bitter thing there on the lonely sea.

In time to come, his father told him, he'd meet with people of the name of Claridge. They were merchants, and the owners of ships; they had branches and agents in all the large ports of the world; they were so rich that princes might well envy them. The Archers had thought all this power was not rightfully their own. But the sick man would not say as to the reasons for this belief; they concerned matters he'd not have burden the boy at that time. Two generations of Archers had broken their spirits against these things, and it was best that Philip, for a time at least, walk in quieter places.

But his father said to him: should ever a Claridge cross his path, no matter where or when, he must be instantly on his guard. There were none of that name or that blood but was his natural enemy. And should chance or his own purpose ever throw the boy in the way of their man, Hasty, he was to put himself in God's care and keep his wits sharp; for Hasty was crafty and ruthless; he'd never mean anything but evil. The dying man bid Philip keep these words in his mind; some day they might be of service to him. For you are my son, he said, and as my son these people will fear you. More than that, under certain circumstances they'd not hesitate to have your life.

"What more my father might have added to that, I don't know," said Philip Archer. "He grew delirious, and day and night talked mad things, and saw strange visions. But he did not die until we came to anchor at a place in Martinique, which was a port of call in our voyage. We buried him in a little graveyard, in the shadow of a lime-washed church; in a few days the *General Wolfe* sailed away."

"He died," said Charlotte Desfourneaux, "and you were left alone?"

There was a tremble in her voice, and the brightness of her eyes dimmed with tears. It stirred his heart to think she felt grief for the lonely boy of those far days; and he looked at her with grateful eyes.

"All alone," he said to her. "And I had not dreamed the sea could be so desolate."

But when, in the course of another half year, the ship returned to New Orleans, and he went to live at the house of Madame Fouquet, he was easier in his mind, and happier. It was in his father's written will that he should go to her; and she seemed to expect him. He well remembered the day he arrived at her house; it had high windows, and little balconies with railings of black iron; and she stood at the open door.

"I am Philip Archer," he told her, "and my father is dead." She kissed him on the cheek, the first and last caress he ever had from her, and took him into a high-ceilinged room where there was a portrait of the King of France over the mantel. She was a thin woman, dark and tall; and she talked very little; but after a time spent in her house the boy had the feeling that she knew a great deal—especially about his family. She'd sit of an evening after their supper, while he studied his Latin grammar, and she'd look at him; sometimes she'd shake her head as though the things she thought were not very pleasant; but she'd never speak; her lips were tight shut.

"But she cared for you greatly," said Charlotte Desfourneaux. "I sense that. You were but a boy, and her heart was heavy with thinking what your fortune in the world might be."

He smiled; there was a warm look in his eyes; he was pleased that she felt this.

Yes, Madame Fouquet cared for him a deal; he came to know that after a while. She had a good soul, though her ways were odd. She taught him to play piquet; they'd sit at a little table in the candlelight, and she was very severe with him when he was careless in his game. Every night, at ten, she opened a table drawer and took out a leather-covered book which had a lock upon it; she had the key upon a thin gold chain about her neck. She'd unlock the book and write in it carefully with a long-pointed quill and in very black ink.

He had a room on the third floor that overlooked a beautiful garden; it was a wide room with a small bed and a polished floor. There was a bookcase holding books in English and French and Spanish, which he read of nights by candlelight after he'd gone to bed. Upon the wall of this room there was the picture of a beautiful woman, a woman of dark loveliness, with coiled masses of shining hair, and eyes that followed him wherever he might go. He tried this very often: first he'd stand directly before the painting; he'd move to one side, then to the other; but the eyes would still be upon him, gentle, anxious; sometimes he'd blow out the candle and lie in his bed in the darkness; he'd feel the eyes searching for him, and so real was this that once, in a sort of agony that she should think he was hiding from her, he called out that he was there.

"Do not weep," he said. "Do not grieve. I shall not go away."

He had been with Madame Fouquet perhaps a year when one evening he stood before a long mirror, a candle on each side of him, tying his neckcloth; it may have been the shadows holding so peculiarly to the line of light, it may have been some small movement of his head, but he saw, in one brief flash, something in his own face that was like the woman's in the painting; his heart pounded; he seemed not to breathe.

Madame Fouquet sat at the piquet table when he came down; she saw his white face and startled eyes, but looked at him, calmly.

"The picture!" he said. "The picture in my room. It is my mother!"

She pointed to a chair at the opposite side of the card table and told him to sit down. She sat opposite him, the cards in her lean, steady hands. Yes, it was his mother, she said; the mother he had never seen. Madame said she'd often thought to tell him of the picture, but she never had, because she knew it would one day tell him itself. And later that night this strange, tight-lipped woman, as he stood with a candle at the foot of the balustraded stairs, told him of the book in which she wrote each night.

It contained an account of things she had witnessed and heard; she was setting them down so that those who came after her would know what had taken place. Some day, she said, he might sit with this book and with certain papers that would be with it, and marvel at what they held. And, if he was fortunate, this knowledge might do him great good.

He often thought of this book and longed to have it in his hand, to open and read it. But there were many long years to pass before he got his wish. Should he not be of legal age when she died, Madame Fouquet told him, all the things that were his, through his father and grandfather, and all the things that belonged to her, were to be put into the keeping of Nicholas Fortune, a friend to his family, a gun founder who had a furnace and forge in the city.

At twelve years of age Philip was sent to the school of St. Philip of Jesus. He was known there as the "ship captain's son"; his English name marked him in that place of French and Spaniards, and upon one occasion a family concerned in the government complained he was not of the sort to be accepted at an institution where people of consequence sent their sons.

At that, Madame Fouquet visited the place; as he'd said, she was tall and spare, and the gown she wore that day being of the tightest, her angularity increased. To that she had a small hat with a single feather, long, slender, and upstanding. Fiercely partisan though the boy was, he acknowledged to himself she had a weird look; but no one smiled, for she held them with her flashing glance. Erect and proud, she was magnificent. Her hand on the boy's shoulder, she said that in all the sixteen provinces of France that faced the sea there was no better blood than his. She would say nothing against the Spanish families then in New Orleans; but their claim to a superior

condition was a thing to smile over. She requested that there
be no more such occasions as the one just past; the school had
been selected by her because she thought it to be one that
would give satisfaction. Nothing could have been more superb
than her way of saying this. She would not care to take any
action, she said, but let there be one more such absurd complaint and she would do so. She would take him from the
school instantly, and he would never return.

He was with her for eight years. Eight years of that high old
house; eight years of the garden behind it, with books and
learned padres; with Corporal Brotot, who taught him the
sword; eight years with the feeling that he had been hidden.

"Hidden!" said Charlotte Desfourneaux. "From what?"

He was not sure. However, the feeling he always had was
that Madame Fouquet was guarding him; that Corporal Brotot, when they faced each other, small-sword in hand, was
teaching him against a time when he'd be ringed with danger.
No, he was not sure, but this he knew; it was the thing his
father had spoken of when he lay dying in the cabin of the
General Wolfe; it was the thing Madame Fouquet wrote of each
night in the locked book. He remained eight years in New
Orleans; and then, because of small matters that seemed, at
the time, vastly important, he went away; he went to sea in a
Portuguese ship that carried a letter-of-marque but was little
better than a buccaneer. This vessel carried merchandise,
but he found her armed heavily enough to contend with sloops-
of-war. In the waters off Cayenne he'd refused to sight a gun
against a helpless Dutch galiot, and when a mate aimed a blow
at him, he'd struck the man to the deck and leaped into the
sea.

"A mere boy!" said Charlotte Desfourneaux. "To do such a
thing!"

"I was eighteen," said Philip, "and almost a man grown."

He was picked up two hours afterward by an English ship
trading with the East, and some time later found himself in

the China Sea. And after that he was in vessels sailing among the Asiatic Islands, ships with crews made up of all the peoples of the earth; craft with strange rigs, barbarous, ravaging ships in which a man's life had no value, and no property, however mean, was his own unless he was strong and had a quick eye and struck hard. Philip had the small beginnings of navigation from his father; and an old Scotch captain, in a leaky brig working between London and ports in the Arabian Sea, taught him the remainder. Afterwards he was mate in a French craft, then in others owned in Antwerp, in Rio, in Martinique, in New Orleans.

At New Orleans he learned Madame Fouquet was dead. They showed him the place where she rested; and when after a little he turned away, he found Corporal Brotot standing near by. The letters Philip had written Madame had been received; she'd read and reread them and kept them always near her. What matters she'd left behind were in the care of Nicholas Fortune, as she'd always planned, and held in trust. But Nicholas had gone out of New Orleans two years before; he was then in Philadelphia, where he'd built another furnace, and carried on his trade.

"Within three months," said Philip, "my ship was in Philadelphia port, and I spoke with Nicholas. My father's chest, which I'd taken as a boy to Madame Fouquet's, was in his possession; the black-covered book with the lock was there, and also the key with its thin gold chain. There was a long letter from Madame, full of advice and prayers for my good conduct in life. I must read what she'd written in the book, she said; I must read every word, missing nothing; and then I must read what my father and grandfather had written. After that, I must acquaint myself, as they charged me, with all the documents they left behind, and judge soberly what action I'd take with regard to them."

"And you did," said Charlotte Desfourneaux, her eyes upon him.

The chest and all the other things were put into the cabin of his ship and went to sea with him. In long afternoons he'd sit at the stern windows, slowly making his way through the stiff writing; while the ship was becalmed in hot seas he'd lie in a hammock slung on deck and read; in crowded rivers where the sea-stained hulls ground together and ships' masts lifted thick as forest trees, he went on reading. And at last he mastered all: and sat back to think what was best to do. It was a vast weight to take upon one's shoulders: old struggles, old hatreds, old crimes; the bitter venom of covetous men; sordid mining beneath one's feet, corrupt judges, decisions at law that must have appalled God himself; sleepless nights, rage kindled and re-kindled; murder!

"No," said Charlotte Desfourneaux, as she half arose. "No!"

"Murder," he repeated. "I have word of it written down, proving it to me beyond all question."

He frowned and stirred as he sat on the table's edge; he smoothed his shaven chin and stared at the candle that threw its tiny flame between them. There was a pause; and then the girl said:

"These Claridges, of whom your father warned you, what contacts have you had with them?"

He looked at her with a new caution; he'd talked freely, so freely that, now he thought of it, he was surprised. For she knew De Chaulnes; Hasty's name had been mentioned in connection with her; and he now recalled a thing James Archer, his grandfather, had written upon the flyleaf of his last journal.

"No matter how attractive the thing, or how genial and compelling the person, if a Claridge has touched hand to it, or them—take care! God himself scarce can save you if you venture in where you cannot see!"

She was beautiful; her eyes were of a like such as he'd never seen before; her color had the loveliness of deep afternoons; there was a quietness about her that calmed his spirit; but, for all, when he answered her, he did it feeling the value of each word he said.

He'd remembered the name, and in his voyages around about the world he often came upon it. He saw it for the first time over the door of a counting house in a Chinese port and questioned a Venetian merchant with whom he was talking. The man replied with vast respect. It was a great house, he said. Its riches were untold. It was a firm known wherever trade was carried on, and was powerful in ships and influence. There had, perhaps, never been such a mercantile concern since Venice was in the height of its greatness.

In Calcutta he'd come upon the name again; then in the Mediterranean ports; at Bordeaux, Lisbon, London, among the islands of the Atlantic. He marked their ships; he saw them at anchor, or going into, or out of, harbors; they were built of oak or teak, were wide sailed, with towering masts, full crewed, and with striding, frowning officers who, so it was said, demanded the utmost of their vessels and would see a sail whipped to ribbons before they'd give the word to take it in.

"It must have been some time ago," said the girl, "that you came into the possession of the locked book of Madame Fouquet and the papers left by your father. Have you made no effort to approach your enemies until now?"

He shook his head.

"Those who follow the sea are usually poor," he said. "I had to sail around the world, you may say, and contrive and fetch and carry, to gain enough money to set myself free. Before I moved in the matter, or spoke a word, I must make sure of what I had and where I stood."

"And now," she said, and leaned toward him ever so little, "you have done all that?"

"All of it, as far as one unlearned in the law may go," he said.

"You mean to go up to the city to-morrow to speak with John Claridge?"

"Yes," he said, and looked at her attentively, a something that was in her voice catching his ear.

She was silent for a few moments; and when she spoke again she had gone white, and her hand was outheld as though in appeal.

"How long ago was this—this murder done that you spoke of? Was it in these later years or long ago?"

"It was in New Orleans. My father was a boy of no more than fourteen. He was awakened in the night by a dreadful cry; leaping out of bed, his heart pounding, he went part way down a flight of stairs. There were a number of candles burning in the hall below, and he saw Campbell, a rugged, short-spoken Scotsman whom his father had placed to watch over him, lying dead on the floor. It was," and the young man reflected, "all of fifty years ago; not in the time of the present head of the Claridge house, but his father's."

There was a look of relief in her face, but only for an instant; then the outheld hand touched his sleeve.

"What has once happened," she said, "can happen again. When you reach the city, do as your father bid you do; be always on your guard. John Claridge will be within hand's reach of you; and John Claridge is a man to fear."

CHAPTER V

PHILIP ARCHER learned, as he sat at breakfast next morning, that Mr. Hasty and De Chaulnes had departed during the night; and that Charlotte Desfourneaux was also gone. He speculated over this as he drank his ale and munched his toast and bacon, but could make little of it.

"The two men had horses put to a carriage at past midnight," said the landlord. "The girl did the same shortly after dawn. I was surprised that she should speak to this man," he added, rubbing his nose with the edge of a forefinger; "one would say she'd not tolerate the sight of him, even, for some time to come."

"Do you mean the Frenchman?" said Philip, frowning at him.

"None other; they gathered in the passage just before the men drove away, she and Mr. Hasty and this ruffian who saw fit to put hands upon me and who," said the host with a deal of satisfaction, "wore a bandage about his head where you struck him so shrewdly."

Philip drank his ale and made what progress he could with the crisp bits of bacon and the good, wholesome bread; but he was puzzled; he continued to frown.

His belongings were put upon the coach top and strapped securely; he sat with the driver on the box seat, and all day they drove, with stoppages to change horses, the lengths of dusty roads, along the river, through miles of wood, past farms and through hamlets. In late afternoon Philip found himself in Philadelphia, installed in a room at the Penny Pot Tavern, overlooking the river; and a smart maid in a white cap went clicking about, making it ready.

46

"You'll find this a choice room, sir," she said. "There do be a good breeze from the river. And the view is beautiful; as you sit at the window you'll see the ships come up the river around the bend, and they'll delight the eyes of you, especially if you are a seafaring gentleman, which you do look like, sir, and that's true. Here, in the jug, is hot water for your shaving; you have clean sheets on the bed, and the room is swept and dusted and aired."

"Thank you," said Philip, good-humoredly, and gave her a small silver bit. "But the road has me famished; when will supper be served?"

"In a little while now, sir; you'll hear the bell which they do ring at the foot of the stairs."

Philip poured out the hot water into a basin after she'd gone; he got out an ebony case with a silver soap cup, a round mirror of about the size of his two hands, and a pair of ivory-handled razors. These things had been his father's. He shaved himself very carefully, and as he looked into the mirror he thought how often it must have reflected his father's face in days that were past. And while he was a deal like his mother, as he'd discovered that night years before at Madame Fou-quet's, he was also like his father; he had the same nose, the same eyes, the same small ears set close to the head. He nodded at himself gravely. God send he was half the man his father had been, that he'd even a little of that steady purpose, of that ready hand, of that strong, good heart.

"There've not been many like him," he said. "What a hand with a ship; what a front for danger! And such a generous spirit for anyone who'd favored him, even in a small measure. And such a pitying eye for any poor soul who'd lost his way in the world."

The landlord was drawing a flagon of ale in the bar when Philip passed the door; and a black boy in livery stood near by.

"Mr. Archer, sir!" called the host. "A message for you." To the black boy, he said: "This is the gentleman, now."

"A letter, m'sieu," said the boy in island French. He held out a folded and sealed paper. Philip opened it wonderingly; it was written in long, sloping letters of elegant shape.

MONSIEUR:

Pardon this message from one with whom you are unacquainted. But word has just reached me of your arrival in the city, and I take this means of claiming your immediate attention.

The boy who hands you this will conduct you to where I may be found. Word of the Vision of St. John *still exists in the world, and I know you will not fail me.*

LOUISE BARREAUT.

Philip Archer put the refolded missive into the breast pocket of his coat; and he looked at the black boy attentively.

"I am to take M'sieu to Madame," said the boy. He had a smooth black skin and a cropped head; his manners were those of a trained servant.

"Very well," said Philip. He glanced regretfully into the supper room, where the waiters were already beginning to stir; the doors to the kitchen were continuously opening and closing, and the delicious smell of cookery filled the air. "Go on."

A handsome carriage with a span of high-bred horses stood at the door of the Penny Pot; the door of this was opened, and Philip got in; then the black boy swung himself up behind. The coachman spoke to his horses, and they were off. They turned into Front Street and then into Chestnut; at Second Street they drew up before a handsome house of brick and stone, broad fronted and with high windows and a spacious doorway. A sloop-of-war lay in Dock Creek, taking in its stores; a number of carters were unloading some brass guns which were also to be put on board.

Philip stood in the wide hall for a space; it was a lavish place, rich and shining, not the sort he'd associated in his mind with this sober city of the Quakers; it was foreign; with the touch the island French gave their houses, opulent, a breath overdone. Then the black boy returned and led him upstairs. In a room whose windows overlooked the creek with its market sloops, a handsome, dark-eyed woman half reclined upon a silken couch. The air was heavy with a rich scent; the rugs were deep and soft; there were costly hangings and beautiful paintings upon the wall. The woman half arose, and held out her hand.

"Monsieur," she said, "I am gratified. That you should put such confidence in me is indeed a compliment."

Philip held the hand and looked down at her. He smiled. She was tall: he noted that. If she stood beside him she'd have been well above his shoulder. She had languorous Creole eyes; they were magnificent; the thin silken robe she wore clung to her, showing her shapely length.

"Your name caught my attention, madame," he said. "For there have been Barreauts in my family's days for generations."

She smiled up at him.

"It is true. And there have been Archers moving upon the horizon of the Barreauts for as long. There have been Barreauts," she said, "who, as children, have had their nurses frighten them by mentioning your name. 'Be good,' these creatures would say, 'or the Archers will get you.'"

She smiled; her teeth were of perfect whiteness.

"Sit down," she said, indicating a chair near the couch. She supported herself upon one elbow; the wide, rich sleeve fell back from her arm, showing its white perfection; there was a necklace about her throat, of lustrous jewels.

"As I said in my note," she went on, "I heard of your arrival in the city only a few hours ago. And I at once had my people begin a search among the inns for you. I am glad I found you in good time," she said.

Again Philip smiled; he crossed one knee over the other and leaned back in the chair; his powerful body, his strong, sea-beaten face seemed out of place amid the scented richness of the room; but he was at his ease and studied young Madame Barreaut with valuing eyes.

"You have spoken, perhaps, with Mr. Hasty," he said. "It was he who told you I was in the city."

But she shook her head; one white hand gestured all idea of Hasty away.

"That old man!" she said. "That old rogue! No! He knows better than to come to me with his villainies. No; it was Charlotte who spoke of you—she whom you met at the inn at New Castle, last night." She dropped back upon the silken cushions and laughed; there was a delicious chuckling sound in her throat; her beautiful eyes shone with amusement. "I scold Charlotte," she said. "I speak to her, oh, so seriously and severely! But she is incorrigible. She *will* do such things. She will so deceive people." The girl again arose upon one elbow, the smile gone. "It was a wicked thing to do, to question you so," she said. "To lure you on—for that is what she really did. For you are young," her eyes full of compassion, one hand held out as though to touch him. "You have not yet reached the place in your years where you distrust people. Especially," she said warmly, "you do not distrust women. It is wrong to take advantage of anyone who is like that."

Philip frowned. The smile was gone from his face, and his strong fingers locked.

"I talked with a girl last night—at the Two Pilots, in New Castle. I had the good fortune to be of service to her."

Madame Barreaut laughed with charming abandon.

"Forgive me," she said, breathlessly, both hands over her face, and she lying prone. "Forgive me! But it *is* comic! She will romance so. Charlotte should have been an actress; she has a wonderful talent; she makes everything so real, so natural. I am vexed with her. Often I could slap her face. But I laugh; I cannot help it." She arose upon her elbow, once more, her hand held out in an appeal. "As God hears me, I will say what is the truth. This young man, he is her lover. He cares for her, oh, so much; and she for him. But, they quarrel, do you understand? They grow furious with each other. It is no wonder you thought the matter serious and struck him down. If I had been a man I should have done the same. Sometimes his manner is such I marvel she stands it."

The furrow between Philip's eyes grew deeper; there were distrust, suspicion, disbelief in them; and yet he listened, a hot anger in his breast.

"Charlotte is her uncle's niece," said Madame Barreaut. "And so, when she learned who you were, she began her masquerading. That old snake, Hasty, had told her you were in the river, and she was ready for you. The things she said you told her!" Madame's arms were flung wide. "It is a shame she should repeat them; they are so intimate, so—so sacred."

Philip's mind darkened. He'd told her of his boyhood; of how his father lay upon death's threshold in the cabin of the *General Wolfe;* of his hopes and fears. He'd told her of his mother's picture!

"It is true I am a Barreaut," said Madame, "made so," smilingly, "by my husband's marrying me. He is now dead, but a Barreaut I remain, cousin to John Claridge, and," with a grimace upon her beautiful face, "with a tradition of great ships behind me. But, monsieur, I am of Martinique; we are generous there; our hearts beat for those who have wrong done them; and I thought to myself: 'What a sin it is to betray the confidence of this young man; to so make game of him; to win his trust and then laugh at him.'"

Suspicion was still in Philip Archer's eyes; and the anger in his breast grew greater. He said nothing, sitting motionless as she went on:

"And so it came into my mind: why should thoughts of the *Vision of St. John* put themselves in my way? Why should I permit a ship that is sunken and gone," she gestured, assuming a look of loathing—"I, who so despise ships—to keep me from speaking as I desire to speak? If this young man has rights of which he's been deprived, I said, shall I be a party to such villainy? I told myself, monsieur, I would not; and at once I set about finding you."

"You are kind," said Philip. He put the frown from his brow; the heat of his anger was disregarded. He smiled once again, his manner unruffled. "A cousin to John Claridge, and yet you go out of your way to do me a service."

"Not being a Barreaut, except by marriage, and having no ties that keep me to the Claridges except commercial ones, I feel myself free to make what friendships I choose," she said. "And your situation, your loneliness, the enemies arrayed against you made my heart sad; and I resolved," she said, "to warn you. Hasty is a serpent; do not trust him. Charlotte Desfourneaux is my friend; she is cousin to my dead husband, whom the blessed saints care for," piously; "but, laugh when you see her. Listen to nothing she says. For, as I have told you just now, John Claridge is her uncle, and she is his niece. There has never been a time when they did not see things with the same eye. De Chaulnes is a sot," she said, "a dissipated wretch; and I am glad you struck him. I do not warn you against him because I can read your eyes; you have expressive eyes," gesturing with one beautiful, jeweled hand, "one can read them like print. You dislike him. That is good. Feel so about them all, and you are safe."

"I thank you," said Philip. "To gain a friend in a strange place is a rich gift from fortune."

There was the sound of wheels from without; they halted. Madame Barreaut arose and stood before him. He also arose. And he'd been right: her height was well above his shoulder. A tall woman, and a marvelously beautiful one. The silken gown still clung to her figure; she had long, shapely lines; her shoulders, her neck, her bosom were splendidly traced; she carried her dark head like a princess.

"There are others," she said, "but I will not mention them

now. I only bid you be careful." She held out her hand. "And now," smiling dazzlingly, "good-bye. I have taken a risk in receiving you here," her eyes full of laughter. "John Claridge, if he knew, would be angry." Then she drew herself up; her face was proud and set in lines suddenly cold. "He may frighten others," she said, "but he cannot frighten me."

The knocker sounded upon the street door; there was a movement below as of a servant passing along the hall. Madame Barreaut went to the stairs with Philip; she descended with him as far as the first landing, where she paused. The staircase was an open one, and the landing commanded the lower hall and the front door.

"Good-bye," said Madame Barreaut. She spoke with great feeling; her brilliant eyes seemed suddenly swimming with tears. "Your loneliness and your peril have touched my heart," she said. "It is as though you were my brother, wandering in a dark place, unguided. Good-bye," she said. "And come again —soon. I shall be expecting you."

Philip went down the remainder of the stairs. The front door was wide, and Charlotte Desfourneaux stood there, drawing off her gloves. He bowed and paused, his face lighting up; but she did not look at him; her head was held high, she was poised splendidly; and she passed him coldly and unseeing.

CHAPTER VI

PHILIP ARCHER ate his supper at the Penny Pot in a gloomy state of mind; it was a good supper of mulled ale and cold beef and cheese and wheaten bread. And after it was done he sat with his pipe at the table, sipping a glass of port and listening to the talk going on about him. A lean man, with big bony hands, sat across from him with a glass of spiced rum and water.

"A seaman, sir?" he said to Philip.

The young man nodded; the big-boned man sipped at his rum and water and looked at him over the rim of the glass.

"High days upon the water, sir," he said, wiping his mouth with the back of his hand. "High, gusty days. By God!" he said, "I wish I could put out beyond the Capes; I'd show them something of my ability."

"You command a ship, then?" said Philip.

"A schooner," said the lean man; "a schooner, sir, that breaks the seas with hardly a ripple. The swiftest, handiest little vessel that ever slipped into the water."

"The schooner is a handy rig," said Philip. "Quick to manage; and God's winds are always generous with them."

"You may say that," said the man. He continued to sip at the mixture in his glass. "And the *Nancy Blake* is the sweetest of them all! I have a long gun in her bow, a gun on a pivot, that'll make the British step if ever I get away. And, also, I have four six-pounders and forty men." There was hunger in the man's eyes. "These are high days at sea," he said, "and here I am shut up in port. It's an ill fortune I'd not expected, sir."

"Who knows," said Philip, "any day now the Capes may open like a pair of doors. The fleet under our sea chief Hopkins is a-cruising, and he may soon take it into his head to steer home and so set you free."

But the lean man shook his head.

"Hopkins will keep his vessels out of danger," he said, "for what is he but a man made by influence? And, for the matter of that, what are his ships but a clutter of dull old merchantmen with some guns mounted in them?"

A smooth-mannered man, stout and with a heavy gold chain across his waistcoat, and who had the appearance of a solid man of affairs, also sat at the table; he had been dividing his attention between a beefsteak pie and the conversation.

"I think, Captain Hawes," he said, "you are a bit too severe upon the commodore, he is not a brilliant man, to be sure, but a very worthy one."

"I would never gainsay his respectability," the privateersman said, "God knows, I'm not one to take the good name from any man. But this gentleman has none of the hawk in him; he is comfortable and fat, dresses his ship reasonably with sails, and likes to sit over his food and drink in the cabin." Again Captain Hawes slapped the table. "You'll never accomplish anything with that breed of man, Mr. Deane: your comfortable, stolid shipman will do naught against the enemy that'll worry him."

"Mr. Hopkins will do well enough," said the other gentleman. He ate of the beefsteak pie and took a swallow of his drink. "The ships we have will answer for the time being. Given pieces of cannon of a proper weight, we'd have little to fear along our coasts, at least."

"If guns of size can be found for private-armed ships," said Philip, and he looked at Captain Hawes, "Congress should have no great trouble procuring them."

"Congress votes large sums," said the privateersman, "but has little moneys at hand. The draftsman who cast the long gun for the *Nancy Blake* is one Nicholas Fortune, a man of no means, and so, unable to serve Congress unless it can contrive to pay money down for his labor and skill."

"Ah, yes, Nicholas!" Philip Archer smiled as he heard the name. "A rare ironmonger. With his furnace and his moulds and his chemicals, he should do much good in a time like this. But, as you say, he is poor and could not carry on long without help."

The privateersman leaned across the table.

"When my need came, I went to Mr. Fortune and I said: 'My desire is to have a long gun for use in the bow of a swift schooner; a far-reaching gun, to swing upon a pivot; an iron gun with solid bands shrunk upon it.' He listened and did not say a word; but with a pen dipped in ink he made a drawing of my exact need. And the finished piece is perfection itself."

"A clever little man," said Philip. "He has the learning of ten, and the readiest hands I've ever seen."

Mr. Deane had his eyes searchingly upon Philip; there was a questioning in them; he cracked the knuckles of his plump hands.

"You are acquainted with him, it would seem," he said. "I fancied you were a stranger in the city,"

"I knew him at New Orleans," said Philip, "some years ago. He did a thriving business there, but, unfortunately, was called upon to serve the needs of all sorts of plundering ruffians; there were French and Spanish and British, and there were half and quarter breeds of various kinds, all desiring sword blades or pike heads, gun locks and cannon, with which to go a-murdering each other upon the seas. And so, unable to tolerate them, he gathered his matters together and left the place behind him."

"I'll warrant most of them were as honest men as you'd care to meet," protested the privateer captain, seeing in this saying a blow at his own profession. "Filling their purses, to be sure; but serving their governments as well."

But Philip made no reply to this.

"A few years ago," said he, "I called at Philadelphia and found Nicholas had established himself on the river above the city. He is still there, I suppose?"

The privateersman said he was.

"A brisk man setting out from this inn," said he, "could reach his furnace in a half hour."

The two talked further; but Mr. Deane was silent; he smoked a pipe and listened, and his eyes were upon Philip with steady attention. In a little while the young man had finished his drink and arose; he bid the captain and Mr. Deane good-evening and left the inn.

CHAPTER VII

PHILIP ARCHER put Vine Street behind him, holding to the river front. This would have been a perilous thing to do had the evening been deeper than dusk, for there were no public lights, and the docks being deeply cut, the roadway ran in and out, unprotected, among them.

The shipyard, as he passed it, was silent; the gaunt skeleton of what was to be a fighting frigate stood in the stocks, lifting high against the sky. Vessels in the stream were already showing lights; there was no wind, and some river sloops drifted with the tide, their sails hanging limp. Passing the next great bend in the river, Philip came abreast of the long, sandy island that lay midway between the Pennsylvania and the New Jersey shores; and on the verge of the water were some low buildings with a tall brick chimney towering above them. A light burned in one of the windows, and Philip looked in. There was a small man bent over a table, his elbows upon it, his chin in his hands, studying what looked like the design of a gun; on the margin of the drawing were long scribblings of figures— definite statements of fact and definite results worked out of them. The little man had a large head, bald in front; and large octagonal lenses were bridged across his nose.

The young man tapped upon the window; the other looked up, staring through the candlelight into the dusk; then he saw and recognized Philip; a smile came into his eyes, and he laughed a welcome. He went instantly to the door and threw it open.

"Philip!" he said, vastly pleased, grasping the hand of the young man in both his own. "Is it you indeed?"

"I am here, Nicholas, as promised," said Philip, not a whit less warm in his greeting.

"Yes, here you are!" said the little man, standing back and gazing at him admiringly. "And looking strong and well; for all your two years' cruising since I saw you last there is not a mark of the sea's anger on you."

"The sea never marks her own," said Philip, smiling. "She knows them without."

The little man shut the door; then he shoved the octagonal spectacles up on his forehead so that he might have a better view. He rubbed his hands together briskly.

"Well, sir," he said, "you are as your father was at your age. You've come, then," and his kindly eyes held steadily to Philip's face, "to do the thing those dead and gone would have you do?"

"I have," said Philip, quietly. "When I spoke to you last I said I'd bide my time until I had money enough to smooth a way for myself; I now have it: sound, heavy Spanish pieces together in a sack and ready to be laid out in any way I decide upon."

There was a wooden settle near the table where the drawing lay, and Nicholas Fortune drew it out from the wall.

"Sit down," he said. "Be comfortable, as Dick Archer's son should be, in my house." As Philip sat down, the little man got a pewter dish from a cupboard and placed upon it a handful of Spanish segars; he put these on the table, together with a short candle in a copper holder; from the same cupboard he took a long-necked bottle of wine and some glasses. "Here is a liquor your grandfather had a taste for: a sound red wine of Bordeaux. Fill up and drink; and then tell me all the things you've done since you were here last."

Philip poured a glass of the wine; he lighted one of the segars, settled comfortably against the high back of the bench, and crossed his legs. Nicholas fired more candles; there was a huge clock that ticked with slow dignity; the room seemed a sort of parlor and workshop combined; it had a sanded floor, there were rows of shelves holding sheep-covered books, and there was a heavy work bench where tools and drawings were cluttered; parts of gun carriages were thrown into corners; from chains in the ceiling hung a twelve-pounder piece, bearing a Spanish legend proclaiming it had been cast in the name of God and to save His holy religion from the Turks.

The young man smoked, and sipped his wine, and told a story of dour toil and struggle against storm, and the niggardliness of shipowners. Vessels had been scarce, but he had persevered. There'd been a voyage to Rio, and then to the Canaries; he'd touched the African coast more than once; he'd been three weeks in Lisbon, and then to Rio once more. Then he voyaged among the islands and in and about the Caribbean and the Gulf.

"Sea wrack and storm," said Nicholas, seated cross-legged upon a stool, the burning end of his segar pointed upward; "and the narrow hearts of vessel owners. Short-handed, I dare say, with food none too good and ships none too safe. And all this to get the small weight of money that will carry your matters through the windings of the law!"

"I'd never saved anything before," said Philip, "and I felt like a churl, putting the pieces so deeply into my pocket."

Nicholas nodded and nursed his folded knees.

"No matter," he said. "It's a thing between God, your father, and yourself. If these affairs of yours were of a kind that strength of body might overcome, all would be different. But the Claridges are rich; and as you must meet them upon ground of their own choosing, money is a needed thing."

As they sat and smoked the long segars, Philip told him of the episode of Charleston harbor and of what happened in the river near New Castle. Nicholas blinked and shook his head.

"To write a letter was a mistake," he said. "In it you warned them of your coming and what you meant to do; and they were waiting for you." He studied the young man through the smoke. "And so you have seen Hasty," he said. "A shrewd old fox: there is little that escapes him."

"It was as much as I could do," said Philip, "to make away with the chest; the captain of the brig, for all his pistols, was not one to fear, but the half-breed was a great swine of a fellow, and dangerous. I had my head laid open, as you can see," parting his hair with his fingers to show his scalp; "and I'll hold Mr. Hasty in mind for that, if for nothing else."

"I was a youth in your grandfather's time," said Nicholas Fortune, "but I remember hearing him say he'd as lief find a serpent in his bed as know the mind of Hasty had taken a fresh turn against him. A rare fox," said Nicholas, half in admiration; "a shrewd, hard flint. I mind him in the old days when he was younger; that was in London, where the Archers and the Claridges were then at grips in the courts. His clever tongue all but drove your grandfather to desperation."

"And yet," said Philip, "I've heard that the old gentleman had a tongue of his own."

Nicholas smoked and nodded.

"He had a gift of speech such as few have equaled. None in the clubs or wine houses of London at that time could match him. But Hasty was a file: he rasped and grated and cut; he had a cold-blooded insistence that would disorder the spleen of any but a rat." There was a silent space; Nicholas motioned toward the bottle. "It is smooth and good," he said. "Drink more of it; it'll never harm you." But as Philip would not, the little man seemed content enough; he blinked his eyes at the lights for a while and then said: "I suppose in the two years passed since you took the papers away, you've studied them a deal."

"Yes," said Philip. "But there was much that perplexed me; and a deal that drenched me like cold water."

"The King's law," said Nicholas Fortune, "whether it be the King of England, or France, or Spain, is like to do that. But, do not let the weight of it bow you down; to be sure, you are but a human man, and the thing is a sorry array of words, but you'll carry through with it, as your father always said you would."

They continued talking until there came a tapping at the door. Nicholas opened it, and at the threshold stood the smooth-looking gentleman who'd talked with Philip and the privateersman at the Penny Pot Tavern only an hour before.

"Good-evening to you, Mr. Deane," said Nicholas, in a most friendly way. "Come in. I was not expecting you these two hours."

"I trust," said Mr. Deane as he entered. "I am not intruding?" He bowed to Philip as he spoke.

"By no means," said Nicholas, affably. "Draw up a chair and take some wine."

The smooth-looking gentleman poured a goblet of the French wine; also he lighted one of the segars; and all the time he kept his gaze upon Philip. Nicholas noticed this and said:

"This is Philip Archer, a friend of many years; his father was the same before him."

Mr. Deane acknowledged the introduction with a bow and a gesture.

"I had the pleasure of speaking with Mr. Archer at supper," he said. He fumbled with his watchguard and examined the young man carefully. "You are in favor of the new government, sir, I take it."

"Quite a deal," said Philip. "I am proud of what Congress has done and said. Mr. Jefferson and Mr. Washington have my highest admiration." Mr. Deane shook his hand with ceremony; they poured out more wine and drank to the new states; all three talked at once; they threw up excited pictures; they dramatized events.

He had never, since God made him, Nicholas said, heard of such a thing as taxation without representation. It was a grisly absurdity, a stupidity without parallel; the joint infamy of a dull-witted minister and a dotard king. The people of

these colonies had been British subjects; the colonies themselves had been British plantations, and the thing contended
for was the very core of the British Constitution. Hadn't
Chatham spoken? hadn't he flayed the ministry at London
and pointed out the peril of what was being done?

No subjects had been more steadfast nor loyal than the
colonists, said Mr. Deane. They were British, deep into the
hearts of them; and they were proud of it; and they had fought
for Britain against the French and Spanish. But they were
people who would not be taxed without a voice in the matter:
as God heard them, they would not!—and that was the end of
it. Into the harbor with the tea! said Mr. Deane. No stamps!
No bleeding of citizens by sharp tradesmen across the water!—
no soft living upon their sweat by the owners of privileges. No
taking them out of their country for trial! No army standing
among them at the beck and call of London; no judges sub-
servient to the Crown and paid out of colonial treasuries! He
was against the writs of assistance; he upheld the Virginia
Resolutions, and the Declaration of Rights and Grievances.

The King's government was no longer inclined to argue,
said Philip in his turn. It was muskets thereafter, and sword
belts; pipe clay and tramping boots; it was horse and artillery,
hussars, high talk, and frowning looks; it was ships swaggering
up and down the coast, with bullet-headed officers placing
themselves above the law, and regarding no man's property
or dignity as superior to their impulses and bigotries. Troops
were to be quartered upon the people. Boston harbor was
closed. Massachusetts charter was abrogated. Canada was
enlarged at the expense of the colonies.

When Mr. Deane heard from Nicholas the part Philip had
played at Charleston harbor, he once more shook hands in his
ceremonious way.

"Sir," he said, "I am proud of your acquaintance. That
engagement was a blow at ministerial arrogance that will not
soon be forgotten."

Nicholas hugged his knees, delightedly; the end of his cigar burned red.

"I can see them lying out beyond the harbor," he said, "with Sir Peter abed with his hurts and cursing in his cabin."

Mr. Deane said to Philip: "I could not but deny what Hawes of the *Nancy Blake*, schooner, said concerning Ezek Hopkins; but, sir, what he said of the ships of our fleet was true enough. They are as dull and as poorly armed a huddle of craft as any man would care to step aboard."

"I've heard them spoken against more than once," said Philip.

"Those of us who had the attention of members," said Mr. Deane, "desired Congress to wait until vessels in other ports could be inspected. Mr. Adams thought it a wise plan, as did Mr. Jefferson and some others. But voices were lifted, protesting delay. It might be fatal, they said! And so, faulty ships were purchased."

"One weighty vessel, of good model," said Nicholas Fortune, "armed with strong guns, would cause more dread than all the ramshackle craft we have on the sea. One good ship under a proper master, and with some gun brigs and floating batteries, would open the port and free us of the enemy in one day's firing. I made special plans," said Nicholas: "fine guns, eighteen-pounders and twelves. I would cast them for the cost of the labor, I said; the metal I would provide at no cost at all: and good honest metal, of the proper parts of copper and tin, zinc and lead. But, no; they would hurry, hurry, hurry!—no time to wait!—the vessels must put to sea! And when they had their small pieces in them and were manned and provisioned, they lay in the river until the ice came; then it was weeks before they got out at all."

"Your day will come," said Philip, encouragingly. "The Congress would win battles with your guns, and they'll find it out before the end is reached."

Nicholas Fortune looked like an ancient gnome as he sat

huddled on his stool, embracing his knees, the big octagonal
lenses high upon his forehead.

"It would be too bad if this were a day when ships were
fought with catapults and onagers," said he. "But God and
the Chineesers gave us gunpowder—though some say 'tis a
fable about the Chinese, and that the monk, Roger Bacon,
made the first of it. Or," said Nicholas, "if it were even the
day of bombards or culverins, we might say the task was too
great to accomplish. But we are in a later time, and the French,
and the Swedes, and the Dutch have done great things with
cannon, with carriages, and with expeditious ways of charging
and firing. There was a time, sirs, when archers thronged the
rails of ships and shot long, pointed shafts against the enemy;
or there were crossbowmen with their bolts; or there were
demi-cannon, bastard muskets, matchlocks, wheelocks, and
other such poor fumblings. Now we have proper pieces, we
have short hand guns and blunderbuss pistols for boarding; the
musket with the bayonet socketed in its barrel has displaced
the pike. And in the face of all this, consider, sirs, a fleet was
permitted to put to sea as that one was!—makeshift ships with
nondescript armament; and we must listen while they tell us
they hope to achieve victory."

He got up, took a drawing from the table, spread it out
upon the floor, and placed a series of flaming candles about
it.

"There is the gun you asked of me, Mr. Deane," he said.
"Cast them as twenty-four pounders, of tough, durable stuff;
mount a score or three dozen to the ship, and you'll drive the
enemy from the sea."

"A splendid piece," said Mr. Deane, admiringly, as he
examined the drawing. He looked at Philip and nodded.
"Twenty-four pounders! That's a weight of metal to set
rattling on a ship's side. What?"

"Good, robust cannon," agreed young Archer. "The
Spaniards have some in their vessels throwing greater weight;

but their barrels are short; they are more like carronades and are for battering, merely."

"There you mark the weakness of all old pieces," said Nicholas Fortune. "With those, engaged vessels come together like gladiators; they grind and roar and fret, but still do but little hurt to each other. With long tubes like this," and he tapped the drawing with a finger, "a shipman of skill may stand away and splinter his enemy's masts and yards and take no risk himself."

"I have spoken of your ideas to some members of Congress," said Mr. Deane, "but there was no eagerness among them. Those from the maritime states listened with interest; but the others were dull to the matter and gave me no encouragement."

Nicholas Fortune wagged his head, cheerfully; there was a smile in his eyes.

"Nothing that has a touch of newness gets official favor immediately," he said. "This gun," said Nicholas, as he rolled the drawing into a cylinder and put it upon the table, "will wait a long time before it speaks upon the sea. I shall be dead, perhaps, and credit for it will go to another."

"We must not lose confidence," said Mr. Deane, smoothly. "I advise against that. When I requested you to put your thought of this arm on paper, Mr. Fortune, I had more than one idea about it. Congress has failed me; but," and he lifted his brows, gesturing with the segar, "I have some hope the King of France will not."

Philip Archer sipped his wine quietly; but there was a cock to his head that told of interest. Nicholas looked at Mr. Deane.

"The help of a strong government like the French would do many things for us," said he.

After some further talk, Mr. Deane arose; he shook Nicholas's hand.

"Use will be made of your skill," he said. "Failing Congress, and failing France, also, there remains the possible private means of which I have spoken to you more than once."

"Captain Conyngham mentioned that to me just before he went to sea," said Nicholas.

"What," said Philip, disappointment in his voice, "has Conyngham gone on a voyage?"

"This month or more," said Nicholas. "But he will return in haste," reassuringly. "His errand is of that kind."

Mr. Deane here extended a cordial hand to Philip.

"We shall meet again, I hope," he said. "And, until then, I suppose I need not say, discretion should be kept well in mind."

Philip assured him he'd be carefulness itself, and Mr. Deane, saluting them from the doorway, took his departure.

"I was about to speak of Conyngham's sudden sailing as Mr. Deane knocked upon the door," said Nicholas to Philip. "He had received your letter and was greatly pleased that something was, at last, to be done. But Congress was gathering, threats were coming across the sea from London, the British forces were being strengthened, and war was all but upon us. None knew better than he how unprepared we were; and so, when the chance came to load his vessel with merchandise and set sail for France, he was away at once. His cargo," said Nicholas, his voice going instinctively to a whisper, "was to be exchanged for gunpowder; also sulphur and nitre for the making of the same; cannon, firearms, bayonets were also to be purchased by him. Warm clothing and boots and blankets for the troops in the field were other matters he was urged to see to."

"I can't regret his absence on such a mission," said Philip. "But," and he looked at the little gun maker questioningly, "I trust Corporal Brotot has not gone off likewise?"

"Brotot is in the city," said Nicholas. "Robust and excellent in spite of his seventy-nine years; seven years older than myself," said the little gun maker admiringly, "and yet as straight as a rifle barrel. His eyes are as sharp, I think, as they were fifty years ago; and his small-sword, when he takes it in hand, is like a flash of light."

"He has not been idle while waiting for me, I dare say," said Philip. "In a chief city, with war growing darker every day, his knowledge must be in large demand."

"I'll warrant you," said Nicholas. "A man of the corporal's skill could not fail but be in demand. As you have quartered yourself at the Penny Pot, you'll find him not far from you, in Water Street. He has transformed an old warehouse into a school of arms, and there he is, working away from dawn until midnight."

"I shall manage a word with him to-night," said Philip. "And do you breakfast with me in the morning. I shall have the corporal there, also; and I can then talk my fill with you and perhaps come to some means of beginning what I have to do."

"I should like," said Nicholas, "to have you speak with a man I've come to know here; a person with a vast knowledge of shipping and of the law covering such things."

"By all means," said Philip. "If it is possible, tell him of our meeting in the morning; perhaps he, too, can contrive to be there."

2

A rain had been falling for some time, and when Philip left Nicholas Fortune's place behind him, it came down in torrents; he took shelter under a tree, and watched the bobbing lights of small vessels anchored in the river as they pitched and tossed in the gusts of wind. The road ran with water; and as he stood, his coat collar turned up and his hat pulled down, he caught the sound of hoofs; turning, he saw two horsemen in long waterproofs, and with the rain streaming from their hat rims, coming at a hard gallop toward him. One of them was a tall man, highshouldered and angular, who, to get as much protection as possible from the downpour, rode close under the trees. He was almost upon Philip, when the young man shouted a warning. The man looked at him, Philip was sure of that, and there was time enough to swerve his horse; the merest trifle would have done it. But the rider made no attempt to do so. The animal's shoulder struck Philip, and he was thrown backward into the muck of the roadside; he arose and looked through the rain after the riders; they did not so much as turn to see if he'd been injured; but as they went on he could hear their laughter. And, full of rage, he set off after them as hard as he could pelt.

CHAPTER VIII

THE cartway was seamed with rivulets of water, and the two horsemen splashed through them; after a space they turned into Vine Street, and then into Water, where they drew up before a large building, apparently once a warehouse, which stood with its back to the river; there was a whale-oil lamp burning above the doorway. A carriage with a pair of horses, fretting and restless in the pouring rain, stood at the door; a man in a streaming tarpaulin held them by the heads, while another had the carriage door open and was inviting the occupants to "step out, madame; there'll be scarcely a drop touch you."

As the horsemen halted beside the carriage, the angular man leaned over and spoke to those inside; instantly a woman's voice, high and vexed, made reply.

"Edward, it is too bad of you! We have been unable to leave the carriage because of the rain and have been wretchedly uncomfortable."

"I am sorry," said Edward, coldly. "A message came from De Chaulnes that I was needed: Hasty desired to speak with me. Why is Brotot not here?" with a sharp glance about. "These people need putting in their places."

He spoke to the groom, who held open the door, with a slurring contempt that made that honest man lift his head, resentfully. De Chaulnes beat with the butt of his riding whip upon the doorposts of the building. But before a reply came, a streaming figure leaped out of the rain and dark, a pair of strong hands reached up and grasped the angular man, plucking him out of his saddle.

"Am I a beggar that you should look me in the eye and ride me down?" said Philip Archer, hotly. He threw the angular young man against the side of the carriage with force enough to rock it upon its leather slings; with his open right hand he struck him upon one side of the face, with the left he struck him upon the other side. Then he stepped back, hooking his thumbs in his belt. "Laugh at that!" he said. "And let me see what you mean to do about it."

The second man slipped out of his saddle. Philip saw that it was De Chaulnes, and that he held the heavy butt of his whip ready to strike; the young man did not move, but looked at him over his shoulder.

"Be so good as to stay where you are," he said. "You are a man of experience and know there is a code covering matters of this sort; the present opportunity belongs to this other gentleman, who seems to think persons afoot have no rights on the road." He looked easily at the angular man, who stood upright and motionless at the carriage door. "I'm awaiting your pleasure, sir," he said.

"It may be," said Edward Claridge, "you are some baker's apprentice, gone mad with revolutionary talk. If that be so, I'll kick you soundly and hand you over to the watch. On the other hand, if you are a person of any consequence, I shall pistol you where you stand."

He went to his horse, which stood, its head hanging, in the rain, and drew a long-barreled pistol from a protected holster; there came a cry at the appearance of the weapon; then Charlotte Desfourneaux, dressed magnificently, with powdered hair and many jewels, was framed in the carriage doorway.

"Edward!" She held out her hand. "Edward! No."

The man held the weapon under his cloak so that the rain would not affect the charge. He paid no attention to the girl, but addressed himself to Philip.

"Now, sir," he said, "your name and station?"

There was a cold authority in the voice that caused Philip to smile; he cocked a humorous eye at the speaker, his thumbs still hooked in his belt, and the rain dripping from him.

"Has it not occurred to you," he said, "that I might not see fit to answer a question put as you put this one? There is a threat in your manner, and I've always made it a practice to meet a thing of that sort with something in kind." He pointed warningly through the rain at Edward Claridge. "I've seen the breath choked out of men with pistols in their hands before this; so be careful what you do and say."

Charlotte was now out of the carriage; De Chaulnes threw his cloak about her, as she put her hand upon the arm of Edward Claridge.

"Edward!" she said. "Listen to me!"

Her lips were close to his ear as she whispered; he started, and his head lifted, his face was intent in the light of the lamps as he stared at Philip. He spoke in a low tone to De Chaulnes, who also stared, surprised, and seeming not at all confident of the situation. Then as the two men conferred, and nothing immediate seemed likely to happen, Philip turned toward the doorway of the building, where a sudden stir had begun; a number of men stood there, small-swords in their hands, and in the midst of them was a short man, old, thick of body, and with powerful shoulders; he wore a sleeveless canvas jacket, and Philip Archer spoke to him at once.

"Brotot!" he said, pleasure in his voice.

The stocky man, with the light gleaming upon his bald head, stiffened; his hand went up in a sharp salute.

"M'sieu," he said. And then: "That is for your grandfather. As you stepped through the rain toward me, I saw him once more." Corporal Brotot moved back a pace or two, and his eyes searched Philip from head to foot.

"You have changed," he said. "The last few years have made a great difference in you." He drew the young man inside; opening from the wide passage was a sort of gun room; there were arms racks upon the walls; pistols, muskets, hangers were suspended in rows. "A year ago," said the old sword master, "I had your letter from Martinique; it came to me at New Orleans. I came here at once, according to instructions, and have been waiting for you."

"I expected to arrive almost immediately," said Philip, "but there has been a great harrying among the islands because of the war; merchants were not sufficiently at rest in their minds to adventure with new cargoes, and more time was needed to gather the money than I thought it would."

Corporal Brotot did not reply; he was looking out into the passage where there was a sudden babble of voices, a stamping of boots, a shaking of wet cloaks. Then he turned his eyes to Philip.

"A moment ago, m'sieu," he said, "I saw you face to face with Edward Claridge."

"Edward Claridge!" Philip looked at the young man in the passage. "He is son to John Claridge, perhaps?"

"A nephew."

Philip scowled at the young man with the high shoulders; there was a quick menace in his eyes.

"He holds his head high, as I've heard his people have always done. If I'd known who he was a moment ago, I'd done more than slap his jaws."

"You struck him!" said Brotot.

"He seems one who takes little account of whom he overturns into a ditch," said Philip; "and I thought it best to make it plain to him that I'm not one to take his mannerisms quietly."

"You have never seen him before to-night?"

"Never."

"You struck him," said Brotot, "and he drew a pistol." He shook his head, a look of something like wonder in his face. "It is the usual beginning, the thing to be expected when an Archer and a Claridge meet."

He looked at the group in the passage, but the eyes of his

mind went back to a scene in the harbor of L'Orient almost a half century before. He'd been a young man then, and on a crisp, bright day he stood on the deck of a French merchant-man—a tall ship with masts like towers, and yards as wide as the great hall of a burgher's exchange. It was a ship owned by the firm of Barreaut Frères, built by them, and engaged in carrying their freight to China and the far India seas. And while he stood there, another Edward Claridge stood there, a tall man, angular, high shouldered, with a cold face and eyes of steel. And before him stood a M'sieu Archer—Philip's grandfather, as supple, as clever, as brave a man as ever stepped; and he was snapping his fingers in Claridge's face! He was as easy and as careless with it as might be, though it was a matter to make one of God's angels tremble; for Edward Claridge stood on his own deck, he had right- and left-hand pistols in his belt, and had death in his face.

"And here, to-night," the corporal thought, "after a half century, the thing, one might say, repeats itself. This present Edward Claridge is very like the other one; and this last of the Archers is as much like the first of them as one sword blade is like another. And when they meet for the first time, a blow is struck, a weapon is drawn. It seems more than a thing of ships and money," shaking his head wonderingly. "It is their spirits that are at war with each other. And it will be so until the end."

As Philip, with Corporal Brotot, left the gun room, he came face to face with Charlotte Desfourneaux; she stood with De Chaulnes, smiling, quite animated, her bronze head gleaming in the yellow of the lamps. Having her treatment of him at Madame Barreaut's well in mind, his manner was guarded; nevertheless, he moved toward her, and as he caught her look he bowed. But she turned her head away without a change of expression; Claridge and De Chaulnes regarded him with cold, sneering looks. Resentment was hot in his heart, and bitter words were upon his lips: but he held himself in check. In his memory, for all his anger, there was the look she'd worn as he talked with her at the Two Pilots the night before; there had been deep sympathy in her voice; more than once he'd seen tears in her eyes as she listened to him. So he stood, his dripping hat in his hand, crushing back his pride; and then De Chaulnes said to him:

"Perhaps, m'sieu, it would be as well if you did not presume upon a meeting the nature of which you do not properly understand."

The heavy blood throbbed in Philip's temples; his hands were clenched. The girl still kept her face averted; the beautiful Madame Barreaut stood at her side, smiling, her dark eyes sparkling; she looked at Philip as though wondering at his dullness. Had she not told him? What fools men were! Had not her words been quite plain? And so, filled with shame and rage, Philip turned and with Brotot at his side walked away.

The drill hall was a huge place, lighted with hanging lamps; in its center was a tanbarked space for horsemen; at regular intervals along the edge of the riding floor were squares of tightly stretched canvas for use in sword play; sabers, small-swords, rapiers, and single-sticks hung upon the walls as in the gun room; also, there were canvas jackets, padded helmets and gloves, muskets with bayonets plugged into their barrels. Wrestling mats were rolled up in corners, and there were vaulting horses, poles for leaping, and other means for training the body and mind for war.

A long line of young men were being put through a sword drill under the direction of a hard-faced old trooper who had a dark, Spanish cast. Philip paused to watch these. A man at his side took out a silver snuffbox, tapped the lid, and offered it to him.

"Ah, once more good-evening to you, Captain Hawes," said the young man, recognizing the privateersman. He took a pinch of the snuff, and Hawes did likewise.

"Here is a thing," said Hawes, and he indicated the line of

young swordsmen. "Here is a thing for every man in the colonies to take note of. It puts heart into one to see it and makes one consider that what has been done by the Congress might not be an empty gesture after all."

"They are raw and awkward," said Philip, as he eyed the line. "But they are earnest, and when you've said that you've said a deal."

The *Nancy Blake's* master nodded.

"You take my meaning at once, sir. They *are* earnest. They stand there before that hardened old devil of a hussar, hour after hour each night; they mount their horses and deploy, ride in files, charge, leap over barriers, and do all manner of things so that the city might have a troop of trained horse soldiers when needed. They are the sons of merchants, of shipowners, of apothecaries, of ironmongers, and merchant's clerks. It may be they'll do little when the test comes, but let that be as it may. It is the intent, sir, that weighs greatest in the end. The same thing being done here to-night is being done in every town from New England to the south; the lads are leaving the plows in the fields and hurrying to arms; the coopers and wharf builders, the sail makers, and porters in the warehouses are searching out old muskets and fowling pieces. It is a great comfort, sir, to see it, and I would to God we had a heavy ship or two so that the harbor might be unsealed and we sailor men be set free upon the waters to do our part."

"That time will come, never fear," said Philip. "Our coast line is long; they haven't enough ships to patrol it all."

"Half face!" The Spanish hussar growled the words in his broken English. "To the left."

Awkwardly the line obeyed; the hussar chattered like a monkey and cursed.

"Elevate."

The long line of blades went out and up, held at an angle of forty-five degrees. Then there were an advance, a retreat, a lunge and parry, both in *quarte* and *tierce*, all gone through with indecision and a scrambling that caused the line to waver and gave the moving blades a ragged look.

The Spanish drill master stopped them; he went, sneeringly, down their length; he mocked them and made uncouth gestures.

"A hard-crusted rascal," said Captain Hawes. "The devil himself to get on with, I'm told." And then, after a moment: "I wonder what does Mr. Adams think of it all. There he sits," indicating a portly, red-faced man of middle age, sitting among a group at some little distance, his knees crossed and his plump fingers drumming impatiently upon the arms of his chair.

"I fancy," said Philip, after watching the famous New Englander for a moment, "it is not the awkwardness of the recruits that makes him impatient so much as the conversation of the people standing near by."

Captain Hawes looked intolerantly at a number of young men and women, elegantly attired, the men with frills at their throats and wrists, with varnished boots, or silk stockings, and handsome coats, high-collared and with wide lapels; the women were beautiful, smiling, gowned perfectly, lolling in chairs; there was a fluttering of fans and fine white handkerchiefs, a posturing and laughing. At those moments when the drilling line of recruits showed itself as especially ragged and unconvincing, this laugh became almost a jeer.

"There is no shortage of Tories in the city," Captain Hawes said, "and they are not always of the timid sort. If anyone with a knowledge of that lot were to comb them out, he'd find few that have not been British taught; and for the most part, I'd dare say, served in the British regiments."

"Edward Claridge, now," said Philip. "I see him among them. What story have you to tell of him?"

"He has been in one of the regiments in New England: in the Carolinas, too, I think. And for three or more years in England. An excellent soldier, they say, but with little that's human in him. I've mastered a vessel owned by the Claridges in my day, and almost came to grips with him more than once."

Corporal Brotot, who had been busy with one of his aides, now spoke.

"At this time, captain, it is best that personal dislikes be put aside," he said. "Edward Claridge has talent that could be used for the public good."

"The Congress will get but little benefit from such as he," said the privateersman, shaking his head.

"You have not heard, then, that he's lately offered himself as an instructor to the new troops," said the corporal. "And Mr. Hancock has accepted him. M'sieu le Duc De Chaulnes, who has led squadrons of cavalry for His Majesty King Louis, has also offered to make suggestions."

They were still talking when the Spanish drill master left his motionless line and swaggered away with his horseman's gait to where Edward Claridge was standing; the two conferred, then the hussar stepped back, saluting. Claridge moved out slowly, superciliously, to the front of the line.

"I had understood," he said, his cold eye valuing the recruits, "that there were some among you who had, at least, the rudiments of the sword." His look went up and down among them, disbelievingly, and he continued: "Some of you have stated in my presence that Brotot has seen little more he could do for you. Of course, that is quite possible," and his look went to the corporal, who stood at Philip's side, erect and silent, "for the professional swordsmen usually come up from the ranks and have little or no firmness at the base of their art."

There was a silence; then a strapping youth, wearing jingling spurs, a heavy leather belt, and carrying a curved sword, stepped out of the line.

"That is all very well, Claridge," he said. "You are London taught and have your prejudices, but I doubt if you've ever engaged with Brotot. They don't breed his type of swordsman where you picked up your learning. And after all, it's the weight of a man's stroke that counts when you face him, sword in hand, and not his station in life."

Claridge smiled his cold-lipped smile.

"It is true," he said, "I have never engaged Corporal Brotot. And I have no doubt he handles his weapon well, but the weight of a stroke is of little consequence unless the blow falls as directed." He leisurely approached the wall upon which the weapons were hung and took down a long blade with a brass hilt. Balancing this in his hand he said: "If the corporal is so minded, I'll strive to show I was quite right when I told Mr. Hancock the methods he used were of the old time."

At this insolent suggestion there was a murmur from those within earshot; everyone looked at Brotot. But he still stood erect, his face almost without expression.

"I will remind M'sieu," he said, "that I teach the sword. I am a professional and do not go upon the floor except as an instructor."

There was a derisive smile upon the face of Claridge; De Chaulnes laughed; the others stirred and whispered together and smiled.

"Of course," said Claridge coldly, "it is for the corporal to say what he will or will not do. I would not influence him in any way. But the representative of a school should, I think, always be willing to defend his method. That, at least, is the custom among gentlemen; though, to be sure, the barrack room may have different ideas."

The corporal kept his erect attitude, his heels together; his hand went to a salute. But he said nothing. Then the strapping youth threw down his sword and seized from the wall one with a blunted point and edge.

"Now, by God, Claridge," he said, hotly, "I think so little of your way of treating a man who is, in a manner of speaking, helpless, that I'll take it upon myself to show you that his method is all that's been claimed for it."

At once the young man's comrades were about him, exclaiming encouragingly; all other matters in the great room ceased;

spectators and those engaged in the drills gathered in a circle.

"Now that," said the privateersman, Captain Hawes, "is a youth of body and pluck. Out he stands with his blade as quick as a whip."

Philip Archer, who had been watching and listening with interested attention, turned quietly to Corporal Brotot.

"You have a champion, at all events, Brotot. And a clever one, I hope?"

But the corporal shook his head.

"He is a good young man," he said. "And earnest. He will make an excellent soldier. But with the sword—no. He has not the feeling for it. He is strong but not swift; and he lacks steadiness."

There was an excited milling in and out, a talking and a measuring of blades; Claridge took no part in this, but talked with De Chaulnes, who stood at the side of Charlotte Desfourneaux. She sat with a fan gently waving, smiling at something Madame Barreaut was saying. Madame looked as supple and handsome as a leopardess, with dazzling skin and flashing eyes; her hair was a glossy black, with never a touch of powder; she wore marvelous jewels; her feet, in red, pointed shoes, were of an amazing and arched smallness.

"It is Madame Barreaut, cousin to Mademoiselle Desfourneaux," said Corporal Brotot.

"A splendid young gypsy," said Philip. "I have had the pleasure of speaking with her."

But his frowning look was upon Charlotte, angry, searching. De Chaulnes was bending over her, she was looking up into his face, her lips parted, her eyes alight.

"Last night," he thought, "I spilt the best part of a flask of wine persuading him to keep his hands from her. But to see them now one would think that none but the most cheerful matters had ever arisen between them."

He'd been clearly overtalkative the night before; he wrinkled his brows and rubbed the side of his nose as he thought of it.

She'd asked him questions; she'd quizzed him; she'd led him on: and he'd been at pains to tell her everything.

"God knows," was his bitter thought, "if I kept anything to myself, I had not meant to. No confession ever made was fuller than the one I made to her. Was there a hope in my mind, or a plan I did not tell her of? I can think of none. Was there a misadventure, an enterprise? Was there an item about my people, or their purposes, their strengths or their failings I didn't relate to her? Not one. And for all my candor, what do I receive? Disdain; a high-held head; a contemptuous look."

For all his anger, his heart was sore in his breast, for as he'd seen her the night before struggling with the Frenchman he'd fancied her greatly. She'd been helpless, but had not lost courage; there'd been a look in her eyes he'd not often seen in a woman's eyes before. And when he'd struck the man, she'd been glad. She'd changed her mind since then. He hated a woman who used her beauty for a mean purpose; but his resentment was mixed with a kind of incredulity; he'd seen the warmth of her eyes; he'd seen a wonderful color in her, and a manner marked by truth; and to think, by God, here she was——

But Edward Claridge now took his place inside the circle of spectators and faced the young trooper who was to oppose him.

"Stand back, señors," said the Spanish hussar in his barking voice. "Make room."

"It may be as Brotot says with this young man," said the master of the privateer; "he may be of poor quality with his weapon. But from the look I see in Mr. Adams' face there is nothing in all these thirteen states of ours he'd not freely give if the youth bore down this supercilious gentleman who stands there so confidently."

Philip looked at Mr. Adams, who was frowning and nodding his head at something that was being said to him; then the blades of the contestants crossed with a ring.

The young trooper was hasty with anger, and lunged at once;

Edward Claridge stepped away with a perfection of ease; he was as straight as a lance shaft. Another hurried thrust: it was parried; another and another, each more furious than the other. The blades grated and rang. Claridge's cold eyes showed the contempt he felt for his opponent's efforts.

"A good workman," said Philip to Corporal Brotot. "A seasoned swordsman, but one of the dulled point, nevertheless."

"The Claridges do not lack courage," said Brotot, steadily.

"Time will show you that. Usually they are cunning, as rats or foxes and ravens are cunning; but when words lose their strength and tricks their power, take care. They are as sudden as leopards and as dangerous."

A cry went up; the young trooper had leaped in behind a series of thrusts; but Edward Claridge had avoided them with ease; then with a darting lunge his blunt point prodded the other's chest, and he stepped easily back. And while the arena was full of sounding talk Mr. Adams summoned Brotot.

"Do not tell me, Corporal," he said, "that this young man is your most finished pupil. Surely you have one capable of mastering this London dandy."

"The youths that come to me, now that troops are being recruited, have no schooling with arms. They can shoot, m'sieu, as all Americans can; but the sword is unknown to them. It is too soon for much to be expected; a long time must pass before they have that joining of eye and hand that makes for skill."

Mr. Adams took a large pinch of snuff; he gestured hopelessly to a man who sat near him.

"A thing like this, Mr. Lazarus, may seem of little consequence; but nevertheless it will leave a bad impression."

Mr. Lazarus was a small man, stooped, with a gray wig and a face seamed with wrinkles. He held a black walking staff with a knob of ivory cut to resemble the head of a fabulous monster.

"Trifles are never unimportant," he said. "My experience, sir, has been wide, and I will say that the things lowest in the moment's estimation have often wrought the larger harm or good."

"I spoke yesterday to Hancock in the matter of young Claridge offering his service here, and said the impression made upon me was not favorable. These fops," and Mr. Adams looked at the group about Edward Claridge, "are usually of a British turn of mind."

Mr. Lazarus was plainly in agreement with this; he nodded his head, and his many wrinkles seemed to grow into many more. He polished the ebony staff with his gnarled fingers and seemed to commune with the ivory monster at its head.

"I think we can safely say, my dear Mr. Adams, they are not in favor of any effective measures for carrying out the plans of Congress."

"You are right, Lazarus. And when finally one of them makes an offer of aid, the motive behind the offer, with me, at least, is one for cogitation."

Mr. Lazarus polished the staff; he seemed to hold it so that the ivory monster was close to his ear.

"These young troopers who have come forward so readily are in the midst of matters not usual to them; and, sir, the young are easily depressed. If charge of their activities is given to a person not in sympathy with them, much harm may be done."

Mr. Adams again took snuff.

"To have this British-taught swordsman and one-time officer in the King's army face down everyone here to-night is, I think, destructive of everything we've lately built up in their minds." He beckoned to Brotot. "Corporal," he said, "take up your blade and dazzle this fellow."

But the old sword master shrugged his shoulders.

"As I have say, it is not for the professional to do this, m'sieu. The mastership of arms is a noble calling, and its followers must treat it with respect. But, m'sieu, if you want the young man beaten, there is a pupil of my own here, an American who has much talent."

"Then, in the name of God, bring him forward!" said Mr. Adams, earnestly. "Let us put a stop to this sniggering behind delicate handkerchiefs. Give him a sword, Brotot, and tell him what to do."

CHAPTER IX

MR. ADAMS was not alone in his resentment of the group of dandies; Philip Archer was watching their posturing gentility, their mincing airs, and detested them. He had seen Charlotte Desfourneaux applaud the popinjay fencing tricks of Edward Claridge: when he'd won and stepped back, she'd offered him her hand. The night before, she'd seemed to despise and fear the Claridges, but now it was quite plain that this stilt-legged jack-a-loon was a sort of hero. A dancing master, by God! And for such as he to take up a blade in the presence of a man like Brotot was absurd. It was scandalous!

And just then the young man felt the touch of Brotot's hand upon his arm.

"It is my wish," said Brotot, "that you take a sword in your hand and teach some manners to this young man who has spoken so slightingly of my years and skill."

Philip smiled; his chin went out, his nose looked more like the beak of a hawk than ever.

"Why, now," he said, "luck is walking at my side. For it was in my mind this very instant I'd like nothing better."

At once he threw off his wet sea coat and turned back his sleeves; Brotot spoke to the hussar who, with a look at Philip, swaggered to one of the arms racks and took down a half dozen long blades. Philip selected one and whipped it through the air until it sang.

"This will do," he said, and wiped it upon his sleeve. "A good blade, and well set into the hilt."

He felt an excited air among the Claridge group; he heard a pattering of hands, an exclaiming, a buzz of talk. And again he saw the eyes of Charlotte Desfourneaux upon him, cold, non-believing. A little breath caught in his throat; his eyes were full of anger.

Then he saw the look of Mr. Adams, and set his jaw, balancing the sword blade in his hand. The eyes of the statesman held to him as he came down the floor.

"Now," said Mr. Adams to Mr. Lazarus, "here is a tall youth who has the look of something. Mark that confident strut! I like a game-cock sort of bearing in anyone as they approach a task, no matter what it is."

The deep, sunken eyes of Lazarus were upon Philip with peculiar fixity; the long yellow fingers clutched at the ebony staff, his blue lips moved as though he were casting up a column of figures.

"A strong young man," he said, "and a very ready one. He has great natural force. He glows like a steel ingot lately taken from the furnace, one that will throw sparks about in a shower, if struck."

Edward Claridge stood cold and unmoved; he picked a sword offered him by the Spanish drill master and spoke to Corporal Brotot.

"It may be," he said, "the small-sword is to be preferred to this type. This is an obsolete weapon, clumsy and with a deal too much material in it." There was smiling derision upon his thin lips as he added: "What does your champion say?"

The corporal spoke to Philip.

"There were times, m'sieu," he said, "when we made play with the sword Mr. Claridge prefers. If your hand still has the feel for it, you may be inclined to oblige him."

Without a word Philip handed his weapon to the drill master; there was a sudden gleam in the eyes of Edward Claridge as he met the glance of De Chaulnes. Mr. Adams brushed some particles of snuff from his shirt frill, frowning his displeasure.

"I feel this is a mistake," he said to Mr. Lazarus. "These

popinjays affect the small-sword much as they do scent and powder. And there is an advantage to Claridge in the exchange, you may be sure."

The Spaniard put aside the long-bladed weapons and now approached with a half dozen small-swords, the hilts held outward; he offered them to the contestants. Claridge looked at Brotot.

"If your friend will be so good," he said with a wave of the hand.

There was a well bred arrogance in the words and action that lifted the hackle of Philip Archer; and when the hussar offered the blades to him in turn, he said:

"The small-sword is of the gentleman's own asking. He shall have every advantage."

There was an instant's pause; then, with a cold lifting of the brows, Edward Claridge chose a weapon, tested it, and moved back. Philip did likewise. Corporal Brotot stood with squared shoulders, looking from one to the other.

"Ready," he said brusquely. Then, as they stepped to the mark, saluting, he added: "Engage."

With the word, young Claridge stepped forward, his blade snapping like a whiplash; the thing had an effrontery in it that caused a gasp of surprise to go up. It was plainly the first move in a studied trick, and was meant to bring the matter to an instant close; but here he had not the honest, cudgeling strokes of the young trooper to deal with. The darting blade was caught upon one that moved like a shadow: the arm behind the blade had the weight of a steel bar, the wrist the suppleness of a python's body; caught off balance by this unexpected power, Claridge was thrown back. Like a cat he recovered himself, but too late; a driving point came at him, such a point as probably he'd never seen before, and Philip Archer prodded him twice upon the chest, then stepped back out of reach and stood waiting.

Instantly Brotot moved between the two, his arms outstretched; but Edward Claridge, his face suddenly white, protested.

"It was a chance," he said. "It could not happen again. One more assault. I'll prove I'm right."

Madame Barreaut was upon her feet, excitedly; but Charlotte Desfourneaux sat waving her fan with slow grace.

"Do you not see?" said Madame. "Edward has been struck."

"He is foolhardy," said the girl. "I warned him, did I not?"

"Charlotte!" said Madame, her eyes flashing, "you are like ice." Then, suddenly, "But this sailor is magnificent; he has the ease of a great bird, swooping. His stroke was like light itself. Poor Edward," she said, clasping her hands, "he will be so chagrined. It is quite dreadful. But, see how his friends gather about him. How they sympathize with him; and how angry he is," with a flashing smile. "He strides like a tiger—up and down, up and down. He would kill that man with a blow if it were possible. He is enraged."

"Edward is given to rages," said the bronze-haired girl. "But they are not important, for he has been taught in a gentle school of manners: a subdued leopard is never very dangerous."

Madame laughed at this; she applauded the winner and cast looks of condolence upon the loser; and over her shapely shoulder she said to Charlotte:

"You are wicked; you have an outrageous tongue. I would not have Edward hear such a thing said of him for the world."

The round face of Mr. Adams was beaming; he rubbed his chubby calves with huge satisfaction.

"This is a youth who will go far!" he said. "This is a youth who has skill and quality! Did you mark the air of him, Lazarus? A game-cock, by God! Quiet until the moment came, and then he was like a thunderbolt!"

"His name," said Lazarus, a crooked look about his mouth, "is Archer. He is one of the Archers of the *Vision of St. John* matter—a thing that had all England, France, and Spain by the ears three generations ago. A great galleon, laden with riches from Porto Bello, was taken at sea, and the plunder has been a matter of controversy ever since."

Brotot approached Philip and repeated Claridge's request; but the young man handed his blade to the drill master and dusted his fingers with an air of finality.

"The gentleman is a novice," he said. "Another assault would be a waste of time."

Like a cold fury, Edward Claridge was at his side.

"Sir," he said, "I have faced the best swords in the British army with no discredit. Do you dare give me another opportunity? Or do you fear it is you who will be shown to be the novice?"

Philip looked at him, good-humoredly.

"I think, sir," he said, "you are taking the matter in bad part." He turned away; then Claridge, in a sudden burst of passion, gripped him by the shoulder, turning him around, holding the blunted sword shortened in his hand. But before he had time to make another motion, Brotot and the drill master had him upon either side; then his friends drew him away.

"Swift work," said Captain Hawes to Philip. "You made him look small enough, and as he is a person of pride and self-admiration, he'll be close to madness for days to come."

There was a step beside them and a voice speaking quietly. It was De Chaulnes, and he was smiling, and nodding his handsome head, his tall figure drawn up splendidly.

"Sir," he said to Philip, "I beg to express my felicitations; your swording is expert, and beautiful to watch." With a light movement of the hand he touched the side of his head. "Hidden here," he said, still smiling, "is the evidence of your blow of last night. It was a shrewd thing enough, as anyone who saw me fall will witness; but, for all that, I am in no way incapacitated. You have just seen fit to refuse my friend, Mr. Claridge, a further chance, but I approach you, thinking you might be of another mind concerning myself."

Philip saw the eyes of Madame Barreaut upon him; he saw
the still averted head of Charlotte Desfourneaux. His expression tightened, and there was a shadow in his look as he
said:

"Do I understand you desire some sort of satisfaction for the
blow you've received?"

"If you please," smiled De Chaulnes, easily. "It is not too
much to ask, I think." The perfection of the man's bearing
was indisputable; he had the crisp elegance of a frequenter of
King Louis's court; but beneath this, the searching eyes of
Philip Archer saw an eagerness, a sort of ferocity. "However,"
said De Chaulnes, "I am not accustomed to the small-sword."
He held out both hands apologetically. "Being by profession a
horse soldier, the saber is my weapon. My purpose here to-
night is to teach the recruits some of the methods of the King's
squadrons in France." His smile was now of the pleasantest.
"There is a possibility, sir, you are accustomed to this weapon;
if so, I've thought you might care to engage with me."

Philip noticed that the circle had tightened once more; there
was a movement of interest, a dying down of the talk; then
he realized the thing was a challenge, and he cocked an eye at
the Frenchman.

"The saber is a deal like the cutlass," he said, "and I've
used more than one of those. But the place for the cutlass is
upon a ship's deck; and the saber, I take it, is the correct arm
only upon a horse's back. Am I to understand, sir, you desire
this test to take place while mounted?"

De Chaulnes' eyes glittered.

"It is customary for such trials to be made that way," he
said. "And," with a gesture that held open mockery, "we will
proceed in the usual way if you do not consider the risk too
great."

A sudden buzz followed this; then a silence. Without a
change of expression, Philip said to Brotot:

"The sabers, Corporal, if you please." He turned away,

pulling his belt tighter; and he said to De Chaulnes, over his shoulder: "The mark I put upon you last night is, I think, upon the left side of your head. I've known before now of blows that unbalanced people's wits and made them say things they otherwise would not have said. A stroke upon the other side of the head may put you upon an even keel once more; and out of kindness I'll see if the thing can't be managed."

"A sharp tongue," said Mr. Adams, greatly amused.

Mr. Lazarus nodded; he held his ebony staff to his thin breast.

"You need the like of him in the public ships," he said. "None but the best will face down these British mastiffs on the sea."

The sabers were brought—heavy, short bladed, with massive hilts, and of the weight of axes; grooms brought the horses forward; the padded helmets and guards were adjusted. De Chaulnes was to ride his own horse, a wicked-looking bay, with a head like a snake and a treacherous eye; the ears were flattened back, and the animal bared its teeth at every movement. The other horse was a strong-looking gray, a bit heavy, but having an air of readiness that caught Philip's eye. He nodded to the corporal that he was satisfied.

Mr. Adams sat back in his chair, disappointed.

"The Frenchman has the better mount," he said, shaking his head.

But the spare Mr. Lazarus seemed of another mind. He stroked his chin with a lean, yellow hand.

"The young man is clever," he said. "And he seems a judge of a horse, sir; this one is not handsome, but it has weight, resolution, and courage. And those are things not to be despised in a joust such as this promises to be."

De Chaulnes was already in the saddle, the bay rearing and tugging at the bridle. Philip mounted and took the gray down the length of the riding ring at a gallop to try his mettle. With the first motions of the horse under him, and the pricking of his ears, he knew he had a cautious brute to deal with, but a steady one.

"I need expect no fire," was his thought as he rode back to the mark, "but he'll go where I take him and do what I ask of him; and that will be enough."

They saluted, and the word was given; they rode at each other, the weapons lifted; the wicked bay, as he leaped forward, lashed out, and the iron-shod feet seemed to flash as they struck at the gray; but Philip swerved his mount, which obeyed cleverly enough, ears up and alert. The bay pivoted about, still lashing out furiously. In spite of De Chaulnes's great weight, it carried him lightly, and the man's handsome, fleshy face was full of hard satisfaction. Again the fiery beast bounded forward; Philip drew the gray back to avoid the shock; at the same time he struck like lightning, and the Frenchman's parry was hurried and weak. Before De Chaulnes could gain sufficient distance for another rush, Philip pulled the gray alongside him, and hung there. His saber again cut wickedly; and again came the hurried parry; once, twice, thrice came the flashing blows; De Chaulnes, dazzled and out of position, could do no more than defend himself; then Philip whirled his horse away and sat quietly, waiting.

His face working with passion, De Chaulnes drew his mount around and again rushed to the attack; there was no lashing of hoofs this time; Philip avoided the weight of the charge and again closed in. The Frenchman cut savagely, but Philip caught the heavy blade and dealt a back-handed stroke in return. The power of both arm and body was in the blow it struck De Chaulnes upon the right side of the head, and in spite of the padded helmet and the dulled edge, a trickle of blood was seen. This seemed to madden the Frenchman; he rode at Philip, his saber swinging axelike above his head. It whistled downward with fearful force, but at a twitch of the rein the gray horse passed under the cut. The Frenchman gained an attacking distance once more, and again he struck; this time the blades met; up and down went De Chaulnes's arm in desperate blows; the gray horse backed steadily away as Philip's defense flashed here and there. De Chaulnes was now like a madman; his blows increased in speed and power, and as they increased, a murmur went up that grew into a shout.

"No man can hold his seat under such an assault, señor," said the Spanish hussar to Brotot. "Your champion is beaten."

But Brotot, erect and calm, replied:

"No good man is beaten without a blow; and note: though M'sieu is being driven back, not one cut has reached him."

The strong arm of the cavalryman continued to work up and down in a fury of strokes, but at last the storm slackened, the cuts were fewer and their power seemed fading.

"See," said Corporal Brotot, "the arm of M'sieu le Duc grows weak. And note how he breathes."

De Chaulnes's mouth was open; he gasped for air, but with all the strength remaining in him, he continued to strike. Steadily, Philip Archer received the blows upon his saber blade or evaded them; he had not attempted a blow since the Frenchman's desperate assault began.

The privateersman stood watching and gnawing his nails, not approving of this.

"What the devil!" he said. "Has he lost his wits? The Frenchman is so taken with weakness he can scarcely lift his arm."

"Do not fear for him, m'sieu," said the sword master; "when the moment comes you shall see what's in his mind."

Slower and slower grew the blows of De Chaulnes; it seemed his gristle was gone and that only his soft flesh remained; the shouting of his friends died away. But still young Archer did not attack; at length the Frenchman, breathless, his face gray, his broad chest heaving, his saber arm hanging at his side, sat gazing at him out of dim but intolerant eyes.

Then Philip drove his mount forward, forcing the bay back until they were directly abreast of the spot where Charlotte

Desfourneaux sat calmly waving her fan. Philip brought the gray alongside De Chaulnes; his weapon did not lift to guard against a possible blow. Expertly he put his foot beneath the other's stirrup, and with a sudden heave threw him from his saddle, almost at the girl's feet. Then, with not so much as a look at her, he slipped down from his horse and walked away.

CHAPTER X

IN THE early hours of the morning the fish market at the foot of High Street was a-bustle with traffic; sloops and schooners were up from the bay, where they'd netted their catch within sight of the topmasts of the enemy's ships, and now were tied up at the wharves, discharging their freight. Drays, filled with shining fish, trundled their way along the dock-heads; market women were stirring briskly; boys and men were washing down pavements and trays, preparing for the day's business. Dogs prowled about; watchmen were beginning to appear upon the decks of vessels anchored in the stream.

Mr. Lazarus turned from Water Street, where his residence was, into High, and then into Front Street; he walked south a bit, and then into Pump Court. A chain maker was working his bellows and making his newly awakened fire roar; a baker, white with flour, stood in his basement door, smoking an early pipe; a boy was taking down the shutters of a chandler's shop across the way; a man with a barrow filled with berries rang a loud bell, looking up at the windows of houses for purchasers of his wares. Mr. Lazarus paused before a coppersmith's and unlocked a side door upon which was lettered:

LAZARUS
IMPORTER
India and the East

He put the big copper key carefully into the skirt pocket of his coat; then he went up a balustraded staircase and let himself into a room at the front. The place was bare and dusty; there were cobwebs in the corners; an old writing table was littered with papers; bills, invoices, and shipping reports hung from hooks on the walls. There was a rickety cupboard with drawers and cubbyholes stuffed with writings. At one side was a strong box fast locked and bolted to the floor.

The windows were put up to let some air into the place; then Mr. Lazarus looked at his watch, a huge bull's-eye of yellow gold; afterwards he took out a second key, blew the dust from it, and unlocked the strong box; he took out a bundle of papers, also a canvas sack which chinked with a heavy fullness as he put it upon the table. Then he sat down, his wrinkled face bent over the papers, which he sorted and re-sorted, studied and re-studied. Apparently satisfied, he emptied out the contents of the sack, a stream of broad, rich pieces, ducats, pistoles, double louis, florins. He took them up one by one, judging their weight and thickness; the ducats were stamped with the round heads of Dutch princes; the pistoles were Swiss and Spanish and Italian—fat pieces holding the deep insignia of power. The florins of Hanover were thick, round, stolid, and of heavy metal; there was a scattering of doubloons, English spade guineas, and a scant handful of Turkish sequins. When these were counted, valued, and arranged in heaps, Mr. Lazarus sat back on his stool and looked at them.

Money to the value of five thousand English pounds; gold money to be carried in a sack across the sea, to be laid out in ship-joining, in mast-stepping, in dresses of sails, in guns.

"There are hangdog ships in the ports of France," said Mr. Lazarus, "that will smarten wonderfully under the warmth of so much money; gold will scrape the foul from their bottoms, cut out the splintered planks, and rig and man them for a-plenty of work on the sea."

Mr. Lazarus sighed; his lips were thin and blue, his deeply wrinkled face had a pinched, fox-like look; the deep-set dark eyes glinted. He pawed among the coins, stacking and restacking them with his yellow fingers. Such solid, rich money, perhaps to be scattered on the seas' bottom; such a fine sum to be spent in broken ships, to poison the air with bursting gunpowder, to drive profitable trade from friendly waters.

The old man drew the back of his hand across his mouth; he fingered the polished ebony of his walking stick; he counseled with the ivory monster at its top. Mr. Deane was to be given charge of this money—Mr. Silas Deane, who had once been a member of Congress, but was now a secret agent for that body. There was a deal of flourish about Mr. Deane; his coats and breeches and neckcloths were a trifle trig, his boots a thought too well varnished, but it might be he was just the man to win the ears of King Louis of France, and De Vergennes, his prime minister. He might be the person to whisper to the best advantage that there were twenty thousand farmers and artisans newly turned soldier, in need of clothing and boots, of muskets and gunpowder, of field pieces and solid shot. Also he might be the man, above all other men, to consult with European ambassadors and ministers; to gain the attention of Spain, of Holland, of the Italian states.

"A clever man could do much," said Mr. Lazarus to the ivory monster. "He would see the value of what he had to give in return for favors; the commerce of what has been the British colonies is to be redistributed, and the most helpful nation would get the greatest share."

Mr. Lazarus was nodding over the gold money upon his table when the sound of wheels was heard from the court. He arose and looked out; a small chariot stood at the door, and Charlotte Desfourneaux was alighting. In a few moments she tapped at his door, and he opened it for her.

"I am sorry," she said. "It is too bad, Mr. Lazarus, that I should get you out so early in the morning."

But Mr. Lazarus smiled and put out a chair for her.

"It is nothing more than the day's routine," he said. "There are few mornings I do not see the sun come up among the topmasts and rigging of the packet ships."

"It's good of you, nevertheless," said the girl. The open

window let in the morning air, and the fresh light from the east touched the dark gold of her hair. "But I could do no better. The Baltimore coach goes in another half hour, and Mr. Deane goes with it."

"It is wise that he take ship from Baltimore," said Mr. Lazarus. He sat down and rubbed his old knees; he fondled the ebony staff, thoughtfully. "He'll have more opportunity of getting out at that place," he said. "The seas are none too quiet; it's a dangerous time to travel."

"He goes in a ship that's armed," said Charlotte Desfourneaux.

The old man looked at her from under his narrowed brows. "Newly armed?" he asked.

"Yes."

He nodded silently; his thin, blue lips were drawn in, making him look like an old vulture.

"You are venturing large sums of money," he said. "This ship of Captain Hawes' has cost a deal to equip, and she's locked here in the river and may never get out. You have a sloop, sailing out of Boston, that has never taken a prize; agents at Martinique, at New Orleans have credits given by you, all meant to privately arm and send out vessels. These are large undertakings."

"I have no fear for the money, as you know," said the girl. "My one dread is that the things I'm striving to do will be of too little consequence. Small privately armed vessels are well enough; but Mr. Fortune is right when he says we need strong public ships, armed as well as, or better than, the British arm theirs."

"That," said Mr. Lazarus, "is true. We have a few such ships already laid down, but the builders are in constant fear; any day the defenses of the bay may be taken, and the new vessels burned as they stand in the stocks."

"Charleston beat back a British fleet," said the girl. "Why could it not happen again?"

"Charleston had rare good fortune," said Mr. Lazarus. "And we must not expect it to continue. There are only a few gun-brigs and shore batteries defending the bay, and their weight will do little against ships-of-the-line."

"As you know," said Charlotte, "I've been thinking Europe is the place best suited to my ideas. The other day I spoke to Dr. Franklin; he, too, has his eyes fixed upon France; he has the firmest hopes of what might be done there. Vessels may be purchased, may be built; they can be taken into British waters in a few hours; prizes can be sold in France, in Holland, in Spain, in Portugal. Wherever this dull English king has bullied and made selfish terms, there he has enemies, and there American ships may find friends. This money," and she nodded at the gold upon the table, "is to be entrusted to Mr. Deane as an earnest of what is to come. When I reach France myself I shall better see what's to be done."

Mr. Lazarus held out his hand, warningly.

"Take care," he said. "Such an adventure has great hazards for a girl."

"In a day's time," said Charlotte, "I shall be aboard the Claridge ship *Trumpeter;* in three weeks I shall be in L'Orient."

He sat silent for a space, the end of his staff held close to his ear; it was as though he were listening to the monster's whispers.

"From what I've seen of your transactions I can form a reasonable estimate of what is in your mind," he said at last. "And your prospects can be carried through, if you continue resolute, even in France."

"Claridge & Company have establishments there," said the girl, composedly. "And you know what is in the will of Antoinette Teresa Barreaut-Desfourneaux. What money I require on the other side of the ocean will be forthcoming, as it is here."

A clock in a neighboring tower struck five; and Mr. Lazarus arose.

"The Baltimore coach will leave in another quarter of an

hour," he said. He put the gold into the sack, and took up his hat. "What final word have you for Mr. Deane?"

"Say to him, if he reaches France first, the matter is entirely in his hands. Also, that more money will be sent if I am much delayed. But," and she looked at the old man steadily, "warn him again he must say nothing of me. My name is not to be mentioned."

He opened the door for her; she went down the stairs, and he followed.

"Good-bye," she said, as the black coachman closed the chariot door.

His bow was almost a salaam; and then as she was driven out of Pump Court, he put the sack of gold under his long coat. And as he went along toward the booking office in Second Street where the Baltimore coach took on its passengers, there was a smile upon his wrinkled face, a crooked smile; his eyes glinted, and the ebony staff struck the ground with a measured beat as he went.

CHAPTER XI

NICHOLAS FORTUNE and Corporal Brotot went to the Penny Pot to breakfast with Philip that same morning. It was sunny, and with a good air in the streets from the river; all the heat of the preceding day had gone with the rain.

They sat in a corner; Nicholas sipped his tea and ate his oaten bread and his eggs and bacon; between mouthfuls he smoked one of his long Spanish segars; and he talked with enjoyment.

"To think," he said, to Philip, "you should meet one of the Claridges like that! And to have him ride you down, as it's in the blood of him to do to anyone; and that you should cuff him about the ears and outsword him, into the bargain!" He filled the air with smoke as he stirred more sugar into his tea. "It's a portent," he said. "Mark what I say; it's an omen of fine fortune to come. You stepped into the matter as a man should, and luck cannot but favor you."

Corporal Brotot had the leg of a fowl, a cut of hot bread, and a mug of ale; and he wore an air of great satisfaction.

"Years ago, m'sieu, at New Orleans," he said to Philip, "when you came to me as a boy, I'd ask myself what rewards or fatalities time had in store for you. You went to school, you were taught French and Spanish and some Latin and Greek; you were taught the art of the sword; it was your father's wish, written plainly in the long letter he left for me, and which I still have, that arms be made familiar to you, that your body and limbs be made strong and skillful." The corporal nodded over his bread and fowl to Nicholas. "He was drilled in the saber, the small-sword, the bayonet and pike; the cudgel was

not unknown to him; he wrestled with a Scot who was cleverness itself. All those things he must know before he met his
enemies." The corporal drained his mug of ale and looked hard
at the waiter until he came to refill it. "You were young,"
he told Philip; "you were deep in your books; you had pleasant
dreams of trees, the bayous, and the river. It hurt me in my
heart," said the old man, and struck himself upon the chest
with an open hand, "for I knew the dangers that were to come.
But, now, I see they were the fears of a man who was already
old. You shall meet these Claridges all, as you've met this first
one; they'll be to you as dried leaves are to the wind."

Philip laughed and cocked a humorous eye at the old sword
master.

"Ah, well, Brotot," he said, "God send the half of what you
say is true. If I can make head through them in some way,
that is all I ask."

He had a cut of ham before him, broiled over red wood coals;
there was a little ring of rice cakes around it, and his ale stood
cold and creaming in a pot beside his plate.

"I am here with you both," he said, "quietly and at our
leisure." He stretched out his long legs; the lines of his face
were slackened; he drew in a great breath and shook his head,
smiling at them, cheerfully. "You were both known to my
father; you both were youths in my grandfather's ships; and
here we are, fast, good friends, all gathered to talk."

"It is a time I've looked forward to," said Nicholas Fortune,
emitting a deal of smoke. "For years I've said to myself: the
day will come when the boy'll be grown up, and then we'll
begin to move about again. Matters will be astir all around
me, and will be settled for good and all."

"John Claridge is here," said Corporal Brotot to Philip.
"You are here. The battle is on."

There was a pause as the two waited for him to speak; but he
sat silent, a wry smile upon his lips, and a little shock of surprise thudding in his mind. For his blood had failed to leap at

this saying; his spirit was quiet; it was sad! He clenched his hands, and frowned, and took counsel with himself. Was this not the great moment—the time for which he'd been trained? Hadn't he, a hundred times in the past, when thought of it came to him, leaped up and set to polishing a sword blade, dropping clear drops of oil into the locks of his pistols, arranging and rearranging his papers? He'd been hot with anticipation, and his muscles tightened with the desire to leap through the months that kept him from his purpose. His eyes went to a window; framed in it was a ship at anchor in the stream, a swift, handy-looking ship, a singing ship, narrow, high-hulled, with masts that reared into lofty pinnacles. He had small desire to face John Claridge or any of his sharp-dealing, ratty-eyed crew; he'd rather step aboard a vessel like this one, with the waters of the world before him and his country's foes to try his courage. Why should he, in a time like this, put his hand and mind to a private war? Why should he jeopardize his life for a sum of money, however great, when—— But seeing the eyes of the others upon him he brought himself up sharply and back to the matter under discussion.

The tip of Nicholas's segar was a cherry red; he wagged his head in approval.

"You are in an excellent state of mind," he said. "A clear thinking state that gives me joy to see. I dreaded you'd come striding into the city demanding your goods and moneys out of hand. That," and he leaned forward, one long finger upheld, "was the way your father would have done. He would not be controlled; and so, in the end, they always beat him off."

"If M'sieu will not be offended at the words of one who served his people many years," said Brotot, "I will add to that: it was the same with your grandfather. It was his habit to win his battles by blows, and to him there was no other way. He scorned his enemies; this great treasure of money was his own, he said, and he'd hold no bargaining with anyone concerning it. He failed to see that government was deep-rooted and strong;

he laughed at people in high office, and they became his
enemies; and the time came when he could make no further
appeal anywhere; his life was safe only at sea, aboard his own
ship."

"In the end," said Philip, soberly, "my father must have
seen the error of this quite clearly; for of a night he'd sit with
me in the cabin of the *General Wolfe*, the candles burning, and
my drawings and spellings and arithmetic on the table before
us, and he'd counsel me. My steps must always be chosen,
he'd say to me. I must never permit anger to overcome me.
If one's foes were deep-thinking and watchful, one must learn
to be like them."

"Ay, like them!" said Nicholas Fortune; "but not too like
them. Better failure itself than that."

Corporal Brotot pushed away the remains of the leg of fowl
and the hot bread and placed his elbows on the table.

"I would not put any man I knew before your father in
a matter of judgment when his mind was cool," said the
corporal. "And when he counseled you so, he spoke with de-
liberation. It was not his thought, as you know, that you
imitate the treachery of the Claridges; it was their steady purpose he was pointing to; their care, their shrewd forethought
before making any move that might involve them. I have little
knowledge of the law," said Brotot, "but I know, m'sieu, it
has devious ways, and it is best to have a guide when one is
venturing into it."

"The Claridges are fortunate in Hasty," said Nicholas;
"from a young man he's given his knowledge to them; he's
toiled and dug and endured. Of course, to his own advantage;
there can be no doubt of that, for he's not one to labor with
no reward. Your grandfather refused advice; your father had
little natural stomach for it; but you will be different," said
Nicholas. "You are more of the proper mind. And against your
coming I have spoken to a man who, above all others, as I said
last night, can be of use to you."

"Oh, yes," said Philip, with interest. "I remember."

"He is a Mr. Lazarus: a Spanish Jew who has been engaged in business here for a dozen or more years past. An importer and exporter, to India, to China, and the Arab seas. His adventures are not many," said Nicholas, "but they are, I'm told, of vast value. He has heard of the matter of the *Vision of St. John*, as all shipmen and those interested in shipping have, and his interest is keen."

"A shrewd man, I suppose," said Philip, "and capable of taking hold of things of weight?"

"As shrewd as a whiplash," said Corporal Brotot. "He is much esteemed, m'sieu, by the officials of the new government; they advise with him in all matters having to do with the navy. You saw him, perhaps, last night, at my academy. He sat with Mr. Adams and was in close talk with him."

"The man to take this case in hand," said Nicholas Fortune, "is one who should have all the proper sorts of knowledge: he must have deep learning in sea changes, in ships, merchants, traders, ports, and the maritime customs of the various nations. It is necessary, also, that he have made a study of trade and the tricks thereof, and this study must reach far into the past."

Philip smiled, gravely.

"That'll be a bill of requirements hard to fill," he said.

"Mr. Lazarus possesses them all," said Nicholas, and Brotot nodded an agreement. "An exceedingly able man, and a shrewd one."

They were still engaged in talk when the door opened and Lazarus came in. Nicholas arose to receive him, and at once introduced him to Philip, who shook his hand.

"I am greatly pleased, sir," said the young man. "Sit down, Mr. Lazarus, and they shall bring you some breakfast."

"A small dish of thin porridge and a little cold water," said Mr. Lazarus to a waiter, when he was seated, his ebony staff between his knees. "I have only the rudiments of a digestion," he said to Philip, "and a very little food satisfies me."

"Here is Philip Archer, come from the sea to claim some millions of gold money now in the possession of Claridge & Company," said Nicholas, while Lazarus ate his porridge carefully. "What word have you for him?"

"Claims upon money are the commonest claims the law knows," said the Spanish Jew. "Claims upon money, involving ships and matters that have come to pass upon the sea, are among the most troublesome. The matter of the *Vision of St. John*," said Lazarus, his deep-set eyes upon Philip, "is the most involved in a century of turmoil; and because of that, because of the difficulties of it, I have studied its history minutely. I have followed it in the Spanish archives; in those of Paris: once I spent a month in New Orleans, Mr. Archer, going over documents, testimony, statements, and records. It is a thing rich in interest," he said, as he pushed away the dish with long, yellow fingers. "I have traced it back and forth, through the hands of this judge and that, one governor and another; princes and kings have set their seals upon it, and yet it is unsettled." He lifted his hands in vast admiration. "It is magnificent!" he said.

"Your interest must have been very great," said Philip; "for you've had a deal of labor in your search. There are not many men who'd have undertaken so much merely to acquire the facts of a case in which they had no personal concern."

Lazarus hugged his staff to his thin chest.

"Every man who has adventures upon the sea is interested in such matters. It happens, perhaps, that I will go further than most to get information. Who shall have a share in a prize seized from an enemy?—in what directions shall salvage go when a vessel in straits is rescued or brought into port when abandoned. The rights of the able and the disabled upon the sea are ever a matter of conjecture. But, as I've said, there is no more vexed or sustained a problem in all the history of maritime adventure, señor, than that of the good Spanish ship, the *Vision of St. John*. She was a large vessel out of Cadiz and had stowed a great cargo of merchandise needed in the Spanish colonies. At Porto Bello she took in gold in bars, in ingots, in nuggets, rich gold to be minted into money, to be made into table services for princes and nobles, into altar pieces for cathedrals, into settings for jewels. The ship was the property of the great firm of Sarraza, in Cadiz, and she was manned by a company of seventy; and her master was Miguel Carrea, than whom Spain had no stouter shipman. And because she had treasure belonging to the King on board, twoscore musketeers and pikemen were put into the ship to guard against an attack of buccaneers, or English sea rovers."

Philip looked at Mr. Lazarus in surprise.

"You have the facts well in hand," he said, "more of them, indeed, than are noted down in my father's or grandfather's papers."

Mr. Lazarus shook his gray wig.

"Your father and grandfather were too hard put to it, keeping what they had, and striving to regain what had been lost," he said. "They had little time to procure more than the most useful facts. Whereas, I had the leisure of the scholar," said Mr. Lazarus; "I gathered my material much as a historian assembles matter for his volumes; port officials, mercantile agents, ship owners, captains in my own vessels, correspondents, all contributed to the sum of my knowledge."

"There's thoroughness!" said Nicholas Fortune. "There's enterprise!" He nodded to Philip. "You could have no better man to advise you."

There was a thin smile upon the blue lips of Mr. Lazarus; the deep-set eyes were fixed steadily upon Philip's face.

"The *Vision of St. John* left Porto Bello on an evening in October, 1724, within a few months of fifty-two years ago; she was four days out, headed north by east, in a choppy sea with some islands off her starboard. There was a sail standing smartly above the horizon, a full rigged ship; Captain Carrea, when he came on deck, gave orders to keep well away from this vessel.

"'We have gold enough on board to buy half the grazing ground in Spain,' he told his chief officer. 'Do not permit any one to approach within three gunshots. If one persists, call all hands, and run out the pieces.'

"The chief officer of the *Vision of St. John* was a man trained in the ships of Barcelona, handy, courageous, and with a wary eye. So he gave much attention to the stranger. She came nearer. He saw from her build she was not English. He knew the English; he bore scars of their making upon his body, and had stood upon decks awash with the sea after their gunfire had been hushed. No, this vessel was not English. She was French. He could tell by the finer lines of her hull, the more graceful rake of her masts, the tautness of her rigging and snug fit of her sails. English vessels were more slovenly; they sat burrowingly in the water and their people were not careful of their trim. And the ship was a merchantman. The first officer of the *Vision of St. John* saw that quite soon; and because of it he permitted her to draw nearer. She carried a sort of banner at her peak; and a youth in one of the tops said it was the insignia of the French firm of Barreaut Frères.

"The vessel drew no nearer; both continued on their way, and night came on, a night with sudden gusts of wind, and with the sea lifting and hissing along their sides. The lights of the French ship could be seen; apparently she was holding to the same course as before. Captain Carrea when he next came on deck watched her. She was French, and he did not give her much thought; a ship of Barreaut's would be nothing but a sturdy merchantman, managed by peaceable people. To be sure, a French vessel, now and then, when tempted by weakness in a rich galleon, had attacked and sometimes taken them; but they were letters-of-marque, or roving ships under little control. And so Captain Carrea went below; entered the day's work in the log, and then to bed."

"I have heard the story of the *Vision of St. John* many times before," said Nicholas Fortune, "but never from the side of the Spaniard."

"The people of the *Prince de Condé* told of that night often enough; and those of the *Sun of India*," said Corporal Brotot. "But the Spanish were all but mute."

"There were reasons for that," said Mr. Lazarus. "Good reasons, too." He polished the ebony staff with his palms and nodded his gray wig. "It was in the night; the wind had lifted, and the seas were running higher; some hours before, the lights of the strange ship had disappeared, and those aboard the *Vision of St. John* had put her out of their minds; the watch on deck was guarding through the night with heavy eyes. Then, of a sudden, there came a great mass, looming in the dark; it was a ship's side, grinning with guns; battle lanthorns flared; there was a roaring of cannon, and solid shot was splintering the housing and masts and spars of the galleon. In an instant's time the decks were cleared; the wheel was abandoned, the ship fell off and lay helpless. Boarders were dropping down upon the Spaniard's decks when Carrea appeared like a lion; his roaring soon rallied his people; the seamen came tumbling on deck; the musketeers formed with their weapons on the high poop; the pikemen lined along the deck, powder and shot was passed up for the guns. The French boarding parties came over the rails; they dropped from the rigging; they clambered over the bows by means of the chains. The night was terrific with cries, and blows, and shots; the deck of the galleon was a very shambles. The attacking vessel," and Mr. Lazarus nodded at Corporal Brotot, "was the *Prince de Condé*, owned by Barreaut Frères, of Bordeaux, and the master of her was Edward Claridge, grandfather of the Edward of whom we saw something last night."

"God knows," said Philip, his brows drawn together, "they

gave but little thought to either property or life in the Caribbean in those days."

"All things were thought fair," said Mr. Lazarus. "And the rich Spaniard, grown weak because of his riches, was considered the prey of all. Most merchant ships sailing those waters in that day had papers from some government or other giving them the right to carry cargo and to cruise searching for richly laden vessels. Barreaut Frères were as strong in ships as some nations, and their power was sometimes given to private war, as well as commerce. The *Prince de Condé* had lain at New Orleans for months, waiting for word of the galleon. This information was given me thirty years ago by an innkeeper at whose house Edward Claridge lived during that time. When the news came that the Spaniard had arrived at Porto Bello, the *Condé* made sail into the gulf and then prowled the sea waiting for her to come out."

"A high-stomached race, these Claridges," said Nicholas Fortune, puffing at his segar. "Planning! Always planning; looking ahead; preparing." He gazed at Philip. "Equal care and desperate fighting will dislodge them, but nothing less."

"The fight upon the decks of the *Vision of St. John*," said Mr. Lazarus, "lasted through the night; the wind grew stronger, and the two ships, now lashed together, ground their timbers, one against the other, like straining monsters. Edward Claridge stood high in the bow of his ship behind a sort of steel buckler and gave his orders; he had a picked crew and outnumbered the galleon's people almost two to one; he poured them over the rails ruthlessly, and his lower-deck guns worked fearful havoc with his victim's hull.

"But Miguel Carrea, as I've said, was a lion: he was of Barcelona, a fat, heavy-browed man who had the vitality of ten. He hoisted brass guns to his high after-deck; loaded with musket balls and broken iron they threw death at his foes; under his eye the musketeers fired steadily in volleys of a score of pieces; his young men swarmed like cats into the rigging and dropped petards with shortened fuses upon the decks and into the open hatches of the *Prince de Condé*. So stout was the resistance of this fine seaman, so desperately resolute were his men, that the French began finally to waver and retreat to their own decks. And at this juncture the chief officer of the galleon let go the whole lower tier of guns in a shattering broadside; the *Prince de Condé's* oaken sides were crushed in; a wild panic followed among her people; and in the midst of this the hooks and chains which held her to the Spaniard were cast off." ·

"Good fighting!" said Philip Archer in admiration; he lifted his mug of ale. "To that fat captain, Miguel Carrea, and may he have a place in heaven fitted to so brave a man."

"The French ship drifted off and lay like a huge, hurt dog, licking its wounds. Claridge, they say, raved like a madman; he cursed his French crew and threatened them, with the brace of pistols he held in his hands. If he'd a company of Englishmen, he told them, he'd had the Spaniard in an hour. A fury took his men at his continued jeers; some of them threw down their arms, the gunners left their pieces; mutiny was swarming through the ship, with Miguel Carrea, in the great galleon, all her guns loaded, drawing down upon them. This Barcelonean master was no longer captain of a peaceful merchantman; he'd been attacked, had beaten off his foe, and was now of the mind to follow and sink him. He was approaching bulkily; his men eager, his guns pointing when a third ship appeared, and spoke a word in what was going forward."

"The *Sun of India*," said Corporal Brotot. "A stout vessel, I've heard."

"A ship with more guns in her than a mere trader should have had," said Mr. Lazarus, and he looked at Philip, nodding the gray wig. "A well managed ship by all accounts, and under scant sail because of the lifting winds. She came out of the darkness with her guns firing into the *Vision of St. John;* and while the *Condé* lay, her men now working frantically to repair the damage done, this stranger took the galleon, drove the crew below decks, and put a score or two of armed seamen aboard of her. And when Edward Claridge was ready to resume the fight there remained nothing for him to do but face what looked like a new and most formidable foe.

"However, he lowered a boat and went aboard the *Sun of India*, and there found she was an English ship, out of Liverpool, with a sort of roving commission, carrying cargo, but armed as a letter-of-marque, and powerfully manned. Her master was an American, James Archer, a young man who seemed to have a deal of confidence in himself.

"'I fought the galleon for more than four hours,' said Edward Claridge as he faced this new personality. 'I had beaten her; in a little while I'd have brought her to terms. She is my prize.'

"But the commander of the *Sun of India* smiled.

"'There were thirty minutes of gunfire before I could close with her,' he said. 'If she was a beaten ship, her people acted in a most peculiar manner.'

"He invited Claridge into his cabin, and they drank, in the course of two hours, as many bottles of Canary as could be put upon the top of a small table. Claridge was like ice, as Claridges are apt to be; his proposals were like those of a god: everything, so it seemed, was to be left to his consideration and mercy; there was to be no voice but his own. But James Archer laughed: wine, so I'm told, always lifted his spirits; he put all the suggestions of Claridge aside.

"'Take your boat,' he said, 'get back to your own ship, and we'll fight it out. Why spoil a comfortable booty by making two parts of it? Let it remain whole, and the victor shall take it all.'

"But Edward Claridge would not agree to that; he came to the matter in another way and maneuvered shrewdly; he bargained and made promises; a paper was to be drawn up, a binding agreement, a document that would hold in all the high courts of Christendom: one half the prize was to go to his owners, Barreaut Frères, and the remaining half to James Archer, owner and master of the *Sun of India*. But James Archer was considering things that might come into the matter in the near future. There had been a deal of freebooting on the sea, and the governments of Europe had made a stand against it; if this rich ship were taken into port, who would condemn her? Who would permit her sale, with Spain clamoring, and shipping people everywhere protesting? Claridge insisted this could be done; but James Archer doubted it more and more, the more he thought of it.

"The master of the galleon was prisoner in Archer's ship and was sent for; stout Miguel Carrea sat at the table with them, a bloody bandage about his head, drank deep of the Canary and talked. James Archer made terms with him; Carrea agreed to pay two thirds of the value of what he had on board the *Vision of St. John* as salvage to the owners of the *Prince de Condé* and the *Sun of India*. As master of a ship in desperate straits he had this power. Edward Claridge, with the others, signed this agreement when drawn up, but he did it in silence.

"Next day a crew made up of men from the French and English ships was put into the galleon, with the chief officers of each sharing command; when repairs were made, sail was put on the ship and she headed away, with the Texal as her agreed upon destination."

Mr. Lazarus looked at the others about the table; he gestured with the ebony staff.

"A deal of what I've just said, you already knew; and what followed is, of course, also known to you. Both the *Sun of India* and the *Prince de Condé* lost sight of the Spanish ship during the next ten hours. There followed several days of storm; on one blustering night the French portion of the crew took the ship and ran her into New Orleans, then a French port. Claim was at once made upon her by Barreaut Frères. Edward

Claridge disclaimed the agreement; the matter was fought in the marine courts at New Orleans and at Dunkerque, and it was decided the galleon was the lawful prize of the *Prince de Condé*, that the interference of the *Sun of India* in the matter was illegal, that the agreement signed was under duress, and gold to the amount of twenty millions of louis was turned over to the French merchants, one of whose daughters was Edward Claridge's wife."

"A fair statement of what happened," said Nicholas Fortune; and Corporal Brotot nodded his head. "A fair statement, with, as has been said, much added matter."

Philip Archer sat with his long legs thrust far under the table; his arms were folded across his chest.

"Fifty and odd years have passed since that time," he said. "And God knows what changes have been made in laws and what written into treaties covering things done in the past. I am here to make yet another struggle for what I know is mine, but what I am to take hold of first, I do not know."

He looked at Mr. Lazarus as he spoke; the Spanish Jew was fondling the ebony staff; the ivory monster was close to his ear, and he seemed listening to its counsel.

"Out of his knowledge of such things," said Nicholas Fortune, who had lighted another segar, "Mr. Lazarus can speak with more authority than anyone else."

Lazarus shook his gray wig; the thin blue lips were muttering; the wrinkles in his face and the stoop of his shoulders made him seem older and frailer than before; but his eyes, deep set under the heavy gray brows, were burning and vital.

"You come at a day when the laws here are in process of change," he said. "It will be a long time before a matter such as this will be heard with any attention. The country is new; no European nation has recognized it; the rights of its citizens cannot be protected, or claims made in foreign places in their behalf. To be sure, your claim in the original was against Barreaut Frères, and the headquarters of Claridge & Company, their successors, is now in this city; but for all that, I would advise, if I were asked an opinion, that the matter be reopened in France, for it was a French court that gave the original judgment."

Philip stirred the ale in his mug and drank of it.

"That procedure has been in my mind more than once," he said. "But, also, I have thought that it would not be out of place if I saw the head of the house of Claridge before I went so far afield. It may be he'll be of a mind to discuss the matter; something might be done by reasoning it out, and a deal of trouble saved."

Mr. Lazarus chuckled; the deep-set eyes gleamed suddenly.

"I have known John Claridge for years," he said; "indeed, I may add, I have been his intimate in many things. And, so, I tell you, he is not a man to reason about anything. His judgments are like the movements of the planets, fixed and unalterable. But," and the chuckle lifted in the scrawny throat of the speaker, "go to him! Go soon. Make your claim to his face, and tell him what thoughts are in your mind. It will do your cause no good," said Mr. Lazarus, "but it will ease your temper and enable you to see what is next to do with more clearness."

"I will see him to-day," said Philip. "Indeed," impulsively, "if I can find him at his place of business, I'll see him within the hour."

Both Nicholas Fortune and the corporal were pleased at this.

"These papers of which you speak," said Mr. Lazarus, as he arose. "Have you them here?"

"In my chest," said Philip, also upon his feet. He told of his experience in the *Racehorse* with Mr. Hasty. "That," he said, "was a warning of what I might expect."

"None are sharper, or cleverer, than Hasty," chuckled Mr. Lazarus. "A capable man, sir; of much value to any cause." And then he fixed Philip with his penetrating eye. "It may so chance, as Mr. Fortune has suggested, I'll be of help to you. If I could have a sight of those documents of yours, these journals, these letters, it would be enlightening. The locked book of Madame Fouquet, of which I have heard, and the confession sworn to by her husband—I would much like to see those."

"Nicholas, who had the care of my papers for so many years, shall show them to you," said Philip. He took a key from his pocket and handed it to the little gun maker. "And while you are engaged with them I'll pay my visit to Mr. Claridge."

He learned from Nicholas that the counting house of Claridge & Company was but a scant five minutes from the Penny Pot; then he shook hands with Mr. Lazarus.

"Fair and easy," said Brotot, as Philip stood framed in the doorway. "Gently at first, as though he were an honest man."

"Facing the India Wharves," said Nicholas, indicating the direction with the burning tip of his Spanish segar. "Just a bit to the south of Tun Alley."

Philip set off without more ado; and as he strode through Market Street, Mr. Lazarus looked after him.

"He'll face Claridge," said Nicholas, nodding his head. "He'll face him for good or ill, as he's never been faced before."

"He has courage," said Mr. Lazarus. "One can see that in his stride and the set of his head. And he has spirits; he's one that's more apt to laugh than grow angry. And now, Mr. Fortune, the papers; let us have the chest open at once, sir, if you please." He smiled as he followed Nicholas. "Papers are strange things. They are read and re-read through generations, but often keep their one vital meaning secret. Who knows?" and the thin lips looked thinner and bluer than before—"it may remain for me to see in these what no one has seen before."

"It may be so," said Nicholas Fortune, over his shoulder, as he trudged up the stair. "And God send it; for a lack of clear sight has caused much suffering to the Archers in the past."

CHAPTER XII

PHILIP ARCHER kept to Water Street until he reached
Tun Alley; here he made his way to the river front. The
sky was high and brilliant, the river was creaming under the
touch of the fresh wind, and lapping against the bows of vessels
anchored in the stream. The tall Indiamen lay at the wharf
above Walnut Street; packet ships, with their noses held fast
in the docks, had a deserted look; laborers and draymen
lounged upon the pierheads; there was no stir or alertness; the
city's foreign trade had slowed almost to stopping.

Claridge & Company's place of business faced the river;
there were huge warehouses—also a row of small buildings
in which the clerkly offices of the firm were carried on. A carriage was standing at the principal entrance; Philip passed in
and found himself in a wide room with men upon tall stools,
or standing at high desks; there were managing clerks seated
upon benches talking with traders, with inland merchants,
with ship captains; a brisk young man approached him and
inquired his business.

"I'd like to speak with Mr. John Claridge," said Philip.

The young man smiled; it was quite plain that many persons, in the course of a day, said the same thing; also it was
evident that few obtained their wish.

"I am sorry," said the brisk clerk. "Mr. John Claridge is
not in the offices to-day. However, Mr. Edward will be here
presently. If your business is anything that might be brought
to his attention——"

"It is not," said Philip. "It is John Claridge I desire to
see. As he is not here, perhaps you might care to say
where he may be found?"

117

The clerk smiled more than ever. He shook his head.

"Mr. Claridge attends to no business except upon those days when he sees fit to come to the counting room. And in these times, when business is so fallen off because of the British warships, he is here no more than once a week."

Philip's glance went about the place; through a partly opened door he had a glimpse of the edge of a silken skirt and a small, perfectly arched foot; he saw a man, tall, harsh-featured, pacing the floor and conversing with the owner of the pretty foot. An instant later he saw Mr. Hasty, who had crossed the counting room, pause at this door, as though about to enter; but at that moment he noted Philip and advanced toward him. He dismissed the clerk with a gesture; there was a bench in a corner by a window, and his next movement invited Philip to sit down, which he did; and Mr. Hasty sat beside him.

"May I ask," said the old attorney, "what brings you here?"

The young man cocked a humorous eye at him.

"There can be only one thing, Mr. Hasty; and that is: to see John Claridge."

The old man settled his lenses across his heavy nose; his shrewd eyes gave Philip their closest attention.

"And when you have seen him, what then?"

Philip drummed with his finger tips upon his knee; his look went about the long counting room and its intently engaged people; there was a sense of permanence in the place, a solidity, a power that impressed one.

"How can I tell?" he said. "First I must hear what replies are made to the questions I ask. My further action, of course, will depend entirely upon those."

"John Claridge," said Mr. Hasty, "is a man who dislikes questioning."

Philip was unmoved by this.

"I could search about in my mind through the whole of a day without finding even the smallest interest in Mr. Claridge's likes or dislikes," he said. "The questions I have to put, Mr. Hasty, require asking, and asked they shall be."

The old counselor stroked his chin. His crafty eyes were narrow behind the big lenses; there was a coldness in his manner, an apartness, a threatening something that Philip did not fail to note.

"Perhaps," said Mr. Hasty, and his voice had a frigid quality equaling his manner, "it would be as well to speak a word of warning to you at this point. Do you realize, thinking as you do, and with the ideas you have in your mind, that you are in danger in this port?"

The gleam of humor was still in Philip's eyes.

"There is danger in every port," he said. "I have been in many of them, and am still sound and whole."

"In times past, John Claridge endured much from your father," said Mr. Hasty. "So much that it has burned itself permanently into his mind; and he is not disposed to suffer anything from you."

Philip's sound, fine teeth showed themselves as he smiled at the man who sat so quietly at the other end of the bench and spoke in such a tone.

"You, Mr. Hasty, have been so long employed by the Claridges that their desires have great weight with you; that they want this or do not want that has high importance in your mind. But, permit me to say, again, that their wishes have no such consequence with me. Also," and the smile grew broader, "it seems to me that I find the traces of a threat in your words. This is a dangerous port for me, says you; implying that the sooner I drop what plans I have and take my departure, the better it will be for me." He clasped his hands about his knee. "You did your best to have me maimed in the *Racehorse*, brig, two days ago, and, I suppose, having failed in that, you'll not hesitate to try something else. I have in mind, Mr. Hasty, a number of things written into my father's and grandfather's journals of happenings that could have on no account come about without some purposeful thought behind them. I especially call to mind a thing of years ago—the murder of Campbell in my grandfather's house at New Orleans—a strongbodied man who had been set to guard a boy whose life was, perhaps, in old Edward Claridge's way."

But the expression of Mr. Hasty was unchanged.

"That matter was sifted by the authorities of the city," he said; "it was shown conclusively that the crime was done by housebreakers."

"You were in New Orleans at the time," said Philip; "and I have no doubt, if the occasion offered, the killing would have been prefaced by threats, used much as you are using these to-day. But my grandfather, if they were made, would have, I think, listened to them with even less attention than I have. So, now, if you know where John Claridge may be found, let us come to that as a matter more deserving of our attention."

"M'sieu," said the voice of Madame Barreaut, and looking up he saw her. "M'sieu, is it possible you are here and desiring to speak with John Claridge?" She clasped her hands, her eyes were shining. "You have courage, and courage is a thing I adore. He desires to talk with John Claridge," she said to Mr. Hasty. "He does not fear him; he will speak to him of what is in his mind, no matter how unpleasant." Her brows went up, there was a smile upon her lips. "He will, perhaps, defy him."

There was a frown between Mr. Hasty's eyes; it was clear her interruption was not to his taste; but she went on, to Philip:

"It is fortunate I also came here to see M'sieu Claridge; and not being successful I mean to visit him at Fairview, where he lives. You shall come with me," she said. Philip had arisen and stood bowing before her. "My carriage is at the door." Mr. Hasty lifted a protesting hand, but she faced him instantly, her head up, her eyes full of wilful purpose. "Do I not tell you I admire courage? M'sieu is brave, and I shall see he gets his wish, no matter how much others are displeased."

Mr. Hasty stood looking at her, and Philip noted a sagging

in the old man's face; he had grown suddenly slack-mouthed; the shrewd eyes had in them a thing like fear.

"Age!" was Philip's thought as he watched him. "He is quite old."

But for all his hand shook as he gestured to Madame Barreaut, Mr. Hasty kept his head high.

"As you please," he said. "But, remember, it is a matter solely of your doing. I give no countenance to it whatsoever."

She did not reply to him, but smiled dazzlingly at Philip.

"In a half hour," she said, "we shall be there. A beautiful drive on a beautiful morning. And," pausing at the door which he held open for her, "you are to be set face to face with what you have so strongly desired." She smiled up at him. "What more could anyone ask?"

Philip handed her into the vehicle and entered after her. They drove along the river front and turned into Chestnut Street; here there were beautiful shade trees and fine, broad-fronted houses.

"It is a prim city," said Madame Barreaut, her beautiful face drawn to a solemn length; then she laughed. "And the people, oh, they are so unhappy. I could not live always in such a place; I would lose my reason."

"It's a thriving city," said Philip. "And, after all, madame, the place we live in is what we make it."

She nodded at him, seriously enough.

"That is true. When I married M'sieu Barreaut he took me to France. I was overjoyed, for I'd heard so much of Paris. But we went to live at L'Orient that we might be near his ships. It was cold and wet. The rain fell all the time; my heart was chilled. I longed for the warm islands, for Martinique, for Havana, for New Orleans, for Charleston, for any of the friendly places I had known. I thought I should die. But I did not." She laughed, brightly. "I tolerated its wetness; I endured its fogs; they killed my husband, who was born among them, but I was spared." They drew out into the open country after a short time; there were farms, and here and there a private park; the road ran through some deep woods. She put a small jeweled hand upon his arm. "That you hate John Claridge is not strange to me," she said.

"I have not told you I hate him," said Philip, composedly.

But she laughed and lifted her dark shining eyes to the rifts of sky showing through the trees.

"M'sieu," she said, "why should you tell me, when I see the thought in your face each time his name is mentioned? And you have cause to hate him. The things he has done to your father!—the cunning, ruthless things, m'sieu. It would be strange if you had any other thought of him in your mind. I have not heard all the matters between your people and his in the past, but what I have heard is enough. It is right that you should hate the Claridges. Also," and she faced him, a new expression in her eyes, "you should hate the Barreauts. For it was not old Edward Claridge alone that seized all the riches of the *Vision of St. John:* his wife, who was a Barreaut, was at one with him. My husband's father was her cousin, and he agreed with them both. I will tell you something," said Madame Barreaut. "The great moneys of that family had come to an end; they were near to ruin. Many merchants for whom they'd built ships had met with misfortune and were bankrupt, with no means of paying their debts; the waters of the near seas were plagued by an armed enemy, and their Indiamen and ships from China were being taken without cessation. So when Edward Claridge formed his plan against the Spaniard they were at eager agreement with him. And when he broke his written word with James Archer, your grandfather, and with the Spanish captain, Miguel Carrea, they supported him, still."

Philip looked at her quietly.

"You do not love the Barreauts?" he said.

"I hate them!" she said, a quick passion in her voice. "I hated their ships, and their never-ending talk of the sea, and trade, and money." And then she smiled, dazzlingly, through the cloud of feeling. "And, as I think I have said to you, I do not love the Claridges, for the same reason."

"And yet," he said, "you seem on most intimate terms with them."

"That," she said, leaning back against the cushion of the carriage, "is because I must. I have moneys involved in Claridge & Company, and I have learned not to trust anyone too much. I would prefer to live in Martinique, or Havana, or even New Orleans, than here. But John Claridge imitates Jehovah so closely I have come to be doubtful concerning him; and I thought it best never to be too far away."

Philip looked at her. She had charm. There was no doubt of that. There was a sparkle, a radiation from her that should have been captivating; her outspokenness should have excited his admiration. But, between his eyes, there was the line of doubt he'd worn the day before.

They had come in sight of a delightful silvery river, flowing at the feet of some low green hills; there were wooded tracts, and farms; on a knoll overlooking the stream was a handsome building much like an English manor house, with a well kept park about it, a keeper's lodge and a number of cottages at some distance, standing in a prim line along a green lane. They passed between two stone pillars, and the wheels grated upon a graveled way.

"The house of John Claridge," said Madame Barreaut, mockery in her eyes. "And a most astonishing house, inside. It might be the dwelling place of a caliph of Bagdad. Magnificence is one of his weaknesses," she said. "I've often wondered why, with his taste, he did not live in Alexandria or Constantinople. But instead," with a gesture of both jeweled hands, "he chooses a city of Quakers. But, really, he did not choose it. It was his father, who was put in charge of the American branch while the firm was still known as Barreaut Frères. That father must have been a clever man of business, for at last the branch grew greater than the parent house; the name of the firm was then changed to Claridge & Company, as it is now."

They got out at a tall white door. There was a broad hall, paneled with inlaid woods; the floor was like worn, hard stone; there was a balustrade, wide, heavy, of an opulent splendor; the stairs were covered with a flowered carpet.

"I will tell him you are here," said Madame Barreaut, motioning the liveried footman aside. She opened the door of what proved a library. "Sit down," she said. "It is cool here. I shall be only a few moments."

When she had gone, Philip looked about him. There was a faint scent in the place that reminded him of the East; there were rugs and hangings upon the walls that he knew to be priceless; the books upon the open shelves were bound in softly colored leather, with an amount of perfect tooling that showed they'd come through the hands of a master of the craft. The young man examined a few of the books; he admired the hangings; then he went to a window and stood looking out. It so chanced he had a view of the drive, and the two stone pillars that marked the entrance; from these the road went winding away to where the timber began. At the far end of this he saw a whirl of dust, a dun-colored column that advanced steadily and left a long, trailing cloud in its rear.

"A carriage," said Philip. "And driven at high speed."

He stood watching it as it advanced; and at last he knew it to be a traveling carriage, with a postilion; there was a single person—a man—seated in it; and when it reached the entrance to Claridge's grounds, it halted and the man got out. As he came along the drive with swift, hardy strides, Philip frowned over a recent memory of him that formed in his mind; and then almost immediately he recognized him. It was the harsh-featured man he'd seen talking with Madame Barreaut at the counting rooms of Claridge & Company less than an hour before.

He felt a touch upon his arm, and looking around saw Madame Barreaut standing beside him.

"John Claridge is in his study," she said. "He will see you."

She glanced through the window as Philip turned from it; at once she caught sight of the harsh-faced man, and her hand reached out instinctively to draw the curtains. Then she laughed.

"It is Gorman, agent for the company," she said. "How unfortunate that he is here; he irritates John Claridge beyond words by his stupidities."

She pushed open a door facing the top of the staircase, and they went in. A man sat at a large table topped with ebony, and in the full light of a west window; he was tall and spare, with big bones and a dead-white face. His dense black hair was brushed back from his forehead, and he sat bolt upright, his eyes, smoldering and intent, fixed upon Philip.

"This," said Madame Barreaut, "is Philip Archer, the young man who has come to visit you."

The man made no reply; he sat motionless, searching Philip's face. The strange eyes had a quality the young man knew; the dead-white face he'd seen many times in far-off Oriental cities. Opium! The black soul of the poppy! The burning dreams, the strange dilation of mind.

"You have come North as you said you would," said John Claridge. "I expected that; if you were an Archer at all I knew you'd make your appearance as promised. And you *are* an Archer." The man nodded his head, the dense, glossy hair gleaming in the sunlight. "You are like your father when I saw him first; you have his face and bearing. It is your purpose to do a great deal; that also was his purpose. But," and the smoldering eyes grew even more fixed, "you will fail as he failed; you will learn there are things here that will break your resolution; you will turn your back, finally, as he turned his: and we'll hear of you no more."

The room was rich in gold ornamentation; there were great splendidly colored maps upon the wall, showing the regions of the East and the waters that lay between; upon a stand was a globe made of agate upon which was traced the lands of the world and the seas of it; upon the walls, also, there were pictures of ships, vessels of admirable distinction, Barreaut models; ships that the Claridges, perhaps, had sailed. One of them, as a gold plate upon its frame said, was the *Prince de Condé;* and as Philip Archer's eyes rested upon it, he smiled.

"There was a deal to break a man's spirit in the things my father faced," said he. "Corrupt judges, perjured witnesses, malevolence that would make the heart sick; but permit me to say, John Claridge, that his resolution kept firm and whole. When he turned his back it was not through loss of hope, or weakening of the thews of his soul; money was needed to fight you who had so much; and death coming upon him before he could bring together what he needed is why you had not to encounter him again."

The dead-white face showed no trace of feeling; but there was an added fire to the somberness of the man's eyes.

"Why are you in my house?" he said. "What word have you to say?"

"I have desired to make no useless step," said Philip. "Before beginning whatever action I may find it necessary to begin, I thought it best to speak to you in person. I have your father's signed word that the cargo of the Spanish ship *Vision of St. John* was to be divided between the owners of the three vessels taking part in the action. Is it still your determination to ignore that word?"

"It is," said John Claridge, unemotionally.

"The weight of a broken word is heavy upon a dead man's soul," said Philip. "You now have a chance to remove it."

"We have denied for many years there had been any voiding of a given pledge in the matter. My father's name," said John Claridge monotonously, "as has been brought out in half a score courts of law, was obtained on that paper under duress. The battle was of his own winning; the galleon was his prize."

"I have read very carefully in the journals in my possession," said Philip; "also in the log of the *Sun of India*, and the testimony at New Orleans in the year 1729. It is shown in all these that Miguel Carrea had made sad work of the *Prince de Condé*, that she was little more than a wreck, with half her people killed and the remainder rising in mutiny when the *Sun of India* appeared in the matter."

"Matter refuting your statement is to be found in the records of every court the case has been heard in," said John Claridge. He looked at Philip, his hands upon the gleaming black top of the table, his face rigid and corpse-like. "Is this all you have to say?"

"It will, possibly, not serve any useful purpose to go further at this moment into a case so old and so much discussed," said Philip. "That I am assured your attitude is the same as in the past, is enough. I can now proceed as I see fit." He bowed to the stark figure before him, and was about to take his leave when there was the sound of low voices at the door: Madame Barreaut came forward and spoke to Claridge.

"M'sieu, Gorman is here, on his way to Baltimore. He is in a great hurry and desires a word with you."

"Let him come in," said John Claridge. Then as Philip was about to turn away he said to him: "Wait. Give me a moment more. Here is a man who knew your father."

The harsh-faced man came into the room; he paused at sight of Philip, looked at John Claridge, and stood motionless. At close hand the man's eyes were a pale green; he had a thin, cruel mouth, and there was a purple birthmark discoloring one side of his jaw.

"Well?" said Claridge.

"The ship *Kingston* sails in three days," said the man. "From Baltimore. It has been directed I go in her, you favoring the order."

"I think you may be useful," said John Claridge. "Go, by all means."

The man fingered his hat.

"There is a possibility I may be needed to see to the adventures moving out of Boston in a fortnight. The matter seems in doubt, and Mr. Coppinger suggested I leave with you my proposed movements in detail for the next two days. This in case you may desire to recall me."

"That is well considered of Coppinger," said John Claridge. He took up a quill and a sheet of paper. "Where will you lie to-night?" he said.

"At the Plough Tavern on the road two hours beyond Chester. It's a place easily found. There is a wood; then a stream with a bridge crossing it; a rider may see the inn's lights all night through. At noon to-morrow I shall stop at the Roast Pig Tavern at Head of Elk; after two hours' waiting for a possible messenger I shall push on, and hope to lie at the White Horse in Baltimore for the night." John Claridge wrote these things upon the sheet of paper; then he read them to the man carefully. "Quite right," said Gorman, with a nod of the head. "And now I shall be off."

He turned, after a salute, and was moving toward the door when Claridge said:

"Gorman, you recall Richard Archer, I suppose?"

"Quite well," said the man, pausing. "A damned madman; and one whom it would have pleased me greatly to have put a leaden ball into."

Claridge, without change of expression, indicated Philip.

"This is his son," he said.

Gorman's pale eyes rested upon the young man for a moment; then he laughed.

"His son!" he said. "In God's name, what trollop did he take up with that he's left a son behind him to trouble decent people?" Then, with a salute to Philip, in which there was complete contempt. "I give you good-day, sir."

He strode through the door without a backward glance. Philip stood poised and motionless, like a hawk before its swoop; his heart cried out to him for a swift and bloody retaliation, but beside this desire there was the whispering counsel of reason.

"His life!" cried his heart, stricken and aghast at the vileness of the man's words. "Hold your hand!" said his reason: "Take great care."

For there was a something in the room that warned him; there was something in its faint odor, the same scent he'd detected in the library on the floor below; there was something in the stillness; in the look of John Claridge's corpse-like face; in the wide eyes of the beautiful Creole. His father, his grandfather before him, had stepped into a circle of peril in dealing with these people; they had entered, blindfolded and bold, into a maze of cunning and treachery; and in spite of all their courage and fortitude they'd been beaten back. This matter of Gorman, and he saw the thing suddenly, like a revelation, was peculiar; it had a shocking unreality that held him fixed in his tracks. And then, after the first hot desire had left him, he turned upon John Claridge and said in a tone like ice:

"I perceive, sir, dimly, but quite sensibly, that this which has just happened is a matter of your doing. Let it be so; only yesterday such a conclusion would have made me dash my fist into your face, and then make after that scoundrel and throttle him. But, now, I leave it to be reckoned up with other matters in the end; and when that time comes, take care of yourself, for I mean to deal with you with all the resentment I have in me."

He left the room and went down the stairs; in the lower hall he heard a light, swift step behind him; it was Madame Barreaut, and she put a small, white hand upon his arm.

"Surely," she said, "oh, surely you do not mean to permit that beast to insult you so, and turn away without a word or a blow!"

Philip looked at her, a frown between his eyes.

"It is in my mind I've permitted a deal more to pass me to-day than a few brutal words."

Her beautiful eyes, full of candor, met his look; the hand tightened upon his arm.

"I hope," she said, "you do not, now or ever, expect anything but denial and disbelief from John Claridge. But," eagerly, "do not let this offense of Gorman's go unpunished. You should take a whip to him." And as he still looked at her, unmoved, she added: "Your father, from what I've heard of him, would never have allowed a thing like that to pass. He would have been out of the house after him; he'd followed him on the road if it took days."

"There were many things which my father did which my judgment sets me against," said Philip. The liveried servant had opened the door; the warm sun and air of high noon came into the wide hall. "Good-day," he said.

"You will return to the city in my carriage?"

"It's very good of you," he said; "but my going back can be managed from the tavern we passed only a short distance along the road."

She stood upon the great white door stone with him.

"I cannot say how displeased I am with what has happened," she said. "I have always known John Claridge was ruthless; but that he'd countenance a thing like this never came into my mind. This man Gorman is——"

"Don't vex your mind about him," said Philip. "He shall be seen to in due course."

He bowed to her, then putting his hat firmly upon his head, he set off down the graveled way. When he reached the two tall pillars, he turned and looked back; at a window he saw John Claridge, haggard, white-faced, looking after him; there was something loathsome in the man's manner, and something a deal like a threat in the gesture of his hand.

CHAPTER XIII

WHEN John Claridge turned from the window, Charlotte Desfourneaux stood in the center of the room. She wore a jacket and skirt of Lincoln green, with copper buttons down the front, a wide-rimmed hat turned up at one side with osprey feathers in it; and in her hand she carried a riding whip.

"Be seated once more," said Claridge, motioning toward a chair beside the table. "I am sorry the arrival of this visitor interrupted us."

The girl sat down; she pulled at her long deerskin gloves and settled the loop of her riding whip about her wrist. John Claridge drew some papers toward him as he, also, sat down; and he frowned blackly at them as he placed them side by side in a row before him.

"A bill," he said, "given to the ship-calking firm of Keith & Lansing: for docking and repairing a vessel; one hundred and twenty pounds."

"Keith & Lansing are excellent work people," said the girl, quietly. "The matter could hardly have been done for less."

There was a crooked look about his thin-lipped mouth, but he kept his eyes upon the sheets of paper.

"Here," he said, "is an item of money, for which you have also given a bill, claimed by the gun founder, Nicholas Fortune. For a pivot gun; for six eight-pounder brass guns, for two six-pounder guns of a sort not stated, there is to be paid the sum of two hundred pounds."

"A small price," said Charlotte Desfourneaux, trifling with the handle of her whip. "Mr. Fortune is a patriot; he desires the country to prove itself upon the sea. And people

131

of a deal of information upon such matters say each piece his forge turns out is of high quality."

"Here," said John Claridge, his eyes never lifting, and his voice keeping to a hard level, "is a bill of three hundred guineas for provisioning a brig sailing out of Boston, the *Goshawk*, equipping her with a new dress of sails, and providing her with three guns. With this is a statement of three heavy sums of money, bills for the payment of which will be presented in Holland, in France, and in Portugal in the near future."

The man put the papers aside, and his smouldering eyes were fixed upon the girl. The sun entering at the westward window fell upon him, turning his white face to a deathly yellow.

"Charlotte," he said, "I have kept from any conversation with you in matters such as these, because my high disapproval of them would be like to make the subject a disagreeable one between us. Hasty has spoken of them to you, and he has regretfully told me you refuse to be guided in any way. He has told you," said John Claridge, one corpse-like hand lifting, "that I disapprove of what you are doing, and still you hold to your course, notwithstanding."

Charlotte looked at him; there was a quiet steadiness in her brown eyes.

"Surely," she said, "that does not surprise you. When I came to you first with my questions, and that was some years ago, you told me I was a deal like Antoinette Teresa Barreaut-Desfourneaux. And she," said the girl, her chin lifted, "was said to be a woman of character and resolution."

"I have been the head of Claridge & Company for twenty years," he said, his eyes burning, as Philip Archer had seen, with the black poison of the East. "And in that time I have permitted no one to put my preferences aside. And," he said, the white, skeleton hands gripping the edges of the table, "I will not permit it now. This money will be paid; but, remember, there must be no more of this folly of yours. Fix that in your mind."

She was not disturbed; even Antoinette Teresa Barreaut-Desfourneaux could not have carried the matter off with a more assured poise.

"Mr. Hasty has already told me something of the kind," she said. "He, also, does not care for what I think so necessary. He considers the sums I have spent," gesturing toward the papers upon the table, "these, and others, are money wasted." She trifled with the riding whip, tracing a pattern with the end of it upon the polished floor. "In his case I can understand it," she said, "for he is naturally a Tory and opposed to the new government. You, however, are friendly to it, are you not?" her brows lifting. "You attend conferences with the members of Congress; your opinions are spoken of with favor. I saw Dr. Franklin himself here not so long ago."

"The affairs of Claridge & Company are in my charge," he said, and the long jaw, yellowed by the sunlight, came forward like that of an angry animal. "And while that is so, its moneys shall be laid out as I direct."

"Mr. Hasty has also told me that from time to time," she said, nodding her head. "But I have never been able to quite understand it. I have had the matter of the money left by my grandmother searched into by a person who has not Mr. Hasty's prejudices, and I find it permits me a voice in the business affairs of the firm. To be sure," with a gesture of the whip, "while I was still a very young girl it was expected I'd be directed what to do; but that time is past." She regarded the man before her with inquiring attention. "I am of legal age and entitled to manage my own affairs. A bill signed by me is, of necessity, honored by the firm of which I am a partner."

"The last to be so honored are here," said John Claridge, and his hand struck the papers upon the table.

"It is not this way you would have spoken to Antoinette Teresa Barreaut-Desfourneaux," said Charlotte, her head up. "She would not have permitted it. And neither will her grand-daughter permit it."

John Claridge smiled, a thin, ugly smile; there was derision in it, there was mockery, there was hate.

"Old Antoinette would have permitted it if her dealings had been with me," he said. "And so long as I am at the head of Claridge & Company, *you* shall permit it."

She drew down her hat upon her head and pulled at her gauntlets; then, putting the handle of her whip into the loop of a bell rope which hung beside the table, she rang the bell.

"If you have made up your mind to that," she said, "the only thing I can do is to remain away, and so give up any small oversight I may have had of the company's affairs." He bowed to her, his hand gesturing mockingly. "However," she said, "if this should prove necessary, I must, in self-defense, name one who will take my place." The derision died in his eyes; he sat still, his hands tightening. At this moment a colored boy in livery came in. "My horse, at once," she said. And when the boy had gone she arose. "Also," she said to John Claridge, "should any bill drawn by myself upon Claridge & Company be dishonored, I shall at once legally require your presence in court, to say why you have done so."

He, too, got upon his feet; the sun in his face gave him a ghastly look; the black, smoothly brushed hair gleamed with a strange vitality.

"Charlotte!" he said.

He walked around the table and stood looking down at her. A tall clock in one corner of the room ticked gravely in the silence; some birds in a spreading sycamore tree outside one of the windows stirred uneasily and twittered in the heat.

"The last time I listened to a threat," he said, "it was uttered by the father of the young man with whom I was just speaking. A matter of that kind was to be expected from him; from you it is not."

"What I have said," she replied, "can in no way be considered a threat. It is a mere statement of a business act following, necessarily, one which you have announced." She looked at him with no trace of unquiet in her face. "If there has been a threat, I think it has been of your own making."

He stood with his burning eyes upon her; his hand shook as he indicated the chair in which she had been seated. But she remained standing.

"From the beginning," said John Claridge, "you have shown a disposition to ignore my advice. I have protested, but it has been of no use. However, what has gone before this has been of small consequence; the things you are now engaged in hold danger to yourself and to all associated with you. This outburst of the colonies against the King will be of short duration; there is scarcely a man of standing in the city, or along the entire seaboard, who is not opposed to it. Merchants find their trade ruined; ship captains can find no employment, as vessels they had been taking to sea are bound up in port; shipbuilders are in desperate straits; importers are at their wit's ends, and craftsmen and mechanics are already finding it hard to procure food for their families. This condition," said John Claridge, "cannot last; it will end in a counter outburst against the villains who have plunged the colonies into a deplorable war; and then, Charlotte, when the King's troops are once more in command, and the King's judges again sit upon the bench, what is to happen? All those who have given aid and encouragement in any outstanding way to the rebels will be held to pitiless account. For the King and his ministers are aroused. They will show no mercy."

"I do not dread the King's government," said the girl. "I have no desire for mercy. The war is a just war; the colonies have endured injustice for years, and as pleadings have done no good they've taken up arms." She looked at him, and there was a light in her eyes he did not like. "I'm sure your acquaintance, Dr. Franklin, agrees with that view of it."

His face was like a bitter mask; there were dark shadows under the burning eyes, the tremor in his hands had increased as he stooped and took the papers from the table.

"Franklin is a dotard, consumed by his own conceit," he said. "Hancock is a crafty self-seeker; Jefferson is a mob leader; if I have any dealings with them at all, it is because I desire to prevent them, as far as possible, from plunging the country into complete ruin before the King's troops can save it." The papers rustled in his hand. "Here are bills calling for moneys to be paid for ships, guns, and materials to assist in this rebellion; the money is to come from Claridge & Company. What countenance am I to assume when I am one day called upon to explain these dealings?"

"You might," she said, "assume the one you now use when in talk with the 'rebels.' So far, it seems to have served you well."

He made no reply to this, though his rigid face told of the fury that filled him. He rang the bell and said to the man:

"Ask Mr. Edward to come in."

Edward Claridge, booted, spurred, and with his blue coat covered with dust, appeared a few moments later. Without speaking, John Claridge handed him the papers.

"Oh, yes," said Edward. He turned his cold eyes upon Charlotte. "I had intended to speak to you of these before now." He sat upon the window ledge, his booted legs crossed, his angular back leaned against the frame. "It is a matter of some difficulty to reason with you, Charlotte," he said, "And, as you have perhaps noticed, I seldom try to do it." He paused as though expecting an answer, but as none came, he said: "As far as I can see, you have fitted out, or assisted in the fitting out, of no less than a dozen small vessels, meant to interfere with British traffic upon the sea, or, and I've heard this expressed, though it seems somewhat impudent, even to engage British warships whenever they might be encountered." There was a smile upon his lips as he surveyed her. "Of course, this is a sheer waste of money, and," here he looked at John Claridge, "as my uncle has no doubt told you, a somewhat dangerous procedure."

"Yes," she said. "He has said that."

"I'm quite content," he said, with the same derisive smile, "to have you a patriot along with the volcanic Sam Adams, the vituperative Patrick Henry, or the hard-riding Colonel Washington. It will do no great harm, for your ships will be blown out of the water and your captains hanged or imprisoned. Uncle," he said, coldly, "is disturbed by the thought that your actions may reflect upon the firm when the matter, as it will, finally comes up for examination; but," with a gesture, "Claridge & Company is strong enough to withstand any such thing, and I am not vexing myself in that direction. Your visit to France, now," and the cold eyes narrowed, "is another matter and deserves examination. That is a dangerous field for the operations of a young woman of your turn of mind; you could do great damage there to our credit and standing. You sail in the Claridge & Company ship, *Trumpeter*, to-morrow; it will have no difficulty in making its way through the British cruisers; we have arranged that. In possibly twenty days' time you will be in London; in two days after that, if you desired, you could be in Paris. May we ask," his voice as cold as ice, "what you mean to do when you reach there?"

She was silent; but her look was steadfast, her head still held high.

"Hasty has been informed," said John Claridge, "that you mean to give yourself to fomenting ill-will in France and Spain against the King's government."

"Mr. Hasty, with his spies, hears a deal," she said, disdainfully.

There was a pause; the two men glanced at each other; Edward lifted his brows and arose; turning his back, he stood looking out into the garden. John Claridge gazed at the girl, his face rigid, his eyes suddenly quiet.

"The *Trumpeter* sails with the tide to-morrow morning," he said. "I understand your baggage is aboard."

"Yes," she said. "I thank you." Her look went from one to the other of them. "Good-bye," she said.

She left the room; and in a few moments Edward Claridge saw her, mounted upon a young bay horse, cantering down the graveled way and into the public road.

2

The young bay tossed his head, tugged at the reins, and fretted with the bit; he loved the summer sun, the long stretch of road and the waving green trees. Charlotte smiled at his eagerness and held him firmly; there were times when she was inclined to let him race, but to-day her mood was downcast, and she had no heart for it.

There was an inn, patronized by the farmers and drovers who made use of the road, standing back among some trees. A clean little place kept by a tidy woman who had two sons. And as the girl went by, she saw one of the sons putting a pair of horses to a light wagon; and near by, his hands behind him, stood Philip Archer. She drew up in the shelter of a hedge and studied him. He was a tall young man and strong; she'd noted that before: tall and strong and with the look of hardihood in his face. She'd heard a deal of the Archers, a fierce-eyed, hawk-nosed race, swaggering, hostile, arms forever within their reach, and high words upon their lips. He was somewhat like that. Her head nodded; but even as it was nodding, she corrected herself. He *could* be like that. But there was another side to him: she'd seen a deal of the boy in him; there had been laughter in his look; when he'd spoken of his mother her heart had melted in her breast at the sadness of it. *She* had not been afraid of him; with her he'd been honest and outspoken and sincere; in the first glimpse she'd had of him, he was arising to her defense!

And De Chaulnes had put his hand upon her! There was anger in her eyes as the instance came back to her: he had dared! And then, with a sick feeling at her heart, she thought of the next night when she'd smiled up into his face; she'd permitted his arm to support her; she'd talked and listened and done everything she could to ask and hold his attention. And when Philip Archer stood before her she'd ignored him, she'd put a contempt and cold insolence into her look that hurt her heart to think of.

She'd been afraid; that'd been the cause of it. She'd been afraid—of a danger that might come to him. As she sat upon the back of the restless young horse, looking at Philip, he standing so dejectedly, a cloud upon his face, her impulse was to spring to the ground, to go to him, to plead with him for forgiveness. Yes, she'd been afraid; dread had never before so taken hold of her, and that is why she'd treated him so. Her heart had shivered and seemed turned to ice when he told her of that night long ago in New Orleans when his father, then a boy, had looked over the stair rail into the hall below, and saw the man who'd been set to guard him, lying still and dead.

Murder! That's what it had been. Murder! And the blow had not been meant for the man, but for the boy who was heir to the Archer claim. The Claridges had struck; they had struck, and a life was scored in red against their name. She'd had dim word of such things, and had always been afraid of them, but she'd never felt such terror as held its place in her thoughts that night and during the next day. John Claridge was hard, ruthless, secretive; there was little mercy in him. Neither he, nor his nephew, nor any of the others concerned, would think a life of importance if death strengthened their hold upon what they called their own. Had she not been a witness to the consternation caused by the letter of Philip Archer announcing his proposed visit to the city? The two Claridges had sat far into the small hours of more than one night, engaged in talk; Mr. Hasty came and went; there had been conferences and dark looks.

At first she'd tried to think these things meant nothing but the anxiety of surprised merchants in the matter of a possible suit-at-law; but Philip's story to her made this impossible; she saw something sinister in every picture her mind recalled. During the whole day after her return from New Castle her fright increased; and then, late in the afternoon, John Claridge came to visit her. He had walked up and down her sitting room, with a black boy holding his horse outside; he kept his hostile eyes upon her; now and then he'd lift one almost transparent hand and smooth back his shining hair.

"I have spoken with Hasty," he'd said. "And with De Chaulnes, also."

His habit was to make a statement of fact, no matter how simple, in the manner of an accusation, and then wait for the words of hasty defense that usually followed. But Charlotte had long since penetrated this.

"Well?" she'd said, and looked at him inquiringly.

"I am given to understand young Archer has arrived," he said. She made no reply to this; he paced the floor, angry, rubbing his hands together. "He struck De Chaulnes."

"At the moment," Charlotte had said, evenly, "I was much agitated and alarmed. I was being forced by a man, almost a stranger, to accompany him on a long journey through the night under, so I was told, your instructions. But I believe Mr. Archer did strike him."

He'd stopped his pacing at that and stood upright and threatening before her.

"I have been told you had a long conversation with this young man. A confidential conversation behind closed doors."

"I spoke with him," said the girl. "I thanked him for being of service to me."

What had she said? John Claridge looked at her, his eyes smouldering, half mad with drugs, and with a thought and purpose suddenly coming to the top of his manner that made her breath catch. What had she told him? And what had his reply been? She had grown accustomed to the man's arrogance and vanity, and of late years had paid little attention to either; but through these things there now showed a deadly, peering purpose; she read it in the stark lines of his face, in the way his almost fleshless hands closed and reclosed. Murder! Murder long ago; and it was to be murder now!

"What questions did he ask you?" said John Claridge, to her. "What did he desire to know?"

Murder! She saw the scarlet sign of the thing in his face as he spoke. He dreaded she'd said something to Philip Archer, some secret, dangerous thing, and because of this, he meant to have the young man's life.

"He asked no questions," she'd said. "He boasted and swaggered, as I've heard the Archers have always done. He told me a deal of things of no consequence. He seemed much younger than his years," she'd said with a smile; "I would not have believed a person of above twenty-five could have spoken so much folly." There was a light contempt in her manner; she'd shrugged her shoulders. "It seems he is also a bully; he told me of brawls and escapades, all having to do with his power of body and skill with the sword. I don't think," she said, "I have ever put in so boresome an hour as the one I spent with him."

"They are all braggarts," said John Claridge, with no change in his look. "But they have also been cunning. Somewhere," he said, "in the thick of his talk he pointed a question so that you'd answer it, perhaps without knowing."

This made her heart almost stop; but she replied with an air of scorn:

"It is not likely he'd trap me so. As you know, I'm not often unguarded."

"Of all the people I've ever had occasion to deal with," said John Claridge, "you have been the most difficult. But an Archer might not find you so," his brows thick and low above the smouldering eyes. "You'd be like to have more sympathy there."

"What questions could he ask?" she'd said. "And, especially, what replies could I make to them? There is no one who

knows less of the doings of Claridge & Company than I do,"
she added, bitterly.

"There are times," said John Claridge, "when I'm not so
sure of that. You have always been close-mouthed, Charlotte;
I've never had more than the meagerest knowledge of what was
in your mind."

"Can you say it has been altogether my fault? Perhaps
a little candor on your part would have helped a deal." He'd
gone out of the room shortly after that, and left the house; his
white face set, his hands clenching and unclenching; a darkness
seemed all about him.

Murder! Charlotte could see it in every step he took, and
for an hour afterward she'd been all but distracted. She sent a
servant to inquire at the inns if one Philip Archer was there,
meaning to go to him the moment he was located. And then
Louise came, purring, smiling, speaking in her soft voice.

"My dear, such an adventure as you must have had! And
that detestable De Chaulnes! They say this stranger struck him
as though he were a stable boy. I'd love to have seen it," clasping her jeweled hands. "How fortunate you are, you courageous thing, to have been there. And you spoke with this
M'sieu Archer. How outrageous! What will John Claridge say
when he has heard of it?"

Charlotte, as she looked at the lovely, smiling creature,
was quite sure she knew John Claridge had been there only an
hour before. But she said nothing; and the beautiful Madame
Barreaut went on:

"To think! He comes upon the same mission his father came
on, years ago." She seemed thrilled. "It is like a tale out of a
book. Charlotte, above all things, I should like to see him.
You are his friend. Ask him to come here; and then ask me,
also." Her gay laugh rang through the place. "It would be
charming. Tell me, quickly: is he handsome? Is he good-
natured? What did he say to you?"

"He said a deal, and to little purpose," said Charlotte.

"Oh, no!" Again the jeweled hands were clasped; her eyes were alight, her beautiful teeth shone. "Surely not! He must have so *much* to tell. But, never mind that," and she shook a pretty finger at Charlotte, "tell me what *you* said to him."

But as Charlotte looked at her coldly and in silence, Madame Barreaut's manner changed; it became suddenly grave, her voice lowered.

"What did you say of these detestable Claridges? I hope you were quite plain-spoken about them, and told how badly they have treated you." As there was still no response from Charlotte, she began laughing once more. "But, there: I am forgetting how reserved you are. Of course, you would say little at a first meeting," the pretty finger shaking. "You'd keep most of it for a later time."

"There will be no later time," said Charlotte. "One meeting with Mr. Archer was quite enough."

The beautiful Madame Barreaut talked with rapid vivacity; she trifled with her rings, her necklace, her bracelets; Charlotte's responses were guarded and brief, but for all that she had a feeling she was saying a deal more than she should. For Madame's eyes were upon her, those quick, beautiful eyes which saw so much; Madame's mind would flash out somewhere in the talk and grasp a small detail; a little later it would grasp something else and put the fragments together. It was her way; and she gained much information by it. She had arisen to go when she said:

"To-night at the drill shed, Edward and M'sieu le duc will take charge of the recruits. Edward requests your presence," said Madame, smilingly. "And De Chaulnes will, I think, ask your pardon."

Two were not enough, then, to examine, to question her! There must be more; Edward must fix his eye upon her, he must value and study her; and then, perhaps, if he saw what he fancied cause for suspicion: murder!

And that afternoon, when Madame Barreaut sent for her so

suddenly. To meet Philip there with Madame's watchful eyes upon them. It was too dreadful! An arranged thing. But she saw it at once, and was on her guard. She'd been disdainful and cold.

And at Brotot's that night! The unfortunate, the poor young man! How pitiful it had been! She thought more than once she'd break down and weep, she had been so utterly wretched. How friendly his eyes had been—how eager! How he'd waited for a word from her, a look! And she'd turned her back upon him. She'd treated him with cold insolence—she had——

But the rumbling of the wagon wheels came at this moment, and she drew still further into the shelter of the hedge; the vehicle passed, and in it she saw Philip sitting moodily beside the driver, his arms folded, his chin upon his breast.

3

When the girl alighted from her horse, a half hour later, before the stable that faced a small green way, she saw Mrs. King beckoning her from the garden.

"My dear," said the good lady, "before you go to your room, please speak to the young man sitting in the passage. He's been here for a half hour or more and seems most impatient."

In the lofty hall of the fine old house, Charlotte found a spare young man with disordered neckcloth and ink-stained fingers.

"What is it, Hunter?" she asked.

He got up hastily and saluted her. From the cuff of his coat he took a folded paper and handed it to her. She unfolded and read it, and her face went white.

"Hunter," she said, "do you know what's in this?"

"I do."

"What are your instructions?"

"To arm myself with a pair of pistols and take to the Baltimore road immediately after I spoke to you."

She stood, pale and much distressed; then she called through an open window to a boy who was taking care of her horse; and when he came quickly to her she said:

"Put the saddle upon the black mare! At once!" and as the boy darted away, she turned to Hunter. "I will go with you," she said.

CHAPTER XIV

PHILIP was driven back to town, and in the public room of the Penny Pot he found Corporal Brotot in conversation with the privateersman, Captain Hawes. The young man's first thought was of Lazarus and the papers, and he inquired if he was still engaged with the contents of the chest.

"Now, that is an unfortunate thing," said Brotot. "He was much interested; indeed, I might say, excited; and as Nicholas threw back the lid of the chest, I never saw a pair of eyes that glinted as his did. But, before he could lay so much as a finger upon a document, there came a call for him by the inn people; a messenger brought in a sealed letter which he read at once; and then he got up in all haste, ordered a carriage, and apologizing for his abruptness, drove away."

For all the heat of the day, Philip ordered brandy and drank it; then he charged a pipe with tobacco and sat with his legs crossed, puffing away and frowning.

"What roads lead out of the city to Baltimore?" he said to Captain Hawes.

The shipman with his finger tip drew a sort of map upon the table.

"It is as direct a way as anyone could wish," he said. "I've traveled it many times: you strike southwest through the city," following the way with his finger, "and you cross the west river here and continue on without impediment; the roads are poor; sometimes travelers must ride in company to protect themselves against highwaymen; in the present unsettled state of things this condition may have grown worse. There's always some ruffian abroad in the countryside who'll risk the hangman in the hope of coming upon a few gold pieces."

Philip smoked his pipe and studied the map with attentive eyes. Then he said to Captain Hawes:

"Among the people employed by Claridge & Company, have you ever met with a man of the name of Gorman?"

The captain replied that he had; and he cursed him with all of a shipman's fervor.

"He was mate with me in a vessel I mastered, owned by Claridge; and so I come to know him well. A damned villain, sir, if ever there was one; how he has gone so far without some exasperated, honest man taking his life, I don't know."

Philip drew moodily at his pipe.

"I knew him for a narrow-eyed rogue directly I put my eyes on him," he said.

Captain Hawes surveyed the young man, shrewdly.

"You've met with him, then?"

"Yes."

"I take it," said the captain, "there was some passage between you?"

"Not that, exactly," said Philip. "I said nothing to him, at all. But he said a thing to me the like of which I never thought to hear."

"But——" said Captain Hawes, and then stopped. "A hurtful thing?" he said.

"A thing which all but burst my heart as I thought of it coming along into the city."

Captain Hawes got up at once.

"A thing of that kind should not be borne by a man of spirit," he said. "It harms the soul and makes many a day of life a thing of ashes. Why did you not stretch him at your feet?" said the captain.

"My first impulse was to do so," said Philip; "but other things came into my mind; things I felt I must consider."

The privateersman shook a finger at him.

"I gather from the corporal you are here in a large matter of money," he said; "but permit me to say this: there can be nothing of so great importance as to cause a man to take a dirty word from such a rascal! But, come with me," said the captain, and hooked his arm beneath Philip's and brought him to his feet. "I know where he lodges; we shall go there and have him out; and you shall beat him until he can no longer stand upright."

But Philip, as he put his pipe upon the table, said:

"I have good reason to think he's not in the city; perhaps he will not be for some time. But what you've said is quite right, Captain," and he shook the privateersman's hand. "I've felt so from the beginning, but this has resolved me."

Without any explanation he turned to Brotot.

"Have them bring out a horse as quickly as possible; a good beast, with plenty of wind and courage, because it may be I'll need to ride him hard."

Once upstairs he kicked off his shoes and drew on a pair of boots; he took a brace of heavy pistols from the chest, carefully loaded them, and placed a small canister of black powder and a dozen leaden balls in his pocket. The horse, an able-looking animal, was at the door when he went down, and while Brotot and the privateersman watched in silence, he put the pistols into the holsters.

"Look for me, perhaps, this time to-morrow, Brotot," he said. Then he waved his hand to Captain Hawes and was off.

He crossed the river at a ford below the ferry, and then struck into a yellow road that wound along through bits of forest and, again, skirted cleared places where cattle and horses were grazing. Just before dusk he found himself upon the edge of a tiny hamlet which proved to be Chester; he got down at a wholesome-looking little tavern for a snack of food. A pleasant-faced girl in a clean apron brought him ale in a toby, and a mug to drink it from, also some bread and cheese, and a pat of good butter which she took out of a white cloth.

"It's a poor road for a horseman," said Philip, as he ate and drank.

The girl said she thought so, too.

"But it's worse for a wagon," she said. "We must take our things to market after harvest each year, and we must go to the city to buy things each spring; and we find it's a long way."

"I suppose," said Philip, "it gets no better as one goes further to the south."

"It's a dreary road, indeed, that way," said the girl; "a good many travel it on the way to and from Baltimore, and they complain of it a deal. And it's a road that's not over safe after nightfall. There are riders going up and down it at times who levy heavy toll upon unprotected people."

"So I've heard," said Philip, eating of his bread and cheese with relish.

"Just now," said the girl, and her voice lowered as she looked deep into the dusk that crept out of the great tangle of forest trees through which the road wound, "Jerry Shuttleworth is riding below there of a night, he who looks so like a parson. He's a dangerous man and defies the laws, and thinks little of God and salvation, though he talks so often of them."

"Highwaymen are much alike in any place and in all countries." He smiled at the serious look in the girl's face. "Salvation means little to them, and God is far away."

He paid his reckoning, after a space, and untied his horse; the landlord and his wife stood with the girl at the tavern door.

"It would be better," said the man, "if you stopped here until morning; there is no fitting place between here and Elks Head where you might lie safely; and you'd not reach that in a night's riding."

"There is the Plough Tavern," said Philip as he got into the saddle. "I've heard of that."

The landlord lifted his brows.

"It is not for me to speak against people who are of the same profession as myself," said he; "but this I will say: if you've heard anything of the Plough but ill, you've been listening to lies."

"Well, at any rate, I must lose no time," said Philip. "But, thank you all; and good-night to you."

He rode on through the dusk; a short space beyond, the road curved away into the wood, and darkness came suddenly upon him. Emerging from this a half hour later, he found the night sky above him glittering with stars and with a small crescent of a moon sailing silently in a sea of dusky purple. He could see plainly enough; his horse cantered on with much willingness, requiring little attention; but suddenly it lifted its head and snuffed the air; then it whinnied loudly. There was a sound of hoofs out of a small byroad that ran along through the wood; and Philip, almost before he realized it, found a horse and rider at his side. More than that, his quick eye, trained to the instant usages of the sea, saw that the man wore a long, dark coat of a clerical cut, and a high white neckcloth; also that his right hand hung straight at his side holding to the butt of a large pistol.

"Good-evening to you, sir," said the young man quietly, checking his horse and making no further move save that of turning his head. "And welcome. This road is strange to me, and I'm glad to come upon a traveler like myself."

The man in the clerical coat chuckled in a pleased sort of way; the hand with the pistol hung motionless.

"It is the graciousness of Providence that brought you here," he said in the singsong manner of a riding preacher. "I am not unfamiliar with the road, friend," he said, "but it had become very lonely to-night, and I'd made up my mind none would be riding this way."

"Why, then," said Philip with good spirits, "here I am, and we'll bear each other company."

Again came the chuckle from the stranger; Philip saw the corners of his mouth curl upward; his strong teeth shone in the light of the fragmentary moon. The arm hanging at his side pressed closer to it; the pistol was all but hidden behind his boot leg.

"So we shall," he said, in his chanting way, "so we shall, brother. We shall bear each other up in the darkness and loneliness of the road; our twin strengths shall keep harm from befalling."

He wheeled his horse to Philip's right side, facing the same way, and as he did so his elbow bent, and the young man knew the long pistol had been thrust back into its holster.

"Forward, then, my young friend, in the name of the all-purposeful, and with the eyes of night fixed upon us."

Philip smiled as the horses carried them on side by side.

"Jerry Shuttleworth," he said to himself. "And it seems I am to be favored with a somewhat extensive acquaintance with him. A clever fellow, too, by the sound of him, and with some quality of humor. Well, at all events, he'll relieve the tediousness of the way; and I trust the night'll not end with me being forced to put a ball through him."

"A stranger, you say," said Jerry Shuttleworth, in his pious tones. "And from the accent of your speech, friend, you are not always where English is spoken."

"No," said Philip. "I follow the sea."

"Ah!" said the highwayman, and turned his eyes upward. "The vast and infinite sea. A life upon its turbulent waters! The great storms, with puny man standing in the hollow of the All-powerful Hand." He looked at Philip, mildly. "So many shipmen ride between Philadelphia and Baltimore since the King's cruisers have taken to guarding the mouths of the bays. Some of them carry matters of large value: in specie, and in minted money."

"So I have heard," said Philip.

"How fortunate a thing that these inland ways are free of the despoiler," said the good Jerry Shuttleworth in his most fervent tones. "How unlike the sea they are—the sea where pirates and other wretches are banded together against the safety of honest people."

Philip's mouth twitched; there was a great laugh in his throat, but he kept his voice steady enough.

"I was saying that very thing to myself as dusk drew on," he said. "To be sure, a seafarer of the kind I am has nothing to lose; but those who carry valuable matters are extremely fortunate in the safe ways of travel, and in the virtuous people they meet as they journey on."

"Right," said Jerry Shuttleworth in his oiliest voice. "Quite right. The companionship of the virtuous is ever a boon." He regarded Philip out of the tail of his eye, trying to read his face in the semi-dark. "You are master of a vessel, I suppose."

"No," said Philip.

"You are meaning to join a ship at Baltimore, though?" persisted the highwayman. "Sent by a merchant or a trader, perhaps," somewhat anxiously, his fingers picking at the pistol butt in the holster at his knee, "with some items of money that had been overlooked?"

"No," said Philip, "I'm journeying rather in the hope I'll not reach Baltimore. To-night I will lie at the Plough; it may be I'll go no further than that."

"The Plough," said Jerry Shuttleworth. "Ah, yes."

"My information is that it's on this road and at no great distance," said Philip. "Do you know it, by any chance?"

"Very well," said the highwayman. He chuckled, and Philip saw his lean head nodding in the starlight. "A comfortable tavern, and with a most obliging landlord. Many is the night, when I and my horse have been worn with haste, we've stopped there and had good attention and soft beds." He pointed to a spot ahead where the road turned. "Just beyond is a small stream with a bridge," he said. "Once across that and the place is in sight." Again Philip felt the sidelong glance upon him, and again the gaunt fingers of the man began caressing the butt of the pistol. "You mean to rest there for the night, you say?"

Philip held his horse close to that of the highwayman so he might be ready to throw himself upon the man if the weapon be drawn. But he had no desire to engage with him at that time, and with the idea of delaying matters, he said:

"Yes, and to sup there. And, if it would not be presuming too much upon a brief acquaintance, I ask you, when we reach there, to get down and sup with me."

Jerry Shuttleworth laughed; he shook his lean head at the stars and swore in a way that sat poorly upon one of his appearance.

"Why, that's good-humored enough," he said, between his fits of cackling. "I've ridden these roads for a half dozen years and met many a traveler upon them, but this is the first time one of them has invited me to take food and drink with him." Both the man's hands were now upon the bridle, and Philip permitted his mount to ease away. "The invitation being generously meant," said the highwayman, "so it is accepted. And there is good brew at the Plough," he added; "and they can broil a fowl in a way that'd do credit to an inn of greater pretensions."

In a little while they rounded the turn, and there before them was the bridge; and some distance further along the road they saw the lighted windows of the Plough Tavern.

CHAPTER XV

A COMFORTABLE sight after the heat of the road," said
Shuttleworth. "At this inn a man may have an ample
chair and may remove his belt and his boots. Of a winter's
night," he said to Philip, "it is even more cheerful. Then
the road is lonely, and bitter blasts are like to drive along
it; a cheerful fire and some hot drink is supporting to the
heart."

They dismounted at the door of the Plough; it was a
neglected-looking building, rambling and shapeless, with low
eaves and small dormer windows projecting upon its sweeping
roof. The landlord, a sandy, furtive-looking man with shifty
eyes and a cringing manner, came out, as a stable boy led away
the horses.

"Good-night to you, Mr. Badger," said Jerry Shuttleworth,
piously. "I trust things have been well with this good house
since I've last halted to partake of its hospitality."

"Only tolerable, sir," said the landlord. "Not anything
to make boast of, indeed. But," and he nodded his head, his
furtive eyes upon Philip, who was speaking with the stable boy,
"we make an occasional profit. Things are never at an actual
standstill."

The highwayman watched Philip as he walked behind the
horses to the barn at the other side of the road. Then he turned
upon the sandy man, lowering his lean head, and speaking in a
threatening tone.

"I've ridden with this young man during the last three
miles," he said, "and have spoken soft and friendly with him
during the whole of the way. There is a weight in the tail pocket

of his coat," said Mr. Shuttleworth, "which can be nothing but a well filled purse, and that I claim as my very own."

The furtive eyes did not meet those of the highwayman; the landlord rubbed his hands and cringed more than ever; but when he spoke there was a something in his voice that would cause anyone to look at him twice.

"Four hours ago," he said, "the Plough had word this traveler was on the way and meant to stop here. That you should come upon him by accident on the road gives you no claim upon him, Mr. Shuttleworth."

The highwayman looked at the landlord, his head held like that of a snake poised to strike.

"If he has a purse upon him, it is mine," he said. "So, be warned, Badger: I'll have no interference."

In the barn, the stable boy, a fat, slow-witted youth, took the saddles from the horses. Philip hung his own upon a wooden peg, and as he did so, slipped one of the holster pistols into the breast pocket of his coat. There was a pair of bay horses, neglected looking, with the sweat dried upon them, tied near the door; also there was a carriage which, in the light of the lantern, looked a deal like the one Gorman had ridden in.

"You have other travelers at the inn," said Philip.

The boy looked at him, a stupid cunning in his face.

"Travelers are always on the road," he said. "And often they stop at the Plough when night overtakes them." He slapped the flank of a horse to move it out of the way. "Maybe you'll be staying until morning?" he said.

"It may be," said Philip. "I don't know." He looked at the carriage and the trappings of the bay horses. "This traveler had an outrider?" he said.

"If he had they'll both be inside," said the stable boy, with the same cunning look. "You'll see them there."

The parlor of the inn was a long, narrow room with low rafters and a huge fireplace of brick, now gloomy and black. The floor was of planks, scrubbed and sanded; the furniture, oaken and heavy, bore the marks of hard usage; the table top was ringed by the countless bottles and glasses that had been placed upon it. The landlord's wife was in the room, a huge woman with bare arms, heavy and lumpy, a small head upon wide, thick shoulders, and eager, hard eyes.

"You'll be wanting supper, sir," she said to Philip, as he hung his hat and riding whip upon the wall.

"We'll both have supper," said the young man, indicating the highwayman, who stood at one of the windows. "You are my guest," said Philip, as the man turned. "You shall, as I've said, sup and drink with me. A pair of fowls," he told the woman, "roasted on the spit; some good ham if you have it, cut cold; and a bit of fish would not be bad if you have such a thing; also any greens you can readily dress." He sat upon a corner of the table, one leg swinging, and looked at the highwayman. "In the matter of drink, now, on a sultry night: what is your wish?"

"Good ale is hearty," said Jerry Shuttleworth, wagging his head, highly pleased, "and an honest drink as well; it lifts the spirit in praise. I've been more thankful for what I've received, with a bellyful of excellent malt, than in any other state I can give name to."

"Ale, then," said Philip to the woman. "And wine."

"We have Portagee wine," said the landlord's wife; "and real French, from a ship Badger knows the mate of."

"A bottle of each, then," said the young man. "And bring them at once."

The place was lighted by a pair of heavy candles burning in iron holders upon the table; the corners were dim and filled with shadows; but the two sat at the table, bottles and glasses upon it, cheerfully enough; and each tossed off a tumbler of the brown wine.

"It's a rich, good drink," said Jerry Shuttleworth, smacking his lips. "I'm beholden to you, sir."

As they sat drinking and awaiting the preparation of the

fowls and other things, Philip talked with the highwayman; but his mind was upon the man he'd come a-seeking. Except for the horses and the carriage there was no sign of him; no rugs nor hats nor any traveling matters were about to indicate his presence in the place. When the woman laid plates and knives and forks and spoons, it was for two persons only.

"We are to have no company, it seems," said Philip to Shuttleworth, over the rim of his refilled glass. "I'm fortunate in the chance that brought about our meeting, otherwise I should have supped quietly enough."

The small eyes of the woman seemed to draw together; she wiped a plate with a clean cloth, and said:

"There are others who'll stop here, sir, through the night. They have been here and gone, but will return, directly."

"The person who came in the carriage I saw outside, I suppose," said Philip.

"Yes, sir," said the woman, readily enough. "A gentleman who often stops here, and travels with a postilion to manage the horses."

Near the empty fireplace there were some billets of wood, sturdy and of good weight. Philip's eyes were upon the largest of these, one that would make a most excellent cudgel.

"He will return directly, you say?"

"That is certain, sir. There was a matter he had to see to, a smith who shod a horse for him the last time he passed this way and must be paid. He'll be here to sup, and then to bed."

As the woman spoke there came a crash from the kitchen, an angry voice, blows, and shrieks of pain. The door of the parlor burst open, and a girl, white-faced, poorly dressed, and with fright in her eyes, rushed in, the landlord pursuing her. At once Philip was up and between the two.

"Now, now," said the young man, amiably, "how is this? Surely, landlord," pointing to an iron spit in the man's hand, "you'd not strike her with such an implement? It is weighty enough to brain a strong man."

"I am tormented with her," said the sandy man. "She's the plague of my life. I have taken her from the poorhouse and given her decent work, and she can be taught nothing. Only now, as she was turning the fowls, she let one of them fall into the fire."

Here the heavy-armed woman reached forward and gave the girl a blow on the side of the head which almost felled her.

"Quietly, now!" said Philip, and his voice was stern. "None of that. The girl looks none too strong."

"Am I to be told my duty in my own house?" said the woman. "Am I to have a stranger——" But her husband took her by the arm and said something to her in a low tone. She at once changed her manner. "The girl is provoking, sir," she said. "She's forever doing some stupid thing because she won't mind her work."

Philip looked into the girl's frightened face: a dull, not overly intelligent face; and he said to her:

"There, it's all over now; you'll not be beaten. Get to your work; and turn the spit carefully. For the fowls are our supper, do you see, and we'd rather not have them garnished with ashes."

"Thank you, sir," she said. "And I'll be careful. I nodded a little, but it was because I was up over late last night with a toothache."

Left to their wine again, Jerry Shuttleworth said:

"Badger has no light hand with his servants. That poor-witted thing has no talent for kitchening, but there is nothing he must pay her sort, and that is why she's here."

After a time the fowls were brought in, also some cuts of cold ham, a dish of lentils, and one of greens; there were hot bread and tall mugs creaming over with ale.

"Now may the all-seeing look upon this with excellent favor," said the highwayman. He carved one of the browned birds with a clever knife while Philip loaded the plates with the other things. "What better way to render thanks for a day's safeguarding than eating heartily at the end of it, and drinking deeply? God's goodness is manifested in various ways, but in no more satisfying a one than a good appetite." He lifted the stone mug and pledged Philip. "To your good health, sir," he said, regarding him steadily over the top of it. "May you prosper, and live to provide as good a repast to every stranger you meet upon the way."

"Not to them all," said Philip, also doing justice to the ale, "for some of them are villains to their heart's core, and kindness would be wasted upon them. But to such as you," pledging him in return. "Well, that's a different matter. May your days be continuous with grace, and may no regret ever come to torment you."

Jerry Shuttleworth drank to this. And he ate with undiminished appetite; but he laughed and chuckled through it all, and sometimes he put down his knife and fork so that he might rub his hands together in glee.

"Life is an excellent joke," he said, "and looked at with proper eyes we can always get humor from it. Sometimes, though," nodding his lean head, mirthfully, "the jest is so keen we all but crack our ribs over it." He grimaced and laughed; he took long pulls at the mug of ale, having it replenished several times; he did not forget the wine bottle, pouring a glass from it now and then. The effects of this began to show before long; he examined Philip with unsteady eyes and began to talk of friendship suddenly come into; finally he reached across the table.

"Shake hands!" he said. Philip readily gripped hands with him. "It is good food we have here," said the man; "generous and handsomely provided. Splendid drink, and bought with a rare good spirit." He fixed Philip with a fishy look. "'You are my guest,' quote you. 'You shall sup and drink with me,' you said. You've treated me like a gentleman, and, by God, sir," smacking his hand upon the table, "no harm shall come to you."

"Harm!" said Philip. "What harm could come to a man at a decent inn?"

Jerry Shuttleworth sat down. The second bottle had been opened, and he filled a glass from it.

"You are not accustomed to these roads," he said, after he'd drunk off the wine. "The inns are not all to be trusted," he said, "and the people you meet with are not always what they seem. But," and he nodded the lean head with comfortable assurance, "you've treated me like a gentleman, and again I say, no harm shall come to you." He reached down and took a long-barreled dueling pistol from his boot leg and put it upon the table. "He who lifts a hand to you," he said, "will have to deal with me."

In the hour or more the two sat at the table, the thick candles had grown shorter, their heavy shrouds flowing over the iron holders. Little by little Philip grew less talkative; a depression came upon his spirit; at those times when Shuttleworth was not speaking the inn was silent; the places in the room beyond reach of the candlelight grew deep with shadow. As the highwayman guzzled his drink the young man's mind drifted back through the years; he saw his father, or his grandfather in his present situation. Would they have sat as patiently as he was doing? He was sure they wouldn't have. They'd been out of their saddles the instant they reached the inn door, demanding the man they sought; not receiving a sufficient answer they'd have ranged through the house, pistol in hand; failing in this, they'd have had the ratty landlord by the throat.

"But here I sit," was Philip's thought, "a good deal like an old woman might at a church door."

Had the Archer blood grown thin in him that he should do this so willingly? Should he not up with him and——! But, no! Wait! The thought that had held his mind as he received Gorman's vile insult at John Claridge's came to the front once more; his whole intelligence was re-lit with it. Prearrange-

ment! That's what it was! Why had Gorman followed him to
Claridge's place? Why had Madame Barreaut tried instinctively to close the curtains at the library window when she saw
him alighting from his carriage? Why had Gorman so carefully
told John Claridge where he might be found that night on the
road to Baltimore? And why had Claridge repeated it word for
word as he wrote it down?

"They knew my father," was Philip's thought; "they knew
his temperament and counted upon my being like him; but
also they counted upon a caution in me which would hold me
in check for time enough to permit the man to get safely away
upon the road! And the girl?" he said to himself. "The beautiful Madame Barreaut? How swiftly she slipped down the
stairs after me; how earnestly she counseled with me; how
cleverly she knew the impulse that was in me and played upon
it. Be after him! That was her advice. Be after him and have
your satisfaction!"

And here he was! He smiled with a humorous grimness.
Here he was, with night settled down, in a place of no savory
repute, dining with a drunken highwaymen, the windows wide
open, his back to one of them, a fair mark for——

There was a sound from outside, a creeping, stealthy sound,
and with a quickness born of many dangerous situations he
threw both the candles to the floor, plunging the place into
darkness.

"What!" said Jerry Shuttleworth, hiccuping in the blackness. "What the devil!"

"Sh-h-h!" Philip leaned across the table and put his hand
upon the man's shoulder. "Keep still."

He heard a stir in the darkness, then a sharp click; he knew
the man had taken up the dueling pistol and cocked it.

"No harm shall come to you," said the highwayman. "You
have treated me cleverly, and you have the word of Jerry
Shuttleworth that your purse'll be safe."

Philip took the holster pistol from his breast pocket and

approached one of the windows; he stood at one side of it, peering out until his eyes had grown accustomed to the darkness. But he saw nothing and heard nothing.

Then a sound from within the room caused him to turn, his weapon lifted. But it was only Jerry Shuttleworth snoring; and Philip could see him with his arms upon the table, his head resting upon them. And at that moment a long strip of light fell across the room, a narrow strip, dull, as though coming from a single candle; the face of the inn servant appeared, at a slightly opened door. The darkness of the room seemed to frighten her, there was terror in her eyes, and she was about to close the door when Philip spoke.

"What is it?" he said.

She gasped, her grubby hand over her mouth.

"Oh, I'm glad there's nothing amiss with you, sir!" She whispered the words; they were so low he barely heard them. "But come away: don't stay here." She entreated him with a gesture. "There do be death in that room, sir. Do not stay there."

He crossed to the door, the folds of his coat hiding the pistol; and in a moment he was in the passage.

"Where are the people of the inn?" he asked.

With clasped hands she implored him to speak lower.

"They have gone," she whispered. "They have been gone for some time. But they will return—when you are dead, sir!" horror in her voice. "They will come back, then, and take your money."

"Someone thinks to do away with me, then," said Philip, his eyes going here and there in the passage. "Who is it?"

"The man who came this afternoon," said the inn servant. "He came in a carriage with a postilion. He was here when you ordered your supper. I heard them talk afterwards, and I was frightened; that's why I let the fowl fall from the spit into the fire."

Philip's hand tightened upon the pistol butt. This, now, was a matter more to his liking; no more patient waiting; there was a prospect of blows. Some little distance along the passage was a door, its bottom edge fringed with light: Philip pointed to this.

"Who is there?" he asked.

"It is not the man," said the trembling girl. "It is the ladies."

"Ladies!" said Philip, a frown between his eyes.

"One of them came this afternoon," said the girl; "the other arrived since dark set in. She must have come on foot from somewhere, maybe through the woods, for her clothes were torn, and she was out of breath."

The young man stood for a space, pondering; then he went quietly down the hall and paused at the door; there was a voice —a woman's voice, pitched low and, though he could not catch the words, full of shaking anger. There were sobs, deep, convulsive, full of fear, there were assurances and protestations murmured between the sobs. Philip stood for a moment at the door; then he saw the latch was not in its groove, and quietly he pushed it open, little by little, until he had a view of the room. He saw Madame Barreaut huddled in a deep chair, her face wet with tears; facing her was Charlotte Desfourneaux, cold, white, her eyes full of anger.

He had but the briefest glimpse of them, then a shot sounded through the place, and he whirled, his pistol lifted. Down the passage he saw the kitchen girl, her face distorted in the dim candlelight, and she was pointing to the door of the room he'd quitted a few moments before. In a leap or two he reached and opened it: darkness met him; and silence. He waited for a moment, not moving, his pistol ready, but the place continued still. In the passage he took down the candle from its holder in the wall and went back into the parlor. And then he saw the figure of Jerry Shuttleworth upon the floor, a bullet hole in the side of his head.

He was standing, the candle held high above his head so he

might get a better view, looking at the dead highwayman, when there came a sudden rush of hoofs and the grind of wheels. It was Gorman! Gorman was making away. He put the candle upon the table, leaped through the open window and raced toward the barn. The sound indicated that the carriage was going in the direction of the city; and thrusting the pistol into his belt, Philip entered the dark stable in search of his horse. He was groping his way about when there came a flutter of light, dim and small; he saw the inn servant, her vacant face turned toward him, the stub of a candle in her hand.

"Quick, sir," she said. "Get your horse and put the saddle on him. If they see me helping you, I don't know what'll happen to me."

She put down the stump of candle and crept outside, where she crouched in the dark at the side of the barn. In a few moments Philip led out his horse; then, with a word of thanks to her, he mounted and rode away. She put out the candle and listened to the rapid hoofbeats as the horse went galloping down the road. Then, from the barn door, her eyes went to the house; the windows upon that side of it were dark except for the dim illumination from the room where Jerry Shuttleworth's body lay; and as she looked she saw a figure cross between the light and the window, an aged man, thin, stooped, with head bent, carrying a walking staff, the knob of which was held to the side of his face, very close to his ear.

CHAPTER XVI

BUT Philip Archer's dash through the night was without result; the postilion who managed Gorman's horses must have known the road quite well: at any rate, he slipped from it, somewhere, into a byway, and so eluded pursuit.

Becoming convinced of this, Philip reined in his startled horse, and soothed it into a state of quiet; he held carefully along the road for above two hours, when he arrived at Chester, and procured a bed at the inn where he'd stopped at sundown; and he slept soundly until morning.

He reached the city about noon; and a waiter spoke to him in the public room of the Penny Pot.

"There have been messengers here for you several times, sir. And once Mr. Fortune, the gun maker, asked for you; also, at another time, Captain Hawes of the schooner *Nancy Blake* stepped into the bar to see if you'd returned."

Philip thanked the man and took a seat in the coffee room, where he ate a dish of stewed turtle and some biscuits and had a glass of white Flemish wine.

"Mr. Archer, sir," said the waiter, who was a chubby little man with carrot-colored hair, "the people inquiring for you were in great haste. Mr. Fortune was especially anxious-looking."

"I'll speak to him during the afternoon," Philip said.

"Captain Hawes walked up and down the floor while waiting; and he looked at his watch a number of times."

"I'll have a word with the captain," said Philip.

"He's on board, sir," said the waiter. "He told me to tell you that."

Philip's thoughts were bleak; the rages of the previous day

were now but ashes in his mind; however, at the words "on board" he stirred in his chair. His spirit lifted. If Hawes had gone on board the *Nancy Blake* there was something newly come down the wind. The privateersman had lived ashore, so he'd said, while he waited for a chance to get to sea. Philip's look went through the open window and to the vessels lying at anchor, their heads toward Windmill Island: what if the *Nancy Blake* meant to drop down with the tide and make a dash for open water? His blood thrilled with the thought; he arose and was striding to and fro, picturing what brisk proceedings were in store for the schooner's company, when the waiter re-entered, ushering in Madame Barreaut.

"M'sieu!" she said, her dark eyes opened wide, her hands outheld. "Oh, I am glad! I am happy!" She swayed and seemed about to fall; the waiter brought her a chair, and Philip put her into it. And after the man had gone she said: "I cannot tell the relief it gives me, now I see you safe. I do not know what last night was to you, who are so steady of courage, but to me it was one of terror. More than once my heart stopped! In that dreadful place I could not breathe. I desired to speak to you, to warn you. But they would not permit me."

Philip looked down at her, the old unbelief in his eyes.

"I fear," she said, "there is much to explain before you really understand. It is always so," she added emotionally. "One seldom does an impulsive thing which really reaches the hearts of those we would help. When I saw you yesterday at John Claridge's counting house," she said, "I sympathized greatly with you, m'sieu. I pitied you. I said to myself: 'I will not leave him to this cold man,' for Mr. Hasty is like ice, m'sieu. I said: 'This youth desires to see John Claridge, and see him he shall.' And so I took you to Fairview, where he lives. I did this with the best of motives," pleadingly. "I meant it for your good. But I had forgotten," and now her voice was almost at a whisper. "I had forgotten what such a meeting might mean."

"It almost meant my life," said Philip.

"Oh, do I not know? Has not my heart been frightened? For John Claridge is cunning and watchful; he values opportunities. His thoughts run far ahead of those who oppose him. And he has no mercy;when he has made up his mind,he strikes. Who would have supposed Gorman would come into that room where you stood, of a set purpose?" she said, piteously. "Of a fixed and dreadful purpose? I knew so little of it," her voice breaking, "that I urged you to follow him. I knew so little of what your thoughts might be that I did not see you were trying to hold yourself from that very thing. And when I learned what had been planned, late in the afternoon, I feared you had taken my advice; for a moment, m'sieu, I thought I should die. And then I followed you."

"To the Plough Inn?" said Philip, his eyes never leaving her.

"Yes," she said. "I was there. You did not see me, but I was there. I wanted to speak with you, but was not permitted to do so. And, then, I heard the shot." She arose and stood before him, steadying herself. "I do not know how I had the resolution to do it—but I went into the room where you had been; you were gone, and a stranger lay dead upon the floor. Killed by the bullet meant for you."

Philip Archer, as he stood with his back set against the window frame, felt his spirit go sick. He looked into the lovely eyes and found them sleek with treachery; the beautiful face masked falsehood, tears stood upon her lashes, each of them poisoned with deceit. He'd come into a loathly thing, indeed, just as the father, in the long journal, said he'd do; he'd approached it with his eyes wide open, but he'd not seen the depth of it, and only a shadow of the evil. It was like a villainous pit, and he'd all but plunged into it. He had no desire to die, but, like any man of heart and moral substance, he'd die readily enough if there was need of it: but no one desires to die meanly, in the dark, where an honest blow will do no good and courage benefit nothing. Yes, as he stood there looking at the girl, his spirit sickened, a rage rose in him, not at her alone, but also at the circumstances in which he found himself.

Filthy, furtive, slinking! No one with whom he might grapple. Dark ways, sinister, cunning, stealthy approaches. He wished to God he was out of it! To think he must remain and engage in such matters when he might be at sea in a swift ship, with the sky racing overhead, an active crew, guns ready, and a foe standing boldly on the horizon. He felt a sudden passionate longing in his heart; he wanted to be clear of this welter of dishonor, he wanted a flag above his head, a deck beneath his feet; he wanted to slap the breech of a gun with the flat of his hand and feel the weight of a cutlass at his belt. What, after all, was John Claridge, his power, or his ships? What were these lawyer-written pages that had so deviled the Archers of three generations? What fascination had kept his father's and his grandfather's feet to this tortuous path upon which he'd now set his own? this way of deceit, of shameless trickery, of creeping subterfuge?

And now there came a fife squealing down the street, a tapping drum behind it; he turned and saw a file of strapping youths, sun-browned, awkward, with muskets on their shoulders. The sturdy step, the earnest faces, made Philip Archer's mouth tighten; it was a time when the long pleading with the King's ministers had ceased, when all spirited men had put aside private matters and thought only of the public good, only of the forces Lord North was sending across the sea against them. Washington had left his fox-hunting in Virginia, and the cultivation of his plantation; Jefferson, Hancock, and the Adamses had dropped their tasks and come forward; merchants, traders, artificers, preachers were giving their days to strengthening the country against the enemy. Masters of ships were surrendering profitable sailings out of the open ports, that they might get to sea in any craft that promised to hamper Britain's trade. It was a time when all men of good courage should down with a swig of drink, and up with a gun barrel, or

a stout blade. And here he was, mired to his belt buckle! Here
he was, engaged in a half-century old wrangle, giving his mind
and his time to winning back a damned hoard of pirate money;
here he was, his reason being poisoned by effrontery, by lies,
by tears and protestation; in bitter anger he spoke to the girl,
but before he had uttered more than a half dozen words, Mr.
Hasty came into the room, with Gorman at his heels.

"Louise!" said the old attorney, his hand closing upon her
arm. "What have I told you?" She drew out of his grasp,
defiance in her eyes. "Has all my talk been wasted?"

"I am tired of your warnings," said the girl, coldly. "I will
do what I desire to do, and I ask you not to interfere with me."

But his face was set, and his old eyes hard.

"It happens, Louise," he said, "in this case you are not dealing with me. In a. carriage at the door is John Claridge. You
are to leave here at once and go with him to Fairview."

The girl's face grew white; but she held herself proudly.

"You have been talking," she said to Gorman. "You've been
lying and trying to win favor for yourself."

The man smiled; he had an arrogant glint in his eyes, his
manner was one of burly humor.

"I think," he said, with a glance at Philip, "it is you who
are talking. Perhaps less of it would be more to the purpose."

Without further delay he took her by the arm and drew her
toward the door. She did not resist, though her dark eyes
flashed fire; Mr. Hasty followed them. At the front of the inn
was a handsome carriage; in it sat John Claridge with his gaunt
white face and gleaming black hair. He stared straight ahead,
not giving the girl a glance as she was helped into the vehicle.
Mr. Hasty got in, and Gorman was about to follow him when a
hand gripped him by the shoulder and held him back.

"One moment," said Philip Archer. He did not address
Gorman, holding him as one might a struggling dog. "I see you
again, Mr. Claridge," said Philip. "And quite unexpectedly. I
suppose," his hot eyes going from John Claridge to the girl

and back again, "you've heard some time since that, in spite of my resolution for caution in dealing with you, I last night walked into the trap you'd set for me. It was sheer good fortune and not any care of my own that saved me. However, since you all know this, there is no need of my insisting upon it; I only desire to add that my visit to the Plough last night was to get within hand's grasp of this gentleman." He released Gorman and struck him a powerful blow on the side of the head, felling him to the ground. "There he is for you," he said quietly. "Make what further use you can of him."

And with that he turned away, heading along the river toward the forge of Nicholas Fortune.

CHAPTER XVII

NICHOLAS FORTUNE sat in his workroom in the midst of his castings, his wooden gun models, and his drawings, smoking his Spanish segar; there was a stout-built, honest-looking young man with him, a sailor-like young man who had a clear blue eye and a deep, growling voice.

"The *Trumpeter's* people all went aboard last night," said the young man, "and she was ready to sail as the tide swung shortly after dawn. But she did not do so."

"Ah," said Nicholas, blowing out a cloud of smoke, "she is still at her anchorage?"

"We watched her closely," said the young sailor. "Captain Hawes, when dark came down last night, had me take a boat and two men and pull to a point in the shelter of Windmill Island where I could watch her. At the first sign of her getting under way I was to return and report. But she did not show any activity; the tide began to run out after daybreak, but still she lay there. However, at about the last hour of the tide, a boat put out from Claridge's wharf; and I saw the cause of the delay. The passenger was in it; she went aboard at once; and then the anchor came up, sail went on the ship, and she moved on her way down the river."

"There is no great air to-day," said Nicholas. "She'll not make many of those sixty miles to the Cape before you are after her."

"Captain Hawes is fretting a good deal," said the young man, who was second mate of the privateer *Nancy Blake*. "He desires to do what you advise, and told me to tell you so particularly. But he has about given up hope of the young man returning; he fears he's met with a serious delay of some kind."

Nicholas drew hard at his segar and looked anxious.

"I wish I had known what was transpiring when he started away yesterday," he said. "Hawes and Corporal Brotot are fighting men and do not properly consider danger. If I had known the young man was setting out on a venture like that, I'd been suspicious at once and sent a couple of stout fellows after him, with hangers and pistols, and instructions to waste no time when the proper moment arrived."

The mate of the *Nancy Blake* took up his hat.

"The captain sends his compliments, Mr. Fortune, and says we'll get up anchor in another hour, and make our way down the bay."

"I am sorry matters have not fallen as I desire," said Nicholas, regretfully. "It was in my mind the young man would be of much service in an adventure of this sort; but now that he——"

There was a step at the open door, and Philip Archer came in. At once Nicholas got up and saluted him with great pleasure.

"We were talking of you only this instant," said the little gun maker. "Sit down, now, and do you, Mr. Peters," to the mate, "return at once to your ship and say to Captain Hawes that Mr. Archer has arrived. Also," nodding at Philip, "that he'll be aboard within half an hour and give him an answer one way or another."

The mate of the schooner took his leave; and Philip sat down with Nicholas. The little man puffed at his segar until its end was cherry red; he talked; he gesticulated excitedly; he shook his finger; he scowled. The night before, the news had leaked out that a ship of Claridge & Company was to sail—a ship called the *Trumpeter*. How the matter came to be known, Nicholas was unable to tell; and only a few knew of the enterprise at most. As no vessel had gone out of the river in some weeks' time, the sailing was a notable one.

"Also," said Nicholas, "it seemed a most peculiar one. To

the best of my knowledge the vessel had taken in no cargo; she
was in ballast, merely."

Philip elevated his brows.

"To take an empty ship through a lane of enemy cruisers,"
he said. "Yes, I'd say that was peculiar, indeed."

Then a reason for the thing was chanced upon, Nicholas
said. The ship was to take a passenger, a person whom the
British government would be much pleased to get possession of.

"More than one in the city, as I've already said to you,
believe the Claridges have a secret understanding with the
King's agents," said the little gun maker; "so what if the ship
Trumpeter were sailing with the sole thought of betraying the
passenger into the enemy's hands?"

Philip shook his head.

"Admitting the Claridges are secretly in favor of the King's
government: would they risk open discovery of their leanings,
merely to accomplish a thing like that?"

Nicholas held up one bony finger.

"No," he said, "you are quite right. When a Claridge moves
in any matter, it is always for a Claridge's gain. But suppose it
happens, in this case, that the person mentioned is dangerous
to them in a private way? suppose this danger promises to
grow greater as time goes on? Would they not," waving the
segar, "venture a desperate stroke to be rid of such a menace?"

"I think," said Philip, "there is no doubt of it."

"Hawes is informed of this matter," said Nicholas; "he has
no love for these people, and is in a sort of fury to overtake the
Trumpeter before she reaches the lower bay."

With the eyes of his mind, Philip saw the Claridge ship,
under a full dress of sails, moving on her way toward the Capes;
also he saw the keen, shrewdly armed *Nancy Blake* in pursuit,
guns ready, with armed men at the rails; and outside, beyond
the Capes, were the British cruisers, vigilant, strong, waiting.

"By God!" said Philip, his face lighting up, "that's something, indeed! I'd love to have a part in it!"

Nicholas rubbed his hands, gleefully.

"There, now!" he exclaimed. "Said exactly as I expected you to say it. And Captain Hawes has been waiting in the hope you'd come aboard of him."

In a few minutes Nicholas had dispatched a man to have a boat ready at the end of the wharf; and while they were waiting for word of this, Mr. Lazarus, his ebony staff in his hand, appeared in the doorway. He shook hands with Philip and with Nicholas.

"I received your message only a half hour ago," he said to the little gun maker, "and made here in all haste. I slept late to-day because unforeseen matters kept me abroad the greater part of the night." He stroked the smooth black staff, his eyes upon Philip. "At my age one does not readily recover from fatigue," he said.

"Though younger than you by some years," said Nicholas, "I can say the same. The time was when I'd be at my drawings and calculations all through the night, and then during the next day be as fresh as you please. But a little extra effort takes its toll heavily these days. I feel it a deal."

Mr. Lazarus kept his look upon Philip.

"I am sorry," he said, "I was called away yesterday before I could examine the papers which you so kindly placed at my disposal. Another time, perhaps—soon—if you'll extend your permission, we'll come to the matter."

"Most willingly," said Philip, "and the sooner the better."

"To-day, perhaps," said Mr. Lazarus, fondling the staff. "To-day."

"Why, yes, of course," said Philip. "But as I'm to be absent for the next little while, Mr. Fortune," looking at Nicholas, "will go to the inn with you when you are ready."

"To be sure," said Nicholas, willingly. Mr. Lazarus rubbed his hands and nodded his head.

The man who had been sent to order the boat now returned, announcing it was ready. And so Philip bid Lazarus good-day and made his way toward the wharf head, the little gun maker at his side.

"Now, good luck," said Nicholas. "Hawes will give you all necessary information when you get aboard."

They shook hands; Philip took his seat in the stern of the skiff, and the boatmen pulled toward the schooner which lay swinging with the changing tide, about a mile or two below.

2

Philip found the *Nancy Blake* as fine a craft as he'd ever put foot in; she had a razor-like bow, a long, slim hull, tall masts, and lay well out of the water. There was little deck hamper, everything being stowed with the snugness of a ship-of-war; the guns were covered with tarpaulins, and the watch on deck was a robust, ready-looking lot.

Hawes, a look of relief upon his face, greeted Philip with out-held hand.

"I'd given you up," he said. "Mr. Fortune desired me to wait for you, and in doing so I missed the morning tide."

"If I'd only known," said Philip, "I'd have kept to the road, dark as it was, and made the city before morning."

"Well, after all," said Hawes, "it is no serious matter. With so light a wind the vessel I hope to overtake could have made but small headway against the tide."

The anchor was gotten up; the mainsail and a jib were put on the vessel and rustled in the light air; the outgoing tide had, by this time, a decided pull, and the *Nancy Blake* went drifting slowly past Windmill Island, toward the great bend where the river began to widen.

"The schooner sails well in light winds," said Hawes to Philip, "and she'll advance a great deal more than the *Trumpeter*. However, they have a matter of six hours' start of us, and that'll be hard to overcome."

In a little while, more sail was put upon the vessel; the wind swelled in the canvas one moment, but it hung in long wrinkles the next; the tide carried the craft along; an hour passed, then two, then three; they saw the low marsh land on the Pennsylvania shore, with the Schuylkill River opening its wide mouth through it; but, after a little more, the drift halted, and the water gradually gathered force for the flow up river once more. Captain Hawes walked the deck with impatient strides; he snapped his bony fingers.

"The *Trumpeter* is well on her way toward Wilmington," he said. "We've hardly more than steerageway now, and unless the wind picks up we'll not overtake her until she's well within the lower bay. And then anything might happen, for there is a half dozen British war sloops prowling there, any one of them strong enough to engage us."

But the wind grew less; the sun in its arc had crossed the river and was lowering in the west. At last Hawes let go an anchor, fearing to drift upon a shoal.

"Little chance," said the captain, gloomily. "We'll probably be here until the next tide."

They leaned upon the rail, looking out over the widening river.

"I was once in a Portuguese ship trading along the South American coast," said Philip; "and one night while at anchor in a small bay, most of the ship's people being ashore, several galleys came down the river, overpowered the watch, helped themselves to what plunder they could carry, and made away upstream before daybreak. The river was unknown to us, and we dared not take the ship in; so we out with two boats, put an armed crew into each, and followed. We came up with them by nightfall and recovered our merchandise." There was a little pause, and then he added: "You have some excellent boats, Captain; why not do the same?"

Hawes snapped his fingers with a report like the drawing of a cork.

"Well said!" he cried. "Six stout oars to a boat, and we

will come up with them before there's enough of to-morrow's light for them to make us out."

In a few moments the mate's voice was sounding through the schooner; two boats were hoisted out, a dozen men, armed with hangers and pistols, tumbled eagerly into each of them; the master put Philip in command of one, and took the other himself, gave orders to his mate to take advantage of any wind that might arise; and then they pulled away.

The weapons were concealed in the bottoms of the boats; a half dozen men tugged at the oars. Philip sat coatless and hatless in the stern, the evening sun falling upon him. He watched Captain Hawes in the other boat; he could hear him grumbling and asking for more speed and smiled good-humoredly. Philip had a pleasant feeling of lightness, of freedom; here was an adventure to his liking; here was a thing a man might do with credit to himself. He whistled an old tune; and the seamen exchanged looks and grinned.

A drift of white clouds crossed the sky; there seemed to be a current of high air, for they came up buoyantly, foaming into strange, tall shapes. It was like a fleet of ships coming out of a wide sea, a fleet of ghost ships, with high hulls, and sails of great breadth; they moved across the purple of the evening heavens in changing formations. The tide ran heavily against the boats; the seamen pulled hard but made little headway. Dusk came on and the river grayed under it; the red went slowly out of the west, and darkness began to settle down. Now and then Hawes would call to him to know where he was, and finally Philip kindled a lantern and placed it in the bow.

After a few hours the men at the oars were relieved by others. Another hour passed and still another; a deep bell struck the hour of eleven.

"What bell is that?" said Philip of the carpenter's mate who sat beside him.

"It must be Wilmington, sir," said the man. "That place should be abreast of us before long."

Sure enough, the lights of a town began to show, low and widespread, to the starboard; also they saw a number of vessels anchored in the stream. The other boat approached, and Captain Hawes conferred with Philip.

"We'll have to make sure of these," he said. "I am of the opinion the vessel we want is further along; but we must *know*. So, do you take these that you see at hand; I'll question the others. If the *Trumpeter's* among them we'll draw off a bit and arrange what to do."

As the captain's boat pulled away, Philip gave the word, and his own approached the nearest ship. She was a squat-built brig; he flashed the light under her stern and saw the name *Martha Short*, Boston. The next was a sloop which he passed by with scant attention; the nearest then was a square-rigger with a wide-awake lookout on deck who'd, no doubt, been observing their light moving about and now hailed:

"Ahoy! What's wanted there?"

Philip made no reply, steering the boat under the ship's stern; he flashed the light upward, but the hull was an extremely high one, with the name out of the radius of his light. The boat's actions and the refusal to answer caused an alarm on the vessel's deck; there were a running of feet, high-pitched orders, and then the bellowing voice of an officer demanding to know what was going on.

"These be no times for ceremony," stated the voice, boldly. "Sheer off, or I'll throw a pint or two of musket balls into you that'll make you sorry enough."

"We're looking for the ship *Trumpeter*," said Philip as the boat pulled around to the side, a ship's light upon it. "Have you seen anything of her in passing to-day?"

The officer hung over the rail and growled ill-humoredly.

"Why didn't you say that, instead of prowling around with your tongues between your teeth?" said he. "The *Trumpeter* dropped along with the tide some time this afternoon; like as not she's anchored somewhere between here and New Castle."

Nevertheless, Philip inspected the remaining ships; then he drew up with the captain's boat, and they consulted once more. There was a fine young moon drifting high in the sky by now, and the stars gave a sparkle to the lapping water.

"I'll know her in this light as soon as I catch sight of her rig," said Hawes. "She has a narrow hull, also, and other peculiarities of structure that can't be mistaken. So, pull away; we've got the tide now and will make better headway."

The boats drew apart and proceeded down the river; a breeze had come up, and as they pulled along, it grew.

"If they have their wits about them," said Philip to the carpenter's mate, "they'll take advantage of this."

But the man seemed doubtful.

"It's sure to be some under-officer's watch on deck," he said, "and they never care to take too much responsibility. And they don't like to wake the first mate up, for when he comes on deck he's usually in a bad humor."

The breeze grew, and soon the boat was lifting to the movement of the water; they made out several vessels but wasted no time with them as they were small and looked like fishermen; at length Philip heard a hail from Hawes and in a little while the captain was alongside him.

"There she rides," he said, pointing toward a tall ship, dimly outlined against the black glitter of the water. "I was close up on her and knew her at once. Out with your light, and come up to her on the port side; I'll take the starboard. If they hail, make some sort of answer; swarm up on her deck and don't hold your hand if anyone opposes you."

Again the boat left them, pulling away into the shadowy moonshine. Philip spoke to his men, warning them to make no more sound than they must; they were to dip their oars carefully; there was to be no talk among them; they must have their weapons ready for use. The carpenter's mate must see to it that the boat was fast fore and aft before he left it; the others were to follow up the side as best they could.

They crept along slowly; then a voice called out an inquiry from the *Trumpeter*, and Hawes answered it. Knowing the watch would now have their attention fixed upon the starboard side, Philip urged haste; and in a little space, while the captain engaged the deck of the ship in talk, he gained the shadow of the high hull. Tossing a grappling iron upward, it caught, and in a moment he had gained the rail, with a stout young seaman coming up the rope hand over hand after him. Philip heard a startled shout; there was a flashing of lights on the dark deck, a rush of feet, angry, threatening faces; he drew a pistol meaning to strike with the butt of it. He shouted some words, but did not afterwards recall what they were; his men came tumbling over the rail, one by one, and hurrying toward him. And then by the companionway he saw a woman; the light of a ship's lantern was full upon her, and he at once knew the wide, startled dark eyes, the glowing hair, as those of Charlotte Desfourneaux. His marking of her was so instant, the thought had not time to be colored by surprise; then in the rush of the *Trumpeter's* watch, he saw Gorman. He saw hate in the man's face and the deliberate way he lifted a heavy pistol. After that, all was dark, and without motion.

CHAPTER XVIII

PHILIP ARCHER lay in a half-conscious state; he was in torment, and his dulled mind wrestled with mysterious things. There was a great darkness, and a moaning through the world; there was a stirring, as of innumerable gloomy wings, a throbbing, a constant throbbing that could hardly be borne. He felt helpless; his soul was sunken; the world was wide and lonely, and the waters of it were churning in a terrible blackness. He lay like a newly born in the midst of a desolation, and he was troubled and incapable of motion. For there was nothing he understood, nothing that was within the range of his experience. His eyes were closed, because no instinct prompted him to open them; his hands lay at his sides, all unknowing that there were things to grasp and hold. Upon all sides of him there was darkness only, darkness that leaped like leopards at his wretched spirit.

He felt, dimly, that he must move, but he could not; he felt he must make his way through the bleak wastes to a haven whose name he could not remember; for the universe was crying out in a kind of madness; it was torn and convulsed. And then he saw a light: it glimmered between his slightly separated lids and caused him to open them wider. It seemed far off, hung among the turning planets in the vastness of space; it was of yellow gold. Into his consciousness came thoughts of threatening coasts, with their beacons to guide sailormen; this was a lamp, so it seemed, placed by God to light the dim minds of broken creatures crawling under the crust of life. His hands moved; he turned his head, and then a voice spoke to him.

"Do not move, please; it is bad for you."

It was a gentle voice; there was great kindness in it; he felt a hand touch his forehead, a cool hand, soft, quieting. And then he saw a face. He looked at it for a long time; he studied it. The light played upon the hair: gold; dark gold; and the eyes were wide and had a splendor in them he'd known somewhere before. There had been a time when they'd been fixed upon him as they were now; he'd seen gentle loveliness in them; he'd seen resentment of things that had caused him harm; he'd seen encouragement in dark places; he'd seen hope, he'd seen joy when victory came to him.

But something had changed them; a shadow had arisen, a shadow dark with hate; and after that he'd seen disdain in the eyes, aversion, cold contempt. He lifted his hand, weak but clenched, to dash the shadow down; and then the voice came again, very gently:

"No; you must not move. You are badly hurt. Be very still."

He could now see the face distinctly: it was that of a girl, and he knew the light was one she carried in her hand. She placed it upon a table, and bent over him. She was beautiful and of a gentle grace; he knew that, and yet in the shadow that hung between them there were treachery and deadly meaning; there were malice and brutal blows.

"You have been unconscious for two days," she said. Her presence brought wonderful comfort. "Because of the storm, we had to secure you as you are; the wind is very high, and the vessel is tossing badly."

He lay still; but his eyes went about the place. It was a ship's cabin; he was stretched upon a bed, held there by wide bands of canvas; he could hear the mountainous rush of water, and feel the staggering weight of the wind; the vessel pitched like a cork. Then there was a new presence in the cabin; a short man, cheerful, with the smell of the salt sea about him.

"Hah!" said the cheerful man. "Come around, eh? That's very good. I thought he would." He wagged a short-cropped head at Philip. "How do you feel?"

Philip muttered some unintelligible thing, and the cheerful surgeon said with added cheerfulness:

"That's excellent. I knew you would make a fight of it."

To the girl he said: "Has he had the draught?"

"Yes," she said. "An hour ago."

The ship's doctor rubbed his hands together, and was exceedingly well pleased.

"We have an excellent patient: young, and of tough fiber. He has a dangerous wound, but I've seen worse and had them get well. I'll look at the bandages." He undid the canvas bands and drew back the sheet; after a swift examination he seemed immensely gratified. "Matters could not be better," he said. "We are going along amazingly." He arranged the patient once more. "We could do with less wind and a good deal less knocking about; but no matter. Give him a spoonful of the port now and then, and keep regularly to the medicine. In a few days, unless I'm greatly mistaken, we'll see a much different man."

After the surgeon had gone, Philip lay still; he closed his eyes and listened to the shriek of the wind and the dash of the sea; the vessel bore up bravely, buffeted here and there, lifting and falling, and plunging and careening, but acting stanchly in the midst of it all. Though his eyes were closed, Philip knew of the quiet presence in the cabin, moving here and there, shading the light, setting one of the windows open so it would admit air but not expose him to the lashing of the blast. Then he knew she was sitting at his bedside, perhaps with her hands folded; he knew she was watching through the night. And, somehow, a confusion grew up in his mind; this vigil became one with his own in the cabin of the ship, *General Wolfe*, years before. It was his own father who lay ill on the bed, worn, wan, all but spent; the candle burned near him in a tall holder; the crucifix with the Christ upon it, a white, helpless, bleeding figure, hung upon the wall; darkness was all over the lonely sea, the waves leaped about the ship.

She was there with the holy light of the candle shining in

her hair; her beautiful hair of deep red-gold. She had calm eyes, and she was of a loveliness that caught at his heart and held it. He was a boy, and his father lay dying, and there were peace and trust in his breast, there was thankfulness that she was there to give him courage, to whisper words of hope and consolation. He had once seen, in a vast cathedral, a painting of a young angel of God; he had stood gravely before it and considered it with believing eyes; he'd felt it was a messenger of high heaven to earth below. She was like that; and so he had no fear.

He slept a deep sleep that gave him strength; and when he awoke from it, morning had come. He could see the gray sky through one of the round windows; the wind had died down, but the sea was running heavily, and the vessel pitched with the rhythm of a clock. His head was clear now, for the fever had gone from him in his sleep; and when a tall figure came into the cabin he knew it at once for Captain Hawes.

"Well, well," said the privateersman with great relief, "here you are, back with us again." He sat down and patted Philip's limp hand with his own strong rough one. "Now, that's a blessing, indeed. For a space," he said, and shook his head gravely, "it looked as though you'd drift out of the world for good and all. That fellow drove a ball through you of the thickness of my thumb: right through you! And Spangler, our surgeon, says that's what saved you. The wound drained out two ways, and there was no lead in you to do you mischief."

The captain saw the young man's eyes go toward the small window, and he said:

"Spangler bid me not to say overmuch to you; he's of the opinion you're not ready to start thinking of things. But we're at sea," said the captain with much satisfaction, "and have been for some days, and it was our luck to run into as nasty a storm as I've seen in a twelvemonth. I had no thought to try and slip out," he said, "but after we'd got possession of the *Trumpeter*, I found there were two British armed brigs not far from us, which'd evidently crept up the river past the batteries, in the darkness. These had come to take off the *Trumpeter's* passenger; indeed, there was a boat's crew of one of them aboard of her when we went over the rails. I was looking through the ship to see what guns she had, with the idea of making some sort of defense, when what comes into view but the *Nancy Blake*, under a fine spread of sail, making down the river toward us. So with that we made all speed aboard of her. But in the meantime the brigs had gotten above us, and as they were strong-looking vessels, and, as I'd heard, heavily manned, we held a council of war and made up our minds, as a deep cloud-drift had providently darkened the moon, to drop down the bay and make the dash I'd been thinking about for the past fortnight. And," said the captain, a smile upon his lean face, "there was never a hand raised against us; we made open water as easily as I've ever seen it made; and before dawn," with a laugh, "we were bare of canvas except for a close-reefed foresail, and fighting the gale that's been blowing ever since."

Philip slept after this and was awakened by a stir at his bedside. It was the cheerful surgeon, Spangler, with one of the mates, and he greeted him with smiles and nods.

"Sorry to disturb you," said Dr. Spangler, "but we thought we'd drop in before the day got any older and have a look at the dressing."

In high good-humor, whistling as he worked, he removed the bandages and examined the wound.

"As thoroughgoing a hole as I've ever seen," said he, pausing in his whistling and beaming at Philip. "And as clean a one. There hasn't been the slightest trace of devilment in it from the start." He did what was necessary with deft skill, and then they eased the young man back to his former position. "There you are, now! The ball never touched a serious spot," he declared. "For all the bits of machinery you've ticking inside you, thereabouts, it never scratched even the least of them. A rib or two splintered," with a gesture, "but what's that? In a few weeks

you'll be up, taking your food and your ration of rum with the
best of them."

2

Now that the fever had gone, Philip was at rare ease; the
pain from the wound was small, and it gave him no trouble; he
slept a deal through the day, deep, dreamless sleep; it was late
afternoon, and awakening, he saw the westward sun sparkling
on the cabin floor.

The motion of the schooner told him the sea had run down,
and was very placidly rolling with no more than a good breeze
whipping over it. The girl was in the cabin; she sat at his bedside facing him, knitting some fragile thing with quick, sure
fingers. She wore a gray gown that trailed upon the floor, belted
at the waist and open at the throat; her splendid bronze-gold
hair was done in two thick braids which hung down over her
breast.

She looked much as she'd looked that night at the Two
Pilots, quiet and warm-eyed; her lips moved with the rolling
of the vessel, as though she were singing some wordless song of
the sea. Yes, she looked a deal like she'd looked that night when
his spirits had arisen so at the interest she'd shown, and he'd
told her all the small, intimate things of his life. Of his boyhood;
of his mother's picture hung upon the wall of the old house at
New Orleans, of how he'd never been told who it was, and how
his heart had told him in the end.

He'd spoken to her, too, of his days at the Spanish school,
with its wide windows and the magnolia trees growing outside
them. And of the books he'd studied that told of the world, and
the beasts and plants of it, and the races of men who warred
upon each other for trivial things. He'd told her of the narrow-
shouldered young priest who taught him of the silent place we
came from, and how, after years of struggle and suffering and
sin, we returned to it once more: a world, so he'd heard, where
God sat, attended by archangels and cherubim, where death

became a glorious victory and life seemed like a dream that had passed. Books in Greek; books in Latin; the book of numbers with its formulas resolving mysterious elements of time and space into plain forms that anyone might understand; music; poets whose words touched the heart and made it sing. He'd said how lonely he'd been in those years in the city on the wide river: how he'd trudge through the narrow streets among the carts drawn by oxen, or by mules decked with strings of bells, among slave women with trays balanced upon their heads, among swaggering seamen with their pay in their pockets and much strong drink in their bellies: a young boy with eyes of wonder for everything, who marveled at the skill of Madame Fouquet as she played at cards of an evening, or wrote rapidly and easily in her black book, afterwards so securely locked. He'd said how quick the blade of Brotot was when he stood before him to learn the art of fence, of the marvelous conversations with Nicholas Fortune of an afternoon, as they'd sit upon a newly wrought gun at the door of his forge.

And then his days on shipboard. The storms he'd faced, the lashing wind, and the salt, bitter sea; how death had crowded him more than once to the limit of life; how he'd often stood among men who gave no thought to law, or truth, or God; of how he'd felt the planks give way beneath his feet in more than one raging gale, and asked Heaven's mercy as he slipped into the churning waves.

He'd spoken of his enemies, and he'd been made to think they were also her enemies; and he'd used many words in telling her of the gold that was his own, but which was held from him by cunning and device.

But in what spirit had his confidences been taken? At the door to Madame Barreaut's house she'd frozen him with a look; in the rain at Brotot's place she'd ignored him. Now God was good. His blessings were many. He gave great kindnesses, sometimes, where they were little deserved; but did He not sometimes permit the open heart to be cruelly scarred? Did He not sometimes permit the trusting to be overreached and made a jest before everyone?

"I met you fairly, and with an honest spirit," said Philip. "I would not have believed you'd treat me so."

There were tears in her eyes, though she tried to keep them back, great tears that wet her cheeks; but she spoke very quietly to him.

The Claridges had always feared him, she said. And when they'd suspected her of telling him some vital thing, they feared him more than ever: and they'd planned to have his life. She'd denied she'd told him anything, for what was there to tell? But they had not been satisfied. John Claridge had questioned her; Madame Barreaut had done likewise; Edward had angered her by his cold suspicion. She'd striven against the thing that was in their minds; she'd tried to divert their thoughts. And this, she said, her hands over her face, she'd done by speaking slightingly of him; she hoped, by acting as though she held him in little account, they'd come to the belief that their fears had no substance, and would not attempt the dreadful purpose so plainly in their minds.

But news came to her, she said, after his visit to John Claridge at Fairview, that he'd fallen into a trap; and she'd ridden to the Plough Inn on the south road to warn him. He tried to lift himself up at this, but her hand held him back. He'd seen her, he said. He'd seen her as the shot sounded in the room where he'd been at his supper: and then he'd taken horse and made away. And she, so she told him, followed him until she knew he was safe. And while his eyes filled with wonder, she begged him to forgive her for the scorn and coldness she'd shown him.

"It hurt my heart," she said, "it hurt it grievously, because you had protected me when I so needed it. But," and her hands were held out to him, "I thought to save you by it. Indeed, indeed, I did; for you were in a place of peril, with enemies all about you, and I was afraid."

CHAPTER XIX

IN TEN days' time Philip Archer came upon deck; and he'd lie in a hammock for hours, white and wasted, while the schooner drove onward. The sun and the sea air helped him wonderfully. Charlotte saw to it that his food was of the right sort; more often than not she, or her mulatto maid, prepared it. And she'd sit beside him while he ate.

"Your strength is returning to you," she said. "You will soon be well."

He had a cushion beneath his head and soft Spanish leather slippers upon his feet; and he lay stretched out peacefully.

"I am well now," he said. "Though I have not the spring of body or briskness of mind I'd like." He looked out over the expanse of heaving water with the sun upon it. "The sea has always been a mother to me," he said. "It will help you in my cure."

She smiled at him.

"Dr. Spangler has given you his faithful attention," she said. "I have done but little. The sea may help you," and she looked out over it. "It is gentle with some." As he watched her he saw a shadow come upon her face.

"With some?" he said. And then: "You are not afraid of it?"

"Oh, no! That would hardly be possible." She smiled again. "My people have been sailors, or shipbuilders, or traders dealing with places across the seas, for three hundred years. No; I have no fear of it; but," and the beautiful face grew grave once more, "I do not trust it."

He looked at her, understanding in his eyes.

"There are many like that," he said. "They see the ocean with tempests upon it, and it is terrible; and when it is quiet, as it is now, and golden with lights, they cannot forget."

"My grandfather, Jean Bart Desfourneaux, loved the storms," she said. "I have heard it said of him that he'd stand upon the deck of his ship, laughing and holding his arms wide, welcoming the gale as it broke over him. My grandmother has often said to me, and I a small child, that the only thing she was ever really jealous of was the tempests. She sailed with him on many voyages, for she loved him greatly; but in a storm he'd forget even her."

"That," said Philip, "would perhaps be Antoinette Teresa Barreaut-Desfourneaux."

"Yes," she said.

"Of all the Barreauts spoken of in my father's and grandfather's papers," he said, "they pause only at her name with respect."

Charlotte looked at him, her level eyes wide, candid.

"She knew and understood a deal; and, for all her temper was high and her tongue quick, she was just. There were things done by her people in the past, and in her own time, of which she did not approve. The ship *Vision of St. John* brought great moneys to the firm of Barreaut Frères, but she always turned her head away at mention of it."

There was a silence between them for a space; the seas fell apart as the sharp bow struck them; the wind hummed in the sails; the second mate, who had the watch on deck, paced to and fro near by.

"She did not approve of the taking of the ship?" said Philip, quietly.

"No. She scorned Pierre Barreaut, who was head of the house at that time; she said he'd done many things to put a stain upon the name; but the chief cause of her aversion was that though his captain, Edward Claridge, was plainly a pirate, Pierre gave him his daughter in marriage."

"She thought him a pirate!" said Philip.

"Who would attack a merchantman, in a time when the sea was quiet of wars, but a pirate?" said Charlotte Desfourneaux.

He lay still and meditated, his fingers tapping the rug she'd thrown across his knees. Pirate! That thought had been in his own mind more than once. The first Edward Claridge a pirate! Well, why not? Had he not crept up in the night and poured his shot into the Spanish ship; had he not thrown his men upon her decks, cutlass and pistol in hand? For hours he'd fought her people up and down the slippery planks; he'd grasped the ship and held it until stout Miguel Carrea wrested it from him as one might a bone from a dog. But then what had happened? What ship burst through the dawn with its carronades firing? What new plunderer was at the Spaniard's throat?

"It was many a year ago," said Philip. "And matters on the sea were not regarded as they are now." She made no reply to this, but sat looking deep into the westward sky. "Drake had always been free enough in his operations. Morgan took cities as well as ships. And Damphier was never known to hold his hand when a rich merchantman sailed within his sight."

Still she said nothing. He frowned, and his fingers twisted in the fringe of the rug. His grandfather's ship, the *Sun of India*, had carried English papers; she was English built. To be sure, her crew had been a mixed one, hard-visaged, no doubt, and careless of what might be called strictly right; eager for gain. He'd known such crews. And his grandfather—he who was called Long Jim Archer? Jovial, careless, a desperate fighter, a hard drinker, a singer of tavern songs. What would a man of this sort, having a ship of his own, be like to turn his hand to on the sea of that day?

Governments took what pleased them! Why should not their shipmen do the same? Philip saw Long Jim Archer at his ease, smoking a long-stemmed pipe, a jug of hot drink beside him, his hanger and pistols put away as he argued for a free sea and a deal of activity upon it. What justice was in a world where

King and Parliament were permitted to reach to the ocean's farthest brim and take what they would, while their captains who endured tempests and the various blows of fortune must pass rich matters by, with their hands folded, like so many young students of theology?

Pirate money! Philip's frown grew darker; to be sure there were many names a thing might be called, but his grandfather, he felt confident, had never thought the treasure of the Spanish ship anything but the honest earnings of a fortunate day. And his father, with a hand forever plucking at a pistol butt, had seen it only as a thing wrongly withheld from him.

"You, too, think the Spanish ship was wrongfully come by?" he said to the girl.

"Yes," she said, and never took her gaze from the sea.

He'd thought so, too, that day in the Penny Pot, as he listened to the pleading of the beautiful Madame Barreaut; he again heard the beat of the drum, and saw the bronzed young recruits shouldering their pieces in the sun. Pirate money! He'd thought he was wasting his days and the strong purpose of his heart seeking to gain possession of plunder taken from an honest ship. He looked at the girl, so clear-eyed, so resolute, and somehow he visioned again the old days at New Orleans, the high-ceilinged room that had been his as a boy, his mother's picture that hung there, the kind eyes that spoke to him, that pleaded with him, that encouraged him. And, somehow, there was a bitterness in the memory; for he felt sure his mother had shared the belief of Charlotte Desfourneaux.

His eyes went hard, but in a moment softening came to them. How often his mother must have listened with troubled heart to his father's wild plans; with what pained eyes she must have watched the striding up and down, the poring over the papers of the great suit, the cleaning of pistols in preparation for a day to come. It had been pirate money to her. Philip was sure of that, because the part of him that was her still spoke to him, still pleaded.

Yes, his eyes softened, and his heart softened, too; and the voice of the drum as it had throbbed in the street that day summoned him. A ship's deck and the wide sea, a great cause, a name gained; these were greater things than the wealth plundered from a hapless Spaniard. But, and this thought followed instantly upon the other, what of the Claridges? What of that high-headed, evil brood? Were they to be left in possession; were they to be left to smile and sneer, and preen themselves and believe that as a race they were of a tougher fiber than his own? What had John Claridge said—almost the first words he spoke, as his eyes rested upon Philip that day at Fairview?

"You are like your father when I saw him first," the man had said; "you have his face and bearing. It is your purpose to do a great deal: that, also, was his purpose. But you will fail, as he failed; you will learn that there are things here which will break your resolution; you will turn your back, finally, as he turned his, and we will hear of you no more."

Philip looked at the girl; his hawk-like nose had a predatory look, his eyes were much as his father's eyes had been.

"When I've taken from the Claridges the share of the money that was named for my grandfather," he said, "I'll weigh it in my hand and then decide if it be evil or no. But not before."

Still she made no reply, but sat for a long time, dreaming, her eyes fast held to the heaving waters. And then, in silence, she arose and went below.

2

Somehow, there was a difference after that: she cared for him and saw to his food, she smiled and talked with him; but he noted a difference. There was a troubled look in Philip's face as he'd watch her moving about the deck, for he did not understand. But he held up his head as the Archers had always done: he'd ask neither favor nor attention from anyone, not even a woman as beautiful as she.

He talked with Captain Hawes about the prospect of winning France over as an open friend; and the privateersman was confident King Louis would in the end be persuaded.

"In a little while Dr. Franklin will be in Paris," he said; "they are already fitting out the ship that'll carry him. He should gain many friends there, for the French greatly respect learning; and, with people of position already favorably disposed toward him, his calm reasoning will do much good."

The privateersman saw great days ahead on the sea; and while he smoked his pipe of a morning, he talked of them.

"There will be a huddling and a contriving behind the Texel such as they haven't seen for years, and many a ship'll come out of that place that the British will not be pleased to see. L'Orient, too, will have her share of privateers and letters-of-marque, and it's there we are headed. Miss Desfourneaux has relatives in that port and had thought to go there in the *Trumpeter;* and as I have no particular place in view I mean to put her ashore there and make what friends I can with the officials during a brief stay. For L'Orient is an excellent place to carry on any little matter having to do with prizes. There are agents there and merchants who handle things very cleverly; they'll condemn and sell a ship and cargo for you, I'm told, in the twinkling of an eye. But Dunkerque is the place for slipping out to sea," he said, with relish. "You are under the cliffs of England in an hour or two, and her merchant craft sail up under your guns in a manner that's most obliging."

"I think," said Philip, "I may have to make my way to Dunkerque when we reach France. There is a friend of mine who may be there, and whom I much desire to see."

"I had hoped," said the privateersman, "to keep you with me in the schooner. To sail in a handy vessel like this is not a waste of time," he said. "I'll send a hundred thousand pounds' worth of cargo into port before we're a month older."

Twice during the run across the Atlantic, the *Nancy Blake* made sail in pursuit of British merchantmen. Once it had been a ship laden with rum, tallow, and hides; on the other occasion she'd overhauled two brigs, keeping each other close company, and richly stowed with silks, cotton goods, and ironmongery. Prize crews had been put into each vessel with instructions to take them into Baltimore.

"In a little while," said Philip, "I hope to find myself in a ship with some likelihood of service; but, just now, I've my hea..th to see to; also there is the business of which I've already sp..ken to you."

During that afternoon the *Nancy Blake* sighted a ship almost directly ahead, and approached it to get a better view. But before getting too near, the sharp eyes of the second mate made her out to be a heavily armed vessel, possibly a frigate, and so the schooner went speeding away, her sails spreading to the breeze like magic. The wind was excellent; the British ship came bustling eagerly along, but the *Nancy Blake* was a swift and ready sailer, and her great spread of canvas sent her skimming ahead in wonderful fashion.

Philip lay in his hammock watching the frigate, with brooding eyes. Yes, he hoped in a short time to find himself in a ship, but not a prowling, running ship like the *Blake*. It would be, if his voice was listened to, a well settled ship, of weight and substance, not only preying upon unarmed craft, but strong enough to engage an armed enemy like this one. A stout, oaken ship with such guns as Nicholas Fortune could make, mounted in her.

The British vessel proved to be one of good sailing quality and hung grimly on; but night coming on and a half-gale arising, the schooner was able to elude her and once more take her way toward L'Orient.

3

The watch on deck saw the point of coast that projects into the Atlantic, the English Channel on one side, and the Bay of Biscay on the other, through the wet fog of an early morning, when they anchored at L'Orient. Philip was still abed, a pair of lighted candles beside him and a copy of Plutarch in his hands, when he heard the slipping of the chain and the plunge of the great hook into the water.

A little later he heard oars dipping, and voices, but paid no attention. When he went upon deck some time afterwards, Hawes told him Charlotte had left the schooner.

"She asked that her best wishes and kindest regards be given you," said the captain. "And she hoped she'd see you some time again."

CHAPTER XX

PHILIP ARCHER went ashore from the *Nancy Blake* during the course of the afternoon. And before he went, Captain Hawes talked with him in the cabin, and chinked a soft leather bag filled with golden louis.

"You came away rather suddenly," said the privateersman, "and brought nothing of consequence with you, and so I must not see you needing. To be sure," as Philip spoke of agents and merchants in France with whom he'd had dealings, "I understand. And no doubt your credit is excellent with them. But, as I sail in the next few days, we'll be on the safe side. Here are three hundred louis; that will carry you along until you are able to make arrangements of your own."

Without a waste of words, the young man stowed the money away in his pockets. And he gave the captain a bill on Nicholas Fortune at Philadelphia.

"What funds I have," he said, "are in his hands. This instructs him to pay you to the value of three hundred louis immediately you arrive."

"Anything you desire will be satisfactory to me," said the privateersman. "But, and I tell you candidly, your leaving the schooner is not to my liking. I'm off for a profitable cruise and will earn a deal of money. Stay with me and take a share of it."

But Philip explained that this could not be done; he shook hands with Hawes and was set ashore a little later: he had his scant belongings, made up from the schooner's slop chest, sent to an inn near the water front. Here he made inquiries for Captain Conyngham, whom he seemed anxious to see. He was informed that Conyngham had set out from Dunkerque some weeks before. Within a day's time Philip had taken passage in a coasting craft for the same place.

At the Casque d'Or, a comfortable inn at Dunkerque, Philip procured the services of a waiter who knew some English, and sent him to inquire among the taverns of the town for the person he sought. After a half hour the man returned.

"I have seen him, m'sieu," he said. "A seagoing man who shakes his fist and swears. He is at the Anchored Ship, a tavern where Jean Bart drank many a flask of wine with his officers, in the great days of France."

"You told him I had arrived?"

The waiter gestured.

"M'sieu, I did. He was overjoyed, and gave me a piece of silver money. Also, m'sieu," with a pleased expression, "he had the landlord give me a drink of excellent brandy."

Philip ordered a brace of fowl prepared, and some other matters of food; to be served as soon after his guest arrived as possible. While he was talking there was a great bustle on the stairs, and a voice crying out:

"Philip, where are you? Musha, God save us, to think of you being here!"

Philip Archer threw the door open, and in rushed a young man in a blue coat and corded breeches, and with a red neck-cloth smartly tied under his chin. His long hair was "clubbed" and hung down upon his collar; he was deep-chested and strong-armed and had a pair of the merriest and most reckless eyes in the world. In an instant he had Philip by both hands, swearing and calling upon Heaven, in the same breath, to witness his great joy at the meeting.

"Here I am in a strange place," said he, "sobbing the heart out of me, almost, because I hadn't a friend to take a noggin of drink, or smoke a pipe with: And, then, here you step out of nowhere." Suddenly he ceased his wringing of Philip's hands, the expression of his face changed. "God bless us," he said,

anxiously, "what's come to you? You look white, and you're
two stone under the weight you should be."

"I've had a bullet through me in a little matter in Delaware
Bay some weeks ago," said Philip. "And I'm only just now
getting my legs under me again."

"A bullet! Ah, well," with a look of relief, "that'll never
harm the likes of you. I thought maybe it was in love you were;
and that would be the divil's own thing entirely." Philip
smiled; and Conyngham laughed and slapped his shoulder.
"But, trust you for that, also. There's never a colleen anywhere
that'd take the notice of one of your breed while there was work
to do."

They sat down at an open window; the young Irishman filled
his pipe out of Philip's pouch, and they both smoked with
enjoyment.

"I'd come to Philadephia to take up the work where my
father put it down. And I expected to find you somewhere
about; but Nicholas Fortune told me you'd sailed on a mission
to France."

"I'm sorry I couldn't wait," said Conyngham. "For it'd
been a great satisfaction to me to give John Claridge a nudge
with me elbow in a court of law. But, God save us, I couldn't
say no, with all the things about me that needed doing. I heard
of the army with no muskets in their fists; I heard of the navy
—save the mark!—with small pieces of cannon that were pitiful to behold. 'What will we do?' says I to myself. 'What will
we do to save ourselves from the cudgelings of this bla'guard
old King?' And, so, when it was whispered to me if I'd slip
away in a little vessel to Holland, or to France, I could trade
my goods for fine muskets and gunpowder and brass cannon
and send them to the agents of Congress; and so, away I went,
thinking you'd understand the need of it when you came."

"To be sure," said Philip. "I would have done the same
myself."

And then, as they sat and smoked, he told Conyngham of his

adventures from the time the *Racehorse*, brig, took him aboard at Charleston. The young Irishman exclaimed, and dashed his fist upon the window sill a score of times before the narrative was done.

"Heavens above!" he said, "did you ever hear the like before! They cozened you out upon the lonely road and waited to put an end to you! And it was Gorman who tried it. May an angel of God lead me to where I'll sometime cross that fellow's path! But," with an instant change of expression, and a laugh in his throat, "I'd give a purse of gold louis the weight of my boots to have seen you dealing with the cook on the *Racehorse*, and old Hasty looking on! And to outsword the grand Edward!" He roared with glee and pounded Philip softly upon the back. "That was a sight. With all his friends witness to it, too!" And then he shook his head regretfully. "What a chance you missed as old John sat there at his table staring at you with those devils' eyes of his and planning to have your life, that you didn't let him feel the weight of your hand across his face."

But the girl, now? Charlotte Desfourneaux? He wanted to know what Philip thought of her. He knew her, himself; he'd seen and talked with her more than once. She was strongly for the freedom of the colonies. A rare young woman. And beautiful! God save us! he'd never seen a pair of eyes like those before. So, she'd heard there was a plot, and had gone racing the darkening roads to save Philip's life? Now, that was a thing for a strong man to do, let alone a woman! But she had courage: you had only to look at her to see that.

"If I had luck enough to stand where you stand," said Conyngham, nodding his head, "I'd be dancing at this minute. Are you hearkening to me? If I could put a light the like of the one that must have been in her eyes at the time she galloped away on that errand, my heart'd be singing for joy."

"She had no desire to see murder done, to be sure," said Philip. "But I'm afraid it was not altogether on account of me. The Claridges are her relatives in a sense, and so——"

But Conyngham interrupted him.

"Now, may the holy angels have pity on you!" said he. "I sit and wonder at your blindness. To be sure she is related to the Claridges; but that is no fault of hers; and when you say it was to keep their hands free of guilt she rode out that night, you are talking folly itself, and no less."

The room was still full of their talk when the waiter and landlord came in with the dinner; a cloth was spread, and the dishes were set upon it. There were a delicious barley soup, an omelet with mushrooms, the side of a noble fish not long out of the sea, with a hot sauce of garlic and peppers. Then there were the fowls, brown and delicious. Conyngham carved them, and the landlord drew the cork of a bottle of red Burgundy; Philip ate sparingly and drank but little; but Conyngham relished the food with high pleasure.

"Bless us and save us," said he, breathing his hearty content when he had done, "you have no light word with the victuals when ordering them, no matter what else has come over you." He drank his wine and smoked his pipe. "And so," he said, his mind going back to the subject of Charlotte Desfourneaux, "she left the ship early of a morning with never a word to you."

"At dawn," said Philip. "There are some Barreauts at L'Orient, I believe."

"There is a pock-marked bla'guard of that name whom I've seen more than once," said Conyngham. "A bully of a fellow, I hear, who has a habit of stretching his masters and mates on the decks before him, if he's not pleased with the voyages they've made. And so," puffing his pipe, "she only left word for you when she went. Faith, then, if it'd been me I'd expected more than that. But, then," with a twinkle in his eye, "maybe that's the reason I am always paying so much heed to them." He crossed one leg over the other and dandled his foot. "She did not seem to agree with you in the matter of the Spanish ship? I'd have expected that. There're things a woman can never see as a man sees them."

She was troubled, Philip said; she was uneasy. During the last week in the schooner he'd, more than once, noted her looking at him when she thought his attention was taken by something else. There was pain in her eyes; there seemed to be something she desired to say to him.

"Well," said the Celt, "never fear but some day she'll say it. And no doubt it's the matter of the money taken out of the old galleon that's worrying her. But, God bless us, if she puts down a thing like that as villainy, what shipman is there, with a few guns aboard of him and a few papers to show, but is one of the divil's own?"

He poured more wine into both their glasses.

"When your Mr. Lazarus told you to make your beginning with the case here in France he gave you good advice. Heed you, now," and he bent toward Philip, "there is in the harbor beyond a fine lugger called the *Admiral Pocock*, British built and with a little sandy man of the name of Murdock, master of her. In a fortnight," said the Irishman, "I'll be standing on her deck with the pine tree flag over me. But first," and he nodded his head mysteriously, "I must take myself off to Paris to see about the money that's to pay for her."

"Then you are no longer in the vessel in which you left Philadelphia?"

"I had her loaded with saltpeter to be used by Congress in making gunpowder, and with cloth and boots and a plenty of useful stuff; but Lord Sormont, divil take him, made such a phillelew that the Dutch authorities seized the ship; and I was forced to sell both it and the cargo and come here, hoping for better fortune." Again he bent toward Philip. "I must start on my journey to Paris to-morrow. Do you rest yourself for a space at this good inn. Then," said Conyngham, "make your way to Paris. By that time I'll have my ship bargained and paid for; then we'll back to Dunkerque together, and away with us to the near seas with our guns loaded, and many a deed ahead of us."

Philip's eyes lighted.

"There is nothing I'd like more," he said. And then the light died down. "But I don't know. However, I'll see you in Paris; by that time I shall perhaps know what the future is to be."

CHAPTER XXI

PHILIP went from Dunkerque to L'Orient thinking to
hear something of Charlotte. But never a whisper did
he have of her. Then he took a post-carriage for Paris.

That day all the brightness had gone out of the sky, the sun
was hidden, and the clouds were heavy and low. Rain! It had
been falling all night, and now the wind drove it in beating
showers. The Atlantic came foaming into the Bay of Biscay,
and the French coast was drowned in spray; then the gale tore
loose from the sea and whirled inland, stinging, slashing, roaring. And night again began to settle upon the long road from
L'Orient to the capital city of France.

The ditches by the roadside were brimming with water, and
the rain and wind were tearing through the full-leafed trees, as
a carriage with two horses and a postilion approached the inn of
the Three Clocks which stood fronting the road, a full day's
journey from the sea. The horses were taken from the carriage
after Philip Archer alighted; the postilion, sodden with rain
for all his waterproof, disappeared to take his comfort at a fire
and relish his food and drink, while Philip followed the innkeeper into the public room. It was a snug place, contrived for
brawling nights of rain or snow and wind; the floor was sanded;
lanthorns hung from the beams; a fire crackled on the hearth,
for the day had a chill in it; and at the tables there were a number of travelers engaged with their food and wine.

"You have it comfortable and warm here," said Philip as an
attendant hung his hat and cloak upon a peg. "A man might
travel far without seeing so cheery a fire as this."

"I had not thought to light so large a one before the coming of winter," said the innkeeper. "But when the wind and the rain drive in from the sea they bring the cold with them." He indicated a table. "Will M'sieu sit here?"

Philip nodded.

"And I'll have my supper as soon as your kitchen can produce it. For I've been on the road all day without a morsel of anything."

The innkeeper lifted his brows and gestured disapproval of this.

"It is wrong, m'sieu," he said, "to so use the stomach. A wet, gusty day and no food to comfort you! Think, m'sieu, what is life to a man whose system is weakened by neglect?"

Philip had a small glass of brandy brought to him, and tossed it off; its fire at once began to pick up the flagging elements of his blood, and as he enjoyed the generous warmth of it, he looked about the room. At one table, under the light of a pair of lanthorns, was a group of travel-stained, hardy-looking men; their scabbarded blades and pistols hung upon the wall, and they ate and drank with gusto. Near them sat two men, one past middle life, florid and settled looking and with a certain exaggeration in dress that marked him at once. The second man was younger, handsome, elegant of manner, with flashing eyes and hands that were smoothly eloquent as he talked. There was something about the fineness of his linen, the whiteness of his neckcloth, the material and cut of his clothes, the boots of soft Spanish leather, the handsome arrangement of his hair that told of the fop. He handled a gold snuffbox with the grace of an actor while the other man talked.

"I have had agents at Bordeaux, and other places, for the past fortnight," said the other man, in English. "They have been awaiting the arrival of several ships laden with tobacco and rice. These sailed several days before I set out from Baltimore, for I'd told the committee of Congress I'd have constant need of money while in France, and these cargoes were to be sold to so provide me."

"Do not let doubts settle in your mind," said the younger man with a gesture of one finely modeled hand. "If the vessels have not arrived, it is no sign that they have been taken. Though the British swarm in the Channel, vessels are constantly making their way through."

The florid man seemed comforted by this and leaned back in his chair, his hands clasped across his stomach. Philip's eyes were upon him; there was, somehow, a familiar look to him; then suddenly memory of him came: he was the American, Silas Deane, who had come into Nicholas Fortune's place upon that first night at Philadelphia!

"I trust these ships are fortunate," said Mr. Deane, "for if they are not, matters will not be very comfortable with me."

"There will be others," said the younger man. "And, then, money is to be had in various ways. Take heart. There are the cruisers you hope to get to sea; a handy vessel or two of this sort will bring a deal of ready money."

"Yes," said Mr. Deane, "that, of course, is true, M'sieu Beaumarchais. We have some captains here who seem quite alive to the moment." He sat nodding and puffing his cheeks. "I have been making inquiries in various places to learn what is thought of our cause," he said, "and I found that people shook their heads a good deal. They did not know, they said. They could not tell. It is generally thought that in throwing down the gage to England we'd taken a mighty risk; they think, in a war such as this, the odds will be all against us. 'You are weak,' they say; 'Britain is strong. But, of course, you are far away; that is in your favor. It is a difficult matter to decide!'"

But the young Frenchman gestured this away.

"Give no heed to such words," he said. "They form the evasive talk of men who are afraid, or have given the matter no consideration. You may reasonably expect our help," he said, "if only because the present enemy of America has been the natural enemy of France for centuries."

Silas Deane grasped the speaker's hand and shook it warmly. "You cannot know what courage it gives me, m'sieu, to hear this. I will quote your saying in the very next letter I write to Congress; for the attitude of Europe has long been a matter of doubt; and they will be as pleased as I am at your words."

"America has all France's sympathy," said Beaumarchais; "and it is natural it should be so. France is a neighbor to England; only a narrow strip of sea divides them, but they have seldom been on terms of friendship. In the old days of bows and pikes and armored men, England held more than one port of France; many times our squadrons of horse were beaten back to the gates of Paris. But in time matters altered; it was a time when England was pressed by foes without and within, and, so, France took possession of her own.

"But the English are a stout people; they recovered their pride and their power, and the wars re-began. France had wonderful ships, but they were no match on the sea for England. Look back," said Beaumarchais, "and what do you see? French and British fleets engaged until we were left with only floating hulks. Britain was supreme upon the sea. The armies of the two nations faced each other at Ticonderoga, Duquesne, Quebec, Louisburg. The French were defeated everywhere. In India, France had planted strong colonies; she drew riches from the teeming ports of that far-off land, also from the desert caravans dealing with inland peoples. But for a long time the English had been making headway. Clive led them in the field, a whirlwind of energy, a master of craft. Our commanders, Dupleix and La Bourdanaux, were stout soldiers, but they were outfought and outmaneuvered: Hindustan, with its untold riches and millions of producers was lost to France forever. Upon European battlefields it was the same; blow after blow fell upon France; she was beaten down; her communications were destroyed; the British overran all her outlying possessions; the nation was humbled and overwhelmed."

"If the British are proud," said Mr. Deane, "France is

equally so. If the British can arise out of defeat, France can do likewise."

"The shameful treaty of '63!" said Beaumarchais, his eloquent hands gesturing the most painful emotions. "That insufferable document! What Frenchman will ever forget it? All our laboriously built colonies in America were taken from us by its terms; in India we gave up everything; among the isles of the sea we were permitted only a foothold. England was our master. In the face of all this," said the Frenchman, "it might seem that we dare not risk another conflict. But a war now, m'sieu, will do us good. We have nothing to lose that Britain can take; our army is compact, our ships are well furnished and manned; a shrewd blow now, and we may regain much that we've lost."

Mr. Deane again seized him by the hand and shook it warmly.

"Excellent! That may very well be so," he said.

"But," said Beaumarchais, with a warning nod of the head, "we must exercise great care; the King, in whose hands these matters lie, must be approached guardedly. He is naturally cautious and feels his way carefully; he will be led into nothing he does not plainly see. Your early friends in France made some mistakes: they thought to further the cause of America by drawing word pictures of the overtaxed farmer leaving his plow to take up a musket against the armies of King George. This had a bad effect. The monarch at Versailles has no more liking for peasants with guns in their hands than has his neighbor at London. Indeed, I think, at bottom you'd find him more bitter against a populace asking for its rights than he is against the enemy who stripped his country of its territory."

"In the King's minister, De Vergennes, though, we have a fast friend," said Mr. Deane.

"And one who will go far," said Beaumarchais. "He has a keen eye and sees France's opportunity in England's discomfiture. During the whole of his active life he has matched his skill against England's best; and he is now waiting, like a crouched leopard, in the hope of avenging the seven years of disastrous war I have just named."

The rain had continued to pour down, drenching the broad front of the Three Clocks and streaming from the eaves; the fire burned cheerily in the hearth, and the wind muttered in the throat of the chimney. The talk in the public room had gradually died down save for that between Beaumarchais and Deane; the steady beat of the English words had caught the attention of those at the other tables, and Philip had for some time noted a turning of heads and an exchange of inquiring looks. His eyes were especially upon the group before noted, for there was a passage of derisive gestures among them, and looks of mockery; and now a heavy chair grated upon the floor as it was pushed back, and a burly, pock-marked man got upon his feet. His spurs jangled upon the floor, and he drew his broad belt tighter as he looked at the two absorbed men near the fire.

"M'sieu," he said in a harsh voice, "may I be permitted a word in your conversation?" At once Beaumarchais and Deane grew silent and looked at him. "I have been a chance listener," said the burly man, "and beg to inform you, m'sieu, that I take exception to most of what you say. I trust," he said, cocking his eye at his companions, who sat smiling broadly, and with looks of expectation upon their faces, "no offense will be taken. The ideas you have expressed, m'sieus, affect Frenchmen one and all, and I feel I am entitled to disagree with you."

M. Beaumarchais tapped the lid of his elegant snuffbox and took a pinch of its contents; after this he dusted the particles from his silken waistcoat.

"I was not aware," he said coldly, "that our words were being overheard. If you feel you must remark upon what has been said, do so, but I must request you to be as brief as possible."

The pock-marked man approached and leaned upon the table, his face advanced; his hard eyes went from one of them to the other.

"It seems to me," he said, "you are dealing with public matters in an over-ready way; and as a true subject of the King I take it upon myself to protest. I know I am singularly favored by this opportunity," mockingly, "for it is not everyone who can number among his day's efforts the putting of M'sieu Beaumarchais in his place."

"I am awaiting your pleasure, m'sieu," said Beaumarchais, still coldly.

"I gather from your talk," said the pock-marked man, "that you and this American think to settle the foreign affairs of the government between you. Because we have suffered somewhat at the hands of the British, does it follow, m'sieu, that we must take up the cause of every beggar nation that appeals to us?"

Mr. Deane held up one hand in protest.

"M'sieu," he said, "we Americans now in France seeking help did not come in the spirit of beggary. We have behind us the dignity of a people who have been wronged."

"In thinking of your own wrongs have you thought of the wrong you must surely put upon us?" The man glowered at the American commissioner. "France has not yet recovered from her late defeats, and you are trying to persuade her to her destruction in another war."

Again Mr. Deane protested, his hand uplifted; then in a sudden burst of rage the man struck at him. With a spring, Beaumarchais was across the table; but the bully tore a blade from its scabbard on the wall, and its point was at the young man's chest.

"Son of a watchmaker," said he, his face writhing with malice. "Common clown! Do I see you again in a hero's rôle?"

Beaumarchais, his hands at his sides, his head held high, moved forward; the blade drew back, cruel, cold, and bright, and just then Philip Archer, who had drawn a pistol from the loop of a bandolier about his shoulders, leaned his elbow upon the table, and fired.

CHAPTER XXII

AS THE crashing report of the heavy pistol still sounded
through the public room of the Three Clocks, the sword
of Beaumarchais's assailant lay upon the floor; the man was
clutching his arm, his face twisted with pain; the place was
filled with voices, weapons were drawn. But the landlord and
his people were a competent lot; with staves in their hands,
waiters, grooms, and lads from the kitchen, together with some
of the guests, stout fellows accustomed to sudden episodes of
the kind, put the matter down in a few moments; and Philip
found himself with Deane and Beaumarchais in a large room
on the floor above. The landlord wiped his face with a corner
of his apron and regarded them with no great satisfaction.

"A shot has been fired in my tavern," he said; "swords have
been drawn, a man has been wounded. All these things I shall
be required to explain to a King's officer."

"I am sorry to bring trouble upon you," said Philip; "but
the matter was not of our making. A shot was fired, but I leave
it to you to say if it was necessary or no."

"I am not disposed to give the blame to you, m'sieu. You
acted much as anyone might. I knew as soon as M'sieu Barreaut crossed my door-stone just before dark, with his friends,
there would be a matter arise which I would be forced to put
down. That is his reputation. And so I had my people ready."

"Barreaut?" said Philip, and looked at the man. "Is he,
then, one of the family of merchants and shipowners?"

"Yes, m'sieu, and a hard-spoken, violent man. He is of
L'Orient, where there are warehouses of his firm, and often
rides the roads between there and Paris. When he arrived, in

the rain, before nightfall, he inquired if you, m'sieu, and you,"
to Beaumarchais and Deane, "had arrived. He came here with
it in his mind to do what he did; of that I am convinced."

When the landlord had gone out of the room, Beaumarchais
shook Philip by the hand.

"That was a timely shot," said he. "Another moment, and
he'd had his sword in me."

Mr. Deane shook hands with Philip.

"I'd heard some days ago that you were in France," he said,
"though when I saw you through the pistol smoke I was
startled." And seeing Philip's inquiring look he smiled and
added: "I have many ways of getting information; situated as
I am, it is a most necessary thing."

A fire was kindled in the room to take the chill from it; wine
was ordered in, also pipes and tobacco, and the three men
settled down in comfort, with the wind and rain upon the window panes. Beaumarchais talked of France and England and of
America. And as he talked Philip studied him. He'd heard of
him many times, and knew him to be one of the most amazing
characters in Europe.

His proper name was Pierre Augustin Caron; and he was the
son of a watchmaker who had kept a little shop in the Rue de la
Feronnerie, Paris. Pierre Augustin had remained an apprentice
in his father's shop until, at the age of twenty, he had put the
impress of his personality upon his work by the invention of an
escapement greatly improving the accuracy of the watch, and
making it possible to reduce it in size. For all his cleverness
he had the elation of a boy; he could not hold his tongue in the
matter and so safeguard himself, but must needs explain the
nature of his invention to a master watchmaker whom he knew,
and with the utmost promptness this person, who was as mean
a rascal as ever stepped, applied the idea to a watch he was
making and made proclamation in the public prints that it was
his own. No doubt he fancied the obscurity of Pierre Augustin
would make it safe for him to do this; but he did not know the

nature of that young man. The facts were made known, and a great clamor arose; the matter was referred to the Academy of Sciences, and a decision was reached in the youth's favor. At one leap he had become quite celebrated; and in a short time he was made watchmaker to the King. He contrived a watch upon the new principle for King Louis, and so arranged the matter that he was permitted to present it in person; later he made a watch so small it was affixed to a finger ring and presented to the King's favorite, Madame de Pompadour.

After this it became quite the thing for the fops of Paris and the frequenters of the King's court to have a watch of the new construction. The King's daughters were much excited by the delicate workmanship of the good-looking youth; also his wit and vivacity pleased them. And so, little by little, he made himself a firm footing at court; in a little while he was teaching the King's sisters the harp; he had fought a duel with a count who had affronted him; he had purchased letters of nobility, changed his name to Beaumarchais, and used his influence with the King to help Paris du Varney, the financier, in a matter near to that gentleman's heart.

In gratitude, Du Varney set about making the young man's fortune. He loaned him money, advised him. Beaumarchais bought ships, made contracts of large magnitude; at one time he undertook the provisioning of the Spanish army. His name became known throughout Paris; princes were his everyday companions; his sayings were quoted in all the fashionable salons; he wrote verses which were read with much admiration. Having a natural aptitude for the stage, he began writing plays; *Eugénie* was the first result of this; *The Two Friends* came later, both dramas which had caused much excitement and had been viciously attacked by his enemies. It was whispered of him that he'd been employed upon many delicate missions for the government: London, Vienna, Constantinople, Madrid had all seen and admired him and felt his adroit touch; more than once he had been thrown into prison through the

contriving of his foes, but each time he had emerged trium-
phant, reëstablished himself before the world, and plunged
anew into what work and adventure he'd found at his hand.

Mr. Deane spoke to Philip Archer.

"There are many prominent persons in Paris who favor the
American cause, but among them all there is none so outspoken
and so willing to plan operations and carry them through as
M'sieu Beaumarchais. Some day the new nation will rise up
and thank him."

Beaumarchais smiled; his teeth were even and white. He
lifted his glass.

"We'll drink to America," he said. "There is nothing else at
this present time which has the swift impulse of the thought
now taking shape across the sea. Liberty! What an idea,
m'sieus! What a light to throw across the world; but what a
task the upholding of it will be, once it is gained and the first
clean fire has died down."

"Put it once within our grasp," said Mr. Deane, "and God
will give us the power to keep it, forever."

"Just lately," said Beaumarchais to Philip, "I returned
from a journey to London. I visited there as a casual Frenchman, but studied and observed and listened. There was much
of interest in the air."

"There must have been," said Philip. "No doubt they are
greatly astonished that the matter of the colonies has been
carried so far."

"I found Chatham, and Burke, and others prominent in
Parliament, speaking openly against a war carried on against
England's own plantations. I heard murmurs against the government of Lord North by the common people; the shopkeep-
ing class are crying out against the increased taxes levied to
equip military and naval expeditions to such a far-off place."

"They'll sweat under the load, as they are always made to
do," said Philip.

"The state of things I found there," said Beaumarchais,

"can do nothing else but hamper the immediate furthering of the war; and delay," with a gesture of his eloquent hands, "will be of great value to your cause. M'sieu Deane tells me," to Philip, "you are none too well advanced yourselves; it requires a deal of time to arouse an unaccustomed people to a sense of danger, and even more to build up sources of supply."

"Our eyes are upon France!" said Mr. Deane as Philip sat silent and thoughtful; "I have asked with all the power I have."

"Help may be nearer than you think," said Beaumarchais. "But we must not idly depend upon it. We must struggle and fight and make the most of what opportunities we have. To send guns and ammunition, and clothing for your soldiers in the field is a useful and necessary thing; but, m'sieus, an equally necessary thing is to put swift ships upon the sea: kites, falcons with sharp eyes and rending beaks and talons. Strike hard at England's merchants and her insurers of seagoing vessels, and you've dealt a blow that will have lasting value."

"By this time to-morrow," said Mr. Deane, nodding his head, confidently, "you'll have heard a deal. There are great moneys to be had in the matter of such ships. You will be surprised."

"The unexpected has always an attraction," smiled Beaumarchais. "Such things are, for example, the life of a play; it gives that sparkle, that quality that catches at the breath, that thing which makes so for suspense and entertainment."

"I was asked by the person who has this money in control," said Mr. Deane, "to look about in Paris and choose a man for an unusual enterprise, a man of parts," nodding to Philip, "a man who'd been experienced in affairs of consequence and was accustomed to deal with persons of rank. Also, he must be a man of influence; above all, it would be necessary that he sympathize with the American cause. I did not require much time to fix upon him," said Mr. Deane. "In an instant I knew M'sieu Beaumarchais was the man above all others."

The Frenchman gestured gracefully; he was greatly pleased.

"Your belief in me, m'sieu," he said, "is appreciated. I trust, when I learn the nature of the undertaking your principal has in view, I will prove to be the man you think me to be."

Mr. Deane held up one hand.

"Of that I have no doubt," he said. "It is an enterprise, m'sieu, so especially fitted to your talents that one might think it created for you."

Philip smoked, and sipped sparingly at the wine. In a little while their dinners were brought up, and they fell to. All during the meal the talk went on. L'Orient. An unusual adventure. The sea and the ships thereof. Help for the rebelling colonies. Great moneys. An unknown presence behind it all, acute, watchful, of great daring.

When he finally arose and took up the candle that had been brought for him, he shook hands with the two men.

"I have had a long day on the road," he said, "and tomorrow I will have another; and so I must get some sleep. If I don't see you in the morning, good-bye and good fortune."

"We shall meet in Paris, I hope," said Mr. Deane. "It may be to the advantage of us both if you keep me in view. Much is about to happen. You are a shipman, and we may be of use to each other."

"Be sure to visit me, m'sieu," said Beaumarchais. "Ask anyone, anywhere in Paris, where I am to be found; they will tell you at once."

As Philip, a little later, put out his candle and drew the coverlet up under his chin he heard the rain dashing against the stout walls of the inn, and the wind moaning among its chimneys and gables. And as he went off to sleep, a presence was making its way through the gale toward the sea, powerful, beautiful, singularly rich: at its gesture ships appeared upon the waters, swift, strong ships like kites, and falcons. He struggled through the rain and wind, through marsh and broken land; he stood upon bleak shores hoping to see this presence plainly. But he could not. There was a hidden and secret thing, a thing to be kept from him, a thing he was not to be trusted with. He felt wretched and outcast and alone. And then his sleep grew deeper. He rested heavily.

CHAPTER XXIII

THE shipbuilding enterprises of the Barreauts had been carried on at L'Orient during the high days of their trade with the world; and many of the ships of Claridge & Company were still constructed there. In the old town of Port Louis, across the river, the head of the house years before had erected a mansion facing the water front, a large stone building of sturdy construction and design, and the representative of the firm at the port still occupied it.

It was late afternoon of the day following the episode at the Three Clocks; the rain had ceased, and the sun glinted upon the water; the distant sounds from the shipyards came drowsily through the air; a traveling carriage, splashed with mud, drew up at the iron gate at Barreauts', and a gray-haired man with a portfolio under his arm stepped out. He was at once admitted. At the great hall door a liveried foot-man took him in charge; after a few moments he was shown into a wide, sun-lit room where Charlotte Desfourneaux sat at a table with numerous papers before her.

"M'sieu Picon, good-afternoon," she said.

The gray-haired man bowed; he had a pinched face and small eyes and a way of nodding his head as he spoke.

"Mademoiselle, I have but now reached here from Bordeaux. The roads are in terrible condition and greatly delayed me." He opened the portfolio and took out some papers. "I bring you these from M'sieu Constant. Two ships have been bought; clever people have examined them and found them stanch and seaworthy. They will proceed to Dunkerque in two days' time."

The girl took the papers and glanced at them. Then she laid them on the table with the others.

"M'sieu Constant bade me tell you," said Picon, "that there is much espionage. The people of the English minister are as thick in Bordeaux as flies in the August sun. They are suspicious and cunning. The vessels cannot sail without cargoes, for that would attract attention. But we have managed; M'sieu Constant is shrewd and watchful; he makes no mistakes."

Picon was nodding and talking and gesturing; but the girl interrupted him.

"I have had a rider from Paris only an hour ago," she said, "and he brought word that sufficient guns had been secured to arm a half dozen vessels of the class I desire. Please convey that to M'sieu Constant."

"I shall do so, mademoiselle," said Picon, rubbing his hands. "He will be much pleased."

"Also the matter of which I spoke to him and M'sieu Deane, the American commissioner, has now come forward. I shall require you to remain overnight at an inn in the town so that you may take him the details in the morning."

"The face of the sea shall be changed," said Picon, exultantly. "Rich ships shall be brought in and sold; they'll be brought in like fat geese, mademoiselle, and much profit will be had of them."

Charlotte selected certain papers from among those before her; these she handed the man, and he in turn locked them carefully in the portfolio. Picon was standing receiving final directions when the door of the room was heard to close, and looking up Charlotte saw her cousin Henri Barreaut, his right wrist bandaged, and the hand thrust into the breast of his coat. His pock-marked face was set in a scowl, and there was a look of contempt in his eyes as they rested upon the dispatch bearer.

"Another of your riders, I suppose, Charlotte," he said.

"By God, anyone having occasion to observe the house would take it for a posting station. At all hours we have coaches and chariots, horsemen and footmen dashing up in a fury, and afterwards leaving in all haste; you get more dispatches and communications of various kinds than the firm does, and it has been carrying on business these two hundred years."

"To-morrow, Picon," said the girl, quietly; "report to me well before noon."

"Yes, mademoiselle. Thank you." The man bobbed his head to Henri Barreaut, a sly twinkle in his eye. "Good-evening, m'sieu."

When the man had gone out, Barreaut said:

"If you had come to me with your enterprises I would have warned you against that fellow immediately; he is one of the slyest rogues to be met in a day's journey; many a merchant and shipowner has suffered by his dishonesty."

"He serves my purpose rather well," said Charlotte. "He is enterprising and quick-witted. And he can hold his tongue when required to do so."

Barreaut went to the window and looked out; the mud-splashed carriage still stood at the gate, the horses panting, the chin of the driver sunk wearily upon his breast. Picon went down the brick walk with a slinking, fox-like gait, the portfolio held tightly under his arm. The pock-marked man turned back into the room.

"If your highly considered Americans have no more care than you, Charlotte, in the people they select to carry on their affairs, they'll make but poor headway," he said. "He serves your purpose, you say: he will, while it seems to him he is serving his own. But once let him see a more profitable way in the day's business, and you'll quickly learn how true my words are."

"My agent employed him, knowing his characteristics," said the girl, composedly.

"Your agent." The man in a sudden burst of anger struck

the table at which she sat with the flat of his left hand. "In God's name, what have we come to when young girls scarcely out of their convents have agents and couriers, and set themselves up as friends and well wishers of revolutionists?"

"You must not forget, Henri," said the girl, "I am an American by birth; my mother, also, was an American. We think it proper and right to interest ourselves in our country when it is in danger?"

"There is no danger to anyone except those plotting blackguards who'd deny the right of the government, and of the governing class. Mark me well, Charlotte, these matters are sure to fall, and in falling they'll carry down with them everyone taking part in them. What purpose will it serve for your General Washington to marshal his ragamuffins against the word of his legal king? What will it serve to gather half-armed ships and send them to sea in spite of the warnings of experienced persons, who see all too well what fate is in store for them?" The man sat down, holding his right arm with his left hand as though in pain.

"I have had more than one letter from John Claridge, as I've already said to you; and the things he put into writing seemed almost beyond credit: until you came here a fortnight or more ago I did not believe them possible." He leaned toward her, still nursing the injured arm. "I wonder, do you realize, Charlotte, what danger you are plunging the firm into? Do you realize that the British, when they put down these headstrong idiots who have arisen against all reason, may condemn and confiscate all we have on the other side of the sea? And all because of your ill-considered enterprises?"

"John Claridge mentioned that quite often," said Charlotte, meeting his look with her quiet eyes. "In spite of his public attitude favoring the new government, he has no belief in it, and so sees danger in doing anything that may be of assistance to it."

"In a year's time," said Barreaut, "there will be no trace

of this rebellion left, and if you continue as you are doing you will have spent, uselessly, a very large sum of money. So heavy a sum," said the man, "that it may impair the credit of the house."

"What money I have used, and any I may use in the future, is my own," said Charlotte Desfourneaux. "The firm of Claridge & Company has never gone out of its way to consider me; indeed, it has always dealt with me impatiently and with a good deal of contempt. I have not forgotten that."

"These ships which you are arming against the wishes of the French government, and to the alarm of the English? Can you hope to avoid the responsibility they must bring upon you? For you are a Barreaut—you are of the firm of Claridge & Company; you occupy a position which makes concealment impossible. Already the British have your name and your doings on their lists. A dozen times in the past week I've had the agents of Lord Stormont, their minister at Paris, in my counting room, questioning and uttering veiled threats. And more than that," the heavy, pitted face hard with anger: "this wretch, Constant, whom you have at Bordeaux, and this lesser villain, Picon, do not seem perilous enough for you, so you must needs entangle yourself with that most unprincipled rascal, Beaumarchais."

"M'sieu Beaumarchais has been recommended to me by persons of consequence," said Charlotte in the same quiet way.

"You are, perhaps, surprised that I've had word of him in your affairs?" said Henri Barreaut, and again he leaned toward her. "You thought it was not known."

"I am *not* surprised," she said. "And that it is known makes little difference."

His eyes were hot with fury; he arose.

"Well, then," he said, "it may interest you to know that I heard three days ago that this adventurer was about to set out for L'Orient to visit you upon business. Also, it may fur-

ther interest you to know that I set out with a party to in-
tercept him."

"It does not interest me in the least," said the girl, "and
I already know it, Henri. A person in my employ was present
at the Three Clocks when you encountered M'sieu Beaumarchais. It seems you drew your sword upon him, and that
your arm was injured by a pistol bullet."

There had been the sound of wheels at the gate some few
moments before, and now a footman came in.

"The M'sieus Beaumarchais and Deane, mademoiselle,"
he said.

"Have them come up," said Charlotte; and as the man left
the room, she continued, to Barreaut: "You will, perhaps, not
desire to meet them again, Henri?"

He looked at her for a moment without speaking, a searching, valuing look, one which had in it both wonder and malice:
then he said:

"Not just now, Charlotte. But, at another time, it will
be a great pleasure."

In a little space after Henri Barreaut had gone, Mr. Deane
and M. Beaumarchais were shown in. The American commissioner presented the Frenchman.

"M'sieu Beaumarchais," said Charlotte, "I am greatly
pleased that you should consider this matter and think it
worth your while to make the long journey between Paris and
L'Orient."

"Mademoiselle," said the playwright, bowing, "it is a great
satisfaction to find a young lady having such serious matters
under consideration. When M'sieu Deane spoke to me of the
things you had in mind, my interest was instantly taken. It
is a privilege to become concerned with you in such a cause."

They sat down, and Charlotte ordered a refreshment for
them; while they were engaged with this, Beaumarchais talked.
He bade the girl be careful how she laid out, or even spoke
of, money. The seeking after ships and armament by the

agents of Congress, or by private persons desiring to send armed vessels to sea on their own account, had stirred up a greed that was quite formidable. The hawks were up, hungry for profit; many were pressing forward, but with no thought of liberty, no desire to aid a new people into the world as a nation. Broad gold pieces were what they coveted, and they'd have them, even at the price of a people's blood. He implored her, when she reached Paris, to be watchful; to guard herself against the approaches of all save those whom she was sure she could trust.

Mr. Deane spoke in the same strain. In the few weeks he'd been in France he'd found credits hard to secure; few traders or brokers, or makers of needed things, were willing to advance money or material against Congress's promise to pay.

"It was when I found that out," said Mr. Deane, "that the vultures began to tempt me. The clothing they offered was of the worst, the gunpowder of poor quality, the muskets were of the kind made for export and as dangerous in the field to a comrade as to a foe. And all these things at prices so fabulous as to make the spirit sick."

"One of the things of which I desired to speak to you," said Charlotte Desfourneaux, "was that of arms and ammunition for the troops in the field. One man whom I recently talked with is M'sieu de la Tuillerie, who represents an armorer of large dealings. After my own business had been settled, and seeing him so agreeable, I mentioned the matter of Congress. He said he was willing to withdraw fifteen thousand muskets of the model of 1763 from the King's arsenal, for immediate delivery, and to replace them with a like number of pieces of their own make, giving the King my security for his good faith, and taking the word of Congress that he in turn shall be fairly dealt with."

"I am acquainted with M'sieu de la Tuillerie," said Beaumarchais with a graceful gesture of approval. "An honest, far-seeing man."

"It is magnificent," said Mr. Deane, delighted. "Fifteen thousand muskets for immediate delivery! Splendid! I shall make arrangements at once for a ship to carry them; I shall——"

"M'sieu," said Beaumarchais, his well kept hand lifted once more, "one moment, I beg. I think Mademoiselle has not yet told us all."

"A part of the muskets are already on the road to Nantes, where a M'sieu Penet, a man whom Congress trusts, has the matter in charge. A fast sailing, well defended ship is to take them on board." She looked at Mr. Deane. "These things had to be done quickly, and I did not communicate with you, knowing you would be in L'Orient quite soon."

The face of the American commissioner had fallen somewhat at the news that he was not to be concerned in the matter; nevertheless, he applauded the stroke with excellent good-will.

"It could not be better," he said. "After all, to secure the pieces, and ship them, are the principal things."

"M'sieu de la Tuillerie could have supplied brass cannon as well, and on the same terms," said Charlotte; "but these bore the arms of the King of France; if any were afterwards captured it would be known where they'd been had, and that would bring about an awkward situation."

"It is so," said Beaumarchais. "The arms of the King of France upon a gun captured upon an American battlefield would develop a crisis we might not, at the moment, be in position to face."

But, continued M'sieu Beaumarchais, cannon were needed for the armies of this young and hopeful nation! How could any body of military, no matter how brave, fight without them? And small armies, such as he'd heard were in the field in America, being swift moving, needed light guns; guns that could be put promptly into position, operated with speed, and then be made away with out of danger if the enemy proved too eager or too strong. The six-pounder pieces were the pieces most needed for this, he said; lively, small guns which bristled like terriers. And they were to be had: if not in France, then in Holland, or in Spain.

They discussed this possibility; and then Charlotte said:

"In my small experience—of less than a year, m'sieus, I seem to have discovered that a deal can be done with money." The two men smiled and nodded to each other, and she proceeded: "Also, I have learned it gives much less than its full service if there is a lacking of organization." They agreed with this; M'sieu Beaumarchais took snuff with a flourish; Mr. Deane beamed and patted his palms together. "Small measures of help," said Charlotte, "some now, some again, with barren spaces between, will be of no advantage to our sailors or soldiers. And it was because I saw the need of more systematic aid," to Mr. Deane, "that I wrote the letter which resulted in your bringing M'sieu Beaumarchais here."

"Two millions of livres," said Mr. Deane. "Two millions!" He wagged his head, his somewhat red face grew an absolute purple. "I never dreamed of such a sum. It is almost, mademoiselle, the fulcrum Archimedes desired that would enable him to move the world. And," he went on, "immediately I spoke to M'sieu Beaumarchais, as the most likely person to have ideas great enough to balance so heavy a sum of money. He took fire. He demanded to see you at once; he was captivated."

Beaumarchais arose and paced the room; as Charlotte watched him he seemed much like an actor moving about a stage; he gestured, his arms thrown wide, his graceful figure drawn up to its full.

"Mademoiselle," he said, "it is difficult for me to convey to you how magnificently opportune was the visit of M'sieu Deane with your letter. It was like a scene in a comedy, a comedy written by a master who knew the value of surprise." He paused in his pacing, one hand lifted. "For a year I had been endeavoring to gain the attention of M'sieu de Vergennes, the King's foreign minister, in the matter of America. But a man who has the welfare of a government in his keeping is hard to approach; he is full of cautions and fears, every step has its hazards, and every word must be weighed. But in the end, when he had guardedly balanced the needs of America against the security of France, he made up his mind that a victorious revolt of the English colonies would be of inestimable value. At once, mademoiselle, I seized the opportunity! I sat down to draw up a memorial to the King. But I soon saw no words I had ever written were sufficient for this instrument. None were sufficiently clever, none had the eloquence, or were stirring enough for my purpose. As I strove I suddenly saw that words alone would not do. A plan as tremendous as the one I had in view must have the support of a great sum in gold: there must be louis and double louis stacked one upon the other until they reared to the height of Notre Dame. I resolved to ask the King for three millions of livres; also I would request three millions more from the King of Spain. But, as an earnest of the soundness of my enterprise, I must be able to show what would be an almost fabulous private confidence. I surveyed the figures which told the whole of my private fortune, and was in despair. I threw down my pen; I arose from the table." With anguish upon his countenance, Beaumarchais turned away, portraying the manner in which it had been done. "And then," stopping suddenly, amazement, wonder upon his face, "M'sieu Deane appeared at my door with your marvelous letter, and I was saved!"

He paced excitedly up and down. Out of this princely gift, liberty might come for a whole people. He had finished his memorial out of hand; in a few hours' time De Vergennes had it at Versailles and had given it to the King. Eight millions of money! Nine millions when his own fortune and that of some friends were added. It was stupendous. Ships! He'd have such a fleet of ships as never were seen before. French and Spanish ships, sailing to the French islands; there American vessels were to take over the cargoes and carry them smartly through the belt of prowling British frigates, into American ports. His plan was to establish a great commercial house in Paris, a respectable firm, seemingly of wide-flung enterprises; but in reality the trade was to be solely with America. Munitions only were to be dealt in; everything used to equip soldiers in the field. And these goods were not to be given to the colonies. They were to be sold to them. The company was to be strictly a private business, carried on in a business way. It would pay for all it received, and would ask payment from Congress; tobacco, rice, hides, furs, any of the natural products of the country would be accepted; but unlimited credit was to be given; payments were to be made as Congress was able to meet them.

"It is a noble plan," said Mr. Deane to Charlotte. "And most ingenious. And America is not to be placed in the position of a beggar nation. The matter is a commercial transaction; we will be dealing with a house which will make its profits from the business it has with us. Congress will be pleased; the thing may well be the solution of the Colonial cause. Sound supplies from an inexhaustible reservoir, long credits and the continued assurance of strong, though secret, support! It is more—very much more, than we had any reason to hope for at this time."

Charlotte made no reply; she studied Beaumarchais as he went up and down the floor, posturing, gesturing. He was handsome; there was, in spite of his foppish way, something virile about him; his way of dramatizing everything, of seizing upon matters of practical fact as theatrical situations, gave an air of unreality to his words and ideas; but at the same time there was a strength behind them, a grasp, a readiness that was admirable.

"You speak of sound supplies, m'sieu," said the playwright. "With the company I would found, they would be assured.

Men in the field facing a strong enemy must have confidence. The gunpowder we'd send them would be of a sort made by God-fearing men. I have seen inferior kinds carried by brave soldiers into positions of great danger. What will bravery serve in a situation like that? If the musket of a wretched soldier fails, all that remains is for the holy saints in heaven to open their arms and receive him, straight.

"Food, of course, America has; but things such as stout boots, no doubt, are badly needed. Pick your men as you will for courage, let them be as well set as you please, strong of limb and with the lungs of coach horses, but without good boots they are useless. The shortest march is labor; the stones of the road are torture. The resolution of the steadiest will seep out at a break in the heel. A lion with a limping paw, mademoiselle, is a sorry beast indeed. And, then, the matter of uniforms," said M'sieu Beaumarchais. "To be sure, a dress for a soldier is but a thing fashioned by a tailor and provided with a given number of buttons; put it upon a single man and it has no effect at all. But, put it upon a number of men, banded together for a given purpose, and it at once becomes a thing of grave consideration. Many a careless youth has given up his life rather than bring discredit to the stripes upon his sleeve."

2

M'sieu Beaumarchais talked and paced and postured for some time; also he listened with attention to Charlotte when she spoke; and when he, with Mr. Deane, was ready to go, he said:

"Put the affair of the money in the hands of your agent, M'sieu Constant; let him lodge it with any banker he sees fit to deal with in Paris. And in a little while after, you shall see a power grow up, mademoiselle, that will astonish you."

When they had gone, Charlotte rang, and one of the servants answered. She desired that M'sieu Barreaut be asked to come to her at once. This M'sieu Barreaut did, and he stood frowning, expectant, fumbling at his injured arm.

"I shall require two millions of livres by to-morrow," said Charlotte, quietly, busy with the papers before her.

The man was aghast; his pitted face turned a dull purple.

"Two millions of livres!" he said. "Have you lost your reason?"

"I shall expect it before noon," said the girl. "If it is not forthcoming, I shall request M'sieu Constant to inquire why, in due legal form."

He stood for a moment, twitching with fury; then he turned, not trusting himself to speak, and left the room.

CHAPTER XXIV

TUCKED away, deep in the heart of old Paris, fronting upon the Rue Vielle du Temple, was a solid looking building of excellent design known as the Hôtel de Hollande. This had been built years before, when Holland was strong upon the sea, and powerful in the councils of Europe, as the residence of the Dutch ambassador. It had been abandoned long since and stood empty and neglected. But now, to the astonishment of everyone, the great lock was shot back by an energetic hand; the doors and windows were thrown open, dust and rubbish vanished; carpenters sawed and fitted, painters applied color and varnish, porters scrubbed and polished, a great abundance of furniture was taken in; and at last the old place stood with all its magnificence restored, gleaming and filled with fresh life. A great copper plate at the side of the main door told in deeply bitten letters that the new tenants were Roderique Hortalez & Company. Gossip had it that the firm was engaged in shipping; that they were Spanish, were purchasing ships and establishing warehouses and magazines.

Talk at once sprang up among firms engaged in the export trade. What sort of people were in the place? Spanish? Yes, so it was said. Spanish, and a long time in commerce, with establishments in all the principal ports of the Mediterranean and the East. South America, of course, also knew them. Now and then a man spoke over his glass of wine at an inn to remember having dealt with them in the past, but none could produce documents testifying to the fact.

"I've had indigo of them, and rugs from the East, and gums and fine woven stuff," said an ancient trader whose ships prowled here and there across the world. "An aristocratic house, if I remember aright. They were some noble family engaged in trade, though that was not commonly known. The name of Hortalez was merely a shelter for their true identity."

"The Paris house, so I've heard, is considered but a branch; but if it is such, it is a very large one," said a broker in ship insurances. "It has a chain of riders and coaches between the Rue Vieille du Temple and various ports and points on the coast; messages come and go with a swiftness the King's own service can scarcely rival. They rush along the roads from Nantes, Bordeaux, L'Orient, and Dunkerque and some of the Dutch ports, with the swiftness of the wind."

"What need have they of such huge communications," said a bewigged old manager of a Paris house. "In all the history of mercantile doings here, nothing like it has been seen before."

"And who," demanded a sly-looking agent of a Bordeaux wine dealer, "ever saw such foppery in a counting house, or any place that'd been put to the use of trade. Paintings on walls, draperies of silk at the windows; every clerk at every desk combed and polished and brushed as though for a ball."

A stout Fleming, who manufactured boots in a border town, spoke of the unexpectedness of his experience.

"I inquired for Señor Hortalez," he said, "and one of the dancing masters who serve as clerks said he was not then in Paris. When he'd return was not known. But, if I had boots to sell, and if they were good boots and in large enough quantities, I would be received by M'sieu Beaumarchais, who would be pleased to speak with me in the matter."

"A play-actor!" said the bewigged manager. "A writer of verses!"

"I was shown into an inner room," said the Fleming, "and whom do I meet but a gentleman like a person of fashion, with gold buckles on his shoes, lace at his wrists, and powder in his hair. When I entered upon him he sat upon a divan with a lute and was practising the turns of a love song."

"God save us!" said the bewigged man, aghast. "What are things coming to!"

"No trade can prosper in such hands," said a fat man, with a heavy, positive face. "Nothing useful can come of such folly."

"This inner room where I met M'sieu Beaumarchais was less like a place of business than the outer ones, though they were bad enough. All about me was the smell of scent; on the tables were play-books, billets-doux, riding whips, music, and instruments for the playing thereof. And, indeed, m'sieus, once while I spoke to him about the differences in leathers, the man leaped up, asked my pardon, and performed some passages for a comedy which it seems he'd just thought of. And while I was still there a party of young nobles, with their ladies, came in, and the place in a moment was so filled with laughter and the whispering of silks that I could not but feel myself an intruder."

"The days when trading was done by traders and in a trading way were more to my liking," said old big-wig. "What does a fine gentleman like this know of it?"

"Nothing," said the old merchant. "Nothing at all."

But the stout Fleming stroked his chin, and shook his head.

"Well, now, as to that," he said, "I am not so sure. His ways were not the usual ways, I know; but he was no bad man of business, for all. I sold him a great many hundred pairs of boots, and he asked me none but the quietest of questions. However, he had an excellent eye for goodness in material, and there was a shrewdness in his treatment of price that showed a deal of thought."

2

M'sieu Constant, agent for Charlotte Desfourneaux, was a round little man with a pink, cherubic face, and fat, gesturing hands; but he had swift, seeing eyes and most excellent judgment. He sat in his small office in an old building which overlooked the Gironde, at Bordeaux, directed all those matters which came up for his judgment, kept his eyes and ears open, set down many notes in a great book which he kept locked in his desk, and asked questions. There was not much happening in the port which M'sieu Constant did not know; ships came and went, and he had news of all of them.

The house of Roderique Hortalez & Company had been established some three months, when one day, toward late afternoon, Picon came quietly up the stairs and into the room. M'sieu Constant nodded to him, smiled in his good-natured way, and sat back in his comfortable chair, his hands crossed upon his rounded stomach. For Picon was an interesting man; when he came in he always brought something of value; it was a pleasure to listen to him.

Picon took off his hat and from the crown of it brought out a scrap of paper; he stood by the window, for M'sieu Constant's room was none too well lighted, and read:

"On November twenty-ninth there arrived, in Quiberon, the American sloop-of-war *Reprisal*, said to mount sixteen guns; the master of the vessel being one Lambert Wickes. She carries a cargo of indigo. Also there are a number of passengers, among them the American savant, Benjamin Franklin, recently appointed to serve as a commissioner with M'sieu Silas Deane, at Paris."

The look of pacific content left the face of the rotund Constant, and in its place was one of much excitement.

"M'sieu Franklin!" he said. "What a great good fortune! He is the one person needed to carry on the work. A fresh span of horses, Picon; and a carriage with lamps. You travel to-night; this news must reach Mademoiselle Desfourneaux before another day passes." From a table drawer he took a leather pouch, and from it a handful of gold coins which he threw upon the table. "Fresh horses at every posting statlon, Picon," he said. "And postilions of the best. Spare nothing," he said, a sheet of paper before him, and a quill dipping into the ink pot; "Mademoiselle must know these important facts before they become common property."

"Through the night to L'Orient," said Picon, his face twisted into an expression of dislike. "A dreary drive, m'sieu; and these young devils of postilions have little regard for a passenger's safety." He picked up the gold pieces as M'sieu Constant wrote, counting them carefully, made a note of the amount in a small book, and then put them in his waistcoat pocket. "But if Mademoiselle must know of the American's arrival, well and good. To-morrow I shall tell her, and shall place myself at her disposal for whatever service she'll require of me."

M'sieu Constant read what he had written and seemed satisfied with it; he sprinkled sand upon it to dry the ink, then folded it and affixed his seal.

"In another half hour I shall expect to know you've left the town behind you," he said, as he handed the dispatch to his messenger. "So do not delay."

Picon went hurrying down the stairs; M'sieu Constant stood at the window and watched the arched gateway at the Ship and Coach, which stood on the river's edge; he saw Picon enter the way at a trot; and well within the half hour he saw a chariot with a span of bay horses and a young postilion emerge between the two lamps already lighted at the gate. The efficient Picon was inside and waved his hand to his employer in farewell; then, with the forethought of an experienced traveler, he began, as he rolled away, to draw and fasten the curtains against the chill of the night.

3

Word had reached the Secret Committee of Congress at Philadelphia of the operations of Roderique Hortalez & Company; French ships, so the message read, were already taking on board arms, ammunition, and needed equipment for the American forces; a quarter of a million pounds would be given by the French King and others for this purpose before the year came to an end. Dr. Franklin had been named some time before to go to the aid of Deane in France, and at this news it was determined that he start at once. So that none might suspect his mission, he left the city in the night. Sleeping for a few hours at an inn at Chester, he arose quite early next morning and proceeded to Marcus Hook, where the smart sloop *Reprisal* lay awaiting him. As soon as he was aboard, she set sail.

It was the season of the year for storms, and the Atlantic was churned into a fury; the stanch little sloop, with every spar and brace straining and singing, plunged through the waves; sometimes she rolled rail under. Franklin was at this time seventy years of age; his health was not of the best, and he was forced to remain in the cabin during the whole of the passage.

"It is my eighth voyage across the ocean," he told Captain Wickes when that stout master inquired about his health, "and the most disagreeable of them all."

But, ill or well, his interest in science remained; and every day, so it is said, he contrived to take the temperature of the ocean in order to verify anew his discovery of the warmth of the Gulf Stream.

The news Picon carried along the night roads between Bordeaux and L'Orient for Charlotte Desfourneaux, while full of the flare of excitement, did not contain all the facts of the *Reprisal's* crossing. More than once the vessel sighted enemy cruisers; more than once she fled away, finding their weight too great for her; once she beat to quarters in the midst of a driving gale, and with a formidable frigate riding high and grim before her. But the fury of the tempest saved her; in other cases darkness came, and she was able to bear away from strong enemies with all lights out, and so lose herself in the deep night and the tossing storm.

Congress had been at a low ebb for money when Franklin left Philadelphia; indeed, so low were the public funds that the philosopher had, by using every available means, gotten together something like four thousand pounds for which he was personally responsible, and turned it over to the treasurer. So, when aboard ship he was not at all well provided for; and the heavy expenses which he knew would accrue during his stay in Paris troubled him grievously. But fortune was never far from this extraordinary man; when they came in sight of the French coast late in November they also drew near to an English brig laden with lumber and wine, out of Bordeaux and bound for an Irish port. They took her and put a prize crew aboard. A few hours later another vessel was captured, bound from an English port for Hamburg, with brandy and flaxseed. The old philosopher witnessed the takings and was greatly pleased.

"Here," said he, "am I well provided for; the money that these two rich ships will bring will support my office for many a month to come."

The sloop ran into Quiberon Bay, where the commissioner was put off in a fishing boat and landed at Auray, a hamlet with but wretched accommodations. But a carriage was had next day, and he was driven to Nantes, where M'sieu Gruel, admirer of Franklin's writings, had a large country house; and there the old philosopher was installed; he rested and made his plans while arrangements were going forward to convey him to Paris.

4

It was at this suburb of Nantes that Charlotte Desfourneaux, after a hurried journey along the dangerous roads from L'Orient, talked with Franklin.

"My dear Miss Desfourneaux," he said, and held her hand,

"it is because of you and the things you have accomplished that I am here at this time. I have heard of Roderique Hortalez & Company," he said, his eyes full of humor and appreciation. "M'sieu Beaumarchais has told me. It is a wonderful conception and will do much toward our success."

"The credit for that, sir, goes to M'sieu Beaumarchais," she said. "It was his plan, and he has carried it through splendidly."

"His plan, to be sure, for who but the writer of comedies would think of such a thing. But the private financing has been done largely by you. And not only that; I have spoken to some other agents of Mr. Deane, my colleague, and they tell me there are twenty sail of armed ships now in French ports or at sea, which you have provided. At home there are other vessels, out of Boston, out of Baltimore, Charleston, and Philadelphia, all equipped by you and so badgering and infuriating the enemy, so draining him of money and credit, and the means of carrying on his commerce, that great good has come to Congress, and the cause."

Beaumarchais had told the old philosopher of certain magazines at Nantes, containing rich stores of the goods needed in the colonies; also he had pointed out some bluff-bowed vessels loading at a quay, one of them Spanish, another Dutch, and two of them French. Cloth, leather, felt, brass buttons, sword-blades, gunpowder, cases of flintlocks, cannon, gun carriages. All to be cleared for the French islands, there to be discharged and kept safely until certain American ships came for them.

"We have been poor," said Franklin; "now we shall be rich. We have been forced to give back before the advance of the enemy; now we shall stand; a fight shall be made for every rood of ground; and our ways to the sea shall be kept open. And the credit for it all goes to you."

He sat with the girl upon the great sofa in M'sieu Gruel's drawing room, and for upwards of two hours they talked of the needs of the colonies, and the various ways of supplying them. And then at last Charlotte Desfourneaux came to the matter that concerned herself.

"It has been said of me," she said, "that I am providing ships and armament not for the good of the colonies but for my own personal gain. It has been said that these ships are privateers. That I am engaged in a commercial enterprise and benefit largely by my people's activities."

He smiled and patted her hand.

"Do not permit such things to disturb you," he said. "Evil is said about all of us. I have no doubt some of my own doings are taken as efforts for personal profit, and that there are many who gossip of them. Do not vex yourself; these venomous creatures are not worth a moment's thought."

"Would it not be possible," she said, "for you to take over my ships? Could you not have commissions given my captains and so make them officers in the American navy? Then when a vessel taken by them is condemned and sold, the money will not revert to me, but to Congress: and in this way there will be proof that I have no desire for gain in what I do."

The wise old eyes studied her face; he took snuff and sat tapping the lid of the ivory box.

"There is something here more than the gossip of a few fools," he said. "For such a thing would not touch you so deeply as this seems to have done."

She answered very earnestly. There was, indeed, a matter of depth and consequence, a thing which troubled her thoughts and caused her bitter anxiety. He had, no doubt, heard at one time or another—everyone had—of the Spanish treasure ship, *Vision of St. John?* It was a matter of fifty years before, when he was a young man. Yes, he said, he had heard of it: it was a celebrated case, the occasion for great outlays of money, of heart-burning, of hate and revenge.

"A deal of the gold taken from that old vessel came to me," said Charlotte Desfourneaux. "It came to me by the gift of

Antoinette Teresa Barreaut-Desfourneaux, my grandmother. It was money which she hated; and in many ways," said Charlotte, "I am greatly like her."

"A hatred of money in one's possession is not a usual thing," said Dr. Franklin with a smile.

"It was the plunder of what was perhaps a very honest ship," said the girl, her eyes steady, her slender, long-fingered hands clasped tightly together. "And it is this money which is being spent outfitting the vessels I have procured, to get crews for them, and guns, and to carry them out to sea."

The broad face of the old philosopher lighted up.

"Why, then," he said, "if there is any way of using money, come by as this was, so that it might lay comfort to your spirit, the way you have selected is the very one. A struggle for the liberty of a whole people is a filter through which anything may be cleansed."

"I have thought over the method a great deal," said the girl. "And it has appealed to me. But there is something more, and it is in this that the trouble lies. The claim made in the early days upon the money has continued; there is an Archer now in France for the purpose of reopening the case in the maritime courts, perhaps appealing to the King. It has occurred to me," she said, "that he may be adjudged to have more claim upon this money than I: if so, I am doing him a wrong."

A shadow came upon Dr. Franklin's face.

"I understand," he said. And after a moment's thought he added, kindly: "Perhaps it would be as well to go more slowly until the matter is settled. Some of what you have contracted for may still be withdrawn."

"In another week's time," she said, her head up, her fine, strong chin out, "I am going to pay another million of livres into Roderique Hortalez & Company. If I do not I shall have placed M'sieu Beaumarchais in a desperate position, as all his own fortune has gone to establish the house. Also, he has agreed with the French and Spanish governments that this money would be forthcoming: if it is not, they may withdraw the funds they have guaranteed. In that case the firm will collapse; and the American colonies may collapse with it."

"Having just arrived," said the old philosopher, "there is a deal in the balance here in France which I have not been able to value. I had understood that Hortalez & Company was merely a mask for the King's government."

"It is a private enterprise," said Charlotte, "which King Louis has been induced to take part in because sums of money as heavy as his own were guaranteed."

There was a silence; the old doctor reflected.

"You've said you thought gravely before using the treasure for this purpose?"

"I considered it carefully," she answered. "And my resolution was, no matter what came or went, I'd give what help I could to Congress. I had purchased and fitted out a number of ships, I'd already employed an agent to make a beginning for me here in France, when the claimant of the money, Philip Archer, was first heard from. I was startled, for I'd not known there was such a person; they had assured me the Archers were all dead and their cause with them."

She told of her journey to New Castle, of her meeting with Mr. Hasty and what he'd said to her. Of De Chaulnes, the high actions of that gentleman, and the blow that stretched him on the floor. The story Philip Archer told her of his boyhood. Of the attempt upon his life at the Plough Inn; of his injury upon the deck of the *Trumpeter* in rescuing her from the abductors; of her talks with him; of his determination to carry on his father's and grandfather's fight and wrest, if possible, the loot of the *Vision of St. John* from those who held it.

"I do not know how much he has learned of me," she said. "I have told him nothing. And while in the ship *Nancy Blake* I'd look at him and listen to him, and always I felt I was not

being honest; that I was wronging him, that I was taking from
him what, after all, may be said by the courts, or the King,
to be his own."

"And yet," said Dr. Franklin, his shrewd old eyes upon her,
"it is not in your mind to give up your purpose?"

"No," she said. "I shall never do that."

He nodded, understandingly.

"There are people whom I have cherished all my life," he
said, "and whom I have put away because of this war. My
own son threw his fortune in with the King's government, and
I see him no more. I have all but impoverished myself; my
wife, whom I love above all, is living humbly, awaiting my
return. War comes upon us," he said, "and our resolutions
are made; friendships are broken, families are torn asunder;
comfort, peace of mind goes, perhaps never to return."

They talked for a long time, and when she was ready to
leave he went with her to the door. And as he held her hand
he said:

"Many things happen unexpectedly. Perhaps it would be
as well if you did not consider the matter of this young man
too seriously." His old eyes smiled at her. "From what you've
said of him, his thoughts are with Congress. That is a good
deal," nodding his head, "and a good deal more may be made
of it."

CHAPTER XXV

PHILIP ARCHER sat by a window in his Paris lodgings and looked out over the wintry Seine. He had improved greatly since the late summer and was once more the tough-fibered young man of earlier days. Conyngham, with his hands under the tails of his coat, was pacing up and down the room and talking.

"Lord Stormont is the divil to be at a body's heels," said the captain, frowning and shaking his head. "Not a thing can I do but his people are after me, spoiling it with their uproar. The bright slip of a lugger was all I needed, and I thought to be away in her long since, and have my hand up to the elbow in the pockets of the fat English merchants; but such a rattling you never heard as Stormont put out of him. If I'd a fleet of three-deckers, he couldn't have done more."

"There's a deal come to pass since Mr. Franklin arrived," said Philip. "Those things that'd had only a glance of Stormont's eye a while ago, now throw him into a great pitch of excitement."

"Ah, well," said Conyngham, a smile breaking through the clouds upon his face, "let him bluster." He took a paper from his pocket and opened it. "Here I am, God bless you, commander of a ship authorized by Congress, and with a commission in my fist to show for it." The paper had the signature of Mr. Hancock, president of Congress; the remainder of it was made out in another hand. "The hand of Mr. Franklin," said Conyngham. "He has a table drawer full of them, which he brought with him, and they only needing the name of the ship and the captain put into them."

"You managed to get acquainted with Mr. Franklin, then?" said Philip.

"Through Miss Desfourneaux, who took me smartly to him, perhaps to stop my complaints. 'Here is a shipmaster in whom I have a deal of confidence,' says she to him. 'He has an able vessel and would love to be frolicking in the Channel at this minute,' she says. 'But the King's officers have been greatly stirred up by the British minister's complaints, and his ship cannot go out without special papers.'

"And then, as quick as you'd wink your eye, the old gentleman had the table drawer open, a paper out of it, and a pen in his hand; and in another wink he had my name to it, and the name of the lugger, and the thing was done."

Philip handed the commission back to the Irishman.

"Your footing is greatly improved," he said. "As a privateersman you had a deal to contend with that will not bother you now. However," and he shook his head, "there is no magic in Mr. Hancock's signature, handsome as it is; Lord Stormont will have no more respect for it than he'd have for your own. And, remember, King Louis has no mind for a war with England at this time; and because of that he'll give her minister's protestations a deal of attention."

Conyngham's cheerfulness vanished at once; his face took on its former bleak expression.

"I fear what you say is true," he said. "Stormont, may the divil set sail to him, is as active as a porpoise in a morning sea."

Philip smiled at this, for it made no bad picture of that vigorous official. Stormont was of the red-faced, fist-shaking type; he was forever scuttling about, not too keen of perception, and always in fear something had escaped him; he was a man who greatly desired to serve his government; but a wrongheaded man, apt to muddle matters sadly because of a hasty temper. Philip put this gentleman beside Franklin who, though in his seventieth year, was, now that he was again ashore, hale and shrewd and full of the direction of a man of forty.

Franklin was in high favor with the people of France; a frugal race, they could not help but admire the maxims of "Poor Richard," while his fame as a philosopher and scientist filled the minds of the aristocracy with respect. Word had come of the reception he had received on the road from Nantes to Paris; the populace crowded the village ways and seemed delighted that America had sent so celebrated a man to negotiate with their ministers of state.

The Hôtel de Hamburg, in the Rue de l'Université, where the philosopher was lodged, was crowded both day and night with people who came to pay their respects. In this luxurious capital of France, amidst the elegance of fashion, the glitter and pomp and dignity of an old nobility, this steady-eyed old man, wearing no wig, with no trace of powder in his hair, in the simple dress of the Quaker City, firm, kindly, learned, was a revelation. It was as though an antique sage had, in some strange way, come among them.

"No matter what ruse Lord Stormont fixes upon to check action in the near seas," said Philip, "Franklin will master him. In a game of wits he is no match for this deep-thinking old man."

"If Franklin gets me to sea in the *Surprize*, I'll name him an angel itself," said Conyngham. "It's a blistering sin, so it is, to see so fine a ship wallowing in the water, her anchor deep, and her sails furled so tight you'd think never a stir of air would get into them again. God save us, what'll we do at all if there are no victories for us on the sea! Sure, the army at home, brave lads enough, mind you, has no chance until power is put into its hands. And if that power does not come from the sea, it will never come at all."

"Your vessel will sail in the end," said Philip, confidently. "Never fear for that. But, be patient; give the good doctor time to make the proper sort of friends among those about the King; a week or a month is nothing. If you sail out of Dunkerque with the King's word sanctioning your going, you may return any time you choose; and what is more, any prizes you take may be brought in also."

"You say true," said the Irish captain; "but the spirit in me is grievously tired with waiting."

Conyngham had been gone for an hour, perhaps, when the landlady knocked at the door. There were letters for M'sieu Archer; a messenger from M'sieu Deane had just brought them. The letters, addressed to Philip in care of Deane, had come, so a note from that gentleman's secretary said, in a French schooner sailing from Martinique which had arrived at Bordeaux three days before. Philip opened the first of them eagerly. It was from Nicholas Fortune, a long letter written in a fine hand, with a hard-pointed pen. Many things had happened, Nicholas said; dark days had come upon the colonies, and their power seemed doomed to be broken.

"*No doubt,*" said Nicholas, "*you have heard how Washington's army was beaten badly at Long Island, crossed to New York, and fell back to the heights above the city. It was a blow we'd not looked for; and what followed was still less expected, for the general passed the Hudson with his army and, even now, is retreating through the Jerseys, with the British in pursuit. Things there are in a turmoil; Philadelphia itself is in peril, and many are preparing to leave it before the British march in. I, myself, have already gone; a month ago I was called upon by Mr. Hancock and Mr. Adams, who said that though they did not expect the city to fall into the hands of the British, nevertheless, caution was a good thing, and preparations should be made covering certain eventualities.*

"*Some moneys had come to hand,*" wrote Nicholas, "*no great sum, but enough to hearten them in their work; so they proposed that I proceed with the casting of certain guns; also that I undertake the making of carriages for the same.*

"'*But,*' said Mr. Adams, '*we are not inclined to have the work done in the city, for the enemy ships-of-the-line may pass*

*the forts at any time, advance up the river, and lay us under
their fire. There is iron ore and fuel in the back country,
toward the hills; move your furnace there, and you shall have
all the activity you've been craving for.'*

"*And so,*" proceeded the little gun founder, "*here I am,
with all my materials in a clearing, locked in among the moun-
tains. Two dozen men are digging out the ore, and my furnace
is transforming it into usable metal. I am in a high state of
mind, for at last the troops shall have pieces of cannon that
will meet any of their occasions.*"

At the bottom of the last page was the postscript:

"*Your letter asking that certain papers be sent you, also
five hundred pounds in gold money, has been received. The
money has been sent, and will be paid you on demand at the
counting house of Chagnon & Company, Paris. The matter
of the papers will be attended to by Brotot, for I put your chest
and all its contents, save the gold money, in his care when I
left the city. He said he will send you what you require; and I
pray it goes safely.*"

The second letter was from Brotot. The hand was heavier
than that of Nicholas, and the words were a mixture of English and island French; and his picture of conditions was much
the gloomier of the two. Things were very bad. The Congress
was a violent, quarreling body of men; only God himself knew
how anything was accomplished. The officers commanding
the army were better; they had the qualities soldiers should
have, but they had no authority beyond what the individual
colonies choose to give them. The plowboys and farmers, said
Brotot, who had swarmed to the siege of Boston, were no
longer a part of M'sieu Washington's army. Most of them had
gone back to their homes; the volunteers who had fought in
the battles around New York had also dispersed when the
armies passed their borders. To be sure, there were men in

Massachusetts who had gone into the regular line, but these were mostly with M'sieus Montgomery and Arnold in the movement on Canada.

"*I have seen the army now in the Jerseys,*" said Brotot. "*It is in rags; it moves like a horde, and with little discipline; the men are gaunt and bristling, but they are hardy, and they hold to their pieces of cannon with determination; their ammunition trains are watched by eyes that are like hawks'. Much can be done with this force. It is one made up of what the English call ne'er-do-wells, younger sons, apprentices, and adventurers. In time, M'sieu Washington will build up an army about this beginning that will hold the field against all the trained troops sent against them. But time! That is the thing. Thus far the colonial regiments have barely kept out of the jaws of the enemy; they are swift, but they have no power to attack. Do what you can from where you are in France. Strength for us must come from over sea. And Nicholas was right. Ships are what are wanted; strong ships with heavy guns; they will bring us needed things, and will reduce the power of the enemy.*

"*Nicholas,*" the letter continued, "*has sent me your request for the small black book of Madame Fouquet, also the papers referred to in same. Gladly I would send these, for I desire above all things to have you win your cause against the Claridges, whom you know I detest. But all your papers were put at the disposal of M'sieu Lazarus at your request. He was given free access to them; and some of them he took away for examination. As I was not able to find those you asked for, I went to his place of business in Pump Court; but he was not there. Neither was he at his lodgings in Water Street. I made inquiries for him, but no one had seen him for weeks. His affairs, I found, had been put into the hands of an agent, and he had disappeared. Also,*" wrote Brotot, "*the small black book of Madame Fouquet and the papers thereunto belonging, to my great regret, have gone with him.*"

CHAPTER XXVI

NEXT morning M'sieu Beaumarchais stood before a tall mirror in his chambers, located in a fashionable quarter of Paris, adjusting a silken neckcloth. His cheeks were smooth and ruddy from recent shaving, his long hair was pomaded and combed back and tied in a queue. With his lawn sleeves, loose satin waistcoat, tight breeches, fine silken hose, and varnished shoes with golden buckles, he carried himself with an air of elegance.

"Victor," he said, as he finished with the neckcloth, "my coat."

His valet, a youth with sharp, dark eyes and deft hands, took a plum-colored silk coat from the depths of a closet; the sheen of the material was perfect; when the garment was put on it hung admirably.

"I think," said Beaumarchais, as he surveyed it in the high mirror, "Ganaud grows steadily more skillful. There is no tailor in all of Paris who can manage the lines of a coat with a surer touch."

"He is superb, m'sieu," said Victor. "His business grows as more and more of the young nobles learn of his talent. In choosing him as your tailor, m'sieu, you have made his fortune."

"I trust," said Beaumarchais, still examining the coat in the mirror, "his time will not become so greatly occupied that his attention will become slack."

"Oh, no, m'sieu," said the sure-tongued Victor. "You may depend upon Ganaud for that. He is an artist. What he does will always be well done; he slights nothing. And never will he be so busy that you, his benefactor, will not receive his best attention."

Beaumarchais smiled, well pleased. Victor fastened the neckcloth with a gold pin.

"Is Maynard still below?" asked the playwright.

"Yes, m'sieu. And M'sieu Archer arrived a few minutes ago."

"Ask him to come up."

In a few minutes Philip Archer came in; he shook hands with Beaumarchais.

"I have not delayed you, I hope," said Philip.

"Not at all; I have just this minute finished dressing. The rehearsal of my comedy does not begin for an hour. There is plenty of time. And now," as Philip sat down, "if you don't mind, I will have in one of my people." He said to Victor: "Let Maynard enter."

A few moments later there came a tap upon the door; a short man, round of face and body, entered.

"M'sieu," he said, "I am pleased you have come back to Paris. I have waited three days for you."

"There is news, then, Maynard?"

"Yes, m'sieu; news I feel sure will interest you greatly."

"But, first, tell me this: How does it happen De Chaulnes has returned and my people have not reported it to me?"

Maynard gestured with both fat hands.

"M'sieu," he said, with the expression of one grievously hurt, "he has been in Paris only a few hours."

"I should have known of his coming within a day after he set foot in France," said Beaumarchais.

"The ship came in at L'Orient," said Maynard, "and he left it in the dark of night; and he did not stop at an inn until daylight as a Christian man would, but immediately took horse and was off through the night for Paris."

"He saw Barreaut?" asked Beaumarchais.

"For one hour, m'sieu."

"Of what did they speak?"

"M'sieu le duc, so I am informed, was much excited. He had heard of the firm of Roderique Hortalez & Company while still in America; he had heard of Mademoiselle Desfourneaux being concerned in it. He was in a passion of anger; he cursed M'sieu Barreaut; they almost came to blows."

"What is the meaning of his return?"

"One way or another he is to interpose between Hortalez & Company and the King; he is to discredit the company if he can; in the end he is to destroy it."

"M'sieu le duc has large confidence in himself," said Beaumarchais, smoothing the sleeves of his plum-colored coat and looking with much satisfaction at the richness and roll of the collar.

"It would seem," said Maynard, "that Claridge & Company, with whom he is associated, fear the operations of Hortalez & Company will bring France into a war with England and so disturb both trade and credits."

"And, so, he will strive to destroy my work!" Beaumarchais smiled, but there was a glint in his eye. "I admire De Chaulnes as a hard-drinking, hectoring noble; but he must not plot with me, Maynard. Plotting is my trade. We must contrive some surprises for him, my friend."

Maynard held his fat sides and laughed.

"It is not for a wine-drinking duc to outwit you, m'sieu," he said. "Nor is it for a group of money-getting merchants who are his partners. We'll match them, m'sieu, as we've matched their betters before them."

"But, now," said Beaumarchais, "what news have you brought me?"

"Why," said the stout man, "it concerns these very people. The Duc de Chaulnes was closeted last night with Lord Stormont. I have been told but meagerly what was said, but all pressure is to be brought to bear to defeat your plans. Powerful merchants of Bordeaux, and Nantes, and Marseilles were

present and all gave their words against any act, secret or
open, that might lead to war with the English. Roderique
Hortalez & Company was spoken of bitterly."

Beaumarchais nodded, and looked at his watch.

"Have you these matters set down in writing, Maynard?"

"I have, m'sieu."

"Give them to Victor, who will lock them away." He took
his hat from the valet and also a slender cane of polished
wood. "And now, M'sieu Archer," smilingly to Philip, "we
shall be off to the theater."

They descended the broad stairs, the arm of the dandy
through that of Philip. A carriage was at the door; they
stepped in and were whirled away.

2

It was noon, at the Théâtre Français, with its protruding
pulpit-like boxes, its heavy chairs, its painted ceiling, the
lamps lighted only about the stage; and there and then the
lines of the famous comedy, *The Barber of Seville*, were spoken
for the first time. Here stepped the stout and irate Dr. Bar-
tholo, the simpering music master, Don Bazile, the lithe and
cunning Figaro; and at a high desk, the book of the play before him, a lighted candle upon either side, stood the author,
Beaumarchais.

As the comedy went on, the intrigue expanded, the characters showed an astonishing humanity. And the benches at
the sides of the stage and the chairs in the auditorium quite
near to it began to fill. The wits and fops of Paris, and the
critics who interested themselves in such matters, usually presented themselves at that time of day at the Comédie Fran-
çaise when a new piece was in preparation. They took snuff,
they stretched out their silk-stockinged legs, smoothed their
frills, and talked. And now, as the play unfolded, they were
aghast.

"I understood, m'sieu," said a pale young man who affected the airs of a scholar, to Beaumarchais, "that you had written a comedy. Here I plainly see all the elements of farce. The characters you present are clowns or stodgy bourgeoise."

"And," said an elderly fop, "the matter of the play seems different. It departs radically from the classic form. Your people should *tell*, in beautiful French, of the matters which concern them: instead, they *do* them."

"The dialogue is not in verse," said a voice out of the dimness, and from among a group which had come in only a short time before. "How can anything written in prose be a play?" It was the voice of the Duc de Chaulnes, and Philip Archer, who sat near the director's desk, nursed his knee and searched with his eyes in the semi-dark. "It is quite amazing that you should think a form such as this could be placed upon the stage of the Théâtre Français."

The players were resting, gathered in small groups about the stage; Beaumarchais smiled and leaned gracefully upon one elbow.

"M'sieu le duc," he said, "why must a play be like other plays to be acceptable to the Théâtre or to those who patronize it? Why must we be eternally bound by a tradition? Why should not a new view have its place?"

"A play," said the pale young man, leaning forward and appealing to those gathered on the benches, "is a play. When we've said that we've said everything possible concerning it. When an author makes a play unlike a play, it is no play."

A laugh went up; there was a renewed stretching out of silk-stockinged legs, a snapping of snuffbox lids, a gesturing with fine handkerchiefs.

"An excellent stroke!"

"When an author makes a play unlike a play, it is no play," repeated the elderly fop with a deal of gusto. "What more need be said? In that we have the fault of the matter punctured by the point of wit."

"Nothing could be better said," spoke a languid youth.

"What place have shopkeepers in a comedy?" demanded De Chaulnes from the dimness of the auditorium. A clapping of hands went about the group in which he sat. "Comedies are concerned only with the doings of the nobility."

"Must we remain firmly joined to what has been?" asked Beaumarchais. "Because a distant generation chose to base its stage upon the pattern of the Greeks, to adopt, shall we say, puppets as the characters of its drama—to set every history upon its platforms as it had set every other history—to make the smoothing of phrases, the declaiming of lines, the chief purpose of the theatre, must we go on doing the same? Is the stage not to advance, m'sieu? Must I, as a dramatist of this present day, put forward the wooden figures of convention? Must I repeat meaningless rhymed lines, forever and always, to gain your approval?"

There was a storm of utterances at this; some arose; there were hisses. The pale young man shook a finger at the playwright.

"What!" demanded he, "are we to have the rude doings and common thoughts of groundlings paraded in a place dedicated to art? It is barbarous, m'sieu!"

"That is not art which is mean and narrow. Are we to suppose," said Beaumarchais, "a man cannot think, or speak, or have experiences unless he wear a title? Are we to be told that all happenings of interest take place in palaces or châteaux, or within the spaces of walled gardens?"

While the playwright was speaking, a page entered; his step was hasty, and he went directly to the Duc de Chaulnes. At the first word De Chaulnes was upon his feet; and as he followed the page through the auditorium, Philip Archer also arose. There was something in the haste of the thing that caught his attention, and he reached the window-lit corridor beyond the auditorium as the door at the far end closed upon the Frenchman. And then he caught the quick, sharp rustle of silken draperies, and the click of high heels upon the floor: a voice called to him.

"M'sieu Archer!" He turned and saw the beautiful Madame Barreaut, her eyes shining, her white hand outheld to him. "Oh, I am so glad. I saw you there on the stage but had no opportunity to speak to you."

Philip bowed to her, his face cold; he made no attempt to take the outheld hand, and stood silent, his back to a long window that overlooked the street.

"You are surprised to see me here?" she said. "Indeed, I am surprised myself. I do not like France. I had thought, when I left Philadelphia, to go to New Orleans, or perhaps to Havana. But I must come here. John Claridge demanded it," lifting her delicate brows and smiling at him. "John Claridge, who thinks he is so like God, said I must come, and here I am."

Philip stood quite still and made no reply. As she talked and gestured and smiled so fascinatingly, he had a feeling of waste; all this beauty, all this charm was futile. It was impressed upon him that this mind which had all the appearances of quickness was dull. For here she was, working upon him as she had at first; experience had taught her nothing.

"What I endured in that city with its squabbling Congress, its rich Tories forever plotting, and no two people at agreement upon any subject! I could not bear it," said Madame Barreaut. "And then I made up my mind I would go, for any day the British might advance and take the city, and then I'd be unable to make away perhaps for months. So when John Claridge desired me to take ship for Paris, I did so."

"De Chaulnes seems to have been of the same frame of mind," said Philip.

She laughed; her beautiful teeth shone.

"M'sieu le duc was wretched there. He could not remain. For, do you see," lowering her voice, "Charlotte had gone. He was very unhappy. And so he took passage in a ship sailing from Boston. John Claridge does not wholly trust anyone," she said, guardedly. "He desired someone to observe De Chaulnes in any important movements he might make; and that is why I was commanded to follow."

Philip said nothing; he had turned partly from her and was looking out into the street. His spirit turned sick at her words. These people were like rats: slinking, suspicious, full of treachery.

"I sent messengers to your inn several times imploring you to see me once more," said Madame. "I felt I must convince you and show you the way to believe in me. Then word came that you had been killed: I was stricken to the heart. It was Gorman who brought the news. You had been shot, he said, in an episode of some kind in the bay. It was he who shot you, he said, and told just how he did it, and how you fell." She put her hand gently upon his arm. "But I am glad it is not so. For all you have thought ill of me," her lovely eyes looking up at him, "I am glad. I shall never forget the pain of that day when I called to speak to you. Never! You said little, but your look stabbed me. I wept," she said. "When I reached home, I wept for hours."

But Philip was not listening; for in the street below stood an open carriage with De Chaulnes beside it; within sat Henri Barreaut, and with him was Mr. Lazarus, looking shrunken and old, a yellow dispatch box held between his knees. A yellow dispatch box! Philip stared at it. It was just such a receptacle as had been in his sea chest, just such a one as held the little black book of Madame Fouquet.

As Philip gazed down at the group Henri Barreaut laughed; the yellow teeth of Lazarus showed in a thin-lipped grin, and the skinny fingers drummed upon the metal box. De Chaulnes, apparently in high good-humor, stepped back and waved his hand. Philip turned and ran through the corridor and in a few moments was in the street. But the carriage had gone; De Chaulnes had disappeared.

CHAPTER XXVII

IN THE days and weeks that followed Philip Archer searched Paris for Lazarus, but with no success. The police knew nothing of him; he was at none of the inns; no traders, or merchants, or shipping people who knew him by reputation had heard he was in France.

"Maynard shall find him," said Beaumarchais when Philip finally put the matter before him. "He is like a hound for following a track."

"But there is no track," said Philip.

"Never mind. Maynard shall find one."

However, the snow grew deep in the Paris streets; the ice in the Seine locked all sorts of craft in its cold arms, refusing to permit them to stir; and still Lazarus was unfound. Much progress had been made in the opening of the case of Archer vs. Barreaut-Claridge; old clerks and attorneys pricked their ears at sound of the names; old records and files were gone into deeply; the ancients of the mercantile world began to talk. But the councilors who had the matter in charge were dismayed when Philip told them of the loss reported in Brotot's letter.

"It is a calamity!" said one old attorney who had received the case with eager joy. "These documents are new in the matter; this book, sworn to and attested, as it was, before one of the judges of the King of Spain at New Orleans, would have had a great effect. To be sure, we can go on with hope of success; but with the documents of Madame Fouquet our labors would have been enormously less: we could possibly have proven corruption, violence, intimidation, forgery."

"I shall recover them," said Philip.

"Do so. In the meantime we will ask for a delay."

Spring came; the rivers of France were free; ships began to come and go. The doings of Roderique Hortalez & Company had reached an astonishing magnitude; vessels were gathered in this name in all the ports of France. Already cannon to the number of a hundred pieces had safely reached the armies of Congress; twenty-five thousand muskets had been distributed among the American regiments in the field; shiploads of uniforms and boots and blankets and gunpowder had been carried from the French islands into Charleston, Baltimore, and Boston.

Lord Stormont never rested in his protestations. Each packet from England brought him the complaints of the Prime Minister, Lord North, and of the King. Something must be done to prevent this trafficking with the rebellious colonies by the French; each cargo, they said, would add a million pounds to England's final bill. The two vessels captured by the sloop *Reprisal*, which had brought Franklin to France, were made matters of great complaint.

"England and France are at peace," said Lord Stormont, "and yet these rebels are permitted to bring in captured ships —whose takings were plainly acts of piracy, and the French courts go through a mockery of condemnation, stripping British merchants of their property."

The French foreign minister, De Vergennes, replied smoothly. He pointed to the laws governing such things, to treaties, to the difficulties of the separate tribunals, and the rights of nations at war.

"To be sure," said the irate Stormont, "the ship *Reprisal* is from America; but there are others of the same sort fitting at Nantes, at L'Orient, at Dunkerque. This is not to be tolerated; the British government has reached the end of its endurance."

"We have searched all vessels for arms whose presence in

our harbors was at all suspicious," said De Vergennes. "In a number of cases we have seized guns and other equipment."

"I have recently placed before you the matter of the firm of Hortalez & Company," said Lord Stormont. "This infamous concern has dispatched two more ships in the last week; more are loading; every aid and encouragement is being given to the rebellious subjects of the English King. And you do nothing to prevent it."

"My dear sir," said De Vergennes, in his perfect English, "the house of Hortalez is an old one. Its trade is legal, and according to the custom of nations. Their buying of matters of merchandise and sending them in their own ships to the French colonies is not a thing I can interfere with."

"The entire proceedings are a mask," said Stormont, bluntly. "The company is catering to the demands of a band of rascally ingrates."

"France cannot prevent a mercantile house sending out cargoes for trading with any nation, except such as might be at war with France. If you object to the traffickings of Roderique Hortalez & Company, my lord, the British navy is your redress. Blockade all American ports; then trading that has not your countenance will cease to exist."

2

Franklin, suave, adroit, made great headway at Paris; the King and his ministers favored him with increasing indulgence as the months went by. He missed no point of contact that would benefit his country; he was everywhere, he knew everybody; merchants, nobles, women of the highest rank in King Louis's court gave him their deepest sympathy and admiration; there was nothing that strong friends and willing ones could do that was not done. The King listened with astonishing readiness; as a rule public affairs bored him, and the surest way to win his displeasure was to persist in any matter that bordered on the serious. But to Franklin, and Franklin's friends, he was most obliging.

"Never a day passes," said one of his intimates, "that I do not grow more and more astonished. He is amiability itself upon this question of America. Franklin, I think, is a necromancer."

But, nevertheless, amiable as the King seemed, he held firmly to his caution. Though he was exultant at the rebellion of England's colonies, and gave much secret aid, still, beyond this he would not go. For while he favored anything that would weaken England, he did not, as has been said of him, favor revolts. Already the lower classes of France, stirred by the writings of Voltaire and Rousseau, were muttering under their breaths, and the court was not pleased, or made to feel any more secure because of it.

"Also," said the King, "did not these same Americans, some years ago, aid the English in driving my armies from Canada?"

Things of this sort made him hesitate; his generals, too, doubted the quality of the American militia; armed "peasants," they called them, disdainfully. Franklin, seeing the futility of furtive assistance over a long period of months, pleaded for an open stand upon the part of France, but his plea was denied.

"However," said the King, amiably, over a glass of his favorite wine, "if, in the future, the American troops show real ability, a treaty will be made. Let one of their generals win a signal victory, and France will come openly to the help of their country: with armies, fleets, and money."

3

Some nights later, Philip Archer was with Beaumarchais at Roderique Hortalez & Company; as they were talking, a secretary tapped upon the door.

"M'sieu Maynard urgently desires to speak with you," he said to Beaumarchais.

When Maynard came in he was obviously excited; he wiped his face with a broad handkerchief.

"I thank you, m'sieu," he said to Beaumarchais, "and am grieved if I have disturbed you in any important matter. But the affair of M'sieu Archer has come to a sudden head, and I felt I must speak with him at once."

Beaumarchais refreshed himself by drinking down a glass of wine that stood upon a table.

"Have I not told you?" he said to Philip. "Maynard will get track of them—no matter how clever they are."

"I was at your lodgings, m'sieu," said Maynard, "a half hour ago. But only to find you out. It occurred to me that you might be here, and I came swiftly."

"What news?" asked Philip. "What word of M'sieu Lazarus?"

"I have found him," said Maynard, his eyes gleefully upon Beaumarchais. "I have found him, though, to be sure, it was no small task." Beaumarchais, settled in an armed chair near a window, motioned toward the decanter, and Maynard deferentially poured himself a glass of wine and drank it. "In all of Paris there was no such person as this M'sieu Lazarus," he said. "I questioned many whom I thought might have chanced upon the name or the man, but no. 'A Jew!' they'd say, and then they'd shake their heads. They knew nothing of him. The servants at the house of the Duc de Chaulnes had heard nothing of him, nor the police; I spent a deal of time among notaries' clerks and people who do the common work of the courts of justice. Again, no. Once I went to L'Orient and fixed upon the people in the neighborhood of M'sieu Barreaut's mansion. I questioned his servants; but M'sieu Lazarus was a stranger to them all.

"It was then, when I returned to Paris," said Maynard, "that I began to give attention to M'sieu le duc. His acquaintance is large; he led me a devil of a dance, sometimes the whole night through. But yesterday he had a visit from M'sieu Barreaut, and somehow it grew in my mind that at last I'd be rewarded in some degree for all my vigilance."

"And you were!" said Beaumarchais. "You were, of course. Maynard never fails," he said, proudly, to Philip. "As I have told you, he has the scent of a hound."

"M'sieu is too good," said Maynard, highly gratified. "Late yesterday afternoon, after being together for some hours, the Duc de Chaulnes and M'sieu Barreaut entered a carriage and drove off. At once I gave a signal, and my own carriage, which I had waiting at no great distance, came up, and I followed them. Out of the city, along the roads to the south, and at last, coming on night, they drew up behind a screen of trees and sat watching an old house that sat some distance back from the road. They talked a great deal and pointed and conferred; at last they seemed to come to an agreement of some sort, and drove away.

"I did not follow, m'sieus. I knew the house contained something of interest, and so I inquired of a gardener who had paused to rest some little distance away with a barrow full of greens. I was right, m'sieu," bowing to Philip. "There was something interesting in the house. It is there that M'sieu Lazarus has taken up his residence."

CHAPTER XXVIII

THE evening's shadows were falling when Philip Archer pushed out of Paris along the road that led to Fontainebleau; there was a heavy drift of clouds along the sky, and the west had a deep red on its furthest rim. The horse the young man rode was a strong, long-winded beast, with a small head and hardy legs; and its stride carried it rapidly over the ground.

There was a chill in the air; Philip was wrapped in a boat cloak and had heavy gauntlets upon his hands; in the breast of his coat he carried a pair of dueling pistols which Beaumarchais had insisted he take in case of need.

"You are adventuring into a strange place," said the playwright, "and it is as well to be prepared. To be sure, Lazarus, as you've told me, is old; but he is not the only person you may encounter; there may be others, younger and far more dangerous, of whom you know nothing; and a loaded pistol at such a time is no bad thing."

It was an old way, this road to the south; armies had marched its length; great things had happened by its wayside; it was from this direction that the English came from the sea, the English with ranks of pikes, of lines of brawny bowmen, of squadrons of horse. Every King of France, from the time William of Normandy first shut his hand upon Britain, had kept an anxious eye upon the great road that met those which spun out their lengths from the cold, green sea.

In the first hour after dark there were many lights by the way, off in the fields, twinkling among the trees at greater distances; another passed, and the powerful legs of the small-headed horse showed no signs of slackening, nor the breath in his barrel-like chest any threat of giving way; the lights were fewer, and finally there were none at all. The road was deserted; the countryside was still. Philip had questioned Maynard closely and carefully as to the whereabouts of the house he had viewed the day before; the man's answers had been direct and easily followed.

"Only the darkness is against me," said Philip. "But in another hour there will be a moon: that will be of fine advantage."

He had, in the first two hours, covered a score of miles; in the third, all ahead being dense and threatening, he slackened his horse's pace; and when the moon at last shouldered its way above some trees upon a far-away knoll he'd added five more. Then came a village; he knew it at once in the white light; a tavern with a sign at the door of a stag with a coronet upon its horns. Philip clattered through the brief street, and, again out upon the open road, he saw in the distance a single square tower lifting out of some trees; and at that got down from his horse and tied it in a sheltered lane, off the high road; and he made his way across the fields toward the house.

It was a building of the sixteenth century, with a massive roof of gray slate; the moonlight fell upon it with a whitening touch; it stood out stark and ghostly in the silence. The driveway leading to it, Philip found in good condition; the broad stone steps to the front door were as solid as though put down a month before. There was a light in a high window on the second floor, a bright, unwinking light, yellow contrasted with the rays of the moon; and as Philip stood in the doorway he heard the deep baying of dogs a long way off.

He struck two blows upon the knocker; waiting a space, he struck two more. There was no reply. He stepped back into the driveway and looked up at the lighted window; it was yellow and glowing, but blank. Returning to the knocker, he struck sharply there was a note of irritation in the sounds, and they echoed across the fields eloquent of impatience. Still no one answered. He tried the latch of the door; to his surprise it was free, and the door opened under his hand. There was a great wide hall, bare looking and yawning, like the opening of a vault. The moonlight struggled into it, wanly. Philip advanced a half dozen steps, his boots rattling upon the floor, his spurs jingling. He called, but silence followed; he repeated the call, but the result was the same. His eyes, becoming accustomed to the darkness, showed him the huge loom of a staircase, wide, curving, with a massive rail; he felt his way to it and looked up. The great well through which the stairs ascended was dark, but upon the wall some distance above was a faint glimmer as though a small ray of light traveling from a distant point had flattened there, and stuck.

Philip considered a moment. Then he took out one of the long-barreled dueling pistols and set the hammer; and he began to ascend the stairs. There was a tall clock on the first landing, and its pendulum swung backward and forward monotonously. At the level of the second floor he halted; down a long corridor he saw a thin, perpendicular line of light; knew there was a door standing slightly open, with lamps or candles burning in the room beyond. With his pistol held ready he stepped down the corridor, his heels sharp, his spurs ringing; and he pushed open the door.

There were a dozen or more candles burning in the room, tall candles in holders of brass; it was a room with rich hangings and mirrors and pictures, a bedroom with a canopied bed at its far end. In an armchair before one of the mirrors sat Mr. Lazarus, a pistol lying across his knees; he had a basin filled with water standing beside him, water stained red, and he was wiping blood from his face with a towel. He turned his head as Philip entered the room, there was a tightening at one corner of his mouth that pulled it into a wry grin, and his hand fumbled at the grip of the pistol; then, as he stared, the hand fell weakly from the weapon, and there was a croak in his voice as he said:

"It's you, then! I had not thought to see you here. But you have come too late; an hour ago you'd been of some use, but now——" He pawed at the air with his skinny hands, then slid out of the chair, and lay face downward on the floor.

Philip lifted him upon the bed. There was a wound in the side of his neck where a broad blade had been thrust into it; it had bled a deal but did not seem especially dangerous. There was some water in a jug, and Philip cleansed the wound; then he tore some of the bed linen into strips and bound it up. He poured out a little brandy which he found upon a stand, and made the old man drink it.

"I was upon the floor," said Mr. Lazarus, "when I heard your spurs on the stones outside. I thought you were Henri Barreaut—returning. He left me, an hour ago, after driving his sword-blade through me, and I'd lain looking at the ceiling thinking my life had come to an end. But, when I thought I heard him coming back, I made up my mind not to die tamely. I got up, and took a pistol from under my mattress, and began cleansing the blood from myself. I thought to sit there, proudly, as though nothing had happened to me, and let a bullet into him as he came through the door."

Philip gave him more of the brandy.

"It was Henri Barreaut who wounded you?" said the young man.

"Yes," said Mr. Lazarus. "Henri, who is partner to John Claridge, and has charge of the firm's affairs at L'Orient. He has never been overfond of me," said the old man, with the twisted grin upon his lips, "for Henri, like the Claridges, does not care for those he cannot dominate. I suspected him when he came to me at the inn where I went after leaving the ship; he fawned and laughed too much for me to trust him. He followed me to Paris, and thrust himself upon me even there."

"Perhaps," said Philip and looked down at the broken figure upon the bed, "he knew what you'd brought with you."

The skinny old hands picked at the coverlet; the faded eyes opened and shut and opened again.

"You know it too, I see. But then I suppose Brotot has written to you. Yes, Henri knew what I had; a yellow dispatch box once belonging to Long Jim Archer and taken from the sea chest that also had been his." Here the old man laughed, a cackling, choking sound. "Henri tried to bargain with me," he said. "Even before I had obtained a lodging in Paris he took me to the Duc de Chaulnes, who also gave voice in the matter. But I baited them," said Lazarus, a look of glee in his eyes. "I made game of them. I laughed and jeered at them in my thoughts. And when I left Henri, he was convinced he would succeed. I led him on and on; sometimes he'd laugh; at others he'd scowl; and all the time he was hungry for my life."

"How did this man know you had the box?" asked Philip.

"That I did not know until to-night," said Lazarus. "Not until to-night when he sat in that chair, his naked blade in his hand, and told me. I had written a letter which he'd intercepted, and that letter told him all he needed to know."

"Some months have passed since you arrived in France," said Philip. "You had my property in your possession, and yet you made no attempt to find me."

"I had thought to see you at once," said Mr. Lazarus. "It was in my mind you'd taken steps to open your case in the courts, and that is why I'd crossed the sea with the yellow box. For in that," said Mr. Lazarus, "I'd found the book of Madame Fouquet, the secretly written, locked book, and read it with the utmost satisfaction. The papers, sworn to by her husband who was once secretary to your grandfather, are priceless to your cause. I knew this man; he was greatly older than his wife, a fox-like creature who knew many things, and told nothing. I can surmise what happened," said Mr. Lazarus; "she worked with him for years trying to get the truth, and only succeeded as he lay dying. The sworn word of this man would have been of huge value to you; the testimony of this woman would have been almost as great. I was persuaded of this, and for that reason came at once to Paris. But unforeseen matters came up; I was spoken to, gravely, by a person whose name I will not mention, and was prevailed upon to delay. I was cautioned to keep close, show myself not at all, and communicate with no one.

"But Henri is not easily beaten," said Mr. Lazarus. "He found me out and to-night as I sat sipping my warmed wine before going to bed, he came in quietly, and stood grinning at me."

"Have you no servants who might have helped you?" said Philip.

Mr. Lazarus gestured weakly.

"There are two old people, a man and wife; but Henri locked them up somewhere in the building before he came in to me. He told me so as he sat there, gloating. It was in his mind to kill me from the first," said the old man, "because if this had not been so he'd not have told me the things he did. John Claridge is in London." The old man watched Philip's face for his response to this. "Edward is also there; they sailed in a Spanish ship from New Orleans, but upon what errand I can only guess. Henri drank my wine and read a letter from Claridge in which he was bidden to find me at once. 'To the devil with your delay,' said John in his masterful way. 'Get me this old Jew, and have the things of him of which he has unlawful possession.' "

Mr. Lazarus laughed. The sound was like the croak of a crow; his yellow teeth showed themselves bleakly.

"Those were his words as Henri read them to me. The Claridges have always been stanch upholders of the law. Illegal things have always hurt them sorely. John Claridge knew the danger of the signed words of the husband of Madame Fouquet, and when Henri gained possession of them they were to be taken, with the little black book, to London.

"'The sensible thing to do,' said Henri to me, 'would be to build a fire of them there on the hearth; but John Claridge

would not be satisfied with that. He must see them himself;
his must be the hand that destroys them.' "

Philip settled the old man comfortably and then left the
room. In a sort of pantry at the back of the house he found
the two old servants, locked fast, and the key gone. He
splintered the door with an iron bar which he found in the
kitchen, releasing them. They cried out in dismay at the sight
of Mr. Lazarus as he lay so bloodless on his bed, all bandaged,
and with such pale, wide-open eyes.

"You will need a physician," said Philip to the old man.
"On my way back to Paris I shall search one out and send
him to you."

But Mr. Lazarus would not have it so.

"My servants shall bring me one if one be needed," he said.
"You have my thanks, M'sieu Archer, nevertheless. And now,
do not delay. I know you are anxious to reach the city and
spread the alarm among your friends. Good-bye to you, and
again my thanks."

Philip stood looking down at the old man, his mind full of
doubts; there was a deal he was not sure of, and there was
more he did not understand. But these things must wait.
Lazarus was in no condition for questioning; also, there was
no time, just then, to give to it.

He left the place; his steps were still sounding upon the
stones outside the door when Mr. Lazarus beckoned to the old
serving man with one bony finger.

"Pierre," he said, "go, at once, by the back way and knock
at the door of Jules, the woodcutter. Knock softly, mind you,
but have him up quickly. Tell him to saddle the best horse
and wait at the door for a message."

"Yes, m'sieu," said the servant, and went at once

And a little while later, while Philip Archer rode toward
Paris, another horseman with a message in his pocket, the ink
of which was scarcely dry, was headed away on the long road
toward the sea.

CHAPTER XXIX

DAWN was breaking over Paris when Philip reached there; and at once he went to the lodgings of Beaumarchais and astonished that gentleman by knocking sturdily at his door until he had him awake and up.

Huddled in a silken robe, the playwright listened to the young man's story.

"Before anything is thought of," he said, "we must have breakfast. Victor," to his valet, whom Philip's knocking had also roused, "M'sieu Archer will breakfast with me. An omelet, I think, some hot bread with butter, and some chocolate."

He dressed, groaning at the earliness of the hour.

"I detest the gray of the morning sky," he said; "it has a bleak unfriendliness that chills the heart. Night, now, I admire; the violet darkness sits well with me!—the small stars are cheery and encouraging. But morning, before the sun puts its color upon it, is a shuddering thing; it makes me think how the world must have looked when it was young, before there were any of the mellow, heartening matters we now have to help us."

They breakfasted upon the omelet and the hot bread and the chocolate; also there was a measure of red wine for each of them. And while they sat there, Beaumarchais's call to his spies went about Paris. Maynard was among the first; he tied his neckcloth and brushed his hat with his sleeve as he stood in the hall.

"I do not know what matters are abroad," he said in answer to the question of one of his fellows. "But they must be of serious moment to have M'sieu Beaumarchais stirring at such

an hour. Be prepared, my friends; there is a problem of more
than usual toughness ahead of us."

"I would venture that it is some discovery of Milord Stormont," said a second inquisitor, as he tied his breeches at the
knee in a more careful way than his hurry had permitted.
"That gentleman's anger is like a flow of lava. These Americans will be the death of him if he does not take care. A
man of stout habit can only bear with a given amount of
vexation, and he has had a deal more than his portion,
already."

In a few moments, more of the sharp-nosed fraternity had
assembled in the passage; and then Beaumarchais came out
to them.

"The Duc de Chaulnes is well known to you all," he said;
"as are his friends and business associates. Do you, Maynard,
take three men and watch that gentleman's house. Keep
your eye upon all who come and go; lose track of no one. If
there is anyone who seems about to venture upon a journey
of length, have him followed, and send word to me at once.
If you should chance upon information, no matter how slight,
that some one of the duc's intimates is traveling toward the
sea, do not delay an instant; that man must be traced and
kept sight of until I, or M'sieu Archer, whom I now present to
those of you who have not seen him before, have caught up
with him and have taken the matter in hand.

"To you, Capot," he said to a powerful-looking man with
a lowering face, "I entrust an enterprise with a deal more action. Take a carriage and make the best of your time to
L'Orient. Study the departures of all the shipping in the harbor; secure the help of what men you know in that port, and
keep a watch upon the house of the merchant Henri Barreaut.
If he or any of his people attempt to board a vessel bound for
England, prevent them. Use force, if necessary; search them
and bring me all papers you find upon them."

He spoke to others in a like strain, cautioning, abjuring,

directing; at the end of a half hour Victor appeared, bearing a tray upon which was a glittering heap of gold louis; these Beaumarchais counted out with careless freedom, dropping them into the hands of the men as he thought they'd need them.

"Be vigilant," he said, as a last word to them. "Let nothing or no one escape you. For the next fortnight I am to be always found here, or at the counting rooms of Roderique Hortalez & Company. And now, be off."

2

A week passed; ten days; it was a bright Sunday in the autumn when Philip Archer, shaving himself at a window, heard a great clattering of feet ascending the stairs. First one flight, then another, though the second was not taken at the same speed; the third was labored, but still with an effort at lightness; then there was a hard breathing at the door, a cough that told of distress, and a heavy hand beat upon the panels.

"Come in," called Philip, halting and turning his head so that he might see the door. It was instantly opened, and a stout man, wiping his face with a huge, figured handkerchief, stepped in. "What, Maynard!" said Philip. He proceeded with the remainder of his shaving in great haste. "What news?"

"M'sieu," said Maynard, panting, "pardon if I sit down." He dropped into a chair and breathed heavily. "Your stairs, they are steep and long; and I was in great haste."

"Something has happened?" said Philip.

Maynard nodded, and mopped his face.

"I went at once to M'sieu Beaumarchais's as ordered," he said. "He directed me here; I came in a carriage with four horses and a postilion, m'sieu."

"Ah," said Philip, washing the remainder of the soap from

his face and applying a towel vigorously. "You are going on a journey?"

"No." Maynard shook his head. "But, M'sieu Beaumarchais thought *you* might have the desire to do so. Listen," said the spy, "and brush your hair, and pull on your boots. You may be leaping down the stairs the moment after I have finished."

He had been watching the mansion of the Duc de Chaulnes, he said, and by devious ways had found that Henri Barreaut was there and meant to start that day for England. Philip had finished pulling on his boots; he took his pistols from the cupboard. "But," Maynard went on, "I knew they were cunning, and was not persuaded. A little later I found that the journey of Henri was but a blind, undertaken to hide the real messenger. That," said Maynard, "is Madame Barreaut, a beautiful woman from the French islands. She is a guest of the rich Comtesse de la Brillière, a noble woman noted for her friendliness with the English. The Comtesse departed for the coast a half hour ago, meaning to take ship to England. Madame Barreaut has gone with her. Also three of my men are following her."

Philip paced the floor for a moment or two. Then he said:

"I mean to take your carriage and proceed to Dunkerque. As soon as assurance comes as to what port Madame Barreaut sails for, dispatch a swift rider to me at once. Instruct him to go to the inn called the Casque d'Or; if I am not there, someone representing me will be, and any message left will reach my hands."

With eyes wide open, Maynard nodded his head.

"It shall be as you desire, m'sieu," he said.

Without a word more, Philip was hastening down the stairs; he sprang into the carriage, spoke to the postilion; and in a little space he had his back turned upon Paris and was proceeding through clouds of dust toward the port overlooking Dover Strait.

3

At the Casque d'Or, next day, Philip learned that Conyngham's ship *Surprize* was still in the harbor. He had his supper
at the inn; and then made his way along the waterfront. Some
boatmen were gathered under a burning lantern on a quay,
and he drew one of them aside and asked about the *Surprize*.
The man shook his head; there was suspicion in his looks as
he said:

"There are so many ships, m'sieu. I would not know how
to get you aboard any one of them in the night."

"This is an American ship," said Philip; "the commander
is a friend whom I desire to see."

"Ah!" The man's brows went up in the lantern light.
"M'sieu is an American?"

"Yes."

"In that case," said the boatman, "I can try to find your
vessel. Here is my boat, m'sieu," indicating the stout skiff tied
to the wharf. "If you will get in while I light the lantern,
we'll be off."

The man pulled leisurely, with the steady stroke of the
seasoned boatman.

"There is so much going and coming, m'sieu; so much that
one can pass no judgment upon, that one does not know what
to do. The English have their spies all about; a man cannot
step into a wine shop without finding one of them at his elbow,
with his questionings and his small pieces of money. The
Surprize is a ship that has many eyes upon her; and you will
forgive me, m'sieu, if I seemed none too ready."

They saw the lugger at anchor, well out in the harbor, a
bright light burning in her cabin windows. The watch upon the
vessel's deck was vigilant, and as the boat approached it was
hailed.

"Is that the *Surprize?*" inquired Philip, standing up in the
stern of the skiff. "I desire to speak to Captain Conyngham."

It seemed, however, Captain Conyngham was not then on board; but the lieutenant, Mr. Hodge, whom Philip had met in Paris, was called upon deck.

"The captain has gone ashore," said the lieutenant. "But, come aboard, Mr. Archer, and wait for him; he'll return, I know, before midnight."

Mr. Hodge was a thin-chested man, with a large, pale face. He talked of the unfortunate way of things; the vessel hadn't loosened a sail in months, or shotted a gun.

"The commissioners are at great expense maintaining her," said Mr. Hodge; "and money is a scarce thing with them. If it were not that Miss Desfourneaux has such a plentifully supplied purse we'd have to give up all thought of getting to sea. A wonderful young woman," said Mr. Hodge. He nodded toward the companionway. "She is below there, now, with her agent, M'sieu Constant, going over the accounts. A noble head for affairs," said Mr. Hodge; "if she were not a woman she'd be a financier, or a person high in the government."

Philip stood quite still, leaning against the ship's rail; the waters of the harbor broke in long, slow ripples, and the stars edged each of them with a cold light.

"Miss Desfourneaux is on board?" said he.

"Yes. She came some hours ago. It may be," said the lieutenant, "you'd care to see her. Shall I tell her you are here?"

"If you please," said Philip.

The man descended the companionway; and in a little space returned; with him was M'sieu Constant, whose plump, short body was filled with haste, and whose cherubic face was beaming with pleasure.

"M'sieu," he said, gesturing with his fat, white hands, "I am overjoyed. I have heard of you frequently, and it is now so unexpected." He shook hands with Philip. "Mademoiselle is also pleased. She is there," pointing to the companionway. "She is awaiting you."

At this Philip descended to the cabin; Charlotte was seated at the broad oaken table; there were papers strewn upon it, an inkpot, and several quills. The yellow light of a ship's lantern fell upon her red-gold hair; her arms were resting upon the table, her hands clasped, and the wide, beautiful eyes were lifted to him as he stood in the doorway.

"Please come in," she said. She extended one hand to him; he held it a moment, and then sat down at the opposite side of the table. "I am glad to see you," she said. "You have been a good deal in my mind since we were together in the *Nancy Blake*."

He considered her carefully; he marveled at her beauty and quietness, and at the stirring she created in his blood.

"I have been in Paris," he said. "And you have been there quite often, I've been told."

She looked at her hands held so tightly together, at the nails of perfect shape, at the heavy ring, with an emerald burning coldly in a golden bed.

"There was a deal for me to do," she said. "There were many pressing things that would not wait. I would be there for a day and then gone again."

He regarded her moodily; there was a something in both her voice and manner that touched him, a forlorn, wistful something that made him thrill with the desire to speak to her in a quieter, kinder way, to make her lift her eyes which he felt had tears in them.

"Perhaps," said he, "you needed help. If you'd spoken to me, I'd have been at your service."

He was right. There *were* tears in her eyes as she lifted them; they lay glistening in the quiet depths, and there was a small catch in her voice as she answered:

"No," she said. "What I had to do I felt myself able to accomplish. And," the perfect chin pointing outward in sudden firmness, "it was not a matter upon which I could call upon you for help."

"You have been, so I've gathered in various ways, purchasing and arming ships for the use of the colonies. I could have been of use to you in those things. I am experienced with ships; you'd have profited, perhaps, in speaking a word with me."

There was a gentleness in his way of saying this, a wistfulness in his eye that made her turn her head suddenly away; however, when she spoke again, her voice was quite steady.

"This is not your first visit to Dunkerque?" she said.

"No. Directly after leaving the *Nancy Blake* I came here."

"Upon business having to do with Claridge & Company?"

"Conyngham is a witness for me in the matter; I came to speak with him. To-night," he added, "I have come aboard his ship, also upon that business."

Her hands were moving among the papers upon the table, papers that crackled as she touched them.

"I suppose," she said, "your suit at law has taken up most of your time since you came to France?"

"It has taken all of it," said Philip. "Though I had hoped it would be otherwise. It was in my mind, once I had made a beginning, I could leave the matter to the councilors and the courts for a space, and then make away to sea in some ship that was in the service of Congress."

"You thought that," she said, and her beautiful eyes held to his face, steadily.

"In my quiet moments I have thought of little else," he said. "If I could not get command of a vessel, it occurred to me I might ship as a mate, or even as a seaman."

There was again a silence; her eyes were still fixed upon his face.

"It is possible," she said, "your visit to-night with Captain Conyngham—in part—has to do with that?"

But he shook his head.

"No," he said, "I am here solely upon the business I have against the Claridges. A serious thing has happened. The cravings of those gentlemen for my sea chest did not end with that day upon the *Racehorse*, brig. They have greatly desired at least a part of its contents; and Mr. Lazarus may be at the point of death because of it."

"Oh, no!" She was now upon her feet. "No!"

"He lies badly hurt in the old house a score or more miles outside Paris—a house," said Philip, "where he had remained—shall we say hidden?—for some time, at your request."

"What has happened?" she said, her hand held out in a gesture of pleading.

"As he had matters in his possession belonging to me, I went to him some nights ago. But Henri Barreaut had preceded me; he had wounded the old man with a sword stroke, and made away, taking what I desired with him."

She stood very still, her hands covering her face.

"Please call M'sieu Constant," she said. "I must go ashore —I must——"

Philip put her into a chair, for she'd gone suddenly weak. And he summoned M'sieu Constant. The round little agent was much alarmed at sight of her white face.

"Mademoiselle, you are not ill?" he said.

"We start for Paris to-night," she said. "M'sieu Lazarus has been attacked—he is badly hurt. Ask Mr. Hodge to get out a boat; we shall go ashore at once. If possible, send someone ahead to the inn with directions to my maid to pack my things. And order a traveling carriage."

"At once, mademoiselle," said Constant, much distressed. "At once."

He left the cabin, and they could hear his voice, lifted excitedly. The girl turned to Philip.

"They tried to take *your* life that night on the south road beyond Philadelphia; they killed the man at New Orleans,

years ago—the man you told me of. And now it is Mr. Lazarus!"

Philip told her of the work of Beaumarchais's spies, of how
Madame Barreaut was to carry the stolen book of Madame
Fouquet to England, of how he hoped to get news of the
packet ship she'd sail in, and, with Conyngham's help, take
her before she'd crossed the Channel.

Charlotte Desfourneaux grew whiter still as she stood under
the cabin lantern and listened to him. She knew the Channel,
that dark and moody strip of sea, tossed by winds, shadowed
by mists. And the frigates, the sloops-of-war, the swift corvettes that prowled here and there: dangerous, watchful
ships manned by hardy, ready men.

"This is no thing to venture your life in," she said. "One
may risk danger in a fine cause, with credit to himself; but in
this you'll have no credit, nor profit, either."

"I think," he said, "the only way a man may ease his soul
is by standing for what he believes to be right. And so long
as anyone with Claridge blood in him sits with the Archers'
share of that old Spanish money in his hands, just that long
shall my spirit be uneasy."

She took a step nearer to him, one hand held out in a pleading gesture.

"There is nothing, now, that you can do," she said. "No
matter what your efforts are, no matter what the judgments
of the courts, no part of the treasure taken from the *Vision
of St. John* can ever come to you."

The keen eyes, level, fearless, wide open, were upon her,
the wide mouth was set. What thought was in his mind, what
reply he meant to make, she did not learn; for just then the
voice of M'sieu Constant came from the doorway.

"The boat is waiting, mademoiselle," said the man. "And,
already, one has gone with your message to the inn."

She looked at Philip.

"Good-bye," she said.

"But not for long, I trust," said Philip.

"It may be," said Charlotte, "by the time we meet again you will have learned a deal more than you know, now. And," she said, the brown eyes troubled, and with shadowings of tears once more in them, "your desire to see me may be very much less."

CHAPTER XXX

THE bells of the town had already tolled midnight when Conyngham came on board.

"Now, God save us," he said, at sight of Philip, and grasped him by the hand, "what brings you to Dunkerque, and aboard of me, at this hour of the night?"

They sat down in the cabin with a bottle of wine between them, and Philip related the story of Lazarus, the stolen papers, and the proposed crossing of Madame Barreaut.

"Now, here's a thing," said Conyngham, his eyes alight, and his hands gripping the table edge. "Here's a thing to come to me with, and the harbor full of eyes that do be watching me night and day."

"I'd not care to bring danger upon you," said Philip. "If you are so closely watched as all that, there'll be small chance of getting out without a fight."

"Divil take you," said the Celt as he poured out more wine, "is it frightened of a fight you're getting to be? As soon as word comes telling the name of the packet, we'll up anchor and be away. And let those lift a hand against us who will."

They drank, and smoked, and talked until far into the night; and after breakfast next morning Philip went over the vessel. She was two-masted, with broad sails; a stanch-looking ship with lines of speed and an armament of guns that promised lively work when the time came for her to engage.

"I've waited too long already," said Conyngham. "Mr. Franklin urged me to be in no haste, as he wants nothing done that would compromise him. But land-keeping people're always overcautious. It has made my heart bleed to think of the rich ships that have gone up and down the Channel while I've kept my anchor fast in the mud of Dunkerque harbor."

They posted a seaman at the Casque d'Or, awaiting news from Beaumarchais. At the end of the second day they were rewarded; the man came hastily aboard with a youth, booted, spurred, and showing every evidence of hard riding. He handed Philip a letter written in the dramatist's bold hand.

"Madame Barreaut left Paris an hour ago in the traveling carriage of the Comtesse and her party. Their destination is Le Havre where they will board the *Essex Prince* for Deal. This vessel carries guns and is a well mounted, strong ship. The information I have of her is that she sails with the tide on Sunday morning."

"Sunday morning," said Conyngham, as he scanned the letter, "and with the tide. By five o'clock the tide will turn and the Sabbath day will be coming up out of the sea. From Le Havre to Deal, does he say? Well, God save us, she'll sail directly into our arms."

They raised the anchor as soundlessly as possible. With the mainsail and a jib outspread to the wind, they moved out of the harbor, silent, ghost-like under the moonlit sky, and in a few hours they were breasting the cold, rough water of the Strait.

2

The night grew blacker as it grew older; the violet look the sky had worn now changed to a starless gloom; the waves were running high under the whip of the night wind. More sail had been put on the vessel; Conyngham and Philip walked the deck, wrapped in heavy cloaks; the watch below were sound asleep in their hammocks, while those upon deck stood mindfully at their posts. The sky seemed far away; the wind hummed in the straining sails· the cordage vibrated, the blocks creaked and complained.

"No place can be blacker of a black night than the sea," said
Conyngham. "But it will soon begin to gray, and with that
the tide will turn. And then, if the wind holds, as I think it
will, the packet will come strolling along like a dandy out for
a morning walk."

As dawn approached, the wind rose; the seas grew larger,
and under the touch of the wind their crests broke in a vicious
whiteness. The gray in the east broadened and filled the whole
of the sky; the sun showed its rim above the lifting sea; and
then the *Essex Prince* appeared. Her sails were set with jaunty
confidence; three jibs were filled with boisterously pushing
wind, and her square sails were like white walls.

"A clean-looking ship," said Philip, watching her. "And
fast."

The *Surprize* gradually edged toward the packet, and in an
hour they'd dropped the French shore line almost out of sight.
Then Conyngham made directly for the other vessel. The
Surprize was a smart sailer, and the Englishman suspected
nothing; in a short time they were within gunshot, and the
tarpaulins were drawn from the brass pieces; the crew, on
deck for some time, were armed and stood in their places.

Conyngham himself sighted the first gun; a shot went dipping over the swelling sea and across the packet's bow. Her
decks at once fell into confusion; officers shouted orders, men
were hurrying to and fro. Then a second shot went growling
between her masts. The pine-tree flag was now flying at the
lugger's peak, and Conyngham's voice trumpeted across the
intervening space.

"Heave to," he shouted, "or we'll fire into you."

But there was a determined movement in the packet; a
long gun in the bow was turning upon a swivel to bear upon
the *Surprize;* then crash after crash came from the American's
brass pieces, and solid shot went swirling all about the *Essex
Prince*.

"There's nothing like a show of power to take the courage

out of a coaster," said Conyngham. "Look, they've changed
their minds about that long divil of a gun, already. Yes, and
there they come to, as gently as lambs."

The packet lay with flapping sails like a huge, protesting
gull, arrested in flight; already the lugger's longboat was
being swung out, and an armed crew was told off to pull to
the captured craft. Conyngham buckled on a cutlass and stuck
a heavy pistol into his bandolier; then the boat moved away
and soon set him aboard the *Essex Prince*. There seemed a
deal of parleying; the boat, after a space, returned with word
from Conyngham for Philip to come aboard the prize. And he
had no sooner crossed the rail than Conyngham spoke to him.

"Well, now, these people are the villains to deal with!
Never a sign of the Comtesse de la Brillière is there on board;
nor any of her people. As for your beautiful Madame Barreaut,
she never set foot in the ship at all, at all."

Astonished, Philip looked at the packet's commander, who
stood near by.

"The Comtesse and a number of others had arranged for
passage to Deal," said he; "but as they did not appear we were
forced to sail without them."

Conyngham drew Philip aside.

"He speaks truth," said the Irishman. "I've been through
the ship, and they are not in her." He laughed and shook his
head. "M'sieu Beaumarchais, so it seems, is not proof against
the cunning of these friends of yours. He can be fooled as well
as his spies. No doubt the matter was thought carefully out.
The *Essex Prince* was named as their ship when, as a matter
of fact, they meant to go, and possibly have gone, by another."

3

Philip and Conyngham spent some time in the cabin of the
packet discussing what had to be done. Then the master of
the *Surprise* inspected the vessel's papers to learn what man-

ner of cargo was stowed under her hatches. And a prize crew, under the third officer, was put aboard of her, with orders to take her into the Texel.

The lugger bore the captured packet company until past the middle of the day; then she drew away, and nightfall found her hovering close off the English coast.

"I knew this place well in the old days," said Conyngham. "There is a small cove with an entrance to it that's so narrow only a small boat can make way in it. The smugglers used it to run their wines and brandies into. At no great distance there are a fishing village and a tavern; from there you can make shift to find the London coach."

It was well past dark when Philip took his seat in the stern of one of the boats with Conyngham steering, and two men at the oars. There was no moon, but the stars threw their cold light upon the water; in a little while they were among the rocks, which lifted, black, slippery, and dangerous; but they won safely past these and into the cove which Conyngham had mentioned. The shore was silent and rugged, and when the boat's nose touched it, Philip sprang out.

"With good luck," he said, "I'll be in London to-morrow."

Conyngham shook his hand.

"You'll be seeing John Claridge," he said, "and when you do you'll be facing the cunningest of them all. So take care! And have a weapon always where you can put your hand upon it."

Philip watched the boat until it disappeared in the darkness; then he stood, his eyes upon the lights of the lugger; at last they began to move steadily toward deep water; then they disappeared, and he was left alone.

CHAPTER XXXI

PHILIP found the tavern which Conyngham had spoken of, a little place, with a sharp-faced woman in the bar attending to the wants of a group of men who looked like fishermen and coastwise sailors. He ate a good meal, and drank the sound Kentish beer, and smoked a pipe; and when he had reached this point he opened a conversation with the landlady.

"I am going up to London in the morning," he said. "Where may I get a coach? Somewhere near at hand, I hope."

The sharp-faced woman regarded him attentively.

"There is no coach here," she said. "You'd find one leaving Deal early in the morning if it'd be there was a packet in from France."

"Deal is quite a step from here, I think," said Philip. "But, possibly, I could get a horse, or a conveyance of some sort to take me there."

"At four in the morning," said the woman, "my son will be driving there in a pony cart; you could go with him if you'd be stirring at that hour."

Philip thanked her gratefully enough; and as he went to his bed under the rafters, a clean bed, with the linen smelling of lavender, he left word to be called in time for the pony cart's going. At three in the morning he was awake, and dousing his face with cold water; then he had a breakfast of oaten cakes and bacon, with a new egg, paid his score, and climbed into the cart that stood at the door. When he reached Deal he was fortunate in that there was a coach standing in front of the Kentish Arms tavern ready for the journey to Canterbury.

"There," said the red-faced driver, "we meet the coach to Rochester; after that, if it is your need, you can go on to London in the mail."

It was green country on the way to Canterbury, green and rich; the roads were good, and the cottages and villages had a peaceful look; men were plowing the fields; the farms spread out with the regularity of gardens.

At Canterbury the passengers were at their noonday meal in the George and Dragon, a huge, rambling old inn with a great array of peaked roofs and red chimney pots. Philip found himself at a table with a youngish looking man who spoke with a clever-sounding Scottish burr and wore a neckcloth of purple silk.

"The ale in Kent," said this young gentleman, "is so good a man desires only to sit him down, and agree to remain forever."

Philip had a tankàrd of the brew before him and was cutting long, well browned slices of meat from the breast of a fowl.

"Sir," he said, "I respect your taste. English beer of the South country has a flavor all its own. In Scotland, now, you've nothing to compare with it, I know."

The young man agreed with this.

"Ale is not fitted to the Scotch palate," he said. "We have a rugged country there in the north, and need a more ardent drink to keep out the cold and damp. The spirit that's in barley or corn, or other grains, is the spirit of cold places; there needs to be comfort in it of a night as one sits by the fire. We have little taste for wine, either, except when it comes concentrated in the way of brandy."

The Scot was an agreeable talker, had a cocky way with him, and seemed a person of means. Philip soon learned he'd been traveling in France, had landed the day before at Sandwich, and had ridden on to Canterbury to take the coach for Rochester. When the vehicle started they found themselves side by side on its top; and the young man was much edified when he found Philip was an American.

"To be sure, there are many like you, favoring the King's government," he said, nodding his head. "But, as God listens to me, I think you have the wrong of it. I have said this many times, and have been cried down; nevertheless, Mr. Burke, and Chatham, and various others think at one with me. Lord North and the King are men of no great minds, sir, and the burdens they have tried to put upon the colonies have no justice in them."

It was through some casual remark dropped by Philip that the Scot had perceived his nationality; and seeing his opinions, because of his presence in England, were taken to be Tory, he said nothing in contradiction.

"There are a many people in America who side with the King," he told his fellow traveler. "And I am surprised that you dare to be so freely spoken against him here in England."

"Why, sir," said the young Scotsman, "it is the privilege of the people of these islands to speak their minds whatever they might contain. If I see the mistakes of Lord North and hold that they *are* mistakes, who shall say I am not within my rights in saying so?"

"May I ask your name, sir?" said Philip.

"It is Boswell, sir," said the young man. "James Boswell, of Auchinleck, in Ayrshire. A traveler of some small pretensions, and with a smaller claim to scholarship."

They discussed many subjects: trade, politics, poetry, bookselling, science, as the coach journeyed along the road. The young man listened with rapt attention to Philip's tales of the East, of South America, of Africa, with its Moorish corsairs and its slave trade, of the sea round Far Asia, of the merchants of Java, of the Malayan Islands, of the West Indies. When they reached Rochester and got down to take their supper at a comfortable tavern, Mr. Boswell exhaled a great breath.

"You tell me astonishing things, sir," he said, "and you

have lived a most amazing life. And now I see it is not for me to claim credit as a traveler; after all you've gone through, I know no more of the world than a lad who has never left his father's house."

Next day saw them in London, and at Mr. Boswell's recommendation Philip quartered himself at the Miter Tavern, in Fleet Street.

"It is a place of quality," said the Scot, "and of no great expense. The wine and ale are good; and they roast a fowl and grill a chop in a way that'll touch your heart."

Philip found the Miter a roomy place, well aired, and with a landlord of the hearty English kind. He supped there, greatly to his satisfaction, and talked with a heavy-jowled man who had a deal of silver money in his breeches pockets, which he rattled with comfortable satisfaction.

"There are many Americans who have sought refuge in England now that matters have gone so badly in the colonies," the heavy-jowled man told Philip, classifying him much as Mr. Boswell had done on the coach. "However, you'll have no great while to remain a refugee; for the King's government has taken the whole matter smartly up, and it will be over and done in another twelve months."

The landlord of the Miter agreed with this.

"The army and the frigates are great persuaders," said he, "and will do a deal; but after all it is the traders, and traffickers, and merchants who regulate any affairs that come up between commercial countries. A thing happened only the other day," said the host, an expression of great sagacity upon his broad face, "that told me much. There arrived at this inn no less a person than the head of one of the most important mercantile houses in the rebel country. He has been closeted for hours at a time with government officials, and with commanding persons of his own sort who trade from London; matters of consequence are brewing," said the landlord, nodding his head. "I would not be at all surprised if news of a large movement did not reach our ears before a day or two."

Philip swirled the ale in his tankard and looked at the host of the inn.

"A great merchant from the colonies," he said. "It would not be one of the Claridges, by any chance?"

The man chuckled and wagged his head.

"There now!" he said to the heavy-jowled man. "You see I've made no mistake in the standing of my guest. At once our young friend here has him in mind and calls him by name. It is John Claridge and none other," he said to Philip, "and his nephew, who I believe is in the business with him, bears him company."

Some time later Philip sat smoking at a window of the tavern, cogitating, and wondering at the sharp stroke of chance that brought him to the same hostelry as John Claridge and Edward. And while he sat there young Boswell, dapper, perky, and looking greatly interested, came in.

"Now," said the Scot, greatly pleased, "this is most fortunate. Only this afternoon, speaking with some friends, I mentioned the tales you told me atop the Rochester coach; they were quite mad with interest, and all desire to meet you at supper to-night."

But Philip shook his head.

"I'm afraid," he said, "much as I'd like it, my stay in London will be too short to give any of it to social things."

But Mr. Boswell was persistent.

"You will have the opportunity of meeting some rare people here in the Miter," he said. "Scholars, statesmen, artists; Mr. Garrick will be present—Mr. Garrick of the theater in Drury Lane. Also there will be Sir Joshua Reynolds, who paints as well as anyone; Mr. Goldsmith will be there, and Edmund Burke. And I am quite sure of Dr. Johnson."

Philip considered. The prospect was a pleasant one: a gathering of notables such as this was not to be met with every night.

And at his own inn! So, to the gratification of young Boswell, he consented.

"They'll take great pleasure in your company," said the Scot. "Some of them have traveled a deal—Dr. Goldsmith is one—but none have seen the strange lands you tell of. It will be a delightful evening."

2

That night, at about eight, the supper room at the Miter was lit with candles and lamps and thronged with the wit and quality of intellectual London. Philip came into the room with Boswell and was presented here and there. At the young man's right hand was an old fop, wrinkled and shaking, but curled, scented, and marvelously held up by stays.

"By Gad!" he was saying, "it's in my mind most of them are here to listen to Johnson talk. He draws them from all directions. If you could pack them into your theater, Garrick, as he does into a supper room, you'd be a prince for wealth in a year or two."

"That," whispered Mr. Boswell to Philip, "is Horace Walpole. How astonishingly he holds his years. Mr. Garrick, of course, you've heard of: the manager of Drury Lane, and the interpreter of tragic rôles. But here, now, I'll present you to the doctor." The music had ceased, and Mr. Boswell leaned over an unwieldy old man who sat in an armchair, and said: "Dr. Johnson, may I present to you the American of whom I spoke to you this afternoon: Mr. Archer?"

Philip looked into the broad face, blotched by disease, and red and jowely through heavy feeding; the mouth had a quarrelsome look, the eyes were intolerant, and yet, somehow, there was that about the old man that was pleasing.

"An American," said Dr. Johnson. "And pray, sir," to Philip, "what are you doing in this country which your people have used so vilely?"

He was so like a surly, overfed old dog that Philip smiled.

"I am here on some matters of business," he said. "As you know, the war has greatly upset things with us. And our people, also, consider themselves ill used and say the favors they've asked were small ones and easy for the King to grant."

"Sir," said Dr. Johnson, "they are a race of convicts and ought to be thankful for anything we allow them short of hanging."

There was a burst of laughter at this, and a great stirring and lifting of voices.

"Never mind," said Mr. Boswell, somewhat mortified, and drawing Philip away, "here are Sir Joshua and Mr. Burke: they will not say the same to you."

The clever-looking portrait painter and the tall statesman bowed to Philip and shook his hand.

"This is one of the doctor's bad nights," said Sir Joshua. "Do not give him any particular heed. Like as not if you'd see him to-morrow he'd be as sweet as new milk."

"It is a dire burden," said Burke, "to have been born a Tory. It brings fine minds down to a narrow crabbedness, and the treasure of intellect is all but wasted."

Philip met other notables; also a few men in the government, who inquired anxiously as to the state of things across the sea.

"In my opinion," said one earnest young man, "the solution of the matter rests with men like you, sir, who are Americans and still hold stanchly to the King's right to impose laws." Philip said nothing in reply to this, but stood trifling with his watchguard, and the earnest young man proceeded: "Only a half hour ago I had the pleasure of speaking to another American who holds the same sort of opinions—Mr. John Claridge."

There was an eagerness in Philip's eye, and he had difficulty in keeping it out of his voice.

"I have heard of Mr. Claridge," he said.

"He has been in London for some weeks. All during that time I have been trying to see him; and my efforts have been without result until to-night. His health has not been good, and he has denied himself to everyone. But the admiralty office has been interested in getting his opinions, and I kept trying." The earnest young man looked more earnest than ever. "He is quite downcast, sir; and I have heard his affairs have received some appalling blows. But he is a man of courage, and in a short time, he hopes, this folly they call a revolution will come to an end."

Philip fell to questioning the admiralty office young man; the manner of this was casual; he had an offhand air. There was, so the young man told him, a side staircase, and upon the second floor, directly facing it, was the door of a sitting room, and in that room John Claridge was installed with his papers and received those visitors he desired to see.

"I had made up my mind it was no use requesting to speak with him," said the young man, "and awhile ago I went directly up and into the room without so much as saying by your leave to anyone. And why not?" as Philip nodded his approval. "Was I not upon government business? Was there anyone with a more rightful claim upon this gentleman's attention than myself?"

"He was in a downcast mood, you say?" spoke Philip.

"Yes," said the young man, "and he acted strangely. He has odd mannerisms and a disordered way of presenting his ideas." The young man rubbed his chin in a puzzled way. "To say the truth, I made little of him."

Some time later, when the admiralty official had left him, Philip found himself in the wide hall. The idea of a side stair-case interested him greatly; John Claridge installed behind a door facing it, upon the second floor, occupied his attention. Philip loitered beside the huge fireplace, wondering what he might do, when the street door opened; there was a sound of voices, low-pitched, hurried, and anxious. Then out of a flurry of talk there appeared a woman, wrapped in a traveling cloak, a porter upon either side; Philip drew in his breath sharply as he caught sight of her, and shrank back into a shadowy angle beside the fireplace. The woman was Madame Barreaut!

3

The side staircase was curving and seemed long because of its narrowness; and the second floor was quiet after the many voices sounding on the one below. The door facing Philip stood partly open, and he paused before it.

"I have suffered," he heard Madame Barreaut say; "I have endured so much I wonder I have the restraint to speak to you at all. I wonder I do not——"

"Just a moment!" It was the cold voice of Edward Claridge that interrupted her. "Suppose you alter your tone a trifle. You should know by this time we are not accustomed to have anyone approach us in that spirit."

Philip heard Madame Barreaut laugh: a shrill, lifting sound that carried contempt and bitter anger.

"You have been accustomed to dealing with sheep," she said. "You have been small gods among a mild people. If I have ever spoken to you in any way that has made you think I am one of these, I am bitterly regretful."

It was John Claridge who now spoke.

"We have always managed our affairs so as to retain the necessary grasp upon those dealing with us," said he. "And that grasp has been upon you, my dear, whether you know it or not."

Philip heard a sound of a chair being pushed back. Madame Barreaut had been seated and had now arisen.

"All you know about my attitude toward you has been based on what I've said and what I've seemed. My thoughts, John Claridge, have been my own."

"I have not," said John Claridge, "any large interest in your thoughts. Since you have been with us you have carried out what instructions have been given you: that is enough."

There was a rustling for a moment among some papers, then he went on. "Here is a letter written by the Jew, Lazarus, to my niece. I will read you a part of it:

"'I have found the manuscript book, in the sea chest of Philip Archer; it will be rare testimony at the trial; also there are some papers that are part and parcel of it. These were no doubt the matters Hasty sought when he tried to gain possession of the chest aboard the brig Racehorse. The statements of the excellent Madame Fouquet as contained in this volume are priceless! At last something fresh has come into the great case of Archer-Claridge-Barreaut. Madame Fouquet's husband was a wretch! What perfidy! What abandon! While he served the Archers as a man of business, he also was in the pay of the Claridges. It is unspeakable! The infamies he witnessed and countenanced, and which these documents describe, he confessed to his wife when in fear of death. They will startle any court in which they are produced.'"

The voice paused; and after a moment John Claridge said:
"We understand this book and its accompanying papers were handed to you in Paris. Have you brought them?"

There was a sound that indicated Madame Barreaut had thrown the book upon a table; a rustling of pages followed, and John Claridge laughed.

"Won!" he said. "Won again. By God, the Claridges for luck!"

"Perhaps foresight would be a better word," said Edward Claridge, his cold voice holding some of the warmth of satisfaction. "Vigilance: care. We had all the things the Archers lacked." He laughed, and then added: "With this testimony of the Fouquets they had a fresh chance; but with its loss that chance has gone. This last whelp of the breed will curl up as the others have done, and we'll be bothered with no more of them."

Philip's face was set and hard, his eyes were like agates; he put his hand against the door and was about to push it wide, when Madame Barreaut again spoke: and something in her voice made him pause.

"You are taking great comfort to yourselves," she said, bitterly. "As usual, you are sitting back, thinking to enjoy the ease the work of another person has brought you. You have always had people like Hasty, like Gorman, like myself to fetch and carry for you; and you've always credited yourselves with vigilance, with foresight, and care. The Claridges have been a race, say you, who have always been keen enough to know their own, and have had the courage to take it. I have watched you and listened to you," said Madame Barreaut, contempt now added to the bitterness in her voice, "and I have come to think so little of you that I am amazed I've been able to contain myself so long."

"If you do not control that tongue of yours," said Edward Claridge, "I'll see if I cannot do it for you."

"I have very little belief in you, Edward," she said. "You are one of those whose pose promises a deal; but I ceased expecting anything definite from you, some time ago."

"By God!" said John Claridge, "you'll leave the room! I'll speak definitely to you in the morning." Philip heard her laugh.

"It was in my mind as I crossed the Channel," she said, "that I'd spend with you only the time it took to say what I have to say. When I tell what I came to tell, I'll go readily enough. And I'll have nothing to say to you thereafter." There was a pause; then the woman resumed. "You think I crossed from France to bring you the papers of Madame Fouquet. I have brought them. There they are, but they are worthless! And I would not have budged an inch if I had carried *them* alone."

"There is something else, then?" said John Claridge.

"Henri Barreaut has no complete idea of how matters are with Claridge & Company in the colonies," said Madame Barreaut, "and things have happened in France which he has not dared to tell you. He has not mentioned the sums of

money Charlotte Desfourneaux has drawn from his branch of
the firm, and which he had not the courage to refuse her."

"Money!" said John Claridge. "Money!"

"We already know of this," said Edward Claridge, coldly.
"The two millions of livres she spent in the adventure of
Roderique Hortalez & Company have been written against
her name."

"Two millions!" Madame Barreaut laughed. "If that is all
you know of the matter, Henri has indeed a tale to tell you.
That was only the beginning. Since then she has called upon
him for treble that sum, to be paid into the hands of this jack-
in-the-box, Beaumarchais."

"No!" cried John Claridge, his voice lifting to a shriek.
"No!"

"And then the ships, the agents, the spies! She had bought
dozens of vessels to sail under the flag of Congress. One she has
had built at Nantes, a frigate that, fully armed, must have
cost a million, alone."

"She has not dared!" said John Claridge. "Henri Barreaut
has not dared!"

"Henri Barreaut has dared as much as you have—no more,
no less. When Charlotte demanded large sums of money he refused to give them, as you did, in Philadelphia. When she spoke
of the law courts he did what you had done—changed his mind;
and the bills she drew were all honored. What mice you have
been!" she said, bitterly. "All of you! And then you talk of
your foresight, your vigilance! One girl took the upper hand of
you; in spite of your bullying, your posing, your conceit, she
did what she liked with you. When she spoke of the law courts
you cringed in your minds; you knew you had been operating
for years upon her money alone, and dreaded the fact becoming
known."

"It would have been ruin!" said John Claridge in a shaking
voice.

"If you had taken the matter competently in hand a year

ago, you'd have saved yourself. I told you then what the result would be if this girl were not put down; but you delayed and fumbled, you permitted your opportunities to pass. You were afraid of discovery."

"If it had been a man," said John Claridge, "I would not have hesitated an hour."

"Your father, or grandfather, would not have hesitated were it man or woman. For all your posing, you are weak-hearted. The law frightened you. And what I warned you of has come to pass. The firm of Claridge & Company is done; it is wrecked; it has not one piece of gold money left, or one ship it can call its own."

It was at that moment Philip Archer opened the door. He saw John Claridge, his death's face yellow and old, the thick, smoothed mass of hair gleaming in the candlelight, one shaking hand lifted; he was about to speak, but the words died upon his lips at the sight of the young man.

"Bad news," said Philip. He smiled at them, his hawk's nose curving, his eyes glinting upon each side of it. "Wreck and ruin. By God, I'd not thought such a deal of plotting could come to such an end." He nodded to Madame Barreaut, who stood erect, her beautiful eyes ablaze, her lips set, and then indicated the small black-covered book, a number of papers tied to it, which lay upon the table. "These are the things taken from Lazarus, I think." He stepped to the table and quietly put them into his pocket. "I hadn't thought to win them back so easily."

And then he looked at the Claridges, who had not moved or spoken.

"Ruined!" he said. "What a stroke to come out of a sky like yours! The news will make a stir in America when it becomes known. And I suppose it will have spread through the French ports before now."

The smile was still upon his face; he nodded to each of the men, and bowed to Madame Barreaut.

"Good-night," he said.

He had turned toward the door which stood open, as he had left it, but the voice of the woman stopped him.

"You are going back to France?" she said. "You are going back to *her?*"

"In the first," said Philip, "you are right. And I say, plainly, I wish the second were as true."

"You love her," said the woman. "You have loved her from the first. I could see it in your face when you looked at her. I could hear it in your voice when you spoke your insults to me." She came quite close to him; the beautiful eyes narrowed, her hands were clenched. "I hate you for what you've said to me; I hate you for the way you've looked at me. Go back to France; go back to her: but take this with you. This money your people have striven for, and which you hoped and planned for, is gone. You'll never touch a piece of it. It is gone, squandered by Charlotte Desfourneaux."

The smile did not leave his face; his eyes went from one to the other of them. When he spoke there was good-humor in his voice.

"Oh, well, if it is gone, I'm well content. It could be sunk in the sea, and I'd never grieve a moment over it."

He was turning toward the door when he suddenly found Edward Claridge standing before him. He did not pause an instant, but was upon the man like a panther, and struck him down. John Claridge grasped the bell rope and pulled it violently; Philip nodded, smiling, to Madame Barreaut and started leisurely down the stairs.

CHAPTER XXXII

AS PHILIP ARCHER went down the stairs at the Miter Inn, he heard the raging of the bell as John Claridge jerked at its cord; he heard the voice of Madame Barreaut lifted in a scream. The waiters and porters in the passage were much agitated.

"What is it, sir?" asked the landlord, startled out of his composure. "Has anything gone amiss?"

"They have had a slight accident of some sort upon the next floor," said Philip. "It is nothing much, perhaps you'd better have someone to inquire into the matter."

"Thank you, sir," said the host. "I shall do so."

Philip went down the full length of the passage, with no one paying much heed to him; at the street door he paused upon the broad stone step, looking up and down the street; there was a hum of voices, hurrying footsteps sounded; a window was thrown open, and a loud voice demanded the presence of the watch.

A number of chairs and chariots stood before the door; at the end of the line was a carriage with a pair of clever-looking horses, and a coachman sitting stolidly in his place. Philip stepped to the carriage side, and a heavy pistol showed in his hand.

"My friend," he said to the man, "while you are waiting you may as well be of some service. No harm will come to you if you are silent and drive away promptly. If you do not, there is a slug in this barrel that will rip your vitals sadly." He stepped into the vehicle, the weapon in plain view of the frightened coachman.

"Where to, sir?" said the man. "If you have any particular place in mind, give it a name."

"Take the straightest and best road to Rochester," said Philip. "And mind yourself, for I know the way, and the slightest divergence from it will cost you dear."

2

The night slipped by, and the miles with it; farmers' carts were rolling toward Rochester Town, with the first streaks of gray lighting the road, when Philip stepped out of the carriage, gave the relieved driver a piece of money, and saw him started on his journey back to London. The young man entered the town on foot, breakfasted, secured another conveyance, and was off without delay toward the sea. But he was afoot again, and some distance past Faversham when night again covered him; and he saw the stars riding high above that broad stretch of water which marks the Thames's contact with the sea. There were a number of small craft at anchor in a sort of estuary; he waded out to one of these, unfurled its worn sail, lifted the anchor, and in a short time had cleared the land and was headed away toward that great point jutting out toward France—a point Jean Bart liked to hover about in days gone by.

He rounded this in the dim of the early morning, and made away through a mist into the straits, the old sail pulling faithfully. Now and then he'd dimly see the loom of a passing ship, but none near enough to notice him; then, suddenly, as he sat huddled in the stern, holding the craft on her course, he heard a hail, and a swift-looking cutter came out of the fog.

"What boat is that?" demanded a man on the deck of the cutter.

"Name, *Alice*, sir; out of Deal," he replied, promptly.

"Come alongside; we want a word with you," said the man.

The haze was fitful; sometimes the wind got under it and ripped it asunder; again it settled and hid the face of the sea completely. As Philip sat considering what to do the mist thickened; he trimmed his sail and made away into it. He heard voices from the cutter, evidently shouted directions to him, then there was a long pause. He held on, hoping he'd have distanced the craft completely by the time the fog lifted again; but suddenly, as though whipped aside by the hand of a magician, it fell away. He saw the cutter at some distance, her crew gathered at the rails. There were shouts which he did not heed, then the report of a gun. The shot dropped across the intervening seas; then there was a crash as the iron missile struck his bow; the boat plunged and filled and he was left struggling in the water. A pair of long sweeps floated loose; Philip grasped them and held on; the cutter's head turned toward him; and then the mist came down once more.

After a half hour he heard the water rippling around the vessel's foot as she passed close by. The mist held to the water for the best part of an hour; then the sun's rays stabbed through it, and in a very little while began to dissolve it. It was still hanging in ragged shreds, the ends trailing in the sea, when Philip heard the familiar hum of wind through cordage, and the slatting of sails. There was a shout, and the sound of running feet upon a deck. He knew he'd been seen and turned his head; but instead of the cutter there was a small sloop, smart, ably handled, and, a glance showed him, of American build. There was another shout; a line came uncurling toward him; he grasped it and was hauled on board.

3

Philip had a stiff drink of rum and hot water handed him as the officers and crew of the sloop gathered about. The vessel was the *Perch*, of the Massachusetts state navy, a swift craft with a few guns and making for any French port she could slip into. There was an affable young man named Austin, apparently a passenger, who provided Philip with clothes while his own were drying, and who smoked a pipe, and seemed much pleasured by the whole proceedings.

"We thought to get into the Texel, or Dunkerque; but the British armed craft are up and down in a state of great activity. One would think they had the places blockaded."

The crew of the *Perch* were a well-looking lot, and the little vessel stood up under her huge dress of sails like a dancer balanced upon her toes.

It was not long until Philip found she was upon a mission of some sort for the Massachusetts Board of War.

"We have had some news in France of how matters are going in America," said he to the sloop's master, "but there have been many things left to uncertainty. A few days ago a rumor came that the British had taken Philadelphia."

"I am sorry to say it is true," said the captain, a hale little man with a round, bald head. "Washington's onfall at Trenton was a great blow to Howe; for the Hessians and Brunswickers were a sad loss to the English army. And the American victory at Princeton made him feel no better. So, baffled in New Jersey, the British took ship to the Chesapeake, then moved toward Philadelphia. Washington advanced his force, but he was beaten at the Brandywine and fell back to the heights above the city, where he now is."

"That will be a blow to Dr. Franklin," said Philip, shaking his head. "He cannot believe the city was ever endangered."

The master of the sloop gave many details of the fights around the capital city, and the condition of the patriot troops who had mounted their pieces of cannon among the hills. Also, there were many episodes at sea; privateersmen were gaining fine victories; state vessels were getting alertly into action, carrying the new flag to many places; national ships were putting marks upon Britain's ocean traffic that would long be remembered.

"If I were younger," said the captain of the *Perch*, "I'd go harrying the sea. There are merchantmen so fat with goods among the islands, it makes a man's mouth water to think of them."

The vessel's wake could be seen traced whitely upon the water; and Philip leaned against the rail and watched the waves tumbling joyously through Dover Strait. As he stood there the sound of gunfire came from a distance.

"A battle!" said young Austin, who was pacing the deck. "The work, it seems," nodding to Philip, "is being carried forward even here."

Philip, as he stood listening to the far-off voices of the cannon, pictured Conyngham in the *Surprize*, or John Paul Jones, that burly, hard-jawed little man with the unflinching eyes; Wicks in his swift brig, or one of a dozen other hardy adventurers, prowling in the shadows of England's cliffs. He looked at the blue sky with its gigantic billows of white cloud; away in the distance sea and sky met; there, ships were maneuvering with colors flying; shrewd hands were at the sails, keen eyes were behind the guns.

He turned into his bed that night heavy and depressed. However, next morning with the French shore in view, the bright, new air in his nostrils, a sense of ease came to him; in the deeps of sleep his spirit had been quieted. The plunder of the *Vision of St. John* was gone; it had passed completely; it would never vex him again. He drew his tall body up to a fine new height. He was free. The feverish watches, the desperate hopes, the perilous adventures that had tormented his people for a half century, were past. The old rages were done; the frantic, futile journeys, the days and nights of planning, of cursing and striding up and down. The bitter thoughts of revenge were at an end.

"I offer thanks for it," he said to the surging wind and the high sky. "I now stand where I have not stood before: and who knows what may come of it?"

The spires of Nantes became sharply visible in the afternoon; and in the evening they entered the roads. Next morning, the sloop being a small one, they set about ascending the river; with the mainsail and a jib drawing, the *Perch* made her way through the anchored craft which were discharging and taking on cargo. They passed a ship—a gleaming new ship with tall masts raking splendidly, a swift, low hull, armed with batteries of twenty-four-pounders: she was like a pantheress at rest, beautiful in line, and terrible in the suggestion of power.

"What vessel is that?" said Philip to the pilot they'd taken on board.

The man shrugged his shoulders.

"She is called the *Sun of India*," he said. "She was built in Nantes, m'sieu, and put into the water a month ago, and her masts and guns went into her at once. She does not belong to the King. It is said she is American, and that an American woman paid the shipbuilders for their work. But," and again he shrugged his shoulders, "no one is sure. These are strange times. One knows but little about anything."

After the sloop had been moored, Philip had young Austin dine with him at an inn. They had a baked fish, a roasted pullet, and several flasks of Burgundy; and in the midst of the drink, Austin leaned across the table and became confidential.

"My errand in France is an urgent one," he said, "and I have spoken of it to no one because my instructions were to exercise great care." He cleared a space upon the table and set his elbows therein; and he blew out clouds of smoke from the Virginia tobacco he was smoking. "I am," he said, "secretary to the Massachusetts Board of War, as you've heard, and carry news of high importance to Dr. Franklin. It is necessary that I reach him at Paris without delay; and knowing but little of the language here, and nothing of the French people or the roads, I should like, if it were possible, to get the aid of someone who'd be of assistance in these things. If you are going on to Paris, as I've heard you say once or twice you meant to do," said Austin, "and if you will not be too long delayed, I shall be greatly pleased to bear you company."

"My own affairs are of a nature that needs some haste," said Philip, "and I mean to make a night journey of it. If you can get matters in order for yourself within an hour or two, let us travel in company, by all means."

Much gratified, young Austin made haste on board the *Perch* to pack his belongings. Philip sat at one of the windows of the inn, smoking and turning matters over in his mind. The frigate he'd seen in the roads kept in his thoughts; her towering masts and broad yards, the lines of speed, the powerful guns. The *Sun of India!* That could not be chance; there was an intent of some sort in the naming of the craft after his grandfather's old sea hawk. "An American woman paid the shipbuilders for their work," said the pilot. That same woman, then, gave it its name. A woman with rich, coppery hair, and wide, beautiful eyes; a woman with a voice so stirring that even the memory of it——

A waiter spoke to him.

"You are M'sieu Archer?" said the man. "Thank you, m'sieu. There is a gentleman who much desires a word with you. He is ill and begs you to come to him. Shall I show M'sieu the way?"

CHAPTER XXXIII

PHILIP followed the man upstairs and into a room filled with the warm western sun; and deep in a great pillow, upon a settee, he saw the drawn, wrinkled face of Mr. Lazarus.

"I heard your laugh a little space ago," said the old man, his wasted hand lifted in a gesture of greeting, "and thought I could not be mistaken. It had the same ring to it your grandfather's had, years ago, when I first saw him, in New Orleans." The old man's eyes were hollow, there was a heavy bandage about his neck. "You see me now somewhat recovered in strength," he said. "I have a good constitution, but a sword blade passed through one at my age is no small thing."

"It is no small thing with a man of any age," Philip said. "And that you have come off so fortunately as you have is an amazing thing, indeed."

The eyes of Lazarus, bright and vital beyond belief in their hollow sockets, searched Philip's face.

"You are rich with youth," he said. "You are strong and enduring. But I am afraid that news will come to you in a little space that will tax your fiber to the full."

Philip had sat down; he looked grave and quiet; his powerful hands lay, bronzed and still, upon the arms of the chair.

"I think," he said, "you have in your mind the matter of the *Vision of St. John*. I heard, while still in London, Claridge & Company had failed, and the money I hoped to claim had passed beyond my reach."

There was a long silence between them; the sunken eyes of Lazarus still held to Philip's face; and then the old man said:

"The rage that should be in you has died strangely down. I

had not thought to see it so. Meekness is no quality the Archers possessed." There was another pause, this time not so long as the other. "What woman was your mother?" he said.

Philip nodded.

"You are right. I must have a deal of my temperament from her. Quiet, and convent bred; much given to prayer, anxious for my upbringing. I had those things of her from my father; for she died before I well understood who she was."

"It is strange," said Lazarus, "the gifts and curses that come down in a strain of blood. That hard, glowing thing that made the Archers, seemed sure to go on as long as one of the name was left." The old man shook his head. "That gentle mother was strong; and a quiet mind sometimes overcomes great obstacles." He lay still for a few moments. "The family of Sarraza had much fire and purpose," he said. "Generations of them had fought the Moors; they had fought the English and the Dutch; they had traded by caravan and by sea, and were fiery, strong men."

"They were the owners of the galleon *Vision of St. John?*" said Philip.

"The firm had their name," said Mr. Lazarus, "though the last of the family had been dead a dozen years when that ship was taken. There had been a time—years before that— when they grew weak in purse, and had to call for help. It was a Jew who responded, a young man once a slave in a Moorish galley: a branded, silent young man who had earned great moneys in the trade with Africa. He was my ancestor," said Mr. Lazarus: "of honored memory."

"You, then, are of the firm of Sarraza?" said Philip.

"I am."

"I now understand your interest in Archer versus Claridge. But I do not understand why you have never come forward in any of the many trials, and claimed the share of the cargo named for you in the agreement."

"A Sarraza would have leaped into the fight much as the

Archers had done," said Lazarus. "But, as I've said, there were none of that name left; the Lazaruses were alone," sadly; "alone with a memory of the galleys deep in their spirits, with the memory of a thousand years under the lash of fierce peoples. And so they moved cautiously. There were five brothers of us; I had been selected for the work and my life dedicated to it. I studied it carefully; I asked questions; I made friends wherever it was possible. The Archers I always helped," he said; "their cause, to some extent, was my own. It was my purpose to help you when your day came as I had, unknown to them, helped the others."

In all the years he had been studying the case of Archer versus Claridge, Mr. Lazarus told Philip, in all the time he had hovered about the edge of the law courts, he had not had the slightest reason to think the cause might be won until he heard of the locked book of Madame Fouquet; then, when he took it from the Archer sea chest and read it and its attendant papers, hope of victory began to take shape in his mind. He was old, he said, but still had many of the impulses of youth; in his haste and enthusiasm he forgot he had already passed his word in the matter of this hoard of money; he had promised to do nothing that would in any way interfere with certain plans laid down regarding it.

"Not the plans of John Claridge?" said Philip.

No, those of Charlotte Desfourneaux. More than a month before Philip arrived in Philadelphia, the old man said, the girl had come to his counting room in Pump Court. She had learned a thing that John Claridge had never learned—that Lazarus was of the house of Sarraza. She spoke to the old man frankly and with a deal of understanding. She was beautiful. She had a persuasive way. Her grandmother had hated this stolen money, she said, and that hatred had come down to herself. Money got by the blood of honest people had God's frown upon it, and it was in her mind never to touch a penny of it. She told him what she meant to do. The colonies had entered into a just war; they had revolted against an oppressor; ships were needed; without ships, the fight would be lost almost at its beginning. She said she desired to buy vessels and pay for them with this great booty. Could this be done? She inquired of him because he was a man of experience in the law and in maritime practice, and one not likely to be prejudiced in favor of the Claridges.

"And you advised her?" said Philip.

"I told her if she had the courage, she might do as she wished. I did not mention it to her, but the information had come to me some time before that the resources of Claridge & Company had greatly shrunken, and they had, for some years, been operating upon the money the grandmother had left to her. I knew if she drew bills resolutely against them, they would not dare dishonor them; for, once in court, their financial condition would become known, and swift ruin would follow."

"You, then, representing the house of Sarraza, agreed to this use of the money remaining from the loot of the old ship?"

"I did. But do not ascribe to me the same high motives that go to Miss Desfourneaux. The firm of Sarraza had despaired of ever having the money wrested from Claridge & Company by process of law," said Mr. Lazarus. "And we were satisfied to see it go for any purpose that would deprive the Claridges of its use."

Philip smiled, and plucked at his belt to give himself more ease. He leaned back in his chair. The thought of those Spanish Jews was not far removed from his own.

"Never was money better spent," he said to Mr. Lazarus. "And, so, we'll let it go." He studied the old man for a space. "Your merchanting, I would say, has brought you a rich estate; as for me: the seas still flow to the world's rim, and its tides and its winds shall provide all I ask."

After her talk with him, said Mr. Lazarus, Charlotte set about the work she had in mind. She had spent a deal of money in craft of various sorts; the firm of Claridge & Company was already agitated as the bills came in for payment; then suddenly Philip's letter to John Claridge arrived. The mention of the sworn-to statements of Fouquet increased their uneasiness, for this man had possessed many of their secrets, and they'd always been desperately afraid of him; and they determined, if Philip should prove the person he said he was, and was not easily bidden, to have his life.

"My people," said Mr. Lazarus, to Philip, "brought me news of the attempt to be made upon you at the Plough Inn; I sent a warning to Miss Desfourneaux and proceeded there at once with two armed men."

"You, too, were there!" said Philip.

"It was I who found the traveler who'd arrived in your company at the inn, dead upon the floor. My men were lifting him up while the strokes of your horse's hoofs still sounded upon the road. Also," said Mr. Lazarus, "it was my spies who learned of the plan to put Miss Desfourneaux into the hands of the British when she ventured aboard the Claridge ship *Trumpeter*, and in that way prevent her hazardous use of the money left her by old Antoinette Teresa Barreaut-Desfourneaux. I had suspected all was not right in the matter of this ship," said Mr. Lazarus, "and had warned her. But she is venturesome, and made up her mind to go."

"She has courage," said Philip, in admiration; "she ventured a deal in many ways."

Old Lazarus looked at him.

"She hesitated only in those matters which concerned you," he said. "And they troubled her greatly. She was often in an agony of mind because she could not be frank with you. This money which you believed so earnestly to be your own, was vanishing, at her will, and she feared you would——"

"If she had spoken one word of her intent," said Philip fervently, "it would have been enough."

"I urged upon her that this might be so," said the old man. "I am a judge of the purposes of people as expressed in their manners and looks, and fancied you'd see the case eye to eye with her. But women are strange," said the old man, a smile about his pale lips; "at times they are strange beyond all persuading. She wept and remained away from all places where she thought she might meet with you."

"Where is she now?" asked Philip.

"At Paris. Directly after conveying me here, where I am well cared for by a clever physician, she posted off with her maid and Constant, to attend to some matters brought up by M'sieu Beaumarchais."

Philip remained talking with Mr. Lazarus for some time, and then descended to the public room.

Here he found young Austin, his effects about him; and in another half hour they were on the road to Paris.

CHAPTER XXXIV

A NIGHT had passed, and a day had followed; the Hôtel de Hollande was shining with lights, and the Rue Vieille du Temple had an animated look. In one of the long, lofty rooms of the old building, hung with portraits of celebrated actresses, and pictured scenes from the dramas of Corneille and Molière, Charlotte Desfourneaux sat upon a huge tufted sofa, the lights from a candelabra falling upon her. She wore a long trailing costume, open at the throat, and setting off her tall supple figure marvelously. Beside a table was the Count de Vergennes, a spare, dark man of past middle age; his wig and white ruffles, and gold shoe buckles, his flowing coat of yellow brocade, and dress sword, made him a striking figure. His earnest look was upon the girl, and he spoke with a deal of feeling.

"I have been waiting and listening," he said. "My hope has always been in to-morrow; and, when to-morrow came, bringing no promise, then in the next day. 'America must win,' I told myself. 'Her people are young and ardent; they have the fire and the resolve for freedom. True, they have struck and struck, and have failed to bring the enemy down; but it will not always be so.' A religious man would say: 'God is with a just cause'; a materialist might say: 'An enemy so far away cannot be formidable; in the end the revolutionists must win.' It may be some of the truth is in both these things, mademoiselle: I do not know. But up to this time there have been no hopeful results. The King of France is fretting and not assured. He still awaits the signal victory of which he spoke some time ago."

"Was the victory at Trenton not enough? Will he not be satisfied with the one at Princeton? A few ragged regiments of the line, and a gathering of raw militia, made it impossible for the British to remain in the Jerseys," said Charlotte. "If they can do that with everything hopelessly against them, what would they not do with proper support?"

"You are quite right," said De Vergennes; "and I agree with you. But the condition of the American army makes King Louis shake his head. He is not one to tolerate weakness in an ally; a victory of undoubted character is required by him as an evidence of solidity. To be sure, Trenton was a blow that must have made the nation glad; Princeton told of generalship and swift courage; but our King of France is not a soldier, and he cannot put defeats aside. He recalls Long Island, and he recalls the Brandywine; he recalls the report, some time ago, of the fall of Philadelphia; he recalls your militia that so often refuses to cross their own borders, and has so often melted away in the face of danger. But more than anything else he keeps in mind this devastating army of the English General Burgoyne. There, Mademoiselle Desfourneaux, is a peril, indeed. This body of British, together, so I've been told, with other bodies of German mercenaries and savages, have marched from the north country into New York, with the intention of driving a wedge between New England and the colonies to the south, separating them and making it possible to encounter and defeat them in detail. No situation that has threatened your country up to this time has had such possibilities of calamity. When I endeavor to persuade the King and he is at a loss for argument, he draws this peril upon me like a sword, and forces me to silence."

While De Vergennes was speaking, Franklin and Beaumarchais came into the room, the old philosopher in his sober coat, his woolen stockings, and unpowdered hair; the dramatist splendidly displaying the genius of his tailor, a gold-hilted sword at his side, his silk-clad calves gleaming in the candlelight, a magnificent curled wig falling over his shoulders.

"It is a great misfortune that the King is *not* a soldier," said Franklin; "there have been rulers of France who'd have grasped at once the weakness of a large army advanced so far from its base as this one led by Burgoyne. A king who had ridden to his own wars would have recognized this at once, and would know how an opposing general might cleverly turn it to his own account."

Beaumarchais applauded this.

"An able general," he said, "does not wait for the fortunes of war to give him victory. And only a doddering ruler would fail to recognize great power when holding it in his hands. Our navy has been rebuilt; the Channel is once more ours if we would but take it. Youth again fills our regiments; never in the history of France have its banners been carried by stronger hands, nor its muskets rested upon broader shoulders."

"King Louis's mind is not to be changed," said De Vergennes; "I see him sometimes," to Franklin, "sitting with his head bent, a stolid, dull look upon his face. He is thinking of armed revolt; he is thinking of the threatenings that have come creeping from time to time even to Versailles. He is thinking of a people no longer subject to his will, but active and up, and demanding its share of the millions in his strong boxes. At such moments," said the Foreign Minister, "he is bitter in his thoughts against America; he still demands a signal victory, but in his heart hopes it will never be gained."

"A France aroused against its king and government is a frightening thing," said Beaumarchais. "And it is surprising that any muttering of such should reach a man as carefully guarded as Louis."

"Stormont makes it his favorite theme," said Franklin, as he sat opposite De Vergennes. "'Kings should ever have an eye upon their common estate,' he says. 'They should not, by word or deed, encourage the subject classes of another nation in anything that approaches open speaking; for if such an enormity gained a foothold in one country, what is to hinder it

from spreading to another?' says my lord Stormont. 'Kings,'
he says, 'owe jealousy in such matters to each other.'"

The three men talked of the many aspects of the question
before them; and Charlotte Desfourneaux listened. Louis was
a dull, timorous monarch. He was narrow-hearted and without
real generosity. Could the colonies win without his aid? Was
England's power great enough to reach across a sea, and crush
a whole people? Were the colonists stubborn enough to keep
their ground under dreadful blows until such time came as
these blows began to weaken? Had Congress the courage to
resist to the point where resistance became a terror and a madness? Armies. Batteries. Divisions. General officers. And then
ships! And the sea!

The enormous, the great sea! It stretched away, an unend-
ing, heaving blankness, under an empty sky. Charlotte wondered how had she hoped to conquer it? How had she thought
anything she might do would make any difference in its vastness, its terrible monotony? Nothing but defeat had ever come
to those who had accepted the challenge of its great voice.

She had hoped to dot its surface with her sea hawks; she'd
planned that carefully; her privateers were to be everywhere;
their prizes were to be condemned and sold, and the money
was to go into more ships, more guns. And success had followed
her vessels; she'd had a fine pride in them; they'd the darting
fury of dragon flies; they took rich merchantmen and fought
the brigs and corvettes of the British with a boldness that made
people wonder. But this was not enough, for England still put
out her great fleets; the horizon bristled with her masts and
guns.

The three men had a map spread upon the table. That green,
empty vastness upon it was the sea; still unchanged by all her
efforts, still challenging. She had failed! Her spirit grew faint
as she admitted it. The great moneys left by Antoinette
Teresa Barreaut-Desfourneaux had been sunk in this great
emptiness; the fleets sent out by Roderique Hortalez & Com-

pany were but tiny spots in the great design of war; her privateers and letters-of-marque, robust fighters though they were, moved upon this huge expanse like creatures whose small presence altered nothing.

Charlotte tried to shake off this feeling. She studied the face of Franklin with its deep lines, its comprehending eyes, its firm mouth and chin; his body was old and run somewhat to flesh, but there were still traces of his athletic youth. His voice was quiet; he had all the appearances of a man whose mind was searching, a man who knew there was, somewhere, a power which, if properly directed, would surge up under the sunken world and lift it to heights before undreamed of.

De Vergennes, for all his dark look and glinting spirit, was cold; his thoughts played like fire under ice. He followed the words of Franklin with heavy words of his own; his hands, as he gestured, seemed weighted with shackles. But not so Beaumarchais; he stood tall and ready and unabashed; his eyes were animated, his voice was eager and had the ring of conviction. The others were bowed over the map as though the hugeness of its spaces held them down; but not he. The gold snuffbox was in his hand; the snowy handkerchief was in his sleeve; he moved about with graceful posturings; his gestures were perfection.

What was it all? he demanded. What was there in the matter that should depress them so? Granted the King was a half-wit and timorous; granted the English were strong, were there not thousands of active minds and ready hands to uphold the idea of liberty? He'd sailed the seas and knew how wide they were; he'd had to do with armies and knew the money they cost; he'd seen defeat and disaster, and all the bitter blows that came to a man wrongly placed; but there was one thing he'd learned from them all: never to be cast down!—never to permit the spirit to grow faint! the head must always be held up! If France would not help America, what of the Dutch? What of the Spanish? What of the states of Germany? The Russians lay

buried in their snows, but an earnest man, provided with the
right words, might draw them out. The Prussian King, if he
were so minded, might daunt England a deal; Portugal had
high-prowed ships; the Scandinavians could boil and froth in a
most troublesome way. Let King Louis settle himself in a
corner like some ancient dame before an embroidery frame if
he would: money would be provided without him; money could
be had from——

The dramatist's voice ceased to reach Charlotte as her own
thoughts closed her in once more. Money! The great moneys of
the *Vision of St. John* were gone: she had paid them out lav-
ishly; there was not a louis of them left. They were gone, and
the news must some time come to Philip Archer's ears. Not,
and her beautiful head lifted proudly, that she dreaded his
anger; for she'd done what was right; the money had not been
really his to claim any more than it had been her own: and that
it was not her own she knew very well. But a bleakness filled
her spirit; a sob was in her throat; she felt his eyes upon her,
those clear, brave eyes! He'd seen a deal; he'd lived hardly and
faced peril; he had a fiery, lifting soul, but there'd been times
when she'd seen a questioning in his look that brought tears to
her eyes: a wondering look that one might see in a boy.

A clerk came in; he spoke to Beaumarchais.

"M'sieu, some travelers from the coast have arrived and are
requesting to see you."

"Ask them to wait," said Beaumarchais.

The clerk hesitated, and then said:

"One of the gentlemen is M'sieu Archer; and he brings with
him a gentleman from America whose business is with Dr.
Franklin."

"From America?" said Franklin, looking up. Then to Beaumarchais he added: "Pray have them in."

In a few moments Philip Archer and young Austin, travel-
stained and weary from their long journey, were shown in.
Philip paused before Charlotte and bowed; he shook hands with

Dr. Franklin and Beaumarchais and spoke to De Vergennes whom he had met at Roderique Hortalez & Company upon previous visits. He indicated Austin.

"Let me present," said he, "Mr. Jonathan Loring Austin, a young man of Massachusetts, and secretary to the Board of War of that colony. Two days ago he arrived at Nantes, and came immediately to Paris. At your house in the suburbs, sir," to Franklin, "we learned you were here and took the liberty of asking for you, as Mr. Austin's business seems of high importance."

There was a pause, and Dr. Franklin looked at Austin and arose to his feet.

"Sir," he said, "you have come to tell me that, after all, Philadelphia has not fallen."

But Austin shook his head.

"I am sorry, sir," he said. "Howe's army is in possession of the city; and the forts of the Delaware have been taken." The strong old face went gray; the great head was bowed, for this was a thing Franklin had refused to believe. The arm of Beaumarchais supported him. "But I was not sent to tell you that," said Austin. "I do not bring news of a defeat, but of victory. The British under General Burgoyne, gentlemen, have been defeated. And more than that," as he saw the sudden joy in Franklin's face; "Burgoyne's army, with all its officers, guns, and baggage, has been surrendered to the Americans at Saratoga."

2

Midnight had come with its blackness shot through by the rays of the moon. Along the well beaten road from Paris to Versailles, a courier was riding as though for his life. The pallor of the moon came through the trees, lighting the way for the horse's flying feet; the hand upon the bridle was firm. It was a strong horse and a swift one: it was a good rider, a French ex-trooper who had served De Vergennes for many years. There was a leather bag hung across the saddlebow, a bag holding papers written by the foreign minister for the eyes of the King.

"*Sir,*" said the fervent De Vergennes in his written words, "*the thing we have all hoped for, prayed for, has come to pass. The Americans have won the signal victory for which you have asked. God is in his heaven, and the right must triumph.*"

3

In a high room at Roderique Hortalez & Company, a room hung with rich draperies and flashing with the light of scores of candles, Beaumarchais paced up and down between two rows of tables at which sat a dozen clerks. He talked rapidly, with many gestures. The tables were littered with newly written sheets; the clerks dipped their pens into the ink pots, striving feverishly to fix the torrent of words upon the sheets of paper. His sayings bristled with warnings to agents at all the seaports of France: Take care! He bade them to set a guard over their tongues. France, in another half-month, would be at war with England! To the masters of Dutch ships, to Flemish merchants, to the ports of Spain, to the French islands, in care of the masters of vessels about to sail, he wrote:

"*Watch like hawks! Make all speed with laden ships, but delay those which might come to danger. War hovers above us! As you read this, England will be striking at us in the Channel!*"

4

In another room sat De Vergennes and Franklin, long writings before them; terms, agreements, plighted words, declarations of intentions. A treaty was already taking form. A paper was making, even at this early hour, that would release the fleets of France, and set her battalions to moving. Help was coming: money! arms! men! The King, with his thin looks and his scant smile, could not now hold his hand. America was strong: she had proven it. And France must walk at her side!

5

There was a wide balcony to Roderique Hortalez & Company, and it was thick with shadows and spotted with the curious glances of the moon.

"I have never been so contented," said Philip Archer. He looked down into the face of Charlotte Desfourneaux, the beautiful eyes lifted to him. "Never so satisfied before. It is as though this night were a great gate which I'd pushed open, and which has swung fast behind me, leaving me in a garden of strange sweetness."

"But," she said, protesting, "you are poor."

"I've always been poor," he smiled at her, "and so it is no new thing."

"I thought you would hate me," she said.

"There was a time when I did not understand, but that is all. Hate you I never could." He kissed her upon the brow and upon the lips. "Now," he said, "I have you, and I have a free life to do with as I will."

He felt her arms tighten about him.

"And your will, Philip—now?"

"Is for the sea," he said.

She met his look, bravely.

"I knew it would be," she said.

"You have no word to say against it?"

"No. I am glad." It was now his arms tightened about *her*. "I knew it would be. And, Philip, before all the money had gone, I thought of you—I thought of what you might like."

"Yes?" he said, and kissed her softly. "Yes."

"Philip," she said, "there is a ship at Nantes; a beautiful ship."

"I saw her," he said. "I saw her in the harbor in the early morning."

"And you liked her?"

"She was like a splendid leopardess."

"You will do wonderful things at sea, Philip," she said, her hand smoothing his hair. "I'm sure of that. And when you come back, I shall be very proud of you."

THE END